MURDER
❦ FOR ❦
CHRISTMAS

*and other yuletide malfeasance
as perpetrated by*

P9-DHQ-692

Margery Allingham

G.K. Chesterton

Agatha Christie

John Collier

Charles Dickens

Arthur Conan Doyle

Stanley Ellin

Thomas Hardy

H.R.F. Keating

A.A. Milne

James Mines

Baroness Orczy

Ellery Queen

Georges Simenon

graphically illustrated by
GAHAN WILSON

edited and with irrelevant comments by
THOMAS GODFREY

MURDER FOR CHRISTMAS

Abridged Edition

EDITED BY THOMAS GODFREY

Illustrated by Gahan Wilson

THE MYSTERIOUS PRESS

New York • London

Grateful acknowledgement is made for permission to reprint the following:

"Back for Christmas" by John Collier. Copyright © by John Collier. Reprinted by permission A.D. Peters & Co. Ltd.

"The Adventure of the Christmas Pudding" ("The Theft of the Royal Ruby.") Reprinted by permission of Dodd, Mead & Company, Inc. from *Double Sin and Other Stories* by Agatha Christie. Copyright © 1960 by Agatha Christie Ltd., Copyright © 1961 by Christie Copyrights Trust.

"Death on Christmas Eve" by Stanley Ellin. Copyright © 1950 by Stanley Ellin. Reprinted by permission of Curtis Brown Ltd.

"A Christmas Tragedy" by Baroness Orczy. Copyright © by Emmusra Orczy. Reprinted by permission A.P. Watt & Son and the Estate of Baroness Orczy.

"Inspector Ghote and the Miracle Baby" by H.R.F. Keating. Copyright © by H.R.F. Keating. Reprinted by permission of the author.

"Maigret's Christmas" by Georges Simenon. Translated by Lawrence Blochman, from *A Treasury of Great Mysteries*, ed. Haycraft and Beecroft, Simon & Schuster 1957. Copyright © 1951 by Georges Simenon and reprinted with his permission and Harcourt, Brace, Jovanovich, Inc. acting in behalf of the author.

"The Adventure of the Dauphin's Doll" by Ellery Queen. Copyright © by Ellery Queen. Reprinted by permission of the author and the author's agents, Scott Meredith Literary Agency, Inc., 845 Third Ave., New York, New York 10022.

"The Case is Altered" by Margery Allingham. Copyright © 1949 by Margery Allingham. Reprinted by permission of Paul R. Reynolds, Inc., 12 East 41st Street, New York, New York, 10017.

All cartoons copyright © 1982 by Gahan Wilson

Cover illustration by Gahan Wilson

Mysterious Press books are published in association with Warner Books, Inc.
666 Fifth Avenue
New York, N.Y. 10103
A Warner Communications Company

Printed in the United States of America

Originally published in hardcover by The Mysterious Press.
First Mysterious Press Paperback Printing: December, 1987

10 9 8 7 6 5 4 3 2 1

To
Kathy
The Best Thing that ever
Happened to me

Originally published in hardcover by The Mysterious Press.

Warner Books Paperback Printing: December 1988

Contents

Introduction

HERE at last is the perfect present for the person who has everything—and plans to leave it to you: thirteen inspirational tales of seasonal malfeasance designed to keep you in the Christmas spirit all year round.

Come savor the gift-giving suggestions of the great masters of mayhem—imaginative hints to help you turn this year's Yuletide festivities into something the whole family will be talking about for generations to come.

Let Sherlock Holmes, Hercule Poirot and Ellery Queen guide your selection for the special someone on your gift list. This Christmas find the perfect year-ending expression of holiday spirit with the aid of John Collier, Stanley Ellin, and James Mines.

But beware—as G.K. Chesterton's Father Brown will soon remind us—crime does not always pay, even at Christmastime.

Just now, take a moment from the ardors of frenzied holiday gift-wrapping to pull up a chair and sample just a few pages . . . if you dare . . . of Margery Allingham's Albert Campion, Georges Simenon's Inspector Maigret, and H.R.F. Keating's Inspector Ghote.

There . . . That's right . . . Just settle back . . . Relax . . . Forget those holiday cares . . . that peculiar noise in your chimney . . . that odd aftertaste in the brandy . . . that strange red fluid dripping from one of the stockings on the mantelpiece . . . that heavy breathing behind your chair . . . Read on . . . Enjoy . . .

AND GOD HELP US EVERY ONE!

MURDER
❧ FOR ❧
CHRISTMAS

Let us begin our Christmas criminologies at the end. The end of Hermione Carpenter, to be exact. Author John Collier was the master of the story of ordinary people suddenly caught up by a bitterly ironic turn of events, all told in a light, casual tone. Not surprisingly, film director Alfred Hitchcock was among Collier's admirers. He popularized this type of writing in the movies and on television.

It was the start of "black humor," a form of expression that was very popular during the days of the Vietnamese War. Collier, along with Stanley Ellin, Roald Dahl and Robert Bloch, formed the Four Horsemen of Contemporary Crime Fiction, a quartet descended from film noir and Cornell Woolrich, that perfected a distinctive style of mystery-suspense writing that still prevails.

"Back for Christmas" is a masterpiece of contradictions, a literary web that is both light and lethal, immoral and just, logical and absurd. It is as contemporary as the last election, yet more durable than any political career. Hitchcock adapted it for his television series, one of the few shows he directed himself. Ironically Hitchcock's name came to overshadow Collier's, as it did all of the writers he worked with. Yet, even if one forgets the name John Collier, it is unlikely that he will ever forget "Back for Christmas."

Back for Christmas

by John Collier

"**D**OCTOR," said Major Sinclair, "we certainly must have you with us for Christmas." It was afternoon and the Carpenters' living room was filled with friends who had come to say last-minute farewells to the Doctor and his wife.

"He shall be back," said Mrs. Carpenter. "I promise you."

"It's hardly certain," said Dr. Carpenter. "I'd like nothing better, of course."

"After all," said Mr. Hewitt, "you've contracted to lecture only for three months."

"Anything may happen," said Dr. Carpenter.

"Whatever happens," said Mrs. Carpenter, beaming at them, "he shall be back in England for Christmas. You may all believe me."

They all believed her. The Doctor himself almost believed her. For ten years she had been promising him for dinner parties, garden parties, committees, heaven knows what, and the promises had always been kept.

The farewells began. There was a fluting of compliments on dear Hermione's marvellous arrangements. She and her husband would drive to Southampton that evening. They would embark the following day. No trains, no bustle, no last-minute worries. Certainly the Doctor was marvellously looked after. He would be a great success in America. Especially with Hermione to see to everything. She would have a wonderful time, too. She would see the skyscrapers. Nothing like that in Little Godwearing. But she must be very sure to bring him back. "Yes, I will bring him back. You may rely upon it." He mustn't be persuaded. No extensions. No won-

3

derful post at some super-American hospital. Our infirmary needs him. And he must be back by Christmas. "Yes," Mrs. Carpenter called to the last departing guest, "I shall see to it. He shall be back by Christmas."

The final arrangements for closing the house were very well managed. The maids soon had the tea things washed up; they came in, said goodbye, and were in time to catch the afternoon bus to Devizes.

Nothing remained but odds and ends, locking doors, seeing that everything was tidy. "Go upstairs," said Hermione, "and change into your brown tweeds. Empty the pockets of that suit before you put it in your bag. I'll see to everything else. All you have to do is not to get in the way."

The Doctor went upstairs and took off the suit he was wearing, but instead of the brown tweeds, he put on an old, dirty bath gown, which he took from the back of his wardrobe. Then, after making one or two little arrangements, he leaned over the head of the stairs and called to his wife, "Hermione! Have you a moment to spare?"

"Of course, dear. I'm just finished."

"Just come up here for a moment. There's something rather extraordinary up here."

Hermione immediately came up. "Good heavens, my dear man!" she said when she saw her husband. "What are you lounging about in that filthy old thing for? I told you to have it burned long ago."

"Who in the world," said the Doctor, "has dropped a gold chain down the bathtub drain?"

"Nobody has, of course," said Hermione. "Nobody wears such a thing."

"Then what is it doing there?" said the Doctor. "Take this flashlight. If you lean right over, you can see it shining, deep down."

"Some Woolworth's bangle off one of the maids," said Hermione. "It can be nothing else." However, she took the flashlight and leaned over, squinting into the drain. The Doctor, raising a short length of lead pipe, struck two or three times with great force and precision, and tilting the body by the knees, tumbled it into the tub.

He then slipped off the bathrobe and, standing completely naked, unwrapped a towel full of implements and put them into the washbasin. He spread several sheets of newspaper on the floor and turned once more to his victim.

She was dead, of course—horribly doubled up, like a somersaulter, at one end of the tub. He stood looking at her for a very long time, thinking of absolutely nothing at all. Then he saw how much blood there was and his mind began to move again.

First he pushed and pulled until she lay straight in the bath, then he removed her clothing. In a narrow bathtub this was an extremely clumsy business, but he managed it at last and then turned on the taps. The water rushed into the tub, then dwindled, then died away, and the last of it gurgled down the drain.

"Good God!" he said. "She turned it off at the main."

There was only one thing to do: the Doctor hastily wiped his hands on a towel, opened the bathroom door with a clean corner of the towel, threw it back onto the bath stool, and ran downstairs, barefoot, light as a cat. The cellar door was in a corner of the entrance hall, under the stairs. He knew just where the cut-off was. He had reason to: he had been pottering about down there for some time past—trying to scrape out a bin for wine, he had told Hermione. He pushed open the cellar door, went down the steep steps, and just before the closing door plunged the cellar into pitch darkness, he put his hand on the tap and turned it on. Then he felt his way back along the grimy wall till he came to the steps. He was about to ascend them when the bell rang.

The Doctor was scarcely aware of the ringing as a sound. It was like a spike of iron pushed slowly up through his stomach. It went on until it reached his brain. Then something broke. He threw himself down in the coal dust on the floor and said, "I'm through. I'm through."

"They've got no right to come. Fools!" he said. Then he heard himself panting. "None of this," he said to himself. "None of this."

He began to revive. He got to his feet, and when the bell rang again the sound passed through him almost painlessly.

"Let them go away," he said. Then he heard the front door open. He said, "I don't care." His shoulder came up, like that of a boxer, to shield his face. "I give up," he said.

He heard people calling. "Herbert!" "Hermione!" It was the Wallingfords. "Damn them! They come butting in. People anxious to get off. All naked! And blood and coal dust! I'm done! I'm through! I can't do it."

"Herbert!"

"Hermione!"

"Where the dickens can they be?"

"The car's there."

"Maybe they've popped round to Mrs. Liddell's."

"We must see them."

"Or to the shops, maybe. Something at the last minute."

"Not Hermione. I say, listen! Isn't that someone having a bath? Shall I shout? What about whanging on the door?"

"Sh-h-h! Don't. It might not be tactful."

"No harm in a shout."

"Look, dear. Let's come in on our way back. Hermione said they wouldn't be leaving before seven. They're dining on the way, in Salisbury."

"Think so? All right. Only I want a last drink with old Herbert. He'd be hurt."

"Let's hurry. We can be back by half past six."

The Doctor heard them walk out and the front door close quietly behind them. He thought, "Half past six. I can do it."

He crossed the hall, sprang the latch of the front door, went upstairs, and taking his instruments from the washbasin, finished what he had to do. He came down again, clad in his bath gown, carrying parcel after parcel of towelling or newspaper neatly secured with safety pins. These he packed carefully into the narrow, deep hole he had made in the corner of the cellar, shovelled in the soil, spread coal dust over all, satisfied himself that everything was in order, and went upstairs again. He then thoroughly cleansed the bath, and himself, and the bath again, dressed, and took his wife's clothing and his bath gown to the incinerator.

One or two more little touches and everything was in order. It was only quarter past six. The Wallingfords were always late; he had only to get into the car and drive off. It was a pity he couldn't wait till after dusk, but he could make a detour to avoid passing through the main street, and even if he was seen driving alone, people would only think Hermione had gone on ahead for some reason and they would forget about it.

Still, he was glad when he had finally got away, entirely unobserved, on the open road, driving into the gathering dusk. He had to drive very carefully; he found himself unable to judge distances, his reactions were abnormally delayed, but that was a detail. When it was quite dark he allowed himself to stop the car on the top of the downs, in order to think.

The stars were superb. He could see the lights of one or two little towns far away on the plain below him. He was exultant. Everything that was to follow was perfectly simple. Marion was waiting in Chicago. She already believed him to be a widower. The lecture people could be put off with a word. He had nothing to do but establish himself in some thriving out-of-the-way town in America and he was safe forever. There were Hermione's clothes, of course, in the suitcases: they could be disposed of through the porthole. Thank heaven she wrote her letters on the typewriter—a little thing like handwriting might have prevented everything. "But there you are," he said. "She was up-to-date, efficient all along the line. Managed everything. Managed herself to death, damn her!"

"There's no reason to get excited," he thought. "I'll write a few letters for her, then fewer and fewer. Write myself—always expecting to get back, never quite able to. Keep the house one year, then another, then another; they'll get used to it. Might even come back alone in a year or two and clear it up properly. Nothing easier. But not for Christmas!" He started up the engine and was off.

In New York he felt free at last, really free. He was safe. He could look back with pleasure—at least after a meal, lighting his cigarette, he could look back with a sort of pleasure—to the minute he had passed in the cellar listening to the bell, the door, and the voices. He could look forward to Marion.

As he strolled through the lobby of his hotel, the clerk, smiling, held up letters for him. It was the first batch from England. Well, what did that matter? It would be fun dashing off the typewritten sheets in Hermione's downright style, signing them with her squiggle, telling everyone what a success his first lecture had been, how thrilled he was with America but how certainly she'd bring him back for Christmas. Doubts could creep in later.

He glanced over the letters. Most were for Hermione. From the Sinclairs, the Wallingfords, the vicar, and a business letter from Holt & Sons, Builders and Decorators.

He stood in the lounge, people brushing by him. He opened the letters with his thumb, reading here and there, smiling. They all seemed very confident he would be back for Christmas. They relied on Hermione. "That's where they make their big mistake," said the Doctor, who had taken to American phrases. The builders' letter he kept to the last. Some bill, probably. It was:

DEAR MADAM,

We are in receipt of your kind acceptance of estimate as below and also of key.

We beg to repeat you may have every confidence in same being ready in ample time for Christmas present as stated. We are setting men to work this week.

We are, Madam,

Yours faithfully,
PAUL HOLT & SONS

To excavating, building up, suitably lining one sunken wine bin in cellar as indicated, using best materials, making good, etc.

. . . . . . £18/0/0

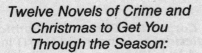

Twelve Novels of Crime and Christmas to Get You Through the Season:

Tied Up In Tinsel by Ngaio Marsh (1971) in which Inspector Roderick Alleyn and his wife Agatha Troy tackle the death of an unpopular servant who disappears after playing Santa Claus.

Red Christmas by Patrick Ruell (1972) in which Murder disrupts a 'Dickensian' Christmas week-end for vacationers at a secluded Victorian inn.

Spence and the Holiday Murders by Michael Allen (1977) in which a rich, young bachelor is blown up in the driveway of his South Coast England home two days before Christmas.

The Gooseberry Fool by James McClure (1974) in which South African police Lt. Tromp Kramer and his Bantu assistant Sgt. Mickey Zondi investigate the death of a government engineer during a Christmas heat wave.

A Corpse for Christmas (Homicide at Yuletide) by Henry Kane (1951) in which hard-boiled private eye Peter Chambers gets involved with a scientist who is supposed to be dead and some ladies who are trying to accommodate him.

The Finishing Stroke by Ellery Queen (1958) in which an unidentified body turns up in the library of a publisher's estate during a twelve day Christmas party.

An English Murder by Cecil Hare (1951) in which members of an English Christmas party are snowbound in a castle with a murderer.

Hercule Poirot's Christmas (Murder for Christmas) by Agatha Christie (1938) in which the famous Belgian sleuth investigates the Christmas Eve slaying of a wealthy old financier with a lot of unhappy relatives.

No Holiday for Murder by Dell Shannon (1973) in which Det. Lt. Luis Mendoza finds his Christmas duty preoccupied with the strange death of a devout Mormon at Los Angeles International Airport.

Rest You Merry by Charlotte MacLeod (1973) in which college professor Peter Shandy finds the body of the assistant college librarian beneath his Christmas tree.

Sadie When She Died by Ed McBain (1972) in which 87th Precinct Det. Steve Carella solves the case of an adulterous wife who appears to be the victim of a local junkie-burglar. The truth arrives as a Christmas gift.

The Christmas Card Murders by David William Meredith (1951) in which four people in a small New Jersey town get identical Christmas cards telling them that they will not live to see the new year.

Robin Hood's Epitaph

Hear undernead dis laith stean
Laiz Robert Earl of Huntington
Nea arcir ver az hie sa geude:
An piple kaud im Robin Heud.
Sic utlawz as hi an iz men,
Wil England never sigh agen.
  Obiit 24 kal. Decembris, 1247.

From a gravestone in
Kirklees Churchyard, Yorkshire.

It is by now catechismic that Conan Doyle wrote the first of his Sherlock Holmes stories while waiting for his medical practice to grow. He must have enjoyed those early works as a welcome relief from the world of intractable physical ailments. What better escape for him after a day of gas pains and 'the vapors' than to open his sketchbook and let his mind wander through the corridors of Baskerville Hall or the moors outside Dartmoor Prison. It provided some needed diversion; it also helped to pay the bills.

No wonder that, when these stories became a chore done at public demand, he considered killing off his detective. The magic and escape were gone. Sherlock Holmes became another obligation not unlike the practice of medicine itself. He turned to mysticism and science fiction, but the public would not have it. They wanted Holmes.

Today these adventures provide a wonderful escape for the contemporary reader. And that, of course, is what detective fiction is largely about: a chance to forget one's own problems and take on those of the royal house of Bohemia or the Red-Headed League.

In that spirit, let us take down our pipes and deerstalker caps, and join the world's greatest consulting detective as he sets off on another adventure down the gas-lit streets of Edwardian England. This time he proposes to cook someone's goose. Or will he? Take a gander at "The Adventure of the Blue Carbuncle."

The Adventure of the Blue Carbuncle

by Sir Arthur Conan Doyle

I HAD CALLED UPON my friend Sherlock Holmes upon the second morning after Christmas, with the intention of wishing him the compliments of the season. He was lounging upon the sofa in a purple dressing-gown, a pipe-rack within his reach upon the right, and a pile of crumpled morning papers, evidently newly studied, near at hand. Beside the couch was a wooden chair, and on the angle of the back hung a very seedy and disreputable hard-felt hat, much the worse for wear, and cracked in several places. A lens and a forceps lying upon the seat of the chair suggested that the hat had been suspended in this manner for the purpose of examination.

"You are engaged," said I; "perhaps I interrupt you."

"Not at all. I am glad to have a friend with whom I can discuss my results. The matter is a perfectly trivial one"—he jerked his thumb in the direction of the old hat—"but there are points in connection with it which are not entirely devoid of interest and even of instruction."

I seated myself in his armchair and warmed my hands before his crackling fire, for a sharp frost had set in, and the windows were thick with the ice crystals. "I suppose," I remarked, "that, homely as it looks, this thing has some deadly story linked on to it—that it is the clue which will guide you in the solution of some mystery and the punishment of some crime."

"No, no. No crime," said Sherlock Holmes, laughing. "Only one of those whimsical little incidents which will happen when you have four million human beings all jostling each other within the space of a few square miles. Amid the action and reaction of so dense a swarm of humanity, every possible combination of events may be expected to take place, and many a little problem will be presented which may be striking and bizarre without being criminal. We have already had experience of such."

"So much so," I remarked, "that of the last six cases which I have added to my notes, three have been entirely free of any legal crime."

"Precisely. You allude to my attempt to recover the Irene Adler papers, to the singular case of Miss Mary Sutherland, and to the adventure of the man with the twisted lip. Well, I have no doubt that this small matter will fall into the same innocent category. You know Peterson, the commissionaire?"

"Yes."

"It is to him that this trophy belongs."

"It is his hat."

"No, no; he found it. Its owner is unknown. I beg that you will look upon it not as a battered billycock but as an intellectual problem. And, first, as to how it came here. It arrived upon Christmas morning, in company with a good fat goose, which is, I have no doubt, roasting at this moment in front of Peterson's fire. The facts are these: about four o'clock on Christmas morning, Peterson, who, as you know, is a very honest fellow, was returning from some small jollification and was making his way homeward down Tottenham Court Road. In front of him he saw, in the gaslight, a tallish man, walking with a slight stagger, and carrying a white goose slung over his shoulder. As he reached the corner of Goodge Street, a row broke out between this stranger and a little knot of roughs. One of the latter knocked off the man's hat, on which he raised his stick to defend himself and, swinging it over his head, smashed the shop window behind him. Peterson had rushed forward to protect the stranger from his assailants; but the man, shocked at having broken the window, and seeing an official-looking person in uniform rushing towards him, dropped his goose, took to his heels, and vanished amid the labyrinth of small streets which lie at the back of Tottenham Court Road. The roughs had also fled at the appearance of Peterson, so that he was left in possession of the field of battle, and also of the spoils of victory in the shape of this battered hat and a most unimpeachable Christmas goose."

"Which surely he restored to their owner?"

"My dear fellow, there lies the problem. It is true that 'For Mrs. Henry Baker' was printed upon a small card which was tied to the bird's left leg, and it is also true that the initials 'H.B.' are legible upon the lining of this hat; but as there are some thousands of Bakers, and some hundreds of Henry Bakers in this city of ours, it is not easy to restore lost property to any of them."

"What, then, did Peterson do?"

"He brought round both hat and goose to me on Christmas morning, knowing that even the smallest problems are of interest to me. The goose we retained until this morning, when there were signs that, in spite of the slight frost, it would be well that it should be eaten without unnecessary delay. Its finder has carried it off, therefore, to fulfil the ultimate destiny of a goose, while I continue to retain the hat of the unknown gentleman who lost his Christmas dinner."

"Did he not advertise?"

"No."

"Then, what clue could you have as to his identity?"

"Only as much as we can deduce."

"From his hat?"

"Precisely."

"But you are joking. What can you gather from this old battered felt?"

"Here is my lens. You know my methods. What can you gather yourself as to the individuality of the man who has worn this article?"

I took the tattered object in my hands and turned it over rather ruefully. It was a very ordinary black hat of the usual round shape, hard and much the worse for wear. The lining had been of red silk, but was a good deal discoloured. There was no maker's name; but, as Holmes had remarked, the initials "H.B." were scrawled upon one side. It was pierced in the brim for a hat-securer, but the elastic was missing. For the rest, it was cracked, exceedingly dusty, and spotted in several places, although there seemed to have been some attempt to hide the discoloured patches by smearing them with ink.

"I can see nothing," said I, handing it back to my friend.

"On the contrary, Watson, you can see everything. You fail, however, to reason from what you see. You are too timid in drawing your inferences."

"Then, pray tell me what it is that you can infer from this hat?"

He picked it up and gazed at it in the peculiar introspective fashion which was characteristic of him. "It is perhaps less suggestive than it might have been," he remarked, "and yet there are a few inferences which are very distinct, and a few others which represent at least a strong balance of probability. That the man was highly intellectual is of course obvious upon the face of it, and also that he was fairly well-to-do within the last three years, although he has now fallen upon evil days. He had foresight, but has less now than formerly, pointing to a moral retrogression, which, when taken with the decline of his fortunes, seems to indicate some evil influence, probably drink, at work upon him. This may account also for the obvious fact that his wife has ceased to love him."

"My dear Holmes!"

"He has, however, retained some degree of self-respect," he continued, disregarding my remonstrance. "He is a man who leads a sendentary life, goes out little, is out of training entirely, is middle-aged, has grizzled hair which he has had cut within the last few days, and which he anoints with lime-cream. These are the more patent facts which are to be deduced from his hat. Also, by the way, that it is extremely improbable that he has gas laid on in his house."

"You are certainly joking, Holmes."

"Not in the least. Is it possible that even now, when I give you these results, you are unable to see how they are attained?"

"I have no doubt that I am very stupid, but I must confess that I am unable to follow you. For example, how did you deduce that this man was intellectual?"

For answer Holmes clapped the hat upon his head. It came right over the forehead and settled upon the bridge of his nose. "It is a question of cubic capacity," said he; "a man with so large a brain must have something in it."

"The decline of his fortunes, then?"

"This hat is three years old. These flat brims curled at the edge came in then. It is a hat of the very best quality. Look at the band of ribbed silk and the excellent lining. If this man could afford to buy so expensive a hat three years ago, and has had no hat since, then he has assuredly gone down in the world."

"Well, that is clear enough, certainly. But how about the foresight and the moral retrogression?"

Sherlock Holmes laughed. "Here is the foresight," said he, putting his finger upon the little disc and loop of the hat-securer. "They are never sold upon hats. If this man ordered one, it is a sign of a certain amount of foresight, since he went out of his way to take this precaution against the wind. But since we see that he has broken the elastic and has not troubled to replace it, it is obvious that he has less foresight now than formerly, which is a distinct proof of a weakening nature. On the other hand, he has endeavored to conceal some of these stains upon the felt by daubing them with ink, which is a sign that he has not entirely lost his self-respect."

"Your reasoning is certainly plausible."

"The further points, that he is middle-aged, that his hair is grizzled, that it has been recently cut, and that he uses lime-cream, are all to be gathered from a close examination of the lower part of the lining. The lens discloses a large number of hair-ends, clean cut by the scissors of the barber. They all appear to be adhesive, and there is a distinct odour of lime-cream. This dust, you will observe, is not the gritty, gray dust of the street but the fluffy brown dust of the house, showing that it has been hung up indoors most of the time; while the marks of moisture upon the inside are proof positive that the wearer perspired very freely, and could therefore hardly be in the best of training."

"But his wife—you said that she had ceased to love him."

"This hat has not been brushed for weeks. When I see you, my dear Watson, with a week's accumulation of dust upon your hat, and when your wife allows you to go out in such a state, I shall fear that you also have been unfortunate enough to lose your wife's affection."

"But he might be a bachelor."

"Nay, he was bringing home the goose as a peace-offering to his wife. Remember the card upon the bird's leg."

"You have an answer to everything. But how on earth do you deduce that the gas is not laid on in his house?"

"One tallow stain, or even two, might come by chance; but when I see no less than five, I think that there can be little doubt that the individual must be brought into frequent contact with burning tallow—walks upstairs at night probably with his hat in one hand and a guttering candle in the other. Anyhow, he never got tallow-stains from a gas-jet. Are you satisfied?"

"Well, it is very ingenious," said I, laughing; "but since, as you said just now, there has been no crime committed, and no harm done save the loss of a goose, all this seems to be rather a waste of energy."

Sherlock Holmes had opened his mouth to reply, when the door flew open, and Peterson, the commissionaire, rushed into the apartment with flushed cheeks and the face of a man who is dazed with astonishment.

"The goose, Mr. Holmes! The goose, sir!" he gasped.

"Eh? What of it, then? Has it returned to life and flapped off through the kitchen window?" Holmes twisted himself round upon the sofa to get a fairer view of the man's excited face.

"See here, sir! See what my wife found in its crop!" He held out his hand and displayed upon the center of the palm a brilliantly scintillating blue stone, rather smaller than a bean in size, but of such purity and radiance that it twinkled like an electric point in the dark hollow of his hand.

Sherlock Holmes sat up with a whistle. "By Jove, Peterson!" said he, "this is treasure trove indeed. I suppose you know what you have got?"

"A diamond, sir? A precious stone. It cuts into glass as though it were putty."

"It's more than a precious stone. It is *the* precious stone."

"Not the Countess of Morcar's blue carbuncle!" I ejaculated.

"Precisely so. I ought to know its size and shape, seeing that I have read the advertisement about it in *The Times* every day lately. It is absolutely unique, and its value can only be conjectured, but the reward offered of £1000 is certainly not within a twentieth part of the market price."

"A thousand pounds! Great Lord of mercy!" The commissionaire plumped down into a chair and stared from one to the other of us.

"That is the reward, and I have reason to know that there are sentimental considerations in the background which would induce the Countess to part with half her fortune if she could but recover the gem."

"It was lost, if I remember aright, at the Hotel Cosmopolitan," I remarked.

"Precisely so, on December 22nd, just five days ago. John Horner, a plumber, was accused of having abstracted it from the lady's jewel-case. The evidence against him was so strong that the case has been referred to the Assizes. I have some account of the matter here, I believe." He rummaged amid his newspapers, glancing over the dates, until at last he smoothed one out, doubled it over, and read the following paragraph:

> "Hotel Cosmopolitan Jewel Robbery. John Horner, 26, plumber, was brought up upon the charge of having upon the 22d inst., abstracted from the jewel-case of the Countess of Morcar the valuable gem known as the blue carbuncle. James Ryder, upper-attendant at the hotel, gave his evidence to the effect that he had shown Horner up to the dressing-room of the Countess of Morcar upon the day of the robbery in order that he might solder the second bar of the grate, which was loose. He had remained with Horner some little time, but had finally been called away. On returning, he found that Horner had disappeared, that the bureau had been forced open, and that the small morocco casket in which, as it afterwards transpired, the Countess was accustomed to keep her jewel, was lying empty upon the dressing-table. Ryder instantly gave the alarm, and Horner was arrested the same evening; but the stone could not be found either upon his person or in his

rooms. Catherine Cusack, maid to the Countess, deposed to having heard Ryder's cry of dismay on discovering the robbery, and to having rushed into the room, where she found matters as described by the last witness. Inspector Bradstreet, B division, gave evidence as to the arrest of Horner, who struggled frantically, and protested his innocence in the strongest terms. Evidence of a previous conviction for robbery having been given against the prisoner, the magistrate refused to deal summarily with the offence, but referred it to the Assizes. Horner, who had shown signs of intense emotion during the proceedings, fainted away at the conclusion and was carried out of court.

"Hum! So much for the police-court," said Holmes thoughtfully, tossing aside the paper. "The question for us now to solve is the sequence of events leading from a rifled jewel-case at one end to the crop of a goose in Tottenham Court Road at the other. You see, Watson, our little deductions have suddenly assumed a much more important and less innocent aspect. Here is the stone; the stone came from the goose, and the goose came from Mr. Henry Baker, the gentleman with the bad hat and all the other characteristics with which I have bored you. So now we must set ourselves very seriously to finding this gentleman and ascertaining what part he has played in this little mystery. To do this, we must try the simplest means first, and these lie undoubtedly in an advertisement in all the evening papers. If this fails, I shall have recourse to other methods."

"What will you say?"

"Give me a pencil and that slip of paper. Now, then:

"Found at the corner of Goodge Street, a goose and a black felt hat. Mr. Henry Baker can have the same by applying at 6:30 this evening at 221B Baker Street.

That is clear and concise."

"Very. But will he see it?"

"Well, he is sure to keep an eye on the papers, since, to a poor man, the loss was a heavy one. He was clearly so scared by his mischance in breaking the window and by the approach of Peterson that he thought of nothing but flight, but since then he must have bitterly regretted the impulse which caused him to drop his bird. Then, again, the introduction of his name will cause him to see it, for everyone who knows him will direct his attention to it. Here you are, Peterson, run down to the advertising agency and have this put in the evening papers."

"In which, sir?"

"Oh, in the *Globe, Star, Pall Mall, St. James's, Evening News Standard, Echo,* and any others that occur to you."

"Very well, sir. And this stone?"

"Ah, yes, I shall keep the stone. Thank you. And, I say, Peterson, just buy a goose on your way back and leave it here with me, for we must have one to give to this gentleman in place of the one which your family is now devouring."

When the commissionaire had gone, Holmes took up the stone and held it against the light. "It's a bonny thing," said he. "Just see how it glints and sparkles. Of course it is a nucleus and focus of crime. Every good stone is. They are the devil's pet baits. In the larger and older jewels every facet may stand for a bloody deed. This stone is not yet twenty years old. It was found in the banks of the Amoy River in southern China and is remarkable in having every characteristic of the carbuncle, save that it is blue in shade instead of ruby red. In spite of its youth, it has already a sinister history. There have been two murders, a vitriol-throwing, a suicide, and several robberies brought about for the sake of this forty-grain weight of crystallized charcoal. Who would think that so pretty a toy would be a purveyor to the gallows and the prison? I'll lock it up in my strong box now and drop a line to the Countess to say that we have it."

"Do you think that this man Horner is innocent?"

"I cannot tell."

"Well, then, do you imagine that this other one, Henry Baker, had anything to do with the matter?"

"It is, I think, much more likely that Henry Baker is an absolutely innocent man, who had no idea that the bird which he was carrying was of considerably more value than if it were made of solid gold. That, however, I shall determine by a very simple test if we have an answer to our advertisement."

"And you can do nothing until then?"

"Nothing."

"In that case I shall continue my professional round. But I shall come back in the evening at the hour you have mentioned, for I should like to see the solution of so tangled a business."

"Very glad to see you. I dine at seven. There is a woodcock, I believe. By the way, in view of recent occurrences, perhaps I ought to ask Mrs. Hudson to examine its crop."

I had been delayed at a case, and it was a little after half-past six when I found myself in Baker Street once more. As I approached the house I saw a tall man in a Scotch bonnet with a coat which was buttoned up to his chin waiting outside in the bright semicircle which was thrown from the fanlight. Just as I arrived the door was opened, and we were shown up together to Holmes's room.

"Mr. Henry Baker, I believe," said he, rising from his armchair and greeting his visitor with the easy air of geniality which he could so readily assume. "Pray take this chair by the fire, Mr. Baker. It is a cold night, and I observe that your circulation is more adapted for summer than for winter. Ah, Watson, you have just come at the right time. Is that your hat, Mr. Baker?"

"Yes, sir, that is undoubtedly my hat."

He was a large man with rounded shoulders, a massive head, and a broad, intelligent face, sloping down to a pointed beard of grizzled brown. A touch of red in nose and cheeks, with a slight tremor of his extended hand, recalled Holmes's surmise as to his habits. His rusty black frock-coat was buttoned right up in front, with the collar turned up, and his lank wrists protruded from his sleeves without a sign of cuff or shirt. He spoke in a slow staccato fashion, choosing his words with care, and gave the impression generally of a man of learning and letters who had had ill-usage at the hands of fortune.

"We have retained these things for some days," said Holmes, "because we expected to see an advertisement from you giving your address. I am at a loss to know now why you did not advertise."

Our visitor gave a rather shamefaced laugh. "Shillings have not been so plentiful with me as they once were," he remarked. "I had no doubt that the gang of roughs who assaulted me had carried off both my hat and the bird. I did not care to spend more money in a hopeless attempt at recovering them."

"Very naturally. By the way, about the bird, we were compelled to eat it."

"To eat it!" Our visitor half rose from his chair in his excitement.

"Yes, it would have been of no use to anyone had we not done so. But I presume that this other goose upon the sideboard, which is about the same weight and perfectly fresh, will answer your purpose equally well?"

"Oh, certainly, certainly," answered Mr. Baker with a sigh of relief.

"Of course, we still have the feathers, legs, crop, and so on of your own bird, so if you wish—"

The man burst into a hearty laugh. "They might be useful to me as relics of my adventure," said he, "but beyond that I can hardly see what use the *disjecta membra* of my late acquaintance are going to be to me. No, sir, I think that, with your permission, I will confine my attentions to the excellent bird which I perceive upon the sideboard."

Sherlock Holmes glanced sharply across at me with a slight shrug of his shoulders.

"There is your hat, then, and there your bird," said he. "By the way, would it bore you to tell me where you got the other one from? I am somewhat of a fowl fancier, and I have seldom seen a better grown goose."

"Certainly, sir," said Baker, who had risen and tucked his newly gained property under his arm. "There are a few of us who frequent the Alpha Inn, near the Museum—we are to be found in the Museum itself during the day, you understand. This year our good host, Windigate by name, instituted a goose club, by which, on consideration of some few pence every week, we were each to receive a bird at Christmas. My pence were duly paid, and the rest is familiar to you. I am much indebted to you, sir, for a Scotch bonnet is fitted neither to my years nor my gravity." With a comical pomposity of manner he bowed solemnly to both of us and strode off upon his way.

"So much for Mr. Henry Baker," said Holmes when he had closed the door behind him. "It is quite certain that he knows nothing whatever about the matter. Are you hungry, Watson?"

"Not particularly."

"Then I suggest that we turn our dinner into a supper and follow up this clue while it is still hot."

"By all means."

It was a bitter night, so we drew on our ulsters and wrapped cravats about our throats. Outside, the stars were shining coldly in a cloudless sky, and the breath of the passers-by blew out into smoke like so many pistol shots. Our footfalls rang out crisply and loudly as we swung through the doctors' quarter, Wimpole Street, Harley Street, and so through Wigmore Street into Oxford Street. In a quarter of an hour we were in Bloomsbury at the Alpha Inn, which is a small public-house at the corner of one of the streets which runs down into Holborn. Holmes pushed open the door of the private bar and ordered two glasses of beer from the ruddy-faced, white-aproned landlord.

"Your beer should be excellent if it is as good as your geese," said he.

"My geese!" The man seemed surprised.

"Yes. I was speaking only half an hour ago to Mr. Henry Baker, who was a member of your goose club."

"Ah! yes, I see. But you see, sir, them's not *our* geese."

"Indeed! Whose, then?"

"Well, I got the two dozen from a salesman in Covent Garden."

"Indeed? I know some of them. Which was it?"

"Breckinridge is his name."

"Ah! I don't know him. Well, here's your good health, landlord, and prosperity to your house. Good-night.

"Now for Mr. Breckinridge," he continued, buttoning up his coat as we came out into the frosty air. "Remember, Watson, that though we have so homely a thing as a goose at one end of this chain, we have at the other a man who will certainly get seven years' penal servitude unless we can establish his innocence. It is possible that our inquiry may but confirm his guilt; but, in any case, we have a line of investigation which has been missed by the police, and which a singular chance has placed in our hands. Let us follow it out to the bitter end. Faces to the south, then, and quick march!"

We passed across Holborn, down Endell Street, and so through a zigzag of slums to Covent Garden Market. One of the largest stalls bore the name of Breckinridge upon it, and the proprietor, a horsy-looking man, with a sharp face and trim side-whiskers, was helping a boy to put up the shutters.

"Good-evening. It's a cold night," said Holmes.

The salesman nodded and shot a questioning glance at my companion.

"Sold out of geese, I see," continued Holmes, pointing at the bare slabs of marble.

"Let you have five hundred to-morrow morning."

"That's no good."

"Well, there are some on the stall with the gas-flare."

"Ah, but I was recommended to you."

"Who by?"

"The landlord of the Alpha."

"Oh, yes; I sent him a couple of dozen."

"Fine birds they were, too. Now where did you get them from?"

To my surprise the question provoked a burst of anger from the salesman.

"Now, then, mister," said he, with his head cocked and his arms akimbo, "what are you driving at? Let's have it straight, now."

"It is straight enough. I should like to know who sold you the geese which you supplied to the Alpha."

"Well, then, I shan't tell you. So now!"

"Oh, it is a matter of no importance; but I don't know why you should be so warm over such a trifle."

"Warm! You'd be as warm, maybe, if you were as pestered as I am. When I pay good money for a good article there should be an end of the business; but it's 'Where are the geese?' and 'Who did you sell the geese to?' and 'What will you take for the geese?' One would think they were the only geese in the world, to hear the fuss that is made over them."

"Well, I have no connection with any other people who have been making inquiries," said Holmes carelessly. "If you won't tell us the bet is off, that is all. But I'm always ready to back my opinion on a matter of fowls, and I have a fiver on it that the bird I ate is country bred."

"Well, then, you've lost your fiver, for it's town bred," snapped the salesman.

"It's nothing of the kind."

"I say it is."

"I don't believe it."

"D'you think you know more about fowls than I, who have handled them ever since I was a nipper? I tell you, all those birds that went to the Alpha were town bred."

"You'll never persuade me to believe that."

"Will you bet, then?"

"It's merely taking your money, for I know that I am right. But I'll have a sovereign on with you, just to teach you not to be obstinate."

The salesman chuckled grimly. "Bring me the books, Bill," said he.

The small boy brought round a small thin volume and a great greasy-backed one, laying them out together beneath the hanging lamp.

"Now then, Mr. Cocksure," said the salesman, "I thought that I was out of geese, but before I finish you'll find that there is still one left in my shop. You see this little book?"

"Well?"

"That's the list of the folk from whom I buy. D'you see? Well, then, here on this page are the country folk, and the numbers after their names are where their accounts are in the big ledger. Now, then! You see this other page in red ink? Well, that is a list of my town suppliers. Now, look at that third name. Just read it out to me."

"Mrs. Oakshott, 117, Brixton Road—249," read Holmes.

"Quite so. Now turn that up in the ledger."

Holmes turned to the page indicated. "Here you are, 'Mrs. Oakshott, 117 Brixton Road, egg and poultry supplier.'"

"Now, then, what's the last entry?"

"'December 22d. Twenty-four geese at 7s. 6d.'"

"Quite so. There you are. And underneath?"

"'Sold to Mr. Windigate of the Alpha, at 12s.'"

"What have you to say now?"

Sherlock Holmes looked deeply chagrined. He drew a sovereign from his pocket and threw it down upon the slab, turning away with the air of a man whose disgust is too deep for words. A few yards off he stopped under a lamp-post and laughed in the hearty, noiseless fashion which was peculiar to him.

"When you see a man with whiskers of that cut and the 'Pink 'un' protruding out of his pocket, you can always draw him by a bet," said he. "I daresay that if I had put £100 down in front of him, that man would not have given me such complete information as was drawn from him by the idea that he was doing me on a wager. Well, Watson, we are, I fancy, nearing the end of our quest, and the only point which remains to be determined is whether we should go on to this Mrs. Oakshott to-night, or whether we should reserve it for to-morrow. It is clear from what that surly fellow said that there are others besides ourselves who are anxious about the matter, and I should—"

His remarks were suddenly cut short by a loud hubbub which broke out from the stall which we had just left. Turning round we saw a little rat-faced fellow standing in the centre of the circle of yellow light which was thrown by the swinging lamp, while Breckinridge, the salesman, framed in the door of his stall, was shaking his fists fiercely at the cringing figure.

"I've had enough of you and your geese," he shouted. "I wish you were all at the devil together. If you come pestering me any more with your silly talk I'll set the dog at you. You bring Mrs. Oakshott here and I'll answer her, but what have you to do with it? Did I buy the geese off you?"

"No; but one of them was mine all the same," whined the little man.

"Well, then, ask Mrs. Oakshott for it."

"She told me to ask you."

"Well, you can ask the King of Proosia, for all I care. I've had enough of it. Get out of this!" He rushed fiercely forward, and the inquirer flitted away into the darkness.

"Ha! this may save us a visit to Brixton Road," whispered Holmes. "Come with me, and we will see what is to be made of this fellow." Striding through the scattered knots of people who lounged round the flaring stalls, my companion speedily overtook the little man and touched him upon the shoulder. He sprang round, and I could see in the gas-light that every vestige of colour had been driven from his face.

"Who are you, then? What do you want?" he asked in a quavering voice.

"You will excuse me," said Holmes blandly, "but I could not help overhearing the questions which you put to the salesman just now. I think that I could be of assistance to you."

"You? Who are you? How could you know anything of the matter?"

"My name is Sherlock Holmes. It is my business to know what other people don't know."

"But you can know nothing of this?"

"Excuse me, I know everything of it. You are endeavoring to trace some geese which were sold by Mrs. Oakshott, of Brixton Road, to a salesman named Breckinridge, by him in turn to Mr. Windigate, of the Alpha, and by him to his club, of which Mr. Henry Baker is a member."

"Oh, sir, you are the very man whom I have longed to meet," cried the little fellow with outstretched hands and quivering fingers. "I can hardly explain to you how interested I am in this matter."

Sherlock Holmes hailed a four-wheeler which was passing. "In that case we had better discuss it in a cosy room rather than in this wind-swept market-place," said he. "But pray tell me, before we go farther, who it is that I have the pleasure of assisting."

The man hesitated for an instant. "My name is John Robinson," he answered with a sidelong glance.

"No, no; the real name," said Holmes sweetly. "It is always awkward doing business with an alias."

A flush sprang to the white cheeks of the stranger. "Well, then," said he, "my real name is James Ryder."

"Precisely so. Head attendant at the Hotel Cosmopolitan. Pray step into the cab, and I shall soon be able to tell you everything which you would wish to know."

The little man stood glancing from one to the other of us with half-frightened, half-hopeful eyes, as one who is not sure whether he is on the verge of a windfall or of a catastrophe. Then he stepped into the cab, and in half an hour we were back in the sitting-room at Baker Street. Nothing had been said during our drive, but the high, thin breathing of our new companion, and the claspings and unclaspings of his hands, spoke of the nervous tension within him.

"Here we are!" said Holmes cheerily as we filed into the room. "The fire looks very seasonable in this weather. You look cold, Mr. Ryder. Pray take the basket-chair. I will just put on my slippers before we settle this little matter of yours. Now, then! You want to know what became of those geese?"

"Yes, sir."

"Or rather, I fancy, of that goose. It was one bird, I imagine, in which you were interested—white, with a black bar across the tail."

Ryder quivered with emotion. "Oh, sir," he cried, "can you tell me where it went to?"

"It came here."

"Here?"

"Yes, and a most remarkable bird it proved. I don't wonder that you should take an interest in it. It laid an egg after it was dead—the bonniest, brightest little blue egg that ever was seen. I have it here in my museum."

Our visitor staggered to his feet and clutched the mantelpiece with his right hand. Holmes unlocked his strongbox and held up the blue carbuncle, which shone out like a star, with a cold, brilliant, many-pointed radiance. Ryder stood glaring with a drawn face, uncertain whether to claim or to disown it.

"The game's up, Ryder," said Holmes quietly. "Hold up, man, or you'll be into the fire! Give him an arm back into his chair, Watson. He's not got blood enough to go in for felony with impunity. Give him a dash of brandy. So! Now he looks a little more human. What a shrimp it is, to be sure!"

For a moment he had staggered and nearly fallen, but the

brandy brought a tinge of colour into his cheeks, and he sat staring with frightened eyes at his accuser.

"I have almost every link in my hands, and all the proofs which I could possibly need, so there is little which you need tell me. Still, that little may as well be cleared up to make the case complete. You had heard, Ryder, of this blue stone of the Countess of Morcar's?"

"It was Catherine Cusack who told me of it," said he in a crackling voice.

"I see—her ladyship's waiting-maid. Well, the temptation of sudden wealth so easily acquired was too much for you, as it has been for better men before you; but you were not very scrupulous in the means you used. It seems to me, Ryder, that there is the making of a very pretty villain in you. You knew that this man Horner, the plumber, had been concerned in some such matter before, and that suspicion would rest the more readily upon him. What did you do, then? You made some small job in my lady's room—you and your confederate Cusack—and you managed that he should be the man sent for. Then, when he had left, you rifled the jewel-case, raised the alarm, and had this unfortunate man arrested. You then—"

Ryder threw himself down suddenly upon the rug and clutched at my companion's knees. "For God's sake, have mercy!" he shrieked. "Think of my father! of my mother! It would break their hearts. I never went wrong before! I never will again. I swear it. I'll swear it on a Bible. Oh, don't bring it into court! For Christ's sake, don't!"

"Get back into your chair!" said Holmes sternly. "It is very well to cringe and crawl now, but you thought little enough of this poor Horner in the dock for a crime of which he knew nothing."

"I will fly, Mr. Holmes. I will leave the country, sir. Then the charge against him will break down."

"Hum! We will talk about that. And now let us hear a true account of the next act. How came the stone into the goose, and how came the goose into the open market? Tell us the truth, for there lies your only hope of safety."

Ryder passed his tongue over his parched lips. "I will tell

you it just as it happened, sir," said he. "When Horner had been arrested, it seemed to me that it would be best for me to get away with the stone at once, for I did not know at what moment the police might not take it into their heads to search me and my room. There was no place about the hotel where it would be safe. I went out, as if on some commission, and I made for my sister's house. She had married a man named Oakshott, and lived in Brixton Road, where she fattened fowls for the market. All the way there every man I met seemed to me to be a policeman or a detective; and, for all that it was a cold night, the sweat was pouring down my face before I came to the Brixton Road. My sister asked me what was the matter, and why I was so pale; but I told her that I had been upset by the jewel robbery at the hotel. Then I went into the back yard and smoked a pipe, and wondered what it would be best to do.

"I had a friend once called Maudsley, who went to the bad, and has just been serving his time in Pentonville. One day he had met me, and fell into talk about the ways of thieves, and how they could get rid of what they stole. I knew that he would be true to me, for I knew one or two things about him; so I made up my mind to go right on to Kilburn, where he lived, and take him into my confidence. He would show me how to turn the stone into money. But how to get to him in safety? I thought of the agonies I had gone through in coming from the hotel. I might at any moment be seized and searched, and there would be the stone in my waistcoat pocket. I was leaning against the wall at the time and looking at the geese which were waddling about round my feet, and suddenly an idea came into my head which showed me how I could beat the best detective that ever lived.

"My sister had told me some weeks before that I might have the pick of her geese for a Christmas present, and I knew that she was always as good as her word. I would take my goose now, and in it I would carry my stone to Kilburn. There was a little shed in the yard, and behind this I drove one of the birds—a fine big one, white, with a barred tail. I caught it, and, prying its bill open, I thrust the stone down its throat as far as my finger could reach. The bird gave a gulp, and I felt the stone pass along its gullet and down into its crop. But the creature flapped and struggled, and out came my sister to know what was the matter. As I turned to speak to her the brute broke loose and fluttered off among the others.

"'Whatever were you doing with that bird, Jem?' says she.

"'Well,' said I, 'you said you'd give me one for Christmas, and I was feeling which was the fattest.'

"'Oh,' says she, 'we've set yours aside for you—Jem's bird, we call it. It's the big white one over yonder. There's twenty-six of them, which makes one for you, and one for us, and two dozen for the market.'

"'Thank you, Maggie,' says I; 'but if it is all the same to you, I'd rather have that one I was handling just now.'

"'The other is a good three pound heavier,' said she, 'and we fattened it expressly for you.'

"'Never mind. I'll have the other, and I'll take it now,' said I.

"'Oh, just as you like,' said she, a little huffed. 'Which is it you want, then?'

"'That white one with the barred tail, right in the middle of the flock.'

"'Oh, very well. Kill it and take it with you.'

"Well, I did what she said, Mr. Holmes, and I carried the bird all the way to Kilburn. I told my pal what I had done, for he was a man that it was easy to tell a thing like that to. He laughed until he choked, and we got a knife and opened the goose. My heart turned to water, for there was no sign of the stone, and I knew that some terrible mistake had occurred. I left the bird, rushed back to my sister's, and hurried into the back yard. There was not a bird to be seen there.

"'Where are they all, Maggie?' I cried.

"'Gone to the dealer's, Jem.'

"'Which dealer's?'

"'Breckinridge, of Covent Garden.'

"'But was there another with a barred tail?' I asked, 'the same as the one I chose?'

"'Yes, Jem; there were two barred-tailed ones, and I could never tell them apart.'

"Well, then, of course I saw it all, and I ran off as hard as my feet would carry me to this man Breckinridge; but he had sold the lot at once, and not one word would he tell me as to where they had gone. You heard him yourselves to-night. Well, he has always answered me like that. My sister thinks that I am going mad. Sometimes I think that I am myself. And now—and now I am myself a branded thief, without ever having touched the wealth for which I sold my character. God help me! God help me!" He burst into convulsive sobbing, with his face buried in his hands.

There was a long silence, broken only by his heavy breathing, and by the measured tapping of Sherlock Holmes's finger-tips upon the edge of the table. Then my friend rose and threw open the door.

"Get out!" said he.

"What, sir! Oh, Heaven bless you!"

"No more words. Get out!"

And no more words were needed. There was a rush, a clatter upon the stairs, the bang of a door, and the crisp rattle of running footfalls from the street.

"After all, Watson," said Holmes, reaching up his hand for his clay pipe, "I am not retained by the police to supply their deficiencies. If Horner were in danger it would be another thing; but this fellow will not appear against him, and the case must collapse. I suppose that I am commuting a felony, but it is just possible that I am saving a soul. This fellow will not go wrong again; he is too terribly frightened. Send him to jail now, and you make him a jail-bird for life. Besides, it is the season of forgiveness. Chance has put in our way a most singular and whimsical problem, and its solution is its own reward. If you will have the goodness to touch the bell, Doctor, we will begin another investigation, in which, also, a bird will be the chief feature."

"I've just told Fettle about the will."

Like so many Americans, my sole acquaintance with wassail was through the song "Wassail, Wassail, all over the town," and occasional mention of a wassail bowl. As neither my parents nor their friends seemed to partake of wassail at Christmas, I came to suspect it was either lewd, illegal, or at the very least, unsanitary.

Egg Nog was always the drink on hand at Christmastime. Although there might be some dispute as to whether it should be spiked with rum or brandy, there was always a dash of nutmeg on top to give it some spice.

I have since read of a lady in Brixton who added ground glass to her nogs to give them some tang, but I think this is generally to be avoided, unless you have a limited amount and wish to discourage seconds.

The gentleman pictured discovered that an extract of mistletoe berries gave egg nog a certain festive quality. So successful was his recipe, that he was persuaded to enter it in a Festival of Britain Cookery competition where he was given first prize and 'the Chair.'

Her heroes were an eccentric windbag and a meddlesome old lady. Her writing seldom got more violent than a good bump on the head. She was hopelessly unconvincing describing anyone under thirty. And her approach to sex and passion was that of two arthritic porcupines mating. Yet she was the most successful author of mystery stories that the world has yet produced.

What made Agatha Christie the writing phenomenon of her time? Plotting. No one could wring as many possibilities out of a murder as she. And, because she couched them all in cozy, English gentility, she caught her reader napping, more often than not.

When "The Adventure of the Christmas Pudding" (also called "The Theft of the Royal Ruby") was first collected, she included an introductory memoir. The story, prefaced by her remarks, begins on the next page.

The Adventure of the Christmas Pudding

by Agatha Christie

The Adventure of the Christmas Pudding is an indulgence of my own, since it recalls to me, very pleasurably, the Christmases of my youth. After my father's death, my mother and I always spent Christmas with my brother-in-law's family in the north of England—and what superb Christmases they were for a child to remember! Abney Hall had everything! The garden boasted a waterfall, a stream, and a tunnel under the drive! The Christmas fare was of gargantuan proportions. I was a skinny child, appearing delicate, but actually of robust health and perpetually hungry! The boys of the family and I used to vie with each other as to who could eat most on Christmas Day. Oyster Soup and Turbot went down without undue zest, but then came Roast Turkey, Boiled Turkey and an enormous Sirloin of Beef. The boys and I had two helpings of all three! We then had Plum Pudding, Mince-pies, Trifle and every kind of dessert. During the afternoon we ate chocolates solidly. We neither felt, nor were, sick! How lovely to be eleven years old and greedy!

What a day of delight from "Stockings" in bed in the morning, Church and all the Christmas hymns, Christmas dinner, Presents, and the final Lighting of the Christmas Tree!

And how deep my gratitude to the kind and hospitable hostess who must have worked so hard to

*make Christmas Day a wonderful memory to me
still in my old age.*

*So let me dedicate this to the memory of Abney
Hall—its kindness and its hospitality.*

And a happy Christmas to all who read (it).

Agatha Christie

I regret exceedingly—" said M. Hercule Poirot.

He was interrupted. Not rudely interrupted. The interruption was suave, dexterous, persuasive rather than contradictory.

"Please don't refuse offhand, M. Poirot. There are grave issues of State. Your co-operation will be appreciated in the highest quarters."

"You are too kind," Hercule Poirot waved a hand, "but I really cannot undertake to do as you ask. At this season of the year—"

Again Mr. Jesmond interrupted. "Christmas time," he said, persuasively. "An old-fashioned Christmas in the English countryside."

Hercule Poirot shivered. The thought of the English countryside at this season of the year did not attract him.

"A good old-fashioned Christmas!" Mr. Jesmond stressed it.

"Me—I am not an Englishman," said Hercule Poirot. "In my country, Christmas, it is for the children. The New Year, that is what we celebrate."

"Ah," said Mr. Jesmond, "but Christmas in England is a great institution and I assure you at Kings Lacey you would see it at its best. It's a wonderful old house, you know. Why, one wing of it dates from the fourteenth century."

Again Poirot shivered. The thought of a fourteenth-century English manor house filled him with apprehension. He had suffered too often in the historic country houses of England. He looked round appreciatively at his comfortable modern flat with its radiators and the latest patent devices for excluding any kind of draught.

"In the winter," he said firmly, "I do not leave London."

"I don't think you quite appreciate, M. Poirot, what a very serious matter this is." Mr. Jesmond glanced at his companion and then back at Poirot.

Poirot's second visitor had up to now said nothing but a polite and formal "How do you do." He sat now, gazing down at his well-polished shoes, with an air of the utmost dejection on his coffee-coloured face. He was a young man, not more than twenty-three, and he was clearly in a state of complete misery.

"Yes, yes," said Hercule Poirot. "Of course the matter is serious. I do appreciate that. His Highness has my heartfelt sympathy."

"The position is one of the utmost delicacy," said Mr. Jesmond.

Poirot transferred his gaze from the young man to his older companion. If one wanted to sum up Mr. Jesmond in a word, the word would have been discretion. Everything about Mr. Jesmond was discreet. His well-cut but inconspicuous clothes, his pleasant, well-bred voice which rarely soared out of an agreeable monotone, his light-brown hair just thinning a little at the temples, his pale serious face. It seemed to Hercule Poirot that he had known not one Mr. Jesmond but a dozen Mr. Jesmonds in his time, all using sooner or later the same phrase—"A position of the utmost delicacy."

"The police," said Hercule Poirot, "can be very discreet, you know."

Mr. Jesmond shook his head firmly.

"Not the police," he said. "To recover the—er—what we want to recover will almost inevitably invoke taking proceedings in the law courts and we know so little. We *suspect*, but we do not *know*."

"You have my sympathy," said Hercule Poirot again.

If he imagined that his sympathy was going to mean anything to his two visitors, he was wrong. They did not want sympathy, they wanted practical help. Mr. Jesmond began once more to talk about the delights of an English Christmas.

"It's dying out, you know," he said, "the real old-fashioned type of Christmas. People spend it at hotels nowadays. But an English Christmas with all the family gathered round, the children and their stockings, the Christmas tree, the turkey and plum pudding, the crackers. The snow-man outside the window—"

In the interests of exactitude, Hercule Poirot intervened.

"To make a snow-man one has to have the snow," he remarked severely. "And one cannot have snow to order, even for an English Christmas."

"I was talking to a friend of mine in the meteorological office only today," said Mr. Jesmond, "and he tells me that it is highly probable there *will* be snow this Christmas."

It was the wrong thing to have said. Hercule Poirot shuddered more forcefully than ever.

"Snow in the country!" he said. "That would be still more abominable. A large, cold, stone manor house."

"Not at all," said Mr. Jesmond. "Things have changed very much in the last ten years or so. Oil-fired central heating."

"They have oil-fired central heating at Kings Lacey?" asked Poirot. For the first time he seemed to waver.

Mr. Jesmond seized his opportunity. "Yes, indeed," he said, "and a splendid hot water system. Radiators in every bedroom. I assure you, my dear M. Poirot, Kings Lacey is comfort itself in the winter time. You might even find the house *too* warm."

"That is most unlikely," said Hercule Poirot.

With practised dexterity Mr. Jesmond shifted his ground a little.

"You can appreciate the terrible dilemma we are in," he said, in a confidential manner.

Hercule Poirot nodded. The problem was, indeed, not a happy one. A young potentate-to-be, the only son of the ruler of a rich and important native State had arrived in London a few weeks ago. His country had been passing through a period of restlessness and discontent. Though loyal to the father whose way of life had remained persistently Eastern, popular opinion was somewhat dubious of the younger generation. His follies had been Western ones and as such looked upon with disapproval.

Recently, however, his betrothal had been announced. He was to marry a cousin of the same blood, a young woman who, though educated at Cambridge, was careful to display no Western influence in her own country. The wedding day was announced and the young prince had made a journey to England, bringing with him some of the famous jewels of his house to be reset in appropriate modern settings by Cartier. These had included a very famous ruby which had been removed from its cumbersome old-fashioned necklace and had been given a new look by the famous jewellers. So far so good, but after this came the snag. It was not to be supposed that a young man possessed of much wealth and convivial tastes, should not commit a few follies of the pleasanter type. As to that there would have been no censure. Young princes were supposed to amuse themselves in this fashion. For the prince to take the girl friend of the moment for a walk down Bond Street and bestow upon her an emerald bracelet or a diamond clip as a reward for the pleasure she had afforded him would have been regarded as quite natural and suitable, corresponding in fact to the Cadillac cars which his father invariably presented to his favourite dancing girl of the moment.

But the prince had been far more indiscreet than that. Flattered by the lady's interest, he had displayed to her the famous ruby in its new setting, and had finally been so unwise as to accede to her request to be allowed to wear it—just for one evening!

The sequel was short and sad. The lady had retired from their supper table to powder her nose. Time passed. She did not return. She had left the establishment by another door and since then had disappeared into space. The important and distressing thing was that the ruby in its new setting had disappeared with her.

These were the facts that could not possibly be made public without the most dire consequences. The ruby was something more than a ruby, it was a historical possession of great significance, and the circumstances of its disappearance were such that any undue publicity about them might result in the most serious political consequences.

Mr. Jesmond was not the man to put these facts into simple language. He wrapped them up, as it were, in a great deal of verbiage. Who exactly Mr. Jesmond was, Hercule Poirot did not know. He had met other Mr. Jesmonds in the course of his career. Whether he was connected with the Home Office, the

Foreign Secretary or some more discreet branch of public service was not specified. He was acting in the interests of the Commonwealth. The ruby must be recovered.

M. Poirot, so Mr. Jesmond delicately insisted, was the man to recover it.

"Perhaps—yes," Hercule Poirot admitted, "but you can tell me so little. Suggestion—suspicion—all that is not very much to go upon."

"Come now, Monsieur Poirot, surely it is not beyond your powers. Ah, come now."

"I do not always succeed."

But this was mock modesty. It was clear enough from Poirot's tone that for him to undertake a mission was almost synonymous with succeeding in it.

"His Highness is very young," Mr. Jesmond said. "It will be sad if his whole life is to be blighted for a mere youthful indiscretion."

Poirot looked kindly at the downcast young man. "It is the time for follies, when one is young," he said encouragingly, "and for the ordinary young man it does not matter so much. The good papa, he pays up; the family lawyer, he helps to disentangle the inconvenience; the young man, he learns by experience and all ends for the best. In a position such as yours, it is hard indeed. Your approaching marriage—"

"That is it. That is it exactly." For the first time words poured from the young man. "You see she is very, very serious. She takes life very seriously. She has acquired at Cambridge many very serious ideas. There is to be education in my country. There are to be schools. There are to be many things. All in the name of progress, you understand, of democracy. It will not be, she says, like it was in my father's time. Naturally she knows that I will have diversions in London, but not the scandal. No! It is the scandal that matters. You see it is very, very famous, this ruby. There is a long trail behind it, a history. Much bloodshed—many deaths!"

"Deaths," said Hercule Poirot thoughtfully. He looked at Mr. Jesmond. "One hopes," he said, "it will not come to that?"

Mr. Jesmond made a peculiar noise rather like a hen who has decided to lay an egg and then thought better of it.

"No, no indeed," he said, sounding rather prim. "There is no question, I am sure, of anything of *that* kind."

"You cannot be sure," said Hercule Poirot. "Whoever has the ruby now, there may be others who want to gain possession of it, and who will not stick at a trifle, my friend."

"I really don't think," said Mr. Jesmond, sounding more prim than ever, "that we need enter into speculation of that kind. Quite unprofitable."

"Me," said Hercule Poirot, suddenly becoming very foreign, "me, I explore all the avenues, like the politicians."

Mr. Jesmond looked at him doubtfully. Pulling himself together, he said, "Well, I can take it that is settled, M. Poirot? You will go to Kings Lacey?"

"And how do I explain myself there?" asked Hercule Poirot.

Mr. Jesmond smiled with confidence.

"That, I think, can be arranged very easily," he said. "I can assure you that it will all seem quite natural. You will find the Laceys most charming. Delightful people."

"And you do not deceive me about the oil-fired central heating?"

"No, no, indeed." Mr. Jesmond sounded quite pained. "I assure you you will find every comfort."

"*Tout confort moderne,*" murmured Poirot to himself, reminiscently. "*Eh bien,*" he said, "I accept."

II

The temperature in the long drawing-room at Kings Lacey was a comfortable sixty-eight as Hercule Poirot sat talking to Mrs. Lacey by one of the big mullioned windows. Mrs. Lacey was engaged in needlework. She was not doing *petit point* or embroidered flowers upon silk. Instead, she appeared to be engaged in the prosaic task of hemming dishcloths. As she sewed she talked in a soft reflective voice that Poirot found very charming.

"I hope you will enjoy our Christmas party here, M. Poirot. It's only the family, you know. My granddaughter and a grandson and a friend of his and Bridget who's my great niece, and Diana who's a cousin and David Welwyn who is a very old friend. Just a family party. But Edwina Morecombe said that that's what you really wanted to see. An old-fashioned Christmas. Nothing could be more old-fashioned than we are! My husband you know, absolutely lives in the past. He likes everything to be just as it was when he was a boy of twelve years old, and used to come here for his holidays." She smiled to herself. "All the same old things, the Christmas tree and the stockings hung up and the oyster soup and the turkey —two turkeys, one boiled and one roast—and the plum pudding with the ring and the bachelor's button and all the rest of it in it. We can't have sixpences nowadays because they're not pure silver any more. But all the old desserts, the Elvas plums and Carlsbad plums and almonds and raisins, and crystallised fruit and ginger. Dear me, I sound like a catalogue from Fortnum and Mason!"

"You arouse my gastronomic juices, Madame."

"I expect we'll all have frightful indigestion by to-morrow evening," said Mrs. Lacey. "One isn't used to eating so much nowadays, is one?"

She was interrupted by some loud shouts and whoops of laughter outside the window. She glanced out.

"I don't know what they're doing out there. Playing some game or other, I suppose. I've always been so afraid, you know, that these young people would be bored by our Christmas here. But not at all, it's just the opposite. Now my own son and daughter and their friends, they used to be rather sophisticated about Christmas. Say it was all nonsense and too much fuss and it would be far better to go out to a hotel somewhere and dance. But the younger generation seems to find all this terribly attractive. Besides," added Mrs. Lacey practically, "schoolboys and schoolgirls are always hungry, aren't they? I think they must starve them at these schools. After all, one does know children of that age eat about as much as three strong men."

Poirot laughed and said, "It is most kind of you and your husband, Madame, to include me in this way in your family party."

"Oh, we're both delighted, I'm sure," said Mrs. Lacey. "And if you find Horace a little gruff," she continued, "pay no attention. It's just his manner, you know."

What her husband, Colonel Lacey, had actually said was: "Can't think why you want one of these damned foreigners here cluttering up Christmas? Why can't we have him some other time? Can't stick foreigners! All right, all right, so Edwina Morecombe wished him on us. What's it got to do with *her.* I should like to know? Why doesn't *she* have him for Christmas?"

"Because you know very well," Mrs. Lacey had said, "that Edwina always goes to Claridge's."

Her husband had looked at her piercingly and said, "Not up to something, are you, Em?"

"Up to something?" said Em, opening very blue eyes. "Of course not. Why should I be?"

Old Colonel Lacey laughed, a deep, rumbling laugh. "I wouldn't put it past you, Em," he said. "When you look your most innocent is when you *are* up to something."

Revolving these things in her mind, Mrs. Lacey went on: "Edwina said she thought perhaps you might help us. . . . I'm sure I don't know quite how, but she said that friends of yours had once found you very helpful in—in a case something like ours. I—well, perhaps you don't know what I'm talking about?"

Poirot looked at her encouragingly. Mrs. Lacey was close on seventy, as upright as a ramrod, with snow-white hair, pink cheeks, blue eyes, a ridiculous nose and a determined chin.

"If there is anything I can do I shall only be too happy to do it," said Poirot. "It is, I understand, a rather unfortunate matter of a young girl's infatuation."

Mrs. Lacey nodded. "Yes. It seems extraordinary that I should—well, want to talk to you about it. After all, you *are* a perfect stranger . . ."

"*And* a foreigner," said Poirot, in an understanding manner.

"Yes," said Mrs. Lacey, "but perhaps that makes it easier, in a way. Anyhow, Edwina seemed to think that you might perhaps know something—how shall I put it—something useful about this young Desmond Lee-Wortley."

Poirot paused a moment to admire the ingenuity of Mr.

Jesmond and the ease with which he had made use of Lady Morecombe to further his own purposes.

"He has not, I understand, a very good reputation, this young man?" he began delicately.

"No, indeed, he hasn't! A very bad reputation. But that's no help so far as Sarah is concerned. It's never any good, is it, telling young girls that men have a bad reputation? It—it just spurs them on!"

"You are so very right," said Poirot.

"In my young day," went on Mrs. Lacey. "(Oh dear, that's a very long time ago!) We used to be warned, you know, against certain young men, and of course it *did* heighten one's interest in them, and if one could possibly manage to dance with them, or to be alone with them in a dark conservatory—" she laughed. "That's why I wouldn't let Horace do any of the things he wanted to do."

"Tell me," said Poirot, "exactly what it is that troubles you?"

"Our son was killed in the war," said Mrs. Lacey. "My daughter-in-law died when Sarah was born so that she has always been with us, and we've brought her up. Perhaps we've brought her up unwisely—I don't know. But we thought we ought always to leave her as free as possible."

"That is desirable, I think," said Poirot. "One cannot go against the spirit of the times."

"No," said Mrs. Lacey, "that's just what I felt about it. And, of course, girls nowadays do do these sort of things."

Poirot looked at her inquiringly.

"I think the way one expresses it," said Mrs. Lacey, "is that Sarah has got in with what they call the coffee-bar set. She won't go to dances or come out properly or be a deb or anything of that kind. Instead she has two rather unpleasant rooms in Chelsea down by the river and wears these funny clothes that they like to wear, and black stockings or bright green ones. Very thick stockings. (So prickly, I always think!) And she goes about without washing or combing her hair."

"*Ça, c'est tout à fait naturelle,*" said Poirot. "It is the fashion of the moment. They grow out of it."

"Yes, I know," said Mrs. Lacey. "I wouldn't worry about *that* sort of thing. But you see she's taken up with this Desmond Lee-Wortley and he really has a *very* unsavoury reputation. He lives more or less on well-to-do girls. They seem to go quite mad about him. He very nearly married the Hope girl, but her people got her made a ward in court or something. And of course that's what Horace wants to do. He says he must do it for her protection. But I don't think it's really a good idea, M. Poirot. I mean, they'll just run away together and go to Scotland or Ireland or the Argentine or somewhere and either get married or else live together without getting married. And although it may be contempt of court and all that—well, it isn't really an answer, is it, in the end? Especially if a baby's coming. One has to give in then, and let them get married. And then, nearly always, it seems to me, after a year or two there's a divorce. And then the girl comes home and usually after a year or two she marries someone so nice he's almost dull and settles down. But it's particularly sad, it seems to me, if there is a child, because it's not the same thing, being brought up by a stepfather, however nice. No, I think it's much better if we did as we did in my young days. I mean the first young man one fell in love with was *always* someone undesirable. I remember I had a horrible passion for a young man called—now what was his name now? —how strange it is, I can't remember his Christian name at all! Tibbitt, that was his surname. Young Tibbitt. Of course, my father more or less forbade him the house, but he used to get asked to the same dances, and we used to dance together. And sometimes we'd escape and sit out together and occasionally friends would arrange picnics to which we both went. Of course, it was all very exciting and forbidden and one enjoyed it enormously. But one didn't go to the—well, to the *lengths* that girls go nowadays. And so, after a while, the Mr. Tibbitts faded out. And do you know, when I saw him four years later I was surprised what I could *ever* have seen in him! He seemed to be such a *dull* young man. Flashy, you know. No interesting conversation.

"One always thinks the days of one's own youth are best," said Poirot, somewhat sententiously.

"I know," said Mrs. Lacey. "It's tiresome, isn't it? I mustn't be tiresome. But all the same I *don't* want Sarah, who's a dear girl really, to marry Desmond Lee-Wortley. She and David

Welwyn, who is staying here, were always such friends and so fond of each other, and we did hope, Horace and I, that they would grow up and marry. But of course she just finds him dull now, and she's absolutely infatuated with Desmond."

"I do not quite understand, Madame," said Poirot. "You have him here now, staying in the house, this Desmond Lee-Wortley?"

"That's *my* doing," said Mrs. Lacey. "Horace was all for forbidding her to see him and all that. Of course, in Horace's day, the father or guardian would have called round at the young man's lodgings with a horse whip! Horace was all for forbidding the fellow the house, and forbidding the girl to see him. I told him that was quite the wrong attitude to take. 'No,' I said. 'Ask him down here. We'll have him down for Christmas with the family party.' Of course, my husband said I was mad! But I said, 'At any rate, dear, let's *try* it. Let her see him in *our* atmosphere and *our* house and we'll be very nice to him and very polite, and perhaps then he'll seem less interesting to her'!"

"I think, as they say, you *have* something there, Madame," said Poirot. "I think your point of view is very wise. Wiser than your husband's."

"Well, I hope it is," said Mrs. Lacey doubtfully. "It doesn't seem to be working much yet. But of course he's only been here a couple of days." A sudden dimple showed in her wrinkled cheek. "I'll confess something to you, M. Poirot. I myself can't help liking him. I don't mean I *really* like him, with my *mind*, but I can feel the charm all right. Oh yes, I can see what Sarah sees in him. But I'm an old enough woman and have enough experience to know that he's absolutely no good. Even if I *do* enjoy his company. Though I do think," added Mrs. Lacey, rather wistfully, "he has *some* good points. He asked if he might bring his sister here, you know. She's had an operation and was in hospital. He said it was so sad for her being in a nursing home over Christmas and he wondered if it would be too much trouble if he could bring her with him. He said he'd take all her meals up to her and all that. Well now, I do think that *was* rather nice of him, don't you, M. Poirot?"

"It shows a consideration," said Poirot, thoughtfully, "which seems almost out of character."

"Oh, I don't know. You can have family affections at the same time as wishing to prey on a rich young girl. Sarah will be *very* rich, you know, not only with what we leave her—and of course that won't be very much because most of the money goes with the place to Colin, my grandson. But her mother was a very rich woman and Sarah will inherit all her money when she's twenty-one. She's only twenty now. No, I do think it was nice of Desmond to mind about his sister. And he didn't pretend she was anything very wonderful or that. She's a shorthand typist, I gather—does secretarial work in London. And he's been as good as his word and does carry up trays to her. Not all the time, of course, but quite often. So I think he has some nice points. But all the same," said Mrs. Lacey with great decision, "I don't want Sarah to marry him."

"From all I have heard and been told," said Poirot, "that would indeed be a disaster."

"Do you think it would be possible for you to help us in any way?" asked Mrs. Lacey.

"I think it is possible, yes," said Hercule Poirot, "but I do not wish to promise too much. For the Mr. Desmond Lee-Wortleys of this world are clever, Madame. But do not despair. One can, perhaps, do a little something. I shall at any rate, put forth my best endeavours, if only in gratitude for your kindness in asking me here for this Christmas festivity." He looked round him. "And it cannot be so easy these days to have Christmas festivities."

"No, indeed," Mrs. Lacey sighed. She leaned forward. "Do you know, M. Poirot, what I really dream of—what I would love to have?"

"But tell me, Madame."

"I simply long to have a small, modern bungalow. No, perhaps not a bungalow exactly, but a small, modern, easy to run house built somewhere in the park here, and live in it with an absolutely up-to-date kitchen and no long passages. Everything easy and simple."

"It is a very practical idea, Madame."

"It's not practical for me," said Mrs. Lacey. "My husband *adores* this place. He *loves* living here. He doesn't mind being slightly uncomfortable, he doesn't mind the inconveniences and he would hate, simply *hate*, to live in a small modern house in the park!"

"So you sacrifice yourself to his wishes?"

Mrs. Lacey drew herself up. "I do not consider it a sacrifice, M. Poirot," she said. "I married my husband with the wish to make him happy. He has been a good husband to me and made me very happy all these years, and I wish to give happiness to him."

"So you will continue to live here," said Poirot.

"It's not really too uncomfortable," said Mrs. Lacey.

"No, no," said Poirot, hastily. "On the contrary, it is most comfortable. Your central heating and your bath water are perfection."

"We spent a lot of money in making the house comfortable to live in," said Mrs. Lacey. "We were able to sell some land. Ripe for development, I think they call it. Fortunately right out of sight of the house on the other side of the park. Really rather an ugly bit of ground with no nice view, but we got a very good price for it. So that we have been able to have as many improvements as possible."

"But the service, Madame?"

"Oh, well, that presents less difficulty than you might think. Of course, one cannot expect to be looked after and waited upon as one used to be. Different people come in from the village. Two women in the morning, another two to cook lunch and wash it up, and different ones again in the evening. There are plenty of people who want to come and work for a few hours a day. Of course for Christmas we are very lucky. My dear Mrs. Ross always comes in every Christmas. She is a wonderful cook, really first-class. She retired about ten years ago, but she comes in to help us in any emergency. Then there is dear Peverell."

"Your butler?"

"Yes. He is pensioned off and lives in the little house near the lodge, but he is so devoted, and he insists on coming to wait on us at Christmas. Really, I'm terrified, M. Poirot, because he's so old and shaky that I feel certain that if he carries anything heavy he will drop it. It's really an agony to watch him. And his heart is not good and I'm afraid of his doing too much. But it would hurt his feelings dreadfully if I did not let him come. He hems and hahs and makes disapproving noises when he sees the state our silver is in and within three days of being here, it is all wonderful again. Yes. He is a dear faithful friend." She smiled at Poirot. "So you see, we are all set for a happy Christmas. A white Christmas, too," she added as she looked out of the window. "See? It is beginning to snow. Ah, the children are coming in. You must meet them, M. Poirot."

Poirot was introduced with due ceremony. First, to Colin and Michael, the schoolboy grandson and his friend, nice polite lads of fifteen, one dark, one fair. Then to their cousin, Bridget, a black-haired girl of about the same age with enormous vitality.

"And this is my granddaughter, Sarah," said Mrs. Lacey.

Poirot looked with some interest at Sarah, an attractive girl with a mop of red hair; her manner seemed to him nervy and a trifle defiant, but she showed real affection for her grandmother.

"And this is Mr. Lee-Wortley."

Mr. Lee-Wortley wore a fisherman's jersey and tight black jeans; his hair was rather long and it seemed doubtful whether he had shaved that morning. In contrast to him was a young man introduced as David Welwyn, who was solid and quiet, with a pleasant smile, and rather obviously addicted to soap and water. There was one other member of the party, a handsome, rather intense-looking girl who was introduced as Diana Middleton.

Tea was brought in. A hearty meal of scones, crumpets, sandwiches and three kinds of cake. The younger members of the party appreciated the tea. Colonel Lacey came in last, remarking in a non-committal voice:

"Hey, tea? Oh yes, tea."

He received his cup of tea from his wife's hand, helped himself to two scones, cast a look of aversion at Desmond Lee-Wortley and sat down as far away from him as he could. He was a big man with bushy eyebrows and a red, weather-beaten face. He might have been taken for a farmer rather than the lord of the manor.

"Started to snow," he said. "It's going to be a white Christmas all right."

After tea the party dispersed.

"I expect they'll go and play with their tape recorders now," said Mrs. Lacey to Poirot. She looked indulgently after her grandson as he left the room. Her tone was that of one who says "The children are going to play with their toy soldiers."

"They're frightfully technical, of course," she said, "and very grand about it all."

The boys and Bridget, however, decided to go along to the lake and see if the ice on it was likely to make skating possible.

"*I* thought we could have skated on it this morning," said Colin. "But old Hodgkins said no. He's always so terribly careful."

"Come for a walk, David," said Diana Middleton, softly.

David hesitated for half a moment, his eyes on Sarah's red head. She was standing by Desmond Lee-Wortley, her hand on his arm, looking up into his face.

"All right," said David Welwyn, "yes, let's."

Diana slipped a quick hand through his arm and they turned towards the door into the garden. Sarah said:

"Shall we go, too, Desmond? It's fearfully stuffy in the house."

"Who wants to walk?" said Desmond. "I'll get my car out. We'll go along to the Speckled Boar and have a drink."

Sarah hesitated for a moment before saying:

"Let's go to Market Ledbury to the White Hart. It's much more fun."

Though for all the world she would not have put it into words, Sarah had an instinctive revulsion from going down to the local pub with Desmond. It was, somehow, not in the tradition of Kings Lacey. The women of Kings Lacey had never frequented the bar of the Speckled Boar. She had an obscure feeling that to go there would be to let old Colonel Lacey and his wife down. And why not? Desmond Lee-Wortley would have said. For a moment of exasperation Sarah felt that he ought to know why not! One didn't upset such old darlings as Grandfather and dear old Em unless it was necessary. They'd been very sweet, really, letting her lead her own life, not understanding in the least why she wanted to live in Chelsea in the way she did, but accepting it. That was due to Em of course. Grandfather would have kicked up no end of a row.

Sarah had no illusions about her grandfather's attitude. It was not his doing that Desmond had been asked to stay at Kings Lacey. That was Em, and Em was a darling and always had been.

When Desmond had gone to fetch his car, Sarah popped her head into the drawing-room again.

"We're going over to Market Ledbury," she said. "We thought we'd have a drink there at the White Hart."

There was a slight amount of defiance in her voice, but Mrs. Lacey did not seem to notice it.

"Well, dear," she said. "I'm sure that will be very nice. David and Diana have gone for a walk, I see. I'm so glad. I really think it was a brainwave on my part to ask Diana here. So sad being left a widow so young—only twenty-two—I do hope she marries again *soon*."

Sarah looked at her sharply. "What are you up to, Em?"

"It's my little plan," said Mrs. Lacey gleefully. "I think she's just right for David. Of course I know he was terribly in love with *you*, Sarah dear, but you'd no use for him and I realise that he isn't your type. But I don't want him to go on being unhappy, and I think Diana will really suit him."

"What a matchmaker you are, Em," said Sarah.

"I know," said Mrs. Lacey. "Old women always are. Diana's quite keen on him already, I think. Don't you think she'd be just right for him?"

"I shouldn't say so," said Sarah. "I think Diana's far too—well, too intense, too serious. I should think David would find it terribly boring being married to her."

"Well, we'll see," said Mrs. Lacey. "Anyway, *you* don't want him, do you, dear?"

"No, indeed," said Sarah, very quickly. She added, in a sudden rush, "You *do* like Desmond, don't you, Em?"

"I'm sure he's very nice indeed," said Mrs. Lacey.

"Grandfather doesn't like him," said Sarah.

"Well, you could hardly expect him to, could you?" said

Mrs. Lacey reasonably, "but I dare say he'll come round when he gets used to the idea. You mustn't rush him, Sarah dear. Old people are very slow to change their minds and your grandfather *is* rather obstinate."

"I don't care what Grandfather thinks or says," said Sarah. "I shall get married to Desmond whenever I like!"

"I know, dear, I know. But do try and be realistic about it. Your grandfather could cause a lot of trouble, you know. You're not of age yet. In another year you can do as you please. I expect Horace will have come round long before that."

"You're on my side aren't you, darling?" said Sarah. She flung her arms round her grandmother's neck and gave her an affectionate kiss.

"I want you to be happy," said Mrs. Lacey. "Ah! there's your young man bringing his car round. You know, I like these very tight trousers these young men wear nowadays. They look so smart—only, of course, it does accentuate knock knees."

Yes, Sarah thought, Desmond *had* got knock knees, she had never noticed it before. . . .

"Go on, dear, enjoy yourself," said Mrs. Lacey.

She watched her go out to the car, then, remembering her foreign guest, she went along to the library. Looking in, however, she saw that Hercule Poirot was taking a pleasant little nap, and smiling to herself, she went across the hall and out into the kitchen to have a conference with Mrs. Ross.

"Come on, beautiful," said Desmond. "Your family cutting up rough because you're coming out to a pub? Years behind the times here, aren't they?"

"Of course they're not making a fuss," said Sarah, sharply as she got into the car.

"What's the idea of having that foreign fellow down? He's a detective, isn't he? What needs detecting here?"

"Oh, he's not here professionally," said Sarah. "Edwina Morecombe, my grandmother, asked us to have him. I think he's retired from professional work long ago."

"Sounds like a broken-down old cab horse," said Desmond.

"He wanted to see an old-fashioned English Christmas, I believe," said Sarah vaguely.

Desmond laughed scornfully. "Such a lot of tripe, that sort of thing," he said. "How can you stand it I don't know."

Sarah's red hair was tossed back and her aggressive chin shot up.

"I enjoy it!" she said defiantly.

"You can't, baby. Let's cut the whole thing to-morrow. Go over to Scarborough or somewhere."

"I couldn't possibly do that."

"Why not?"

"Oh, it would hurt their feelings."

"Oh, bilge! You know you don't enjoy this childish sentimental bosh."

"Well, not really perhaps, but—" Sarah broke off. She realised with a feeling of guilt that she was looking forward a good deal to the Christmas celebration. She enjoyed the whole thing, but she was ashamed to admit that to Desmond. It was not the thing to enjoy Christmas and family life. Just for a moment she wished that Desmond had not come down here at Christmas time. In fact, she almost wished that Desmond had not come down here at all. It was much more fun seeing Desmond in London than here at home.

In the meantime the boys and Bridget were walking back from the lake, still discussing earnestly the problems of skating. Flecks of snow had been falling, and looking up at the sky it could be prophesied that before long there was going to be a heavy snowfall.

"It's going to snow all night," said Colin. "Bet you by Christmas morning we have a couple of feet of snow."

The prospect was a pleasurable one.

"Let's make a snow-man," said Michael.

"Good lord," said Colin, "I haven't made a snow-man since—well, since I was about four years old."

"I don't believe it's a bit easy to do," said Bridget. "I mean, you have to know how."

"We might make an effigy of M. Poirot," said Colin. "Give it a big black moustache. There is one in the dressing-up box."

"I don't see, you know," said Michael thoughtfully, "how M. Poirot could ever have been a detective. I don't see how he'd ever be able to disguise himself."

"I know," said Bridget, "and one can't imagine him running about with a microscope and looking for clues or measuring footprints."

"I've got an idea," said Colin. "Let's put on a show for him!"

"What do you mean, a show?" asked Bridget.

"Well, arrange a murder for him."

"What a gorgeous idea," said Bridget. "Do you mean a body in the snow—that sort of thing?"

"Yes. It would make him feel at home, wouldn't it?"

Bridget giggled.

"I don't know that I'd go as far as that."

"If it snows," said Colin, "we'll have the perfect setting. A body and footprints—we'll have to think that out rather carefully and pinch one of Grandfather's daggers and make some blood."

They came to a halt and oblivious to the rapidly falling snow, entered into an excited discussion.

"There's a paintbox in the old schoolroom. We could mix up some blood—crimson-lake, I should think."

"Crimson-lake's a bit too pink, *I* think," said Bridget. "It ought to be a bit browner."

"Who's going to be the body?" asked Michael.

"I'll be the body," said Bridget quickly.

"Oh, look here," said Colin, "*I* thought of it."

"Oh, no, no," said Bridget, "it must be me. It's got to be a girl. It's more exciting. Beautiful girl lying lifeless in the snow."

"Beautiful girl! Ah-ha," said Michael in derision.

"I've got black hair, too," said Bridget.

"What's that got to do with it?"

"Well, it'll show up so well on the snow and I shall wear my red pyjamas."

"If you wear red pyjamas, they won't show the blood-stains," said Michael in a practical manner.

"But they'd look so effective against the snow," said Bridget, "and they've got white facings, you know, so the blood could be on that. Oh, won't it be gorgeous? Do you think he will really be taken in?"

"He will if we do it well enough," said Michael. "We'll

have just your footprints in the snow and one other person's going to the body and coming away from it—a man's, of course. He won't want to disturb them, so he won't know that you're not really dead. You don't think," Michael stopped, struck by a sudden idea. The others looked at him. "You don't think he'll be *annoyed* about it?"

"Oh, I shouldn't think so," said Bridget, with facile optimism. "I'm sure he'll understand that we've just done it to entertain him. A sort of Christmas treat."

"I don't think we ought to do it on Christmas Day," said Colin reflectively. "I don't think Grandfather would like that very much."

"Boxing Day then," said Bridget.

"Boxing Day would be just right," said Michael.

"And it'll give us more time, too," pursued Bridget. "After all, there are a lot of things to arrange. Let's go and have a look at all the props."

They hurried into the house.

III

The evening was a busy one. Holly and mistletoe had been brought in in large quantities and a Christmas tree had been set up at one end of the dining-room. Everyone helped to decorate it, to put up the branches of holly behind pictures and to hang mistletoe in a convenient position in the hall.

"I had no idea anything so archaic still went on," murmured Desmond to Sarah with a sneer.

"We've always done it," said Sarah, defensively.

"What a reason!"

"Oh, don't be tiresome, Desmond. *I* think it's fun."

"Sarah my sweet, you *can't!*"

"Well, not—not really perhaps but—I do in a way."

"Who's going to brave the snow and go to midnight mass?" asked Mrs. Lacey at twenty minutes to twelve.

"Not me," said Desmond. "Come on, Sarah."

With a hand on her arm he guided her into the library and went over to the record case.

"There are limits, darling," said Desmond. "Midnight mass!"

"Yes," said Sarah. "Oh yes."

With a good deal of laughter, donning of coats and stamping of feet, most of the others got off. The two boys, Bridget, David and Diana set out for the ten minutes' walk to the church through the falling snow. Their laughter died away in the distance.

"Midnight mass!" said Colonel Lacey, snorting. "Never went to midnight mass in my young days. *Mass*, indeed! Popish, that is! Oh, I beg your pardon, Mr. Poirot."

Poirot waved a hand. "It is quite all right. Do not mind me."

"Matins is good enough for anybody, I should say," said the colonel. "Proper Sunday morning service. 'Hark the herald angels sing', and all the good old Christmas hymns. And then back to Christmas dinner. That's right, isn't it, Em?"

"Yes, dear," said Mrs. Lacey. "That's what *we* do. But the young ones enjoy the midnight service. And it's nice, really, that they *want* to go."

"Sarah and that fellow don't want to go."

"Well, there dear, I think you're wrong," said Mrs. Lacey. "Sarah, you know, *did* want to go, but she didn't like to say so."

"Beats me why she cares what that fellow's opinion is."

"She's very young, really," said Mrs. Lacey placidly. "Are you going to bed, M. Poirot? Good night. I hope you'll sleep well."

"And you, Madame? Are you not going to bed yet?"

"Not just yet," said Mrs. Lacey. "I've got the stockings to fill, you see. Oh, I know they're all practically grown up, but they do *like* their stockings. One puts jokes in them! Silly little things. But it all makes for a lot of fun."

"You work very hard to make this is a happy house at Christmas time," said Poirot. "I honour you."

He raised her hand to his lips in a courtly fashion.

"Hm," grunted Colonel Lacey, as Poirot departed. "Flowery sort of fellow. Still—he appreciates you."

Mrs. Lacey dimpled up at him. "Have you noticed, Horace,

that I'm standing under the mistletoe?" she asked with the demureness of a girl of nineteen.

Hercule Poirot entered his bedroom. It was a large room well provided with radiators. As he went over towards the big four-poster bed he noticed an envelope lying on his pillow. He opened it and drew out a piece of paper. On it was a shakily printed message in capital letters.

DON'T EAT NONE OF THE PLUM PUDDING.

ONE AS WISHES YOU WELL.

Hercule Poirot stared at it. His eyebrows rose. "Cryptic," he murmured, "and most unexpected."

IV

Christmas dinner took place at 2 p.m. and was a feast indeed. Enormous logs crackled merrily in the wide fireplace and above their crackling rose the babel of many tongues talking together. Oyster soup had been consumed, two enormous turkeys had come and gone, mere carcasses of their former selves. Now, the supreme moment, the Christmas pudding was brought in, in state! Old Peverell, his hands and his knees shaking with the weakness of his eighty years, permitted no one but himself to bear it in. Mrs. Lacey sat, her hands pressed together in nervous apprehension. One Christmas, she felt sure, Peverell would fall down dead. Having either to take the risk of letting him fall down dead or of hurting his feelings to such an extent that he would probably prefer to be dead than alive, she had so far chosen the former alternative. On a silver dish the Christmas pudding reposed in its glory. A large football of a pudding, a piece of holly stuck in it like a triumphant flag and glorious flames of blue and red rising round it. There was a cheer and cries of "Ooh-ah."

One thing Mrs. Lacey had done: prevailed upon Peverell to place the pudding in front of her so that she could help it rather than hand it in turn round the table. She breathed a sigh of relief as it was deposited safely in front of her. Rapidly the plates were passed round, flames still licking the portions.

"Wish, M. Poirot," cried Bridget. "Wish before the flame goes. Quick, Gran darling, quick."

Mrs. Lacey leant back with a sigh of satisfaction. Operation Pudding had been a success. In front of everyone was a helping with flames still licking it. There was a momentary silence all round the table as everyone wished hard.

There was nobody to notice the rather curious expression on the face of M. Poirot as he surveyed the portion of pudding on his plate. *"Don't eat none of the plum pudding."* What on earth did that sinister warning mean? There could be nothing different about his portion of plum pudding from that of everyone else! Sighing as he admitted himself baffled—and Hercule Poirot never liked to admit himself baffled—he picked up his spoon and fork.

"Hard sauce, M. Poirot?"

Poirot helped himself appreciatively to hard sauce.

"Swiped my best brandy again, eh Elm?" said the colonel good-humouredly from the other end of the table. Mrs. Lacey twinkled at him.

"Mrs. Ross insists on having the best brandy, dear," she said. "She says it makes all the difference."

"Well, well," said Colonel Lacey, "Christmas comes but once a year and Mrs. Ross is a great woman. A great woman and a great cook."

"She is indeed," said Colin. "Smashing plum pudding, this. Mmmm." He filled an appreciative mouth.

Gently, almost gingerly, Hercule Poirot attacked his portion of pudding. He ate a mouthful. It was delicious! He ate another. Something tinkled on his plate. He investigated with a fork. Bridget, on his left, came to his aid.

"You've got something, M. Poirot," she said. "I wonder what it is."

Poirot detached a little silver object from the surrounding raisins that clung to it.

"Oooh," said Bridget, "it's the bachelor's button! M. Poirot's got the bachelor's button!"

Hercule Poirot dipped the small silver button into the finger-glass of water that stood by his plate, and washed it clear of pudding crumbs.

"It is very pretty," he observed.

"That means you're going to be a bachelor, M. Poirot," explained Colin helpfully.

"That is to be expected," said Poirot gravely. "I have been a bachelor for many long years and it is unlikely that I shall change that status now."

"Oh, never say die," said Michael. "I saw in the paper that someone of ninety-five married a girl of twenty-two the other day."

"You encourage me," said Hercule Poirot.

Colonel Lacey uttered a sudden exclamation. His face became purple and his hand went to his mouth.

"Confound it, Emmeline," he roared, "why on earth do you let the cook put glass in the pudding?"

"Glass!" cried Mrs. Lacey, astonished.

Colonel Lacey withdrew the offending substance from his mouth. "Might have broken a tooth," he grumbled. "Or swallowed the damn' thing and had appendicitis."

He dropped the piece of glass into the finger-bowl, rinsed it, and held it up.

"God bless my soul," he ejaculated. "It's a red stone out of one of the cracker brooches." He held it aloft.

"You permit?"

Very deftly M. Poirot stretched across his neighbour, took it from Colonel Lacey's fingers and examined it attentively. As the squire had said, it was an enormous red stone the colour of a ruby. The light gleamed from its facets as he turned it about. Somewhere around the table a chair was pushed sharply back and then drawn in again.

"Phew!" cried Michael. "How wizard it would be if it was *real.*"

"Perhaps it is real," said Bridget hopefully.

"Oh, don't be an ass, Bridget. Why a ruby of that size would be worth thousands and thousands and thousands of pounds. Wouldn't it, M. Poirot?"

"It would indeed," said Poirot.

"But what *I* can't understand," said Mrs. Lacey, "is how it got into the pudding."

"Oooh," said Colin, diverted by his last mouthful, "I've got the pig. It isn't fair."

Bridget chanted immediately, "Colin's got the pig! Colin's got the pig! Colin is the greedy guzzling *pig!*"

"I've got the ring," said Diana in a clear, high voice.

"Good for you, Diana. You'll be married first, of us all."

"I've got the thimble," wailed Bridget.

"Bridget's going to be an old maid," chanted the two boys. "Yah, Bridget's going to be an old maid."

"Who's got the money?" demanded David. "There's a real ten shilling piece, gold, in this pudding. I know. Mrs. Ross told me so."

"I think I'm the lucky one," said Desmond Lee-Wortley.

Colonel Lacey's two next door neighbours heard him mutter, "Yes, you would be."

"*I've* got a ring, too," said David. He looked across at Diana. "Quite a coincidence, isn't it?"

The laughter went on. Nobody noticed that M. Poirot carelessly, as though thinking of something else, had dropped the red stone into his pocket.

Mince-pies and Christmas dessert followed the pudding. The older members of the party then retired for a welcome siesta before the tea-time ceremony of the lighting of the Christmas tree. Hercule Poirot, however, did not take a siesta. Instead, he made his way to the enormous old-fashioned kitchen.

"It is permitted," he asked, looking round and beaming, "that I congratulate the cook on this marvellous meal that I have just eaten?"

There was a moment's pause and then Mrs. Ross came forward in a stately manner to meet him. She was a large woman, nobly built with all the dignity of a state duchess. Two lean grey-haired women were beyond in the scullery washing up and a tow-haired girl was moving to and fro between the scullery and the kitchen. But these were obviously mere myrmidons. Mrs. Ross was the queen of the kitchen quarters.

"I am glad to hear you enjoyed it, sir," she said graciously.

"Enjoyed it!" cried Hercule Poirot. With an extravagant foreign gesture he raised his hand to his lips, kissed it, and wafted the kiss to the ceiling.

"But you are a genius, Mrs. Ross! A genius! *Never* have I tasted such a wonderful meal. The oyster soup—" he made an expressive noise with his lips. "—and the stuffing. The chestnut stuffing in the turkey, that was quite unique in my experience."

"Well, it's funny that you should say that, sir," said Mrs. Ross graciously. "It's a very special recipe, that stuffing. It was given me by an Austrian chef that I worked with many years ago. But all the rest," she added, "is just good, plain English cooking."

"And is there anything better?" demanded Hercule Poirot.

"Well, it's nice of you to say so, sir. Of course, you being a foreign gentleman might have preferred the continental style. Not but what I can't manage continental dishes too."

"I am sure, Mrs. Ross, you could manage anything! But you must know that English cooking—*good* English cooking, not the cooking one gets in the second-class hotels or the restaurants—is much appreciated by *gourmets* on the continent, and I believe I am correct in saying that a special expedition was made to London in the early eighteen hundreds, and a report sent back to France of the wonders of the English puddings. 'We have nothing like that in France,' they wrote. 'It is worth making a journey to London just to taste the varieties and excellencies of the English puddings. And above all puddings," continued Poirot, well launched now on a kind of rhapsody, "is the Christmas plum pudding, such as we have eaten to-day. That was a home-made pudding, was it not? Not a bought one?"

"Yes, indeed, sir. Of my own making and my own recipe such as I've made for many years. When I came here Mrs. Lacey said that she'd ordered a pudding from a London store to save me the trouble. But no, Madam, I said, that may be kind of you but no bought pudding from a store can equal a home-made Christmas one. Mind you," said Mrs. Ross, warming to her subject like the artist she was, "it was made too soon before the day. A good Christmas pudding should be made some weeks before and allowed to wait. The longer they're kept, within reason, the better they are. I mind now that when I was a child and we went to church every Sunday, we'd start listening for the collect that begins 'Stir up O Lord we beseech thee' because that collect was the signal, as it were, that the puddings should be made that week. And so they always were. We had the collect on the Sunday, and that week sure enough my mother would make the Christmas puddings. And so it should have been here this year. As it was, that pudding was only made three days ago, the day before you arrived, sir. However, I kept to the old custom. Everyone in the house had to come out into the kitchen and have a stir and make a wish. That's an old custom, sir, and I've always held to it."

"Most interesting," said Hercule Poirot. "Most interesting. And so everyone came out into the kitchen?"

"Yes, sir. The young gentlemen, Miss Bridget and the London gentleman who's staying here, and his sister and Mr. David and Miss Diana—Mrs. Middleton, I should say—All had a stir, they did."

"How many puddings did you make? Is this the only one?"

"No, sir, I made four. Two large ones and two smaller ones. The other large one I planned to serve on New Year's Day and the smaller ones were for Colonel and Mrs. Lacey when they're alone like and not so many in the family."

"I see, I see," said Poirot.

"As a matter of fact, sir," said Mrs. Ross, "it was the wrong pudding you had for lunch to-day."

"The wrong pudding?" Poirot frowned. "How is that?"

"Well, sir, we have a big Christmas mould. A china mould with a pattern of holly and mistletoe on top and we always have the Christmas Day pudding boiled in that. But there was a most unfortunate accident. This morning, when Annie was getting it down from the shelf in the larder, she slipped and dropped it and it broke. Well, sir, naturally I couldn't serve that, could I? There might have been splinters in it. So we had to use the other one—the New Year's Day one, which was in a plain bowl. It makes a nice round but it's not so decorative as the Christmas mould. Really, where we'll get another mould like that I don't know. They don't make things in that size nowadays. All tiddly bits of things. Why, you can't even buy a breakfast dish that'll take a proper eight to ten eggs and bacon. Ah, things aren't what they were."

"No, indeed," said Poirot. "But to-day that is not so. This

Christmas Day has been like the Christmas Days of old, is that not true?"

Mrs. Ross sighed. "Well, I'm glad you say so, sir, but of course I haven't the *help* now that I used to have. Not skilled help, that is. The girls nowadays—" she lowered her voice slightly, "—they mean very well and they're very willing but they've not been *trained,* sir, if you understand what I mean."

"Times change, yes," said Hercule Poirot. "I too find it sad sometimes."

"This house, sir," said Mrs. Ross, "it's too large, you know, for the mistress and the colonel. The mistress, she knows that. Living in a corner of it as they do, it's not the same thing at all. It only comes alive, as you might say, at Christmas time when all the family come."

"It is the first time, I think, that Mr. Lee-Wortley and his sister have been here?"

"Yes, sir." A note of slight reserve crept into Mrs. Ross's voice. "A very nice gentleman he is but, well—it seems a funny friend for Miss Sarah to have, according to our ideas. But there—London ways are different! It's sad that his sister's so poorly. Had an operation, she had. She seemed all right the first day she was here, but that very day, after we'd been stirring the puddings, she was took bad again and she's been in bed ever since. Got up too soon after her operation, I expect. Ah, doctors nowadays, they have you out of hospital before you can hardly stand on your feet. Why, my very own nephew's wife . . ." And Mrs. Ross went into a long and spirited tale of hospital treatment as accorded to her relations, comparing it unfavourably with the consideration that had been lavished upon them in older times.

Poirot duly commiserated with her. "It remains," he said, "to thank you for this exquisite and sumptuous meal. You permit a little acknowledgment of my appreciation?" A crisp five pound note passed from his hand into that of Mrs. Ross who said perfunctorily:

"You really shouldn't do *that,* sir."

"I insist. I insist."

"Well, it's very kind of you indeed, sir." Mrs. Ross accepted the tribute as no more than her due. "And I wish you, sir, a very happy Christmas and a prosperous New Year."

V

The end of Christmas Day was like the end of most Christmas Days. The tree was lighted, a splendid Christmas cake came in for tea, was greeted with approval but was partaken of only moderately. There was cold supper.

Both Poirot and his host and hostess went to bed early.

"Good night, M. Poirot," said Mrs. Lacey. "I hope you've enjoyed yourself."

"It has been a wonderful day, Madame, wonderful."

"You're looking very thoughtful," said Mrs. Lacey.

"It is the English pudding that I consider."

"You found it a little heavy, perhaps?" asked Mrs. Lacey delicately.

"No, no, I do not speak gastronomically. I consider its significance."

"It's traditional of course," said Mrs. Lacey. "Well, good night, M. Poirot, and don't dream too much of Christmas puddings and mince-pies."

"Yes," murmured Poirot to himself as he undressed. "It is a problem certainly, that Christmas plum pudding. There is here something that I do not understand at all." He shook his head in a vexed manner. "Well—we shall see."

After making certain preparations, Poirot went to bed, but not to sleep.

It was some two hours later that his patience was rewarded. The door of his bedroom opened very gently. He smiled to himself. It was as he had thought it would be. His mind went back fleetingly to the cup of coffee so politely handed him by Desmond Lee-Wortley. A little later, when Desmond's back was turned, he had laid the cup down for a few moments on a table. He had then apparently picked it up again and Desmond had had the satisfaction, if satisfaction it was, of seeing him drink the coffee to the last drop. But a little smile lifted Poirot's moustache as he reflected that it was not he but someone else who was sleeping a good sound sleep to-night. "That pleasant young David," said Poirot to himself, "he is worried, unhappy. It will do him no harm to have a night's really sound sleep. And now, let us see what will happen?"

He lay quite still breathing in an even manner with occasionally a suggestion, but the faintest suggestion, of a snore.

Someone came up to the bed and bent over him. Then, satisfied, that someone turned away and went to the dressing-table. By the light of a tiny torch the visitor was examining Poirot's belongings neatly arranged on top of the dressing-table. Fingers explored the wallet, gently pulled open the drawers of the dressing-table, then extended the search to the pockets of Poirot's clothes. Finally the visitor approached the bed and with great caution slid his hand under the pillow. Withdrawing his hand, he stood for a moment or two as though uncertain what to do next. He walked round the room looking inside ornaments, went into the adjoining bathroom from whence he presently returned. Then, with a faint exclamation of disgust, he went out of the room.

"Ah," said Poirot, under his breath. "You have a disappointment, Yes, yes, a serious disappointment. Bah! To imagine, even, that Hercule Poirot would hide something where you could find it!" Then, turning over on his other side, he went peacefully to sleep.

He was aroused next morning by an urgent soft tapping on his door.

"*Qui est là?* Come in, come in."

"Monsieur Poirot, Monsieur Poirot."

"But yes?" Poirot sat up in bed. "It is the early tea? But no. It is you, Colin. What has occurred?"

Colin was, for a moment, speechless. He seemed to be under the grip of some strong emotion. In actual fact it was the sight of the nightcap that Hercule Poirot wore that affected for the moment his organs of speech. Presently he controlled himself and spoke.

"I think—M. Poirot, could you help us? Something rather awful has happened."

"Something has happened? But what?"

"It's—it's Bridget. She's out there in the snow. I think— she doesn't move or speak and—oh, you'd better come and look for yourself. I'm terribly afraid—she may be *dead.*"

"What?" Poirot cast aside his bed covers. "Mademoiselle Bridget—dead!"

"I think—I think somebody's killed her. There's—there's blood and—oh do come!"

"But certainly. But certainly. I come on the instant."

With great practicality Poirot inserted his feet into his outdoor shoes and pulled a fur-lined overcoat over his pyjamas.

"I come," he said. "I come on the moment. You have aroused the house?"

"No. No, so far I haven't told anyone but you. I thought it would be better. Grandfather and Gran aren't up yet. They're laying breakfast downstairs, but I didn't say anything to Peverell. She—Bridget—she's round the other side of the house, near the terrace and the library window."

"I see. Lead the way. I will follow."

Turning away to hide his delighted grin, Colin led the way downstairs. They went out through the side door. It was a clear morning with the sun not yet high over the horizon. It was not snowing now, but it had snowed heavily during the night and everywhere around was an unbroken carpet of thick snow. The world looked very pure and white and beautiful.

"There!" said Colin breathlessly. "I—it's—*there!*" He pointed dramatically.

The scene was indeed dramatic enough. A few yards away Bridget lay in the snow. She was wearing scarlet pyjamas and a white wool wrap thrown round her shoulders. The white wool wrap was stained with crimson. Her head was turned aside and hidden by the mass of her outspread black hair. One arm was under her body, the other lay flung out, the fingers clenched, and standing up in the centre of the crimson stain was the hilt of a large curved Kurdish knife which Colonel Lacey had shown to his guests only the evening before.

"*Mon Dieu!*" ejaculated M. Poirot. "It is like something on the stage!"

There was a faint choking noise from Michael. Colin thrust himself quickly into the breach.

"I know," he said. "It—it doesn't seem *real* somehow, does it? Do you see those footprints—I suppose we mustn't disturb them?"

"Ah yes, the footprints. No, we must be careful not to disturb those footprints."

"That's what I thought," said Colin. "That's why I wouldn't let anyone go near her until we got you. I thought you'd know what to do."

"All the same," said Hercule Poirot briskly, "first, we must see if she is still alive? Is not that so?"

"Well—yes—of course," said Michael, a little doubtfully, "but you see, we thought—I mean, we didn't like—"

"Ah, you have the prudence! You have read the detective stories. It is most important that nothing should be touched and that the body should be left as it is. But we cannot be sure as yet if it *is* a body, can we? After all, though prudence is admirable, common humanity comes first. We must think of the doctor, must we not, before we think of the police?"

"Oh yes. Of course," said Colin, still a little taken aback.

"We only thought—I mean—we thought we'd better get you before we did anything," said Michael hastily.

"Then you will both remain here," said Poirot. "I will approach from the other side so as not to disturb these footprints. Such excellent footprints, are they not—so very clear? The footprints of a man and a girl going out together to the place where she lies. And then the man's footsteps come back but the girl's—do not."

"They must be the footprints of the murderer," said Colin, with bated breath.

"Exactly," said Poirot. "The footprints of the murderer. A long narrow foot with rather a peculiar type of shoe. Very interesting. Easy, I think, to recognise. Yes, those footprints will be very important."

At that moment Desmond Lee-Wortley came out of the house with Sarah and joined them.

"What on earth are you all doing here?" he demanded in a somewhat theatrical manner. "I saw you from my bedroom window. What's up? Good lord, what's this? It—it looks like—"

"Exactly," said Hercule Poirot. "It looks like murder, does it not?"

Sarah gave a gasp, then shot a quick suspicious glance at the two boys.

"You mean someone's killed the girl—what's-her-name—

Bridget?" demanded Desmond. "Who on earth would want to kill her? It's unbelievable!"

"There are many things that are unbelievable," said Poirot. "Especially before breakfast, is it not? That is what one of your classics say. Six impossible things before breakfast." He added: "Please wait here, all of you."

Carefully making a circuit, he approached Bridget and bent for a moment down over the body. Colin and Michael were now both shaking with suppressed laughter. Sarah joined them, murmuring, "What have you two been up to?"

"Good old Bridget," whispered Colin. "Isn't she wonderful? Not a twitch!"

"I've never seen anything look so dead as Bridget does," whispered Michael.

Hercule Poirot straightened up again.

"This is a terrible thing," he said. His voice held an emotion it had not held before.

Overcome by mirth, Michael and Colin both turned away. In a choked voice Michael said:

"What—what must we do?"

"There is only one thing to do," said Poirot. "We must send for the police. Will one of you telephone or would you prefer me to do it?"

"I think," said Colin, "I think—what about it, Michael?"

"Yes," said Michael, "I think the jig's up now." He stepped forward. For the first time he seemed a little unsure of himself. "I'm awfully sorry," he said, "I hope you won't mind too much. It—er—it was a sort of joke for Christmas and all that, you know. We thought we'd—well, lay on a murder for you."

"You thought you would lay on a murder for me? Then this—then this—"

"It's just a show we put on," explained Colin, "to—to make you feel at home, you know."

"Aha," said Hercule Poirot. "I understand. You make of me the April fool, is that it? But to-day is not April the first, it is December the twenty-sixth."

"I suppose we oughtn't to have done it really," said Colin, "but—but—you don't mind very much, do you, M. Poirot?

Come on, Bridget," he called, "get up. You must be half-frozen to death already."

The figure in the snow, however, did not stir.

"It is odd," said Hercule Poirot, "she does not seem to hear you." He looked thoughtfully at them. "It is a joke, you say? You are sure this is a joke?"

"Why yes." Colin spoke uncomfortably. "We—we didn't mean any harm."

"But why then does Mademoiselle Bridget not get up?"

"I can't imagine," said Colin.

"Come on, Bridget," said Sarah impatiently. "Don't go on lying there playing the fool."

"We really are very sorry, M. Poirot," said Colin apprehensively. "We do really apologise."

"You need not apologise," said Poirot, in a peculiar tone.

"What do you mean?" Colin stared at him. He turned again. "Bridget! Bridget! What's the matter? Why doesn't she get up? Why does she go on lying there?"

Poirot beckoned to Desmond. "*You,* Mr. Lee-Wortley. Come here—"

Desmond joined him.

"Feel her pulse," said Poirot.

Desmond Lee-Wortley bent down. He touched the arm—the wrist.

"There's no pulse . . ." he stared at Poirot. "Her arm's stiff. Good God, she really *is* dead!"

Poirot nodded. "Yes, she is dead," he said. "Someone has turned the comedy into a tragedy."

"Someone—who?"

"There is a set of footprints going and returning. A set of footprints that bears a strong resemblance to the footprints *you* have just made, Mr. Lee-Wortley, coming from the path to this spot."

Desmond Lee-Wortley wheeled round.

"What on earth—Are you accusing me? *ME?* You're crazy! Why on earth should I want to kill the girl?"

"Ah—why? I wonder . . . Let us see. . . ."

He bent down and very gently prised open the stiff fingers of the girl's clenched hand.

Desmond drew a sharp breath. He gazed down unbelievingly. In the palm of the dead girl's hand was what appeared to be a large ruby.

"It's that damn thing out of the pudding!" he cried.

"Is it?" said Poirot. "Are you sure?"

"Of course it is."

With a swift movement Desmond bent down and plucked the red stone out of Bridget's hand.

"You should not do that," said Poirot reproachfully. "Nothing should have been disturbed."

"I haven't disturbed the body, have I? But this thing might —might get lost and it's evidence. The great thing is to get the police here as soon as possible. I'll go at once and telephone."

He wheeled round and ran sharply towards the house. Sarah came swiftly to Poirot's side.

"I don't understand," she whispered. Her face was dead white. "I don't *understand*." She caught at Poirot's arm. "What did you mean about—about the footprints?"

"Look for yourself, Mademoiselle."

The footprints that led to the body and back again were the same as the ones just made accompanying Poirot to the girl's body and back.

"You mean—that it was Desmond? Nonsense!"

Suddenly the noise of a car came through the clear air. They wheeled round. They saw the car clearly enough driving at a furious pace down the drive and Sarah recognised what car it was.

"It's Desmond," she said. "It's Desmond's car. He—he must have gone to fetch the police instead of telephoning."

Diana Middleton came running out of the house to join them.

"What's happened?" she cried in a breathless voice. "Desmond just came rushing into the house. He said something about Bridget being killed and then he rattled the telephone but it was dead. He couldn't get an answer. He said the wires must have been cut. He said the only thing was to take a car and go for the police. Why the police? . . ."

Poirot made a gesture.

"Bridget?" Diana stared at him. "But surely—isn't it a joke of some kind? I heard something—something last night. I thought that they were going to play a joke on you, M. Poirot?"

"Yes," said Poirot, "that was the idea—to play a joke on me. But now come into the house, all of you. We shall catch our deaths of cold here and there is nothing to be done until Mr. Lee-Wortley returns with the police."

"But look here," said Colin, "we can't—we can't leave Bridget here alone."

"You can do her no good by remaining," said Poirot gently. "Come, it is a sad, a very sad tragedy, but there is nothing we can do any more to help Mademoiselle Bridget. So let us come in and get warm and have perhaps a cup of tea or of coffee."

They followed him obediently into the house. Peverell was just about to strike the gong. If he thought it extraordinary for most of the household to be outside and for Poirot to make an appearance in pyjamas and an overcoat, he displayed no sign of it. Peverell in his old age was still the perfect butler. He noticed nothing that he was not asked to notice. They went into the dining-room and sat down. When they all had a cup of coffee in front of them and were sipping it, Poirot spoke.

"I have to recount to you," he said, "a little history. I cannot tell you all the details, no. But I can give you the main outline. It concerns a young princeling who came to this county. He brought with him a famous jewel which he was to have reset for the lady he was going to marry, but unfortunately before that he made friends with a very pretty young lady. This pretty young lady did not care very much for the man, but she did care for his jewel—so much so that one day she disappeared with the historic possession which had belonged to his house for generations. So the poor young man, he is in a quandary, you see. Above all he cannot have a scandal. Impossible to go to the police. Therefore he comes to me, to Hercule Poirot. 'Recover for me,' he says, 'my historic ruby.' *Eh bien,* this young lady, she has a friend and the friend, he has put through several questionable transactions. He has been concerned with blackmail and he has been concerned with the sale of jewellery abroad. Always he has been very clever. He is suspected, yes, but nothing can be proved. It comes to my knowledge that this very clever gentleman, he is spending Christmas here in this house. It is important that the pretty young lady, once she has acquired the jewel, should disappear for a while from circulation, so that no pressure can be put upon her, no questions can be asked her. It is arranged, therefore, that she comes here to Kings Lacey, ostensibly as the sister of the clever gentleman——"

Sarah drew a sharp breath.

"Oh, no. Oh, no, not *here!* Not with me here!"

"But so it is," said Poirot. "And by a little manipulation I, too, become a guest here for Christmas. This young lady, she is supposed to have just come out of hospital. She is much better when she arrives here. But then comes the news that I, too, arrive, a detective——a well-known detective. At once she has what you call the wind up. She hides the ruby in the first place she can think of, and then very quickly she has a relapse and takes to her bed again. She does not want that I should see her, for doubtless I have a photograph and I shall recognise her. It is very boring for her, yes, but she has to stay in her room and her brother, he brings her up the trays."

"And the ruby?" demanded Michael.

"I think," said Poirot, "that at the moment it is mentioned I arrive, the young lady was in the kitchen with the rest of you, all laughing and talking and stirring the Christmas puddings. The Christmas puddings are put into bowls and the young lady she hides the ruby, pressing it down into one of the pudding bowls. Not the one that we are going to have on Christmas Day. Oh no, that one she knows is in a special mould. She put it in the other one, the one that is destined to be eaten on New Year's Day. Before then she will be ready to leave, and when she leaves no doubt that Christmas pudding will go with her. But see how fate takes a hand. On the very morning of Christmas Day there is an accident. The Christmas pudding in its fancy mould is dropped on the stone floor and the mould is shattered to pieces. So what can be done? The good Mrs. Ross, she takes the other pudding and sends it in."

"Good lord," said Colin, "do you mean that on Christmas Day when Grandfather was eating his pudding that that was a *real* ruby he'd got in his mouth?"

"Precisely," said Poirot, "and you can imagine the emotions of Mr. Desmond Lee-Wortley when he saw that. *Eh bien,* what happens next? The ruby is passed round. I examine it and I manage unobtrusively to slip it in my pocket. In a careless way as though I were not interested. But one person at least observes what I have done. When I lie in bed that person searches my room. He searches me. He does not find the ruby. Why?"

"Because," said Michael breathlessly, "you had given it to Bridget. That's what you mean. And so that's why—but I don't understand quite—I mean—Look here, what *did* happen?"

Poirot smiled at him.

"Come now into the library," he said, "and look out of the window and I will show you something that may explain the mystery."

He led the way and they followed him.

"Consider once again," said Poirot, "the scene of the crime."

He pointed out of the window. A simultaneous gasp broke from the lips of all of them. There was no body lying on the snow, no trace of the tragedy seemed to remain except a mass of scuffled snow.

"It wasn't all a dream, was it?" said Colin faintly. "I—has someone taken the body away?"

"Ah," said Poirot. "You see? The Mystery of the Disappearing Body." He nodded his head and his eyes twinkled gently.

"Good lord," cried Michael. "M. Poirot, you are—you haven't—oh, look here, he's been having us on all this time!"

Poirot twinkled more than ever.

"It is true, my children, I also have had my little joke. I knew about your little plot, you see, and so I arranged a counter-plot of my own. Ah, *voilà* Mademoiselle Bridget. None the worse, I hope, for your exposure in the snow? Never should I forgive myself if you attrapped *une fluxion de poitrine*."

Bridget had just come into the room. She was wearing a thick skirt and a woolen sweater. She was laughing.

"I sent a *tisane* to your room," said Poirot severely. "You have drunk it?"

"One sip was enough!" said Bridget. *"I'*m all right. Did I

do it well, M. Poirot? Goodness, my arm hurts still after that tourniquet you made me put on it."

"You were splendid, my child," said Poirot. "Splendid. But see, the others are still in the fog. Last night I went to Mademoiselle Bridget. I told her that I knew about your little *complot* and I asked her if she would act a part for me. She did it very cleverly. She made the footprints with a pair of Mr. Lee-Wortley's shoes."

Sarah said in a harsh voice:

"But what's the point of it all, M. Poirot? What's the point of sending Desmond off to fetch the police? They'll be very angry when they find out it's nothing but a hoax."

Poirot shook his head gently.

"But I do not think for one moment, Mademoiselle, that Mr. Lee-Wortley went to fetch the police," he said. "Murder is a thing in which Mr. Lee-Wortley does not want to be mixed up. He lost his nerve badly. All he could see was his chance to get the ruby. He snatched that, he pretended the telephone was out of order and he rushed off in a car on the pretence of fetching the police. I think myself it is the last you will see of him for some time. He has, I understand, his own ways of getting out of England. He has his own plane, has he not, Mademoiselle?"

Sarah nodded. "Yes," she said. "We were thinking of—" She stopped.

"He wanted you to elope with him that way, did he not? *Eh bien*, that is a very good way of smuggling a jewel out of the country. When you are eloping with a girl, and that fact is publicised, then you will not be suspected of also smuggling a historic jewel out of the country. Oh yes, that would have made a very good camouflage."

"I don't believe it," said Sarah. "I don't believe a word of it!"

"Then ask his sister," said Poirot, gently nodding his head over her shoulder. Sarah turned her head sharply.

A platinum blonde stood in the doorway. She wore a fur coat and was scowling. She was clearly in a furious temper.

"Sister my foot!" she said, with a short unpleasant laugh. "That swine's no brother of mine! So he's beaten it, has he, and left me to carry the can? The whole thing was *his* idea! He put me up to it! Said it was money for jam. They'd never prosecute because of the scandal. I could always threaten to say that Ali had *given* me his historic jewel. Des and I were to have shared the swag in Paris—and now the swine runs out on me! I'd like to murder him!" She switched abruptly. "The sooner I get out of here—Can someone telephone for a taxi?"

"A car is waiting at the front door to take you to the station, Mademoiselle," said Poirot.

"Think of everything, don't you?"

"Most things," said Poirot complacently.

But Poirot was not to get off so easily. When he returned to the dining-room after assisting the spurious Miss Lee-Wortley into the waiting car, Colin was waiting for him.

There was a frown on his boyish face.

"But look here, M. Poirot. *What about the ruby?* Do you mean to say you've let him get away with it?"

Poirot's face fell. He twirled his moustaches. He seemed ill at ease.

"I shall recover it yet," he said weakly. "There are other ways. I shall still—"

"Well, I do think!" said Michael. "To let that swine get away with the ruby!"

Bridget was sharper.

"He's having us on again," she cried. "You are, aren't you, M. Poirot!"

"Shall we do a final conjuring trick, Mademoiselle? Feel in my left-hand pocket."

Bridget thrust her hand in. She drew it out again with a scream of triumph and held aloft a large ruby blinking in crimson splendour.

"You comprehend," explained Poirot, "the one that was clasped in your hand was a paste replica. I brought it from London in case it was possible to make a substitute. You understand? We do not want the scandal. Monsieur Desmond will try and dispose of that ruby in Paris or in Belgium or wherever it is that he has his contacts, and then it will be discovered that the stone is not real! What could be more excellent? All finishes happily. The scandal is avoided, my princeling receives his ruby back again, he returns to his country and makes a sober and we hope a happy marriage. All ends well."

"Except for me," murmured Sarah under her breath.

She spoke so low that no one heard her but Poirot. He shook his head gently.

"You are in error, Mademoiselle Sarah, in what you say there. You have gained experience. All experience is valuable. Ahead of you I prophesy there lies happiness."

"That's what *you* say," said Sarah.

"But look here, M. Poirot," Colin was frowning. "How did you know about the show we were going to put on for you?"

"It is my business to know things," said Hercule Poirot. He twirled his moustache.

"Yes, but I don't see how you could have managed it. Did someone split—did someone come and tell you?"

"No, no, not that."

"Then how? Tell us how?"

They all chorused, "Yes, tell us how."

"But no," Poirot protested. "But no. If I tell you how I deduced that, you will think nothing of it. It is like the conjurer who shows how his tricks are done!"

"Tell us, M. Poirot! Go on. Tell us, tell us!"

"You really wish that I should solve for you this last mystery?"

"Yes, go on. Tell us."

"Ah, I do not think I can. You will be so disappointed."

"Now, come on, M. Poirot, tell us. *How did you know?*"

"Well, you see, I was sitting in the library by the window in a chair after tea the other day and I was reposing myself. I had been asleep and when I awoke you were discussing your plans just outside the window close to me, and the window was open at the top."

"Is that all?" cried Colin, disgusted. "How simple!"

"Is it not?" said Hercule Poirot, smiling. "You see? You *are* disappointed!"

"Oh well," said Michael, "at any rate we know everything now."

"Do we?" murmured Hercule Poirot to himself. "*I* do not. I, whose business it is to know things."

He walked out into the hall, shaking his head a little. For perhaps the twentieth time he drew from his pocket a rather dirty piece of paper. "DON'T EAT NONE OF THE PLUM PUDDING. ONE AS WISHES YOU WELL."

Hercule Poirot shook his head reflectively. He who could explain everything could not explain this! Humiliating. Who had written it? *Why* had it been written? Until he found that out he would never know a moment's peace. Suddenly he came out of his reverie to be aware of a peculiar gasping noise. He looked sharply down. On the floor, busy with a dustpan and brush was a tow-headed creature in a flowered overall. She was staring at the paper in his hand with large round eyes.

"Oh sir," said this apparition. "Oh, *sir. Please,* sir."

"And who may you be, *mon enfant?*" inquired M. Poirot genially.

"Annie Bates, sir, please sir. I come here to help Mrs. Ross. I didn't mean, sir, I didn't mean to—to do anything what I shouldn't do. I did mean it well, sir. For your good, I mean."

Enlightenment came to Poirot. He held out the dirty piece of paper.

"Did you write that, Annie?"

"I didn't mean any harm, sir. Really I didn't."

"Of course you didn't, Annie." He smiled at her. "But tell me about it. Why did you write this?"

"Well, it was them two, sir. Mr. Lee-Wortley and his sister. Not that she *was* his sister, I'm sure. None of us thought so! And she wasn't ill a bit. We could all tell *that.* We thought—we all thought—something queer was going on. I'll tell you straight, sir. I was in her bathroom taking in the clean towels, and I listened at the door. *He* was in her room and they were talking together. I heard what they said plain as plain. 'This detective,' he was saying. 'This fellow Poirot who's coming here. We've got to do something about it. We've got to get him out of the way as soon as possible.' And then he says to her in a nasty, sinister sort of way, lowering his voice, 'Where did you put it?' And she answered him *'In the pudding.'* Oh sir, my heart gave such a leap I thought it would stop beating. I thought they meant to poison you in the Christmas pudding.

I didn't know *what* to do! Mrs. Ross, she wouldn't listen to the likes of me. Then the idea came to me as I'd write you a warning. And I did and I put it on your pillow where you'd find it when you went to bed." Annie paused breathlessly.

Poirot surveyed her gravely for some minutes.

"You see too many sensational films, I think, Annie," he said at last, "or perhaps it is the television that affects you? But the important thing is that you have the good heart and a certain amount of ingenuity. When I return to London I will send you a present."

"Oh thank you, sir. Thank you very much, sir."

"What would you like, Annie, as a present?"

"Anything I like, sir? Could I have anything I like?"

"Within reason," said Hercule Poirot prudently, "yes."

"Oh sir, could I have a vanity box? A real posh slap-up vanity box like the one Mr. Lee-Wortley's sister, wot wasn't his sister, had?"

"Yes," said Poirot, "yes, I think that could be managed.

"It is interesting," he mused. "I was in a museum the other day observing some antiquities from Babylon or one of those places, thousands of years old—and among them were cosmetic boxes. The heart of woman does not change."

"Beg pardon, sir?" said Annie.

"It is nothing," said Poirot, "I reflect. You shall have your vanity box, child."

"Oh thank you, sir. Oh thank you very much indeed, sir."

Annie departed ecstatically. Poirot looked after her, nodding his head in satisfaction.

"Ah," he said to himself. "And now—I do. There is nothing more to be done here."

A pair of arms slipped round his shoulders unexpectedly.

"If you *will* stand just under the mistletoe—" said Bridget.

Hercule Poirot enjoyed it. He enjoyed it very much. He said to himself that he had had a very good Christmas

"Well, we found out what's been clogging your chimney since last December, Miss Emmy."

Perhaps the greatest of Georges Simenon's considerable achievements has been his mastery of a literary form that had become almost the exclusive province of English-speaking writers. When one considers that Simenon's art has constantly been at the mercy of translators, it becomes apparent that his stories in their original French must be durable stuff indeed.

This Belgian born writer now has over 200 novels to his credit in a career that spans over sixty years. By far the most popular of these works are the Inspector Maigret adventures which constitute a hefty percentage of his production.

Maigret's success gives cause for consideration, too. He is neither flamboyant nor eccentric, just an average middle class government worker earning a living, and getting by, in a simple, honest fashion.

Simenon's style is likewise clean and "sec", in a way that is agreeably Gallic. Like the great wines of France, the Maigret stories are an acquired taste. But also, like those wines, a taste well worth the acquisition.

Maigret's Christmas

by Georges Simenon

Translated by Lawrence G. Blochman

THE ROUTINE never varied. When Maigret went to bed he must have muttered his usual, "Tomorrow morning I shall sleep late." And Mme. Maigret, who over the years should have learned to pay no attention to such casual phrases, had taken him at his word this Christmas day.

It was not quite daylight when he heard her stirring cautiously. He forced himself to breathe regularly and deeply as though he were still asleep. It was like a game. She inched toward the edge of the bed with animal stealth, pausing after each movement to make sure she had not awakened him. He waited anxiously for the inevitable finale, the movement when the bedspring, relieved of her weight, would spring back into place with a faint sigh.

She picked up her clothing from the chair and turned the knob of the bathroom door so slowly that it seemed to take an eternity. It was not until she had reached the distant fastness of the kitchen that she resumed her normal movements.

Maigret had fallen asleep again. Not deeply, not for long. Long enough, however, for a confused and disturbing dream. Waking, he could not remember what it was, but he knew it was disturbing because he still felt vaguely uneasy.

The crack between the window drapes which never quite closed became a strip of pale, hard daylight. He waited a while longer, lying on his back with his eyes open, savoring the fragrance of fresh coffee. Then he heard the apartment door open and close, and he knew that Mme. Maigret was hurrying downstairs to buy him hot *croissants* from the bakery at the corner of the Rue Amelot.

He never ate in the morning. His breakfast consisted of black coffee. But his wife clung to her ritual: on Sundays and holidays he was supposed to lie in bed until mid-morning while she went out for *croissants*.

He got up, stepped into his slippers, put on his dressing gown, and drew the curtains. He knew he was doing wrong. His wife would be heartbroken. But while he was willing to make almost any sacrifice to please her, he simply could not stay in bed longer than he felt like it.

It was not snowing. It was nonsense, of course, for a man past 50 to be disappointed because there was no snow on Christmas morning; but then middle-aged people never have as much sense as young folks sometimes imagine.

A dirty, turbid sky hung low over the rooftops. The Boulevard Richard-Lenoir was completely deserted. The words *Fils et Cie.*, *Bonded Warehouses* on the sign above the porte-cochére across the street stood out as black as mourning crêpe. The *F*, for some strange reason, seemed particularly dismal.

He heard his wife moving about in the kitchen again. She came into the dining room on tiptoe, as though he were still asleep instead of looking out the window. He glanced at his watch on the night table. It was only ten past 8.

The night before the Maigrets had gone to the theatre. They would have loved dropping in for a snack at some restaurant, like everyone else on Christmas Eve, but all tables were reserved for *Réveillon* supper. So they had walked home arm in arm, getting in a few minutes before midnight. Thus they hadn't long to wait before exchanging presents.

He got a pipe, as usual. Her present was an electric coffee pot, the latest model that she had wanted so much, and, not to break with tradition, a dozen finely embroidered handkerchiefs.

Still looking out the window, Maigret absently filled his new pipe. The shutters were still closed on some of the windows across the boulevard. Not many people were up. Here and there a light burned in a window, probably left by children who had leaped out of bed at the crack of dawn to rush for their presents under the Christmas tree.

In the quiet Maigret apartment the morning promised to be a lazy one for just the two of them. Maigret would loiter in his dressing gown until quite late. He would not even shave. He would dawdle in the kitchen, talking to his wife while she put the lunch on the stove. Just the two of them.

He wasn't sad exactly, but his dreams—which he couldn't remember—had left him jumpy. Or perhaps it wasn't his dream. Perhaps it was Christmas. He had to be extra-careful on Christmas Day, careful of his words, the way Mme. Maigret had been careful of her movements in getting out of bed. Her nerves, too, were especially sensitive on Christmas.

Oh, well, why think of all that? He would just be careful to say nothing untoward. He would be careful not to look out the window when the neighborhood children began to appear on the sidewalks with their Christmas toys.

All the houses in the street had children. Or almost all. The street would soon echo to the shrill blast of toy horns, the roll of toy drums, and the crack of toy pistols. The little girls were probably already cradling their new dolls.

A few years ago he had proposed more or less at random: "Why don't we take a little trip for Christmas?"

"Where?" she had replied with her infallible common sense.

Where, indeed? Whom would they visit? They had no relatives except her sister who lived too far away. And why spend Christmas in some second-rate country inn, or at a hotel in some strange town?

Oh, well, he'd feel better after he had his coffee. He was never at his best until he'd drunk his first cup of coffee and lit his first pipe.

Just as he was reaching for the knob, the door opened noiselessly and Mme. Maigret appeared carrying a tray. She looked at the empty bed, then turned her disappointed eyes upon her husband. She was on the verge of tears.

"You got up!" She looked as though she had been up for hours herself, every hair in place, a picture of neatness in her crisp clean apron. "And I was so happy about serving your breakfast in bed."

He had tried a hundred times, as subtly as he could, to make her understand that he didn't like eating breakfast in bed. It made him uncomfortable. It made him feel like an invalid or a senile old gaffer. But for Mme. Maigret breakfast in bed was the symbol of leisure and luxury, the ideal way to start Sunday or a holiday.

"Don't you want to go back to bed?"

No, he did not. Decidedly not. He hadn't the courage.

"Then come to breakfast in the kitchen. And Merry Christmas."

"Merry Christmas! . . . You're not angry?"

They were in the dining room. He surveyed the silver tray on a corner of the table, the steaming cup of coffee, the golden-brown *croissants*. He put down his pipe and ate a *croissant* to please his wife, but he remained standing, looking out the window.

"It's snowing."

It wasn't real snow. It was a fine white dust sifting down from the sky, but it reminded Maigret that when he was a small boy he used to stick out his tongue to lick up a few of the tiny flakes.

His gaze focused on the entrance to the building across the street, next door to the warehouse. Two women had just come out, both bareheaded. One of them, a blonde of about 30, had thrown a coat over her shoulders without stopping to slip her arms into the sleeves. The other, a brunette, older and thinner, was hugging a shawl.

The blonde seemed to hesitate, ready to turn back. Her slim little companion was insistent and Maigret had the impression that she was pointing up toward his window. The appearance of the concierge in the doorway behind them seemed to tip the scales in favor of the little brunette. The blonde looked back apprehensively, then crossed the street.

"What are you looking at?"

"Nothing . . . two women. . . ."

"What are they doing?"

"I think they're coming here."

The two women had stopped in the middle of the street and were looking up in the direction of the Maigret apartment.

"I hope they're not coming here to bother you on Christmas Day. My housework's not even done." Nobody would have guessed it. There wasn't a speck of dust on any of the polished furniture. "Are you sure they're coming here?"

"We'll soon find out."

To be on the safe side, he went to comb his hair, brush his teeth, and splash a little water on his face. He was still in his room, relighting his pipe, when he heard the doorbell. Mme. Maigret was evidently putting up a strong hedgehog defense, for it was some time before she came for him.

"They insist on speaking to you," she whispered. "They claim it's very important and they need advice. I know one of them."

"Which one?"

"The skinny little one, Mlle. Doncoeur. She lives across the street on the same floor as ours. She's a very nice person and she does embroidery for a firm in the Faubourg Saint-Honoré. I sometimes wonder if she isn't in love with you."

"Why?"

"Because she works near the window, and when you leave the house in the morning she sometimes gets up to watch you go down the street."

"How old is she?"

"Forty-five to fifty. Aren't you getting dressed?"

Doesn't a man have the right to lounge in his dressing gown, even if people come to bother him at 8:30 on Christmas morning? Well, he'd compromise. He'd put his trousers on underneath the robe.

The two women were standing when he walked into the dining room.

"Excuse me, mesdames . . ."

Perhaps Mme. Maigret was right. Mlle. Doncoeur did not blush; she paled, smiled, lost her smile, smiled again. She opened her mouth to speak but said nothing.

The blonde, on the other hand, was perfectly composed. She said with a touch of humor: "Coming here wasn't my idea."

"Would you sit down, please?"

Maigret noticed that the blonde was wearing a house dress under her coat and that her legs were bare. Mlle. Doncoeur was dressed as though for church.

"You perhaps wonder at our boldness in coming to you like this," Mlle. Doncoeur said finally, choosing her words carefully. "Like everyone in the neighborhood, we are honored to have such a distinguished neighbor. . . ." She paused, blushed,

and stared at the tray. "We're keeping you from your breakfast."

"I've finished. I'm at your service."

"Something happened in our building last night, or rather
this morning, which was so unusual that I felt it was our duty
to speak to you about it immediately. Madame Martin did not
want to disturb you, but I told her—"

"You also live across the street, Madame Martin?"

"Yes, Monsieur." Madame Martin was obviously unhappy
at being forced to take this step. Mlle. Doncoeur, however,
was now fully wound up.

"We live on the same floor, just across from your windows." She blushed again, as if she were making a confession. "Monsieur Martin is often out of town, which is natural
enough since he is a traveling salesman. For the past two
months their little girl has been in bed, as a result of a silly
accident. . . ."

Maigret turned politely to the blonde. "You have a daughter?"

"Well, not a daughter exactly. She's our niece. Her mother
died two years ago and she's been living with us ever since.
The girl broke her leg on the stairs. She should have been up
and about after six weeks, but there were complications."

"Your husband is on the road at present?"

"He should be in Bergerac."

"I'm listening, Mlle. Doncoeur."

Mme. Maigret had detoured through the bathroom to regain
the kitchen. The clatter of pots and pans had resumed. Maigret stared through the window at the leaden sky.

"I got up early this morning as usual," said Mlle. Doncoeur, "to go to first mass."

"And you did go to church?"

"Yes. I stayed for three masses. I got home about 7:30 and
prepared my breakfast. You may have seen the light in my
window."

Maigret's gesture indicated he had not been watching.

"I was in a hurry to take a few goodies to Colette. It's very
sad for a child to spend Christmas in bed. Colette is Madame
Martin's niece."

"How old is she?"

"Seven. Isn't that right, Madame Martin?"

"She'll be seven in January."

"So at 8 o'clock I knocked at the door of their apartment—"

"I wasn't up," the blonde interrupted. "I sometimes sleep rather late."

"As I was saying, I knocked. Madame Martin kept me waiting for a moment while she slipped on her négligée. I had my arms full, and I asked if I could take my presents in to Colette."

Maigret noted that the blonde was making a mental inventory of the apartment, stopping occasionally to dart a sharp, suspicious glance in his direction.

"We opened the door to her room together. . . ."

"The child has a room of her own?"

"Yes. There are two bedrooms in the apartment, a dressing room, a kitchen, and a dining room. But I must tell you—No, I'm getting ahead of myself. We had just opened the door and since the room was dark, Madame Martin had switched on the light . . ."

"Colette was awake?"

"Yes. It was easy to see she'd been awake for some time, waiting. You know how children are on Christmas morning. If she could use her legs, she would certainly have got up long since to see what Father Christmas had brought her. Perhaps another child would have called out. But Colette is already a little lady. She's much older than her age. She thinks a lot."

Now Madame Martin was looking out the window. Maigret tried to guess which apartment was hers. It must be the last one to the right, the one with the two lighted windows.

"I wished her a Merry Christmas," Mlle. Doncoeur continued. "I said to her, and these were my exact words, 'Darling, look what Father Christmas left in my apartment for you.'"

Madame Martin was clasping and unclasping her fingers.

"And do you know what she answered me, without even looking to see what I'd brought? They were only trifles, anyhow. She said, 'I saw him.'"

"'Whom did you see?'"

"'Father Christmas.'"

"'When did you see him?' I asked. 'Where?'"

"'Right here, last night. He came to my room.'"

"That's exactly what she said, isn't it, Madame Martin? With any other child, we would have smiled. But as I told you, Colette is already a little lady. She doesn't joke. I said, 'How could you see him, since it was dark?'"

"'He had a light.'"

"'You mean he turned on the electricity?'"

"'No. He had a flashlight. Look, Mama Loraine.'"

"I must tell you that the little girl calls Madame Martin 'Mama,' which is natural enough, since her own mother is dead and Madame Martin has been taking her place."

The monologue had become a confused buzzing in Maigret's ears. He had not drunk his second cup of coffee and his pipe had gone out. He asked without conviction: "Did she really see someone?"

"Yes, Monsieur l'Inspector. And that's why I insisted that Madame Martin come to speak to you. Colette did see someone and she proved it to us. With a sly little smile she threw back the bedsheet and showed us a magnificent doll . . . a beautiful big doll she was cuddling and which I swear was not in the house yesterday."

"You didn't give your niece a doll, Madame Martin?"

"I was going to give her one, but mine was not nearly as nice. I got it yesterday afternoon at the Galeries, and I was holding it behind me this morning when we came into her room."

"In other words, someone *did* come into your apartment last night."

"That's not all," said Mlle. Doncoeur quickly; she was not to be stopped. "Colette never tells lies. She's not a child who imagines things. And when we questioned her, she said the man was certainly Father Christmas because he wore a white beard and a bright red coat."

"At what time did she wake up?"

"She doesn't know—sometime during the night. She opened her eyes because she thought she saw a light. And there was a light, shining on the floor near the fireplace."

"I can't understand it," sighed Madame Martin. "Unless my husband has some explanation . . ."

But Mlle. Doncoeur was not to be diverted from her story.

It was obvious that she was the one who had questioned the child, just as she was the one who had thought of Maigret. She resumed:

"Colette said, 'Father Christmas was squatting on the floor, and he was bending over, as though he were working at something.'"

"She wasn't frightened?"

"No. She just watched him. This morning she told us he was busy making a hole in the floor. She thought he wanted to go through the floor to visit the people downstairs—that's the Delormes who have a little boy of three—because the chimney was too narrow. The man must have sensed she was watching him, because he got up, came over to the bed, and gave Colette the big doll. Then he put his finger to his lips."

"Did she see him leave?"

"Yes."

"Through the floor?"

"No, by the door."

"Into what room does this door open?"

"Directly into the outside hall. There is another door that opens into the apartment, but the hall door is like a private entrance because the room used to be rented separately."

"Wasn't the door locked?"

"Of course," Madame Martin intervened. "I wouldn't let the child sleep in a room that wasn't locked from the outside."

"Then the door was forced?"

"Probably. I don't know. Mlle. Doncoeur immediately suggested we come to see you."

"Did you find a hole in the floor?"

Madame Martin shrugged wearily, but Mlle. Doncoeur answered for her.

"Not a hole exactly, but you could see that the floor boards had been moved."

"Tell me, Madame Martin, have you any idea what might have been hidden under the flooring?"

"No, Monsieur."

"How long have you lived in this apartment?"

"Since my marriage, five years ago."

"And this room was part of the apartment then?"

"Yes."

"You know who lived there before you?"

"My husband. He's 38. He was 33 when we were married, and he had his own furniture then. He liked to have his own home to come back to when he returned to Paris from the road."

"Do you think he might have wanted to surprise Colette?"

"He is six or seven hundred kilometers from here."

"Where did you say?"

"In Bergerac. His itinerary is planned in advance and he rarely deviates from his schedule."

"For what firm does he travel?"

"He covers the central and southwest territory for Zenith watches. It's an important line, as you probably know. He has a very good job."

"There isn't a finer man on earth!" exclaimed Mlle. Doncoeur. She blushed, then added, "Except you, Monsieur l'Inspecteur."

"As I understand it then, someone got into your apartment last night disguised as Father Christmas."

"According to the little girl."

"Didn't you hear anything? Is your room far from the little girl's?"

"There's the dining room between us."

"Don't you leave the connecting doors open at night?"

"It isn't necessary. Colette is not afraid, and as a rule she never wakes up. If she wants anything, she has a little bell on her night table."

"Did you go out last night?"

"I did not, Monsieur l'Inspecteur." Madame Martin was annoyed.

"Did you receive visitors?"

"I do not receive visitors while my husband is away."

Maigret glanced at Mlle. Doncoeur whose expression did not change. So Madame Martin was telling the truth.

"Did you go to bed late?"

"I read until midnight. As soon as the radio played *Minuit, Chrétiens,* I went to bed."

"And you heard nothing unusual?"

"Nothing."

"Have you asked the concierge if she clicked the latch to let in any strangers last night?"

"I asked her," Mlle. Doncoeur volunteered. "She says she didn't."

"And you found nothing missing from your apartment this morning, Madame Martin? Nothing disturbed in the dining room?"

"No."

"Who is with the little girl now?"

"No one. She's used to staying alone. I can't be at home all day. I have marketing to do, errands to run. . . ."

"I understand. You told me Colette is an orphan?"

"Her mother is dead."

"So her father is living. Where is he?"

"Her father's name is Paul Martin. He's my husband's brother. As to telling you where he is—" Madame Martin sketched a vague gesture.

"When did you see him last?"

"About a month ago. A little longer. It was around All Saint's Day. He was finishing a novena."

"I beg your pardon?"

"I may as well tell you everything at once," said Madame Martin with a faint smile, "since we seem to be washing our family linen." She glanced reproachfully at Mlle. Doncoeur. "My brother-in-law, especially since he lost his wife, is not quite respectable."

"What do you mean exactly?"

"He drinks. He always drank a little, but he never used to get into trouble. He had a good job with a furniture store in the Faubourg Saint-Antoine. But since the accident . . ."

"The accident to his daughter?"

"No, to his wife. He borrowed a car from a friend one Sunday about three years ago and took his wife and little girl to the country. They had lunch at a roadside inn near Mantes-la-Jolie and he drank too much white wine. He sang most of the way back to Paris—until he ran into something near the Bougival bridge. His wife was killed instantly. He cracked his own skull and it's a miracle he's still alive. Colette escaped without a scratch. Paul hasn't been a man since then. We've practically adopted the little girl. He comes to see her occasionally when he's sober. Then he starts over again. . . ."

"Do you know where he lives?"

Another vague gesture. "Everywhere. We've seen him loitering around the Bastille like a beggar. Sometimes he sells papers in the street. I can speak freely in front of Mlle. Doncoeur because unfortunately the whole house knows about him."

"Don't you think he might have dressed up as Father Christmas to call on his daughter?"

"That's what I told Mlle. Doncoeur, but she insisted on coming to see you anyhow."

"Because I see no reason for him to take up the flooring," said Mlle. Doncoeur acidly.

"Or perhaps your husband returned to Paris unexpectedly. . . ."

"It's certainly something of the sort. I'm not at all disturbed. But Mlle. Doncoeur—"

Decidedly Madame Martin had not crossed the boulevard lightheartedly.

"Do you know where your husband might be staying in Bergerac?"

"Yes. At the Hotel de Bordeaux."

"You hadn't thought of telephoning him?"

"We have no phone. There's only one in the house—the people on the second floor, and they hate to be disturbed."

"Would you object to my calling the Hotel de Bordeaux?"

Madame Martin started to nod, then hesitated. "He'll think something terrible has happened."

"You can speak to him yourself."

"He's not used to my phoning him on the road."

"You'd rather he not know what's happening?"

"That's not so. I'll talk to him if you like."

Maigret picked up the phone and placed the call. Ten minutes later he was connected with the Hotel de Bordeaux in Bergerac. He passed the instrument to Madame Martin.

"Hello. . . . Monsieur Martin, please. . . . Yes, Monsieur Jean Martin. . . . No matter. Wake him up."

She put her hand over the mouthpiece. "He's still asleep. They've gone to call him."

Then she retreated into silence, evidently rehearsing the words she was to speak to her husband.

"Hello? . . . Hello   darling. . . . What? . . . Yes,   Merry Christmas! . . . Yes, everything's all right. . . . Colette is fine. . . . No, that's not why I phoned. . . . No, no, no! Nothing's wrong. Please don't worry!" She repeated each word separately. "Please . . . don't . . . worry! I just want to tell you about a strange thing that happened last night. Somebody dressed up like Father Christmas and came into Colette's room. . . . No, no! He didn't hurt her. He gave her a big doll. . . . Yes, *doll!* . . . And he did queer things to the floor. He removed two boards which he put back in a hurry. . . . Mlle. Doncoeur thought I should report it to the police inspector who lives across the street. I'm there now. . . . You don't understand? Neither do I. . . . You want me to put him on?" She passed the instrument to Maigret. "He wants to speak to you."

A warm masculine voice came over the wire, the voice of an anxious, puzzled man.

"Are you sure my wife and the little girl are all right? . . . It's all so incredible! If it were just the doll, I might suspect my brother. Loraine will tell you about him. Loraine is my wife. Ask her. . . . But he wouldn't have removed the flooring. . . . Do you think I'd better come home? I can get a train for Paris at three this afternoon. . . . What? . . . Thank you so much. It's good to know you'll look out for them."

Loraine Martin took back the phone.

"See, darling? The inspector says there's no danger. It would be foolish to break your trip now. It might spoil your chances of being transferred permanently to Paris. . . ."

Mlle. Doncoeur was watching her closely and there was little tenderness in the spinster's eyes.

". . . I promise to wire you or phone you if there's anything new. . . . She's playing quietly with her new doll. . . . No, I haven't had time yet to give her your present. I'll go right home and do it now."

Madame Martin hung up and declared: "You see." Then, after a pause, "Forgive me for bothering you. It's really not my fault. I'm sure this is all the work of some practical joker . . . unless it's my brother-in-law. When he's been drinking there's no telling what he might do."

"Do you expect to see him today? Don't you think he might want to see his daughter?"

"That depends. If he's been drinking, no. He's very careful never to come around in that condition."

"May I have your permission to come over and talk with Colette a little later?"

"I see no reason why you shouldn't—if you think it worthwhile. . . ."

"Thank you, Monsieur Maigret!" exclaimed Mlle. Doncoeur. Her expression was half grateful, half conspiratorial. "She's such an interesting child! You'll see!"

She backed toward the door.

A few minutes later Maigret watched the two women cross the boulevard. Mlle. Doncoeur, close on the heels of Madame Martin, turned to look up at the windows of the Maigret apartment.

Mme. Maigret opened the kitchen door, flooding the dining room with the aroma of browning onions. She asked gently:

"Are you happy?"

He pretended not to understand. Luckily he had been too busy to think much about the middle-aged couple who had nobody to make a fuss over this Christmas morning.

It was time for him to shave and call on Colette.

He was just about to lather his face when he decided to make a phone call. He didn't bother with his dressing gown. Clad only in pajamas, he dropped into the easy chair by the window—*his* chair—and watched the smoke curling up from all the chimney pots while his call went through.

The ringing at the other end—in headquarters at the Quai des Orfèvres—had a different sound from all other rings. It evoked for him the long empty corridors, the vacant offices, the operator stuck with holiday duty at the switchboard. . . . Then he heard the operator call Lucas with the words: "The boss wants you."

He felt a little like one of his wife's friends who could imagine no greater joy—which she experienced daily—than lying in bed all morning, with her windows closed and curtains drawn, and telephoning all her friends, one after the other. By the soft glow of her night-light she managed to maintain a constant state of just having awakened. "What? Ten o'clock already? How's the weather? Is it raining? Have you been out yet? Have you done all your marketing?" And as she established telephonic connection with the hurly-burly of the workaday world, she would sink more and more voluptuously into the warm softness of her bed.

"That you, Chief?".

Maigret, too, felt a need for contact with the working world. He wanted to ask Lucas who was on duty with him, what they were doing, how the shop looked on this Christmas morning.

"Nothing new? Not too busy?"

"Nothing to speak of. Routine. . . ."

"I'd like you to get me some information. You can probably do this by phone. First of all, I want a list of all convicts released from prison the last two or three months."

"Which prison?"

"All prisons. But don't bother with any who haven't served at least five years. Then check and see if any of them has ever lived on Boulevard Richard-Lenoir. Got that?"

"I'm making notes."

Lucas was probably somewhat bewildered but he would never admit it.

"Another thing. I want you to locate a man named Paul Martin, a drunk, no fixed address, who frequently hangs out around the Place de la Bastille. I don't want him arrested. I don't want him molested. I just want to know where he spent Christmas Eve. The commissariats should help you on this one."

No use trying. Maigret simply could not reproduce the idle mood of his wife's friend. On the contrary, it embarrassed him to be lolling at home in his pajamas, unshaven, phoning from his favorite easy chair, looking out at a scene of complete peace and quiet in which there was no movement except the smoke curling from the chimney pots, while at the other end of the wire good old Lucas had been on duty since six in the morning and was probably already unwrapping his sandwiches.

"That's not quite all, old man. I want you to call Bergerac long distance. There's a traveling salesman by the name of

Jean Martin staying at the Hotel de Bordeaux there. No, Jean. It's his brother. I want to know if Jean Martin got a telegram or a phone call from Paris last night or any time yesterday. And while you're about it, find out where he spent Christmas Eve. I think that's all."

"Shall I call you back?"

"Not right away. I've got to go out for a while. I'll call you when I get home."

"Something happen in your neighborhood?"

"I don't know yet. Maybe."

Mme. Maigret came into the bathroom to talk to him while he finished dressing. He did not put on his overcoat. The smoke curled slowly upward from so many chimney pots blended with the gray of the sky and conjured up the image of just as many overheated apartments, cramped rooms in which he would not be invited to make himself at home. He refused to be uncomfortable. He would put on his hat to cross the boulevard, and that was all.

The building across the way was very much like the one he lived in—old but clean, a little dreary, particularly on a drab December morning. He avoided stopping at the concierge's lodge, but noted she watched him with some annoyance. Doors opened silently as he climbed the stairs. He heard whispering, the padding of slippered feet.

Mlle. Doncoeur, who had doubtless been watching for him, was waiting on the fourth floor landing. She was both shy and excited, as if keeping a secret tryst with a lover.

"This way, Monsieur Maigret. She went out a little while ago."

He frowned, and she noted the fact.

"I told her that you were coming and that she had better wait for you but she said she had not done her marketing yesterday and that there was nothing in the house. She said all the stores would be closed if she waited too long. Come in."

She had opened the door into Madame Martin's dining room, a small, rather dark room which was clean and tidy.

"I'm looking after the little girl until she comes back. I told Colette that you were coming to see her, and she is delighted. I've spoken to her about you. She's only afraid you might take back her doll."

"When did Madame Martin decide to go out?"

"As soon as we came back across the street, she started dressing."

"Did she dress completely?"

"I don't understand."

"I mean, I suppose she dresses differently when she goes downtown than when she merely goes shopping in the neighborhood."

"She was quite dressed up. She put on her hat and gloves. And she carried her shopping bag."

Before going to see Colette, Maigret stepped into the kitchen and glanced at the breakfast dishes.

"Did she eat before you came to see me?"

"No. I didn't give her a chance."

"And when she came back?"

"She just made herself a cup of black coffee. I fixed breakfast for Colette while Madame Martin got dressed."

There was a larder on the ledge of the window looking out on the courtyard. Maigret carefully examined its contents: butter, eggs, vegetables, some cold meat. He found two uncut loaves of fresh bread in the kitchen cupboard. Colette had eaten *croissants* with her hot chocolate.

"How well do you know Madame Martin?"

"We're neighbors, aren't we? And I've seen more of her since Colette has been in bed. She often asks me to keep an eye on the little girl when she goes out."

"Does she go out much?"

"Not very often. Just for her marketing."

Maigret tried to analyze the curious impression he had had on entering the apartment. There was something in the atmosphere that disturbed him, something about the arrangement of the furniture, the special kind of neatness that prevailed, even the smell of the place. As he followed Mlle. Doncoeur into the dining room, he thought he knew what it was.

Madame Martin had told him that her husband had lived in this apartment before their marriage. And even though Madame Martin had lived there for five years, it had remained a bachelor's apartment. He pointed to the two enlarged photographs standing on opposite ends of the mantelpiece.

"Who are they?"

"Monsieur Martin's father and mother."

"Doesn't Madame Martin have photos of her own parents about?"

"I've never heard her speak of them. I suppose she's an orphan."

Even the bedroom was without the feminine touch. He opened a closet. Next to the neat rows of masculine clothing, the woman's clothes were hanging, mostly severely tailored suits and conservative dresses. He did not open the bureau drawers but he was sure they did not contain the usual trinkets and knickknacks that women collect.

"Mademoiselle Doncoeur!" called a calm little voice.

"Let's talk to Colette," said Maigret.

The child's room was as austere and cold as the others. The little girl lay in a bed too large for her, her face solemn, her eyes questioning but trusting.

"Are you the inspector, Monsieur?"

"I'm the inspector, my girl. Don't be afraid."

"I'm not afraid. Hasn't Mama Loraine come home yet?"

Maigret pursed his lips. The Martins had practically adopted their niece, yet the child said "Mama Loraine," not just "Mama."

"Do you believe it was Father Christmas who came to see me last night?" Colette asked Maigret.

"I'm sure it was."

"Mama Loraine doesn't believe it. She never believes me."

The girl had a dainty, attractive little face, with very bright eyes that stared at Maigret with level persistence. The plaster cast which sheathed one leg all the way to the hip made a thick bulge under the blankets.

Mlle. Doncoeur hovered in the doorway, evidently anxious to leave the inspector alone with the girl. She said: "I must run home for a moment to make sure my lunch isn't burning."

Maigret sat down beside the bed, wondering how to go about questioning the girl.

"Do you love Mama Loraine very much?" he began.

"Yes, Monsieur." She replied without hesitation and without enthusiasm.

"And your papa?"

"Which one? Because I have two papas, you know—Papa Paul and Papa Jean."

"Has it been a long time since you saw Papa Paul?"

"I don't remember. Perhaps several weeks. He promised to bring me a toy for Christmas, but he hasn't come yet. He must be sick."

"Is he often sick?"

"Yes, often. When he's sick he doesn't come to see me."

"And your Papa Jean?"

"He's away on a trip, but he'll be back for New Year's. Maybe then he'll be appointed to the Paris office and won't have to go away any more. That would make him very happy and me, too."

"Do many of your friends come to see you since you've been in bed?"

"What friends? The girls in school don't know where I live. Or maybe they know but their parents don't let them come alone."

"What about Mama Loraine's friends? Or your papa's?'

"Nobody comes, ever."

"Ever? Are you sure?"

"Only the man to read the gas meter, or for the electricity. I can hear them, because the door is almost always open. I recognize their voices. Once a man came and I didn't recognize his voice. Or twice."

"How long ago was that?"

"The first time was the day after my accident. I remember because the doctor just left."

"Who was it?"

"I didn't see him. He knocked at the other door. I heard him talking and then Mama Loraine came and closed my door. They talked for quite a while but I couldn't hear very well. Afterward Mama Loraine said it was a man who wanted to sell her some insurance. I don't know what that is."

"And he came back?"

"Five or six days ago. It was night and I'd already turned off my light. I wasn't asleep, though. I heard someone knock, and then they talked in low voices like the first time. Mademoiselle Doncoeur sometimes comes over in the evening, but

I could tell it wasn't she. I thought they were quarreling and I was frightened. I called out, and Mama Loraine came in and said it was the man about the insurance again and I should go to sleep."

"Did he stay long?"

"I don't know. I think I fell asleep."

"And you didn't see him either time?"

"No, but I'd recognize his voice."

"Even though he speaks in low tones?"

"Yes, that's why. When he speaks low it sounds just like a big bumblebee. I can keep the doll can't I? Mama Loraine bought me two boxes of candy and a little sewing kit. She bought me a doll, too, but it wasn't nearly as big as the doll Father Christmas gave me, because she's not rich. She showed it to me this morning before she left, and then she put it back in the box. I have the big one now, so I won't need the little one and Mama Loraine can take it back to the store."

The apartment was overheated, yet Maigret felt suddenly cold. The building was very much like the one across the street, yet not only did the rooms seem smaller and stuffier, but the whole world seemed smaller and meaner over here.

He bent over the floor near the fireplace. He lifted the loose floor boards, but saw nothing but an empty, dusty cavity smelling of dampness. There were scratches on the planks which indicated they had been forced up with a chisel or some similar instrument.

He examined the outside door and found indications that it had been forced. It was obviously an amateur's work, and luckily for him, the job had been an easy one.

"Father Christmas wasn't angry when he saw you watching him?"

"No, Monsieur. He was busy making a hole in the floor so he could go and see the little boy downstairs."

"Did he speak to you?"

"I think he smiled at me. I'm not sure, though, because of his whiskers. It wasn't very light. But I'm sure he put his finger to his lips so I wouldn't call anybody, because grown-ups aren't supposed to see Father Christmas. Did you ever see him?"

"A very long time ago."

"When you were little?"

Maigret heard footsteps in the hallway. The door opened and Madame Martin came in. She was wearing a gray tailored suit and a small beige hat and carried a brown shopping bag. She was visibly cold, for her skin was taut and very white, yet she must have hurried up the stairs, since there were two pink spots on her cheeks and she was out of breath. Unsmiling, she asked Maigret:

"Has she been a good girl?" Then, as she took off her jacket, "I apologize for making you wait. I had so many things to buy, and I was afraid the stores would all be closed later on."

"Did you meet anyone?"

"What do you mean?"

"Nothing. I was wondering if anyone tried to speak to you."

She had had plenty of time to go much farther than the Rue Amelot or the Rue du Chemin-Vert where most of the neighborhood shops were located. She had even had time to go across Paris and back by taxi or the Metro.

Mlle. Doncoeur returned to ask if there was anything she could do. Madame Martin was about to say no when Maigret intervened: "I'd like you to stay with Colette while I step into the next room."

Mlle. Doncoeur understood that he wanted her to keep the child busy while he questioned the foster-mother. Madame Martin must have understood, too, but she gave no indication.

"Please come in. Do you mind if I take off my things?"

Madame Martin put her packages in the kitchen. She took off her hat and fluffed out her pale blonde hair. When she had closed the bedroom door, she said; "Mlle. Doncoeur is all excited. This is quite an event, isn't it, for an old maid—particularly an old maid who cuts out every newspaper article about a certain police inspector, and who finally has the inspector in her own house. . . . Do you mind?"

She had taken a cigarette from a silver case, tapped the end, and snapped a lighter. The gesture somehow prompted Maigret's next question:

"You're not working, Madame Martin?"

"It would be difficult to hold a job and take care of the

house and the little girl, too, even when the child is in school. Besides, my husband won't allow me to work."

"But you did work before you met him?"

"Naturally. I had to earn a living. Won't you sit down?"

He lowered himself into a rude raffia-bottomed chair. She rested one thigh against the edge of a table.

"You were a typist?"

"I have been a typist."

"For long?"

"Quite a while."

"You were still a typist when you met Martin? You must forgive me for asking these personal questions."

"It's your job."

"You were married five years ago. Were you working then? Just a moment. May I ask your age?"

"I'm thirty-three. I was twenty-eight then, and I was working for a Monsieur Lorilleux in the Palais-Royal arcades."

"As his secretary?"

"Monsieur Lorilleux had a jewelry shop. Or more exactly, he sold souvenirs and old coins. You know those old shops in the Palais-Royal. I was salesgirl, bookkeeper, *and* secretary. I took care of the shop when he was away."

"He was married?"

"And father of three children."

"You left him to marry Martin?"

"Not exactly. Jean didn't want me to go on working, but he wasn't making very much money then and I had quite a good job. So I kept it for the first few months."

"And then?"

"Then a strange thing happened. One morning I came to work at 9 o'clock as usual, and I found the door locked. I thought Monsieur Lorilleux had overslept, so I waited...."

"Where did he live?"

"Rue Mazarine with his family. At half-past 9 I began to worry."

"Was he dead?"

"No. I phoned his wife, who said he had left the house at 8 o'clock as usual."

"Where did you telephone from?"

"From the glove shop next door. I waited all morning. His

wife came down and we went to the commissariat together to report him missing, but the police didn't take it very seriously. They just asked his wife if he'd ever had heart trouble, if he had a mistress—things like that. But he was never seen again, and nobody ever heard from him. Then some Polish people bought out the store and my husband made me stop working."

"How long was this after your marriage?"

"Four months."

"Your husband was already traveling in the southwest?"

"He had the same territory he has now."

"Was he in Paris when your employer disappeared?"

"No, I don't think so."

"Didn't the police examine the premises?"

"Nothing had been touched since the night before. Nothing was missing."

"Do you know what became of Madame Lorilleux?"

"She lived for a while on the money from the sale of the store. Then she bought a little dry-goods shop not far from here, in the Rue du Pas-de-la-Mule. Her children must be grown up now, probably married."

"Do you still see her?"

"I go into her shop once in a while. That's how I know she's in business in the neighborhood. The first time I saw her there I didn't recognize her."

"How long ago was that?"

"I don't know. Six months or so."

"Does she have a telephone?"

"I don't know. Why?"

"What kind of man was Lorilleux?"

"You mean physically?"

"Let's start with the physical."

"He was a big man, taller than you, and broader. He was fat, but flabby, if you know what I mean. And rather sloppy-looking."

"How old?"

"Around fifty. I can't say exactly. He had a little salt-and-pepper mustache, and his clothes were always too big for him."

"You were familiar with his habits?"

"He walked to work every morning. He got down fifteen

minutes ahead of me and cleared up the mail before I arrived. He didn't talk much. He was a rather gloomy person. He spent most of the day in the little office behind the shop."

"No romantic adventures?"

"Not that I know of."

"Didn't he try to make love to you?"

"No!" The monosyllable was tartly emphatic.

"But he thought highly of you?"

"I think I was a great help to him."

"Did your husband ever meet him?"

"They never spoke. Jean sometimes came to wait for me outside the shop, but he never came in." A note of impatience, tinged with anger, crept into her voice. "Is that all you want to know?"

"May I point out, Madame Martin, that you are the one who came to get me?"

"Only because a crazy old maid practically dragged me there so she could get a close-up look at you."

"You don't like Mlle. Doncoeur?"

"I don't like people who can't mind their own business."

"People like Mlle. Doncoeur?"

"You know that we've taken in my brother-in-law's child. Believe me or not, I've done everything I can for her. I treat her the way I'd treat my own child. . . ." She paused to light a fresh cigarette, and Maigret tried unsuccessfully to picture her as a doting mother. ". . . And now that old maid is always over here, offering to help me with the child. Every time I start to go out, I find her in the hallway, smiling sweetly, and saying, 'You mustn't leave Colette all alone, Madame Martin. Let me go in and keep her company.' I sometimes wonder if she doesn't go through my drawers when I'm out."

"You put up with her, nevertheless."

"How can I help it? Colette asks for her, especially since she's been in bed. And my husband is fond of her because when he was a bachelor, she took care of him when he was sick with pleurisy."

"Have you already returned the doll you bought for Colette's Christmas?"

She frowned and glanced at the door to the child's bedroom. "I see you've been questioning the little girl. No, I haven't taken it back for the very good reason that all the big department stores are closed today. Would you like to see it?"

She spoke defiantly, expecting him to refuse, but he said nothing. He examined the cardboard box, noting the price tag. It was a very cheap doll.

"May I ask where you went this morning?"

"I did my marketing."

"Rue Amelot or Rue du Chemin-Vert?"

"Both."

"If I may be indiscreet, what did you buy?"

Furious, she stormed into the kitchen, snatched up her shopping bag, and dumped it on the dining room table. "Look for yourself!"

There were three tins of sardines, butter, potatoes, some ham, and a head of lettuce.

She fixed him with a hard, unwavering stare. She was not in the least nervous. Spiteful, rather.

"Any more questions?"

"Yes. The name of your insurance agent."

"My insurance. . . ." She was obviously puzzled.

"Insurance agent. The one who came to see you."

"I'm sorry. I was at a loss for a moment because you spoke of *my* agent as though he were really handling a policy for me. So Colette told you that, too? Actually, a man did come to see me twice, trying to sell me a policy. He was one of those door-to-door salesmen, and I thought at first he was selling vacuum cleaners, not life insurance. I had a terrible time getting rid of him."

"Did he stay long?"

"Long enough for me to convince him that I had no desire to take out a policy."

"What company did he represent?"

"He told me but I've forgotten. Something with 'Mutual' in it."

"And he came back later?"

"Yes."

"What time does Colette usually go to sleep?"

"I put out her light at 7:30, but sometimes she talks to herself in the dark until much later."

"So the second time the insurance man called, it was later than 7:30?"

"Possibly." She saw the trap. "I remember now I was washing the dishes."

"And you let him in?"

"He had his foot in the door."

"Did he call on other tenants in the building?"

"I haven't the slightest idea, but I'm sure you will inquire. Must you cross-examine me like a criminal, just because a little girl imagines she saw Santa Claus? If my husband were here——"

"By the way, does your husband carry life insurance?"

"I think so. In fact, I'm sure he does."

Maigret picked up his hat from a chair and started for the door. Madame Martin seemed surprised.

"Is that all?"

"That's all. It seems your brother-in-law promised to come and see his daughter today. If he should come, I would be grateful if you let me know. And now I'd like a few words with Mlle. Doncoeur."

There was a convent smell about Mlle. Doncoeur's apartment, but there was no dog or cat in sight, no antimacassars on the chairs, no bricbrac on the mantelpiece.

"Have you lived in this house long, Mlle. Doncoeur?"

"Twenty-five years, Monsieur l'Inspecteur. I'm one of the oldest tenants. I remember when I first moved in you were already living across the street, and you wore long mustaches."

"Who lived in the next apartment before Martin moved in?"

"A public works engineer. I don't remember his name, but I could look it up for you. He had a wife and daughter. The girl was a deaf-mute. It was very sad. They went to live somewhere in the country."

"Have you been bothered by a door-to-door insurance agent recently?"

"Not recently. There was one who came around two or three years ago."

"You don't like Madame Martin, do you?"

"Why?"

"I asked if you liked Madame Martin?"

"Well, if I had a son . . ."

"Go on."

"If I had a son I don't think I would like Madame Martin for a daughter-in-law. Especially as Monsieur Martin is such a nice man, so kind."

"You think he is unhappy with his wife?"

"I wouldn't say that. I have nothing against her, really. She can't help being the kind of woman she is."

"What kind of woman is she?"

"I couldn't say, exactly. You've seen her. You're a better judge of those things than I am. In a way, she's not like a woman at all. I'll wager she never shed a tear in her life. True, she is bringing up the child properly, decently, but she never says a kind word to her. She acts exasperated when I tell Colette a fairy tale. I'm sure she's told the girl there is no Santa Claus. Luckily Colette doesn't believe her."

"The child doesn't like her either, does she?"

"Colette is always obedient. She tries to do what's expected of her. I think she's just as happy to be left alone."

"Is she alone much?"

"Not much. I'm not reproaching Madame Martin. It's hard to explain. She wants to live her own life. She's not interested in others. She doesn't even talk much about herself."

"Have you ever met her brother-in-law—Colette's father?"

"I've seen him on the landing, but I've never spoken to him. He walks with his head down, as if he were ashamed of something. He always looks as if he slept in his clothes. No, I don't think it was he last night, Monsieur Maigret. He's not the type. Unless he was terribly drunk."

On his way out Maigret looked in at the concierge's lodge, a dark cubicle where the light burned all day.

It was noon when he started back across the boulevard. Curtains stirred at the windows of the house behind him. Curtains stirred at his own window, too. Mme. Maigret was watching for him so she would know when to put the chicken in the oven. He waved to her. He wanted very much to stick out his tongue and lick up a few of the tiny snow flakes that were drifting down. He could still remember their taste.

"I wonder if that little tike is happy over there," sighed

Mme. Maigret as she got up from the table to bring the coffee from the kitchen.

She could see he wasn't listening. He had pushed back his chair and was stuffing his pipe while staring at the purring stove. For her own satisfaction she added: "I don't see how she could be happy with that woman."

He smiled vaguely, as he always did when he hadn't heard what she said, and continued to stare at the tiny flames licking evenly at the mica windows of the salamander. There were at least ten similar stoves in the house, all purring alike in ten similar dining rooms with wine and cakes on the table, a carafe of cordial waiting on the sideboard, and all the windows pale with the same hard, gray light of a sunless day.

It was perhaps this very familiarity which had been confusing his subconscious since morning. Nine times out of ten his investigations plunged him abruptly into new surroundings, set him at grips with people of a world he barely knew, people of a social level whose habits and manners he had to study from scratch. But in this case, which was not really a case since he had no official assignment, the whole approach was unfamiliar because the background was too familiar. For the first time in his career something professional was happening in his own world, in a building which might just as well be his building.

The Martins could easily have been living on his floor, instead of across the street, and it would probably have been Mme. Maigret who would look after Colette when her aunt was away. There was an elderly maiden lady living just under him who was a plumper, paler replica of Mlle. Doncoeur. The frames of the photographs of Martin's father and mother were exactly the same as those which framed Maigret's father and mother, and the enlargements had probably been made by the same studio.

Was that what was bothering him? He seemed to lack perspective. He was unable to look at people and things from a fresh, new viewpoint.

He had detailed his morning activities during dinner—a pleasant little Christmas dinner which had left him with an overstuffed feeling—and his wife had listened while looking at the windows across the street with an air of embarrassment.

"Is the concierge sure that nobody could have come in from outside?"

"She's not so sure any more. She was entertaining friends until after midnight. And after she had gone to bed, there were considerable comings and goings, which is natural for Christmas Eve."

"Do you think something more is going to happen?"

That was a question that had been plaguing Maigret all morning. First of all, he had to consider that Madame Martin had not come to see him spontaneously, but only on the insistence of Mlle. Doncoeur. If she had got up earlier, if she had been the first to see the doll and hear the story of Father Christmas, wouldn't she have kept the secret and ordered the little girl to say nothing?

And later she had taken the first opportunity to go out, even though there was plenty to eat in the house for the day. And she had been so absent-minded that she had bought butter, although there was still a pound in the cooler.

Maigret got up from the table and resettled himself in his chair by the window. He picked up the phone and called Quai des Orfèvres.

"Lucas?"

"I got what you wanted, Chief. I have a list of all prisoners released for the last four months. There aren't as many as I thought. And none of them has lived in the Boulevard Richard-Lenoir at any time."

That didn't matter any more now. At first Maigret had thought that a tenant across the street might have hidden money or stolen goods under the floor before he was arrested. His first thought on getting out of jail would be to recover his booty. With the little girl bedridden, however, the room was occupied day and night. Impersonating Father Christmas would not have been a bad idea to get into the room. Had this been the case, however, Madame Martin would not have been so reluctant to call in Maigret. Nor would she have been in so great a hurry to get out of the house afterwards on such a flimsy pretext. So Maigret had abandoned that theory.

"You want me to check each prisoner further?"

"Never mind. Any news about Paul Martin?"

"That was easy. He's known in every station house between

the Bastille and the Hotel de Ville, and even on the Boulevard Saint-Michel."

"What did he do last night?"

"First he went aboard the Salvation Army barge to eat. He's a regular there one day a week and yesterday was his day. They had a special feast for Christmas Eve and he had to stand in line quite a while."

"After that?"

"About 11 o'clock he went to the Latin Quarter and opened doors for motorists in front of a night club. He must have collected enough money in tips to get himself a sinkful, because he was picked up dead drunk near the Place Maubert at 4 in the morning. He was taken to the station house to sleep it off, and was there until 11 this morning. They'd just turned him loose when I phoned, and they promised to bring him to me when they find him again. He still had a few francs in his pocket."

"What about Bergerac?"

"Jean Martin is taking the afternoon train for Paris. He was quite upset by a phone call he got this morning."

"He got only one call?"

"Only one this morning. He got a call last night while he was eating dinner."

"You know who called him?"

"The desk clerk says it was a man's voice, asking for Monsieur Jean Martin. He sent somebody into the dining room for Martin but when Martin got to the phone, the caller had hung up. Seems it spoiled his whole evening. He went out with a bunch of traveling salesmen to some local hot-spot where there were pretty girls and whatnot, but after drinking a few glasses of champagne, he couldn't talk about anything except his wife and daughter. The niece he calls his daughter, it seems. He had such a dismal evening that he went home early. Three A.M. That's all you wanted to know, Chief?"

When Maigret didn't reply, Lucas had to satisfy his curiosity. "You still phoning from home, Chief? What's happening up your way? Somebody get killed?"

"I still can't say. Right now all I know is that the principals are a seven-year-old girl, a doll, and Father Christmas."

"Ah?"

"One more thing. Try to get me the home address of the manager of Zenith Watches, Avenue de l'Opera. You ought to be able to raise somebody there, even on Christmas Day. Call me back."

"Soon as I have something."

Mme. Maigret had just served him a glass of Alsatian plum brandy which her sister had sent them. He smacked his lips. For a moment he was tempted to forget all about the business of the doll and Father Christmas. It would be much simpler just to take his wife to the movies. . . .

"What color eyes has she?"

It took him a moment to realize that the only person in the case who interested Mme. Maigret was the little girl.

"Why, I'm not quite sure. They can't be dark. She has blonde hair."

"So they're blue."

"Maybe they're blue. Very light, in any case. And they are very serious."

"Because she doesn't look at things like a child. Does she laugh?"

"She hasn't much to laugh about."

"A child can always laugh if she feels herself surrounded by people she can trust, people who let her act her age. I don't like that woman."

"You prefer Mlle. Doncoeur?"

"She may be an old maid but I'm sure she knows more about children than that Madame Martin. I've seen *her* in the shops. Madame Martin is one of those women who watch the scales, and take their money out of their pocketbooks, coin by coin. She always looks around suspiciously, as though everybody was out to cheat her."

The telephone rang as Mme. Maigret was repeating, "I don't like that woman."

It was Lucas calling, with the address of Monsieur Arthur Godefroy, general manager in France for Zenith Watches. He lived in a sumptuous villa at Saint-Cloud, and Lucas had discovered that he was at home. He added:

"Paul Martin is here, Chief. When they brought him in, he started crying. He thought something had happened to his daughter. But he's all right now—except for an awful hangover. What do I do with him?"

"Anyone around who can come up here with him?"

"Torrence just came on duty. I think he could use a little fresh air. He looks as if he had a hard night, too. Anything more from me, Chief?"

"Yes. Call Palais-Royal station. About five years ago a man named Lorilleux disappeared without a trace. He sold jewelry and old coins in the Palais-Royal arcades. Get me all the details you can on his disappearance."

Maigret smiled as he noted that his wife was sitting opposite him with her knitting. He had never before worked on a case in such domestic surroundings.

"Do I call you back?" asked Lucas.

"I don't expect to move an inch from my chair."

A moment later Maigret was talking to Monsieur Godefroy, who had a decided Swiss accent. The Zenith manager thought that something must have happened to Jean Martin for anyone to be making inquiries about him on Christmas Day.

"Most able . . . most devoted . . . I'm bringing him into Paris to be assistant manager next year. . . . Next week, that is . . . Why do you ask? Has anything—? Be still, you!" He paused to quiet the juvenile hubbub in the background. "You must excuse me. All my family is with me today and—"

"Tell me, Monsieur Godefroy, has anyone called your office these last few days to inquire about Monsieur Martin's current address?"

"Yesterday morning, as a matter of fact. I was very busy with the holiday rush, but he asked to speak to me personally. I forget what name he gave. He said he had an extremely important message for Jean Martin, so I told him how to get in touch with Martin in Bergerac."

"He asked you nothing else?"

"No. He hung up at once. Is anything wrong?"

"I hope not. Thank you very much, Monsieur."

The screams of children began again in the background and Maigret said goodbye.

"Were you listening?"

"I heard what you said. I didn't hear his answers."

"A man called the office yesterday morning to get Martin's address. The same man undoubtedly called Bergerac that evening to make sure Martin was still there, and therefore would not be at his Boulevard Richard-Lenoir address for Christmas Eve."

"The same man who appeared last night as Father Christmas?"

"More than likely. That seems to clear Paul Martin. He would not have to make two phone calls to find out where his brother was. Madame Martin would have told him."

"You're really getting excited about this case. You're delighted that it came up, aren't you? Confess!" And while Maigret was racking his brain for excuses, she added: "It's quite natural. I'm fascinated, too. How much longer do you think the child will have to keep her leg in a cast?"

"I didn't ask."

"I wonder what sort of complications she could have had?"

Maigret looked at her curiously. Unconsciously she had switched his mind onto a new track.

"That's not such a stupid remark you just made."

"What did I say?"

"After all, since she's been in bed for two months, she should be up and around soon, barring really serious complications."

"She'll probably have to walk on crutches at first."

"That's not the point. In a few days then, or a few weeks at most, she will no longer be confined to her room. She'll go for a walk with Madame Martin. And the coast will be clear for anyone to enter the apartment without dressing up like Father Christmas."

Mme. Maigret's lips were moving. While listening to her husband and watching his face, she was counting stitches.

"First of all, the presence of the child forced our man to use trickery. She's been in bed for two months—two months for him to wait. Without the complications the flooring could have been taken up several weeks ago. Our man must have had urgent reasons for acting at once, without further delay."

"Monsieur Martin will return to Paris in a few days?"

"Exactly."

"What do you suppose the man found underneath the floor?"

"Did he really find anything? If not, his problem is still as pressing as it was last night. So he will take further action."

"What action?"

"I don't know."

"Look, Maigret, isn't the child in danger? Do you think she's safe with that woman?"

"I could answer that if I knew where Madame Martin went this morning on the pretext of doing her shopping." He picked up the phone again and called Police Judiciaire.

"I'm pestering you again, Lucas. I want you to locate a taxi that picked up a passenger this morning between 9 and 10 somewhere near Boulevard Richard-Lenoir. The fare was a woman in her early thirties, blonde, slim but solidly built. She was wearing a gray suit and a beige hat. She carried a brown shopping bag. I want to know her destination. There couldn't have been so many cabs on the street at that hour."

"Is Paul Martin with you?"

"Not yet."

"He'll be there soon. About that other thing, the Lorilleux matter, the Palais-Royal boys are checking their files. You'll have the data in a few minutes."

Jean Martin must be taking his train in Bergerac at this moment. Little Colette was probably taking her nap. Mlle. Doncoeur was doubtless sitting behind her window curtain, wondering what Maigret was up to.

People were beginning to come out now, families with their children, the children with their new toys. There were certainly queues in front of the cinemas. . . .

A taxi stopped in front of the house. Footsteps sounded in the stairway. Mme. Maigret went to the door. The deep bass voice of Torrence rumbled: "You there, Chief?"

Torrence came in with an ageless man who hugged the walls and looked humbly at the floor. Maigret went to the sideboard and filled two glasses with plum brandy.

"To your health," he said.

The man looked at Maigret with surprised, anxious eyes. He raised a trembling, hesitant hand.

"To your health, Monsieur Martin. I'm sorry to make you come all the way up here, but you won't have far to go now to see your daughter."

"Nothing has happened to her?"

"No, no. When I saw her this morning she was playing with her new doll. You can go, Torrence. Lucas must need you."

Mme. Maigret had gone into the bedroom with her knitting. She was sitting on the edge of the bed, counting her stitches.

"Sit down, Monsieur Martin."

The man had touched his lips to the glass and set it down. He looked at it uneasily.

"You have nothing to worry about. Just tell yourself that I know all about you."

"I wanted to visit her this morning," the man sighed. "I swore I would go to bed early so I could wish her a Merry Christmas."

"I know that, too."

"It's always the same. I swear I'll take just one drink, just enough to pick me up. . . ."

"You have only one brother, Monsieur Martin?"

"Yes, Jean. He's six years younger than I am. He and my wife and my daughter were all I had to love in this world."

"You don't love your sister-in-law?"

He shivered. He seemed both startled and embarrassed.

"I have nothing against Loraine."

"You entrusted your child to her, didn't you?"

"Well, yes, that is to say, when my wife died and I began to slip. . . ."

"I understand. Is your daughter happy?"

"I think so, yes. She never complains."

"Have you ever tried to get back on your feet?"

"Every night I promise myself to turn over a new leaf, but next day I start all over again. I even went to see a doctor. I followed his advice for a few days. But when I went back, he was very busy. He said I ought to be in a special sanatorium."

He reached for his glass, then hesitated. Maigret picked up his own glass and took a swallow to encourage him.

"Did you ever meet a man in your sister-in-law's apartment?"

"No. I think she's above reproach on that score."

"Do you know where your brother first met her?"

"In a little restaurant in the Rue Beaujolais where he used to eat when he was in Paris. It was near the shop where Loraine was working."

"Did they have a long engagement?"

"I can't say. Jean was on the road for two months and when he came back he told me he was getting married."

"Were you his best man?"

"Yes. Loraine has no family in Paris. She's an orphan. So her landlady acted as her witness. Is there something wrong?"

"I don't know yet. A man entered Colette's room last night dressed as Father Christmas. He gave your girl a doll, and lifted two loose boards from the floor."

"Do you think I'm in fit condition to see her?"

"You can go over in a little while. If you feel like it you can shave here. Do you think your brother would be likely to hide anything under the floor?"

"Jean? Never!"

"Even if he wanted to hide something from his wife?"

"He doesn't hide things from his wife. You don't know him. He's one of those rare humans—a scrupulously honest man. When he comes home from the road, she knows exactly how much money he has left, to the last centime."

"Is she jealous?"

Paul Martin did not reply.

"I advise you to tell me what you know. Remember that your daughter is involved in this."

"I don't think that Loraine is especially jealous. Not of women, at least. Perhaps about money. At least that's what my poor wife always said. She didn't like Loraine."

"Why not?"

"She used to say that Loraine's lips were too thin, that she was too polite, too cold, always on the defensive. My wife always thought that Loraine set her cap for Jean because he had a good job with a future and owned his own furniture."

"Loraine had no money of her own?"

"She never speaks of her family. I understand her father died when she was very young and her mother did housework somewhere in the Glacière quarter. My poor wife used to say, 'Loraine knows what she wants.'"

"Do you think she was Lorilleux's mistress?"

Paul Martin did not reply. Maigret poured him another finger of plum brandy. Martin gave him a grateful look, but he did not touch the glass. Perhaps he was thinking that his daughter might notice his breath when he crossed the street later on.

"I'll get you a cup of coffee in a moment. . . . Your wife must have had her own ideas on the subject."

"How did you know? Please note that my wife never spoke disparagingly of people. But with Loraine it was almost pathological. Whenever we were to meet my sister-in-law, I used to beg my wife not to show her antipathy. It's funny that you should bring all that up now, at this time in my life. Do you think I did wrong in letting her take Colette? I sometimes think so. But what else could I have done?"

"You didn't answer my question about Loraine's former employer."

"Oh, yes. My wife always said it was very convenient for Loraine to have married a man who was away from home so much."

"You know where she lived before her marriage?"

"In a street just off Boulevard Sébastopol, on the right as you walk from the Rue de Rivoli toward the Boulevard. I remember we picked her up there the day of the wedding."

"Rue Pernelle?"

"That's it. The fourth or fifth house on the left side of the street is a quiet rooming house, quite respectable. People who work in the neighborhood live there. I remember there were several little actresses from the Châtelet."

"Would you like to shave, Monsieur Martin?"

"I'm ashamed. Still, since my daughter is just across the street. . . ."

"Come with me."

Maigret took him through the kitchen so he wouldn't have to meet Mme. Maigret in the bedroom. He set out the necessary toilet articles, not forgetting a clothes brush.

When he returned to the dining room, Mme. Maigret poked her head through the door and whispered: "What's he doing?"

"He's shaving."

Once more Maigret reached for the telephone. He was certainly giving poor Lucas a busy Christmas Day.

"Are you indispensable at the office?"

"Not if Torrence sits in for me. I've got the information you wanted."

"In just a moment. I want you to jump over to Rue Pernelle. There's a rooming house a few doors down from the Boulevard Sébastopol. If the proprietor wasn't there five years ago, try to dig up someone who lived then. I want everything you can find out on a certain Loraine. . . ."

"Loraine who?"

"Just a minute, I didn't think of that."

Through the bathroom door he asked Martin for the maiden name of his sister-in-law. A few seconds later he was on the phone again.

"Loraine Boitel," he told Lucas. "The landlady of this rooming house was witness at her marriage to Jean Martin. Loraine Boitel was working for Lorilleux at the time. Try to find out if she was more than a secretary to him, and if he ever came to see her. And work fast. This may be urgent. What have you got on Lorilleux?"

"He was quite a fellow. At home in the Rue Mazarine he was a good respectable family man. In his Palais-Royal shop he not only sold old coins and souvenirs of Paris, but he had a fine collection of pornographic books and obscene pictures."

"Not unusual for the Palais-Royal."

"I don't know what else went on there. There was a big divan covered with red silk rep in the back room, but the investigation was never pushed. Seems there were a lot of important names among his customers."

"What about Loraine Boitel?"

"The report barely mentions her, except that she waited all morning for Lorilleux the day he disappeared. I was on the phone about this when Langlois of the Financial Squad came into my office. The name Lorilleux rang a bell in the back of his mind and he went to check his files. Nothing definite on him, but he'd been making frequent trips to Switzerland and back, and there was a lot of gold smuggling going on at that time. Lorilleux was stopped and searched at the frontier several times, but they never found anything on him."

"Lucas, old man, hurry over to Rue Pernelle. I'm more than ever convinced that this is urgent."

Paul Martin appeared in the doorway, his pale cheeks close-shaven.

"I don't know how to thank you. I'm very much embarrassed."

"You'll visit your daughter now, won't you? I don't know how long you usually stay, but today I don't want you to leave until I come for you."

"I can't very well stay all night, can I?"

"Stay all night if necessary. Manage the best you can."

"Is the little girl in danger?"

"I don't know, but your place today is with your daughter."

Paul Martin drank his black coffee avidly, and started for the stairway. The door had just closed after him when Mme. Maigret rushed into the dining room.

"You can't let him go to see his daughter empty-handed on Christmas Day!"

"But—" Maigret was about to say that there just didn't happen to be a doll around the house, when his wife thrust a small shiny object into his hands. It was a gold thimble which had been in her sewing basket for years but which she never used.

"Give him that. Little girls always like thimbles. Hurry!"

He shouted from the landing: "Monsieur Martin! Just a minute, Monsieur Martin!"

He closed the man's fingers over the thimble. "Don't tell a soul where you got this."

Before re-entering the dining room he stood for a moment on the threshold, grumbling. Then he sighed: "I hope you've finished making me play Father Christmas."

"I'll bet she likes the thimble as well as a doll. It's something grownups use, you know."

They watched the man cross the boulevard. Before going into the house he turned to look up at Maigret's windows, as if seeking encouragement.

"Do you think he'll ever be cured?"

"I doubt it."

"If anything happens to that woman, to Madame Martin. . . ."

"Well?"

"Nothing. I was thinking of the little girl. I wonder what would become of her."

Ten minutes passed. Maigret had opened his newspaper and lighted his pipe. His wife had settled down again with her knitting. She was counting stitches when he exhaled a cloud of smoke and murmured: "You haven't even seen her."

Maigret was looking for an old envelope, on the back of which he had jotted down a few notes summing up the day's events. He found it in a drawer into which Mme. Maigret always stuffed any papers she found lying around the house.

This was the only investigation, he mused, which he had ever conducted practically in its entirety from his favorite armchair. It was also unusual in that no dramatic stroke of luck had come to his aid. True, luck had been on his side, in that he had been able to muster all his facts by the simplest and most direct means. How many times had he deployed scores of detectives on an all-night search for some minor detail. This might have happened, for instance, if Monsieur Arthur Godefroy of Zenith had gone home to Zurich for Christmas, or if he had been out of reach of a telephone. Or if Monsieur Godefroy had been unaware of the telephone inquiry regarding the whereabouts of Jean Martin.

When Lucas arrived shortly after 4 o'clock, his nose red and his face pinched with the cold, he too could report the same kind of undramatic luck.

A thick yellow fog, unusual for Paris, had settled over the city. Lights shone in all the windows, floating in the murk like ships at sea or distant beacons. Familiar details had been blotted out so completely that Maigret half-expected to hear the moan of fog horns.

For some reason, perhaps because of some boyhood memory, Maigret was pleased to see the weather thicken. He was also pleased to see Lucas walk into his apartment, take off his overcoat, sit down, and stretch out his frozen hands toward the fire.

In appearance, Lucas was a reduced-scale model of Maigret—a head shorter, half as broad in the shoulders, half as stern in expression although he tried hard. Without conscious imitation but with conscious admiration, Lucas had copied his chief's slightest gestures, postures, and changes of expression —even to the ceremony of inhaling the fragrance of the plum brandy before touching his lips to the glass.

The landlady of the rooming house in the Rue Pernelle had been killed in a subway accident two years earlier, Lucas reported. Luckily, the place had been taken over by the former night watchman, who had been in trouble with the police on morals charges.

"So it was easy enough to make him talk," said Lucas, lighting a pipe much too large for him. "I was surprised that he had the money to buy the house, but he explained that he was front man for a big investor who had money in all sorts of enterprises but didn't like to have his name used."

"What kind of dump is it?"

"Looks respectable. Clean enough. Office on the mezzanine. Rooms by the month, some by the week, and a few on the second floor by the hour."

"He remembers Loraine?"

"Very well. She lived there more than three years. I got the impression he didn't like her because she was tight-fisted."

"Did Lorilleux come to see her?"

"On my way to the Rue Pernelle I picked up a photo of Lorilleux at the Palais-Royal station. The new landlord recognized him right away."

"Lorilleux went to her room often?"

"Two or three times a month. He always had baggage with him, he always arrived around 1 o'clock in the morning, and always left before 6. I checked the timetables. There's a train from Switzerland around midnight and another at 6 in the morning. He must have told his wife he was taking the 6 o'clock train."

"Nothing else?"

"Nothing, except that Loraine was stingy with tips, and always cooked her dinner on an alcohol burner, even though the house rules said no cooking in the rooms."

"No other men?"

"No. Very respectable except for Lorilleux. The landlady was witness at her wedding."

Maigret glanced at his wife. He had insisted she remain in the room when Lucas came. She stuck to her knitting, trying to make believe she was not there.

Torrence was out in the fog, going from garage to garage, checking the trip-sheets of taxi fleets. The two men waited serenely, deep in their easy chairs, each holding a glass of plum brandy with the same pose. Maigret felt a pleasant numbness creeping over him.

His Christmas luck held out with the taxis, too. Sometimes it took days to run down a particular taxi driver, particularly when the cab in question did not belong to a fleet. Cruising drivers were the hardest to locate; they sometimes never even read the newspapers. But shortly before 5 o'clock Torrence called from Saint-Ouen.

"I found one of the taxis," he reported.

"One? Was there more than one?"

"Looks that way. This man picked up the woman at the corner of Boulevard Richard-Lenoir and Boulevard Voltaire this morning. He drove her to Rue de Maubeuge, opposite the Gare du Nord, where she paid him off."

"Did she go into the railway station?"

"No. The chauffeur says she went into a luggage shop that keeps open on Sundays and holidays. After that he doesn't know."

"Where's the driver now?"

"Right here in the garage. He just checked in."

"Send him to me, will you? Right away. I don't care how he gets here as long as it's in a hurry. Now I want you to find me the cab that brought her home."

"Sure, Chief, as soon as I get myself coffee with a stick in it. It's damned cold out here."

Maigret glanced through the window. There was a shadow against Mlle. Doncoeur's curtains. He turned to Lucas.

"Look in the phone book for a luggage shop across from the Gare du Nord."

Lucas took only a minute to come up with a number, which Maigret dialed.

"Hello, this is the Police Judiciaire. Shortly before 10 this morning a young woman bought something in your shop, probably a valise. She was a blonde, wearing a gray suit and beige hat. She carried a brown shopping bag. Do you remember her?"

Perhaps trade was slack on Christmas Day. Or perhaps it was easier to remember customers who shopped on Christmas. In any case, the voice on the phone replied:

"Certainly, I waited on her myself. She said she had to leave suddenly for Cambrai because her sister was ill, and she didn't have time to go home for her bags. She wanted a cheap valise, and I sold her a fiber model we have on sale. She paid me and went into the bar next door. I was standing in the doorway and a little later I saw her walking toward the station, carrying the valise."

"Are you alone in your shop?"

"I have one clerk on duty."

"Can you leave him alone for half an hour? Fine! Then jump in a taxi and come to this address. I'll pay the fare, of course."

"And the return fare? Shall I have the cab wait?"

"Have him wait, yes."

According to Maigret's notes on the back of the envelope, the first taxi driver arrived at 5:50 P.M. He was somewhat surprised, since he had been summoned by the police, to find himself in a private apartment. He recognized Maigret, however, and made no effort to disguise his curious interest in how the famous inspector lived.

"I want you to climb to the fourth floor of the house just across the street. If the concierge stops you, tell her you're going to see Madame Martin."

"Madame Martin. I got it."

"Go to the door at the end of the hall and ring the bell. If a blonde opens the door and you recognize her, make some excuse—You're on the wrong floor, anything you think of. If somebody else answers, ask to speak to Madame Martin personally."

"And then?"

"Then you come back here and tell me whether or not she is the fare you drove to Rue de Maubeuge this morning."

"I'll be right back, Inspector."

As the door closed, Maigret smiled in spite of himself.

"The first call will make her worry a little. The second, if all goes well, will make her panicky. The third, if Torrence has any luck—"

Torrence, too, was having his run of Christmas luck. The phone rang and he reported:

"I think I've found him, Chief. I dug up a driver who picked up a woman answering your description at the Gare du Nord, only he didn't take her to Boulevard Richard-Lenoir. He dropped her at the corner of Boulevard Beaumarchais and the Rue du Chemin-Vert."

"Send him to me."

"He's a little squiffed."

"No matter. Where are you?"

"The Barbès garage."

"Then it won't be much out of your way to stop by the Gare du Nord. Go to the check room. Unfortunately it won't be the same man on duty, but try to find out if a small new valise was checked between 9:30 and 10 this morning. It's made of fiber and shouldn't be too heavy. Get the number of the check. They won't let you take the valise without a warrant, so try to get the name and address of the man on duty this morning."

"What next?"

"Phone me. I'll wait for your second taxi driver. If he's been drinking, better write down my address for him, so he won't get lost."

Mme. Maigret was back in the kitchen, preparing the evening meal. She hadn't dared ask whether Lucas would eat with them.

Maigret wondered if Paul Martin was still across the street with his daughter. Had Madame Martin tried to get rid of him?

The bell rang again. Two men stood at the door.

The first driver had come back from Madame Martin's and had climbed Maigret's stairs behind the luggage dealer.

"Did you recognize her?"

"Sure. She recognized me, too. She turned pale. She ran to close a door behind her, then she asked me what I wanted."

"What did you tell her?"

"That I had the wrong floor. I think maybe she wanted to buy me off, but I didn't give her a chance. But she was watching from the window when I crossed the street. She probably knows I came here."

The luggage dealer was baffled and showed it. He was a middle-aged man, completely bald and equally obsequious. When the driver had gone, Maigret explained what he wanted, and the man objected vociferously.

"One just doesn't do this sort of thing to one's customers," he repeated stubbornly. "One simply does not inform on one's customers, you know."

After a long argument he agreed to call on Madame Martin. To make sure he didn't change his mind, Maigret sent Lucas to follow him.

They returned in less than ten minutes.

"I call your attention to the fact that I have acted under your orders, that I have been compelled——"

"Did you recognize her?"

"Will I be forced to testify under oath?"

"More than likely."

"That would be very bad for my business. People who buy luggage at the last minute are very often people who dislike public mention of their comings and goings."

"You may not have to go to court. Your deposition before the examining magistrate may be sufficient."

"Very well. It was she. She's dressed differently, but I recognized her all right."

"Did she recognize you?"

"She asked immediately who had sent me."

"What did you say?"

"I . . . I don't remember. I was quite upset. I think I said I had rung the wrong bell."

"Did she offer you anything?"

"What do you mean? She didn't even offer me a chair. Luckily. It would have been most unpleasant."

Maigret smiled, somewhat incredulously. He believed that the taxi driver had actually run away from a possible bribe. He wasn't so sure about this prosperous-looking shopkeeper who obviously begrudged his loss of time.

"Thank you for your cooperation."

The luggage dealer departed hastily.

"And now for Number Three, my dear Lucas."

Mme. Maigret was beginning to grow nervous. From the kitchen door she made discreet signs to her husband, beckoning him to join her. She whispered: "Are you sure the father is still across the street?"

"Why?"

"I don't know. I can't make out exactly what you're up to, but I've been thinking about the child, and I'm a little afraid. . . ."

Night had long since fallen. The families were all home again. Few windows across the street remained dark. The silhouette of Mlle. Doncoeur was still very much in evidence.

While waiting for the second taxi driver, Maigret decided to put on his collar and tie. He shouted to Lucas:

"Pour yourself another drop. Aren't you hungry?"

"I'm full of sandwiches, Chief. Only one thing I'd like when we go out: a tall beer, right from the spigot."

The second driver arrived at 6:20. At 6:35 he had returned from across the street, a gleam in his eye.

"She looks even better in her négligée than she does in her street clothes," he said thickly. "She made me come in and asked who sent me. I didn't know what to say, so I told her I was a talent scout for the Folies Bergère. Was she furious! She's a fine hunk of woman, though, and I mean it. Did you get a look at her legs?"

He was in no hurry to leave. Maigret saw him ogling the bottle of plum brandy with envious eyes, and poured him a glass—to speed him on his way.

"What are you going to do next, Chief?" Lucas had rarely seen Maigret proceed with such caution, preparing each step with such care that he seemed to be mounting an attack on some desperate criminal. And yet the enemy was only a woman, a seemingly insignificant little housewife.

"You think she'll still fight back?"

"Fiercely. And what's more, in cold blood."

"What are you waiting for?"

"The phone call from Torrence."

As if on cue, the telephone rang. Torrence, of course.

"The valise is here all right. It feels practically empty. As you predicted, they won't give it to me without a warrant. The check-room attendant who was on duty this morning lives in the suburbs near La Varenne Saint-Hilaire." A snag at last? Or at least a delay? Maigret frowned. But Torrence continued. "We won't have to go out there, though. When he finishes his day's work here, he plays cornet in a *bal musette* in the Rue de Lappe."

"Go get him for me."

"Shall I bring him to your place?"

Maigret hesitated, thinking of Lucas's yearning for a glass of draft beer.

"No, I'll be across the street. Madame Martin's apartment, fourth floor."

He took down his heavy overcoat. He filled his pipe.

"Coming?" he said to Lucas.

Mme. Maigret ran after him to ask what time he'd be home for dinner. After a moment of hesitation, he smiled.

"The usual time," was his not very reassuring answer.

"Look out for the little girl, will you?"

At 10 o'clock that evening the investigation was still blocked. It was unlikely that anyone in the whole building had gone to sleep, except Colette. She had finally dozed off, with her father sitting in the dark by her bedside.

Torrence had arrived at 7:30 with his part-time musician and check-room attendant, who declared:

"She's the one. I remember she didn't put the check in her handbag. She slipped it into a big brown shopping bag." And when they took him into the kitchen he added, "That's the bag. Or one exactly like it."

The Martin apartment was very warm. Everyone spoke in low tones, as if they had agreed not to awaken the child. Nobody had eaten. Nobody, apparently, was even hungry. On their way over, Maigret and Lucas had each drunk two beers in a little cafe on the Boulevard Voltaire.

After the cornetist had spoken his piece, Maigret took Torrence aside and murmured fresh instructions.

Every corner of the apartment had been searched. Even the photos of Martin's parents had been taken from their frames, to make sure the baggage check had not been secreted between picture and backing. The dishes had been taken from their shelves and piled on the kitchen table. The larder had been emptied and examined closely. No baggage check.

Madame Martin was still wearing her pale blue négligée. She was chain-smoking cigarettes. What with the smoke from the two men's pipes, a thick blue haze swirled about the lamps.

"You are of course free to say nothing and answer no questions. Your husband will arrive at 11:17. Perhaps you will be more talkative in his presence."

"He doesn't know any more than I do."

"Does he know as much?"

"There's nothing to know. I've told you everything."

She had sat back and denied everything, all along the line. She had conceded only one point. She admitted that Lorilleux had dropped in to see her two or three times at night when she lived in the Rue Pernelle. But she insisted there had been nothing between them, nothing personal.

"In other words he came to talk business—at 1 o'clock in the morning?"

"He used to come to town by a late train, and he didn't like to walk the streets with large sums of money on him. I already told you he might have been smuggling gold, but I had nothing to do with it. You can't arrest me for his activities."

"Did he have large sums of money on him when he disappeared?"

"I don't know. He didn't always take me into his confidence."

"But he did come to see you in your room at night?"

Despite the evidence, she clung to her story of the morning's marketing. She denied ever having seen the two taxi drivers, the luggage dealer, or the check-room attendant.

"If I had really left a package at the Gare du Nord, you would have found the check, wouldn't you?"

She glanced nervously at the clock on the mantel, obviously thinking of her husband's return.

"Admit that the man who came last night found nothing under the floor because you changed the hiding place."

"I know of nothing that was hidden under the floor."

"When you learned of his visit, you decided to move the treasure to the check room for safekeeping."

"I haven't been near the Gare du Nord. There must be thousands of blondes in Paris who answer my description."

"I think I know where we'll find the check."

"You're so very clever."

"Sit over here at this table." Maigret produced a fountain pen and a sheet of paper. "Write your name and address."

She hesitated, then obeyed.

"Tonight every letter mailed in this neighborhood will be examined, and I'll wager we will find one addressed in your handwriting, probably to yourself."

He handed the paper to Lucas with an order to get in touch with the postal authorities. Much to his surprise, the woman reacted visibly.

"You see, it's a very old trick, Little One." For the first time he called her "Little One," the way he would have done if he were questioning her in his office, Quai des Orfèvres.

They were alone now. Maigret slowly paced the floor, while she remained seated.

"In case you're interested," Maigret said slowly, "the thing that shocks me most about you is not what you have done but the cold-blooded way you have done it. You've been dangling at the end of a slender thread since early this morning, and you still haven't blinked an eye. When your husband comes home, you'll try to play the martyr. And yet you know that sooner or later we'll discover the truth."

"But I've done nothing wrong."

"Then why do you lie?"

She did not reply. She was still far from the breaking point. Her nerves were calm, but her mind was obviously racing at top speed, seeking some avenue of escape.

"I'm not saying anything more," she declared. She sat down and pulled the hem of her négligée over her bare knees.

"Suit yourself." Maigret made himself comfortable in the chair opposite her.

"Are you going to stay here all night?" she asked.

"At least until your husband gets home."

"Are you going to tell him about Monsieur Lorilleux's visits to my room?"

"If necessary."

"You're a cad! Jean knows nothing about all this. He had no part in it."

"Unfortunately he is your husband."

When Lucas came back, they were staring at each other in silence.

"Janvier is taking care of the letter, Chief. I met Torrence downstairs. He says the man is in that little bar, two doors down from your house."

She sprang up. "What man?"

Maigret didn't move a muscle. "The man who came here last night. You might have expected him to come back, since he didn't find what he was looking for. And he might be in a different frame of mind this time."

She cast a dismayed glance at the clock. The train from Bergerac was due in twenty minutes. Her husband could be home in forty. She asked: "You know who this man is?"

"I can guess. I could go down and confirm my suspicion: I'd say it is Lorilleux and I'd say he is very eager to get back his property."

"It's not his property!"

"Let's say that, rightly or wrongly, he considers it his property. He must be in desperate straits, this man. He came to see you twice without getting what he wanted. He came back a third time disguised as Father Christmas. And he'll come back again. He'll be surprised to find you have company. I'm convinced that he'll be more talkative than you. Despite the general belief, men always speak more freely than women. Do you think he is armed?"

"I don't know."

"I think he is. He is tired of waiting. I don't know what story you've been telling him, but I'm sure he's fed up with it. The gentleman has a vicious face. There's nothing quite as cruel as a weakling with his back up."

"Shut up!"

"Would you like us to go so that you can be alone with him?"

The back of Maigret's envelope contained the following note: "10:38 P.M.—she decides to talk."

It was not a very connected story at first. It came out in bits and pieces, fragments of sentences interlarded with venomous asides, supplemented by Maigret's own guesses which she either confirmed or amended.

"What do you want to know?"

"Was it money that you left in the check room?"

"Bank notes. Almost a million."

"Did the money belong to Lorilleux?"

"No more to him than to me."

"To one of his customers?"

"Yes. A man named Julian Boissy."

"What became of him?"

"He died."

"How?"

"He was killed."

"By whom?"

"By Monsieur Lorilleux."

"Why?"

"Because I gave him to understand that if he could raise enough money—real money—I might run away with him."

"You were already married?"

"Yes."

"You're not in love with your husband?"

"I despise mediocrity. All my life I've been poor. All my life I've been surrounded by people who have had to scrimp and save, people who have had to sacrifice and count centimes. I've had to scrimp and sacrifice and count centimes myself." She turned savagely on Maigret, as if he had been responsible for all her troubles. "I just didn't want to be poor any more."

"Would you have gone away with Lorilleux?"

"I don't know. Perhaps for a while."

"Long enough to get your hands on his money?"

"I hate you!"

"How was Boissy murdered?"

"Monsieur Boissy was a regular customer of long standing."

"Pornographic literature?"

"He was a lascivious old goat, sure. So are all men. So is Lorilleux. So are you, probably. Boissy was a widower. He lived alone in a hotel room. He was very rich and very stingy. All rich people are stingy."

"That doesn't work both ways, does it? You, for instance, are not rich."

"I would have been rich."

"If Lorilleux had not come back. How did Boissy die?"

"The devaluation of the franc scared him out of his wits. Like everybody else at that time, he wanted gold. Monsieur Lorilleux used to shuttle gold in from Switzerland pretty regularly. And he always demanded payment in advance. One afternoon Monsieur Boissy came to the shop with a fortune in currency. I wasn't there. I had gone out on an errand."

"You planned it that way?"

"No."

"You had no idea what was going to happen?"

"No. Don't try to put words in my mouth. When I came back, Lorilleux was packing the body into a big box."

"And you blackmailed him?"

"No."

"Then why did he disappear after having given you the money?"

"I frightened him."

"You threatened to go to the police?"

"No. I merely told him that our neighbors in the Palais-Royal had been looking at me suspiciously and that I thought he ought to put the money in a safe place for a while. I told him about the loose floor board in my apartment. He thought it would only be for a few days. Two days later he asked me to cross the Belgian frontier with him."

"And you refused?"

"I told him I'd been stopped and questioned by a man who looked like a police inspector. He was terrified. I gave him some of the money and promised to join him in Brussels as soon as it was safe."

"What did he do with the corpse?"

"He put the box in a taxi and drove to a little country house he owned on the banks of the Marne. I suppose he either buried it there or threw it into the river. Nobody ever missed Monsieur Boissy."

"So you sent Lorilleux to Belgium without you. How did you keep him away for five years?"

"I used to write him, general delivery. I told him the police were after him, and that he would probably read nothing about it in the papers because they were setting a trap for him. I told him the police were always coming back to question me. I even sent him to South America."

"He came back two months ago?"

"About. He was at the end of his rope."

"Didn't you send him any money?"

"Not much."

"Why not?"

She did not reply. She looked at the clock.

"Are you going to arrest me? What will be the charge? I didn't kill Boissy. I wasn't there when he was killed. I had nothing to do with disposing of his body."

"Stop worrying about yourself. You kept the money because all your life you wanted money—not to spend, but to keep, to feel secure, to feel rich and free from want."

"That's my business."

"When Lorilleux came back to ask for money, or to ask you to keep your promise and run away with him, you used Colette as a pretext. You tried to scare him into leaving the country again, didn't you?"

"He stayed in Paris, hiding." Her upper lip curled slightly. "What an idiot! He could have shouted his name from the housetops and nobody would have noticed."

"The business of Father Christmas wasn't idiotic."

"No? The money wasn't under the floor board any longer. It was right here under his nose, in my sewing basket."

"Your husband will be here in ten or fifteen minutes. Lorilleux across the street probably knows it. He's been in touch with Bergerac by phone, and he can read a timetable. He's surely armed. Do you want to wait here for your two men?"

"Take me away! I'll slip on a dress. . . ."

"The check-room stub?"

"General delivery, Boulevard Beaumarchais."

She did not close the bedroom door after her. Brazenly she dropped the négligée from her shoulders and sat on the edge of the bed to pull on her stockings. She selected a woolen dress from the closet, tossed toilet articles and lingerie into an overnight bag.

"Let's hurry!"

"Your husband?"

"That fool? Leave him for the birds."

"Colette?"

She shrugged.

Mlle. Doncoeur's door opened a crack as they passed.

Downstairs on the sidewalk she clung fearfully to the two men, peering into the fog.

"Take her to the Quai des Orfèvres, Lucas. I'm staying here."

She held back. There was no car in sight, and she was obviously frightened by the prospect of walking into the night with only Lucas to protect her. Lucas was not very big.

"Don't be afraid. Lorilleux is not in this vicinity."

"You lied to me! You—you—"

Maigret went back into the house.

The conference with Jean Martin lasted two hours.

When Maigret left the house at one-thirty, the two brothers were in serious conversation. There was a crack of light under Mlle. Doncoeur's door, but she did not open the door as he passed.

When he got home, his wife was asleep in a chair in the dining room. His place at table was still set. Mme. Maigret awoke with a start.

"You're alone?" When he looked at her with amused surprise, she added, "Didn't you bring the little girl home?"

"Not tonight. She's asleep. You can go for her tomorrow morning."

"Why, then we're going to . . ."

"No, not permanently. Jean Martin may console himself with some decent girl. Or perhaps his brother will get back on his feet and find a new wife. . . ."

"In other words, she won't be ours?"

"Not in fee simple, no. Only on loan. I thought that would be better than nothing. I thought it would make you happy."

"Why, yes, of course. It will make me very happy. But . . . but . . ."

She sniffled once and fumbled for her handkerchief. When she couldn't find it, she buried her face in her apron.

"Your tomato surprise, sir."

The Feast of St. Stephen is celebrated on the 26th of December in many countries throughout Europe. St. Stephen became the first Christian martyr when he met a grizzly death at the hands of a barbaric crowd.

On his day, it became the custom to open the alms boxes and distribute the contents to the poor.

In England, where it is a legal holiday, the 26th is known as Boxing Day. It later became common practice for the apprentices of tradesmen to take boxes around to their master's customers to secure tips for their services of the previous year. Hence the name Boxing Day.

This in turn led to the more widespread modern practice of the Christmas bonus. So ingrained is this custom that it is incorporated into many contracts.

The diner pictured here was one of a hardy band of gentlemen who attempted to abolish the custom of the Christmas bonus in Britain. His career as a reformer, however, was rather short-lived.

Baroness Orczy was not born in Barchester Towers, but her readers may be forgiven for thinking so. She was the daughter of a Hungarian musician, but developed a proficiency in her second language, English, that is rivalled only by Joseph Conrad's.

She is best remembered as the creator of Sir Percy Blakeney, the Scarlet Pimpernel, but she also gave us The Old Man in the Corner and Lady Molly of Scotland Yard, who appears in this story.

Lady Molly was among the first female detectives of mystery fiction, and certainly the first female police officer. If her attachment to Scotland Yard remained somewhat vague, her ability to deal with dastardly criminals did not.

Her faithful companion Mary describes some nefarious doings at a cozy English gathering—a familiar setting, to be sure. Dickens and Christie would have felt at home here—a remarkable evocation of an English Christmas from a writer who began life near the banks of the Danube.

The Scarlet Pimpernel was clearly her masterpiece, but this tale of yuletide malfeasance demonstrates that Baroness Orczy's success was no magic fluke.

A Christmas Tragedy

by Baroness Orczy

I<small>T WAS</small> a fairly merry Christmas party, although the surliness of our host somewhat marred the festivities. But imagine two such beautiful young women as my own dear lady and Margaret Ceely, and a Christmas Eve Cinderella in the beautiful ball-room at Clevere Hall, and you will understand that even Major Ceely's well-known cantankerous temper could not altogether spoil the merriment of a good, old-fashioned, festive gathering.

It is a far cry from a Christmas Eve party to a series of cattle-maiming outrages, yet I am forced to mention these now, for although they were ultimately proved to have no connection with the murder of the unfortunate Major, yet they were undoubtedly the means whereby the miscreant was enabled to accomplish the horrible deed with surety, swiftness, and as it turned out afterwards—a very grave chance of immunity.

Everyone in the neighbourhood had been taking the keenest possible interest in those dastardly outrages against innocent animals. They were either the work of desperate ruffians who stick at nothing in order to obtain a few shillings, or else of madmen with weird propensities for purposeless crimes.

Once or twice suspicious characters had been seen lurking about in the fields, and on more than one occasion a cart was heard in the middle of the night driving away at furious speed. Whenever this occurred the discovery of a fresh outrage was sure to follow, but, so far, the miscreants had succeeded in baffling not only the police, but also the many farm hands who had formed themselves into a band of volunteer watchmen, determined to bring the cattle maimers to justice.

We had all been talking about these mysterious events during the dinner which preceded the dance at Clevere Hall; but later on, when the young people had assembled, and when the first strains of "The Merry Widow" waltz had set us aglow with prospective enjoyment, the unpleasant topic was wholly forgotten.

The guests went away early, Major Ceely, as usual, doing nothing to detain them; and by midnight all of us who were staying in the house had gone up to bed.

My dear lady and I shared a bedroom and dressing-room together, our windows giving on the front. Clevere Hall is, as you know, not very far from York, on the other side of Bishopthorpe, and is one of the finest old mansions in the neighbourhood, its only disadvantage being that, in spite of the gardens being very extensive in the rear, the front of the house lies very near the road.

It was about two hours after I had switched off the electric light and called out "Good-night" to my dear lady, that something roused me out of my first sleep. Suddenly I felt very wide-awake, and sat up in bed. Most unmistakably—though still from some considerable distance along the road—came the sound of a cart being driven at unusual speed.

Evidently my dear lady was also awake. She jumped out of bed and, drawing aside the curtains, looked out of the window. The same idea had, of course, flashed upon us both, at the very moment of waking: all the conversations anent the cattle-maimers and their cart, which we had heard since our arrival at Clevere, recurring to our minds simultaneously.

I had joined Lady Molly beside the window, and I don't know how many minutes we remained there in observations, not more than two probably, for anon the sound of the cart died away in the distance along a side road. Suddenly we were startled with a terrible cry of "Murder! Help! Help!" issuing from the other side of the house, followed by an awful, deadly silence. I stood there near the window shivering with terror, while my dear lady, having already turned on the light, was hastily slipping into some clothes.

The cry had, of course, aroused the entire household, but my dear lady was even then the first to get downstairs, and to reach the garden door at the back of the house, whence the weird and despairing cry had undoubtedly proceeded.

That door was wide open. Two steps lead from it to the terraced walk which borders the house on that side, and along these steps Major Ceely was lying, face downwards, with arms outstretched, and a terrible wound between his shoulder-blades.

A gun was lying close by—his own. It was easy to conjecture that he, too, hearing the rumble of the wheels, had run out, gun in hand, meaning, no doubt, to effect, or at least to help, in the capture of the escaping criminals. Someone had been lying in wait for him; that was obvious—someone who had perhaps waited and watched for this special opportunity for days, or even weeks, in order to catch the unfortunate man unawares.

Well, it were useless to recapitulate all the various little incidents which occurred from the moment when Lady Molly and the butler first lifted the Major's lifeless body from the terrace steps until that instant when Miss Ceely, with remarkable coolness and presence of mind, gave what details she could of the terrible event to the local police inspector and to the doctor, both hastily summoned.

These little incidents, with but slight variations, occur in every instance when a crime has been committed. The broad facts alone are of weird and paramount interest.

Major Ceely was dead. He had been stabbed with amazing sureness and terrible violence in the back. The weapon used must have been some sort of heavy, clasp knife. The murdered man was now lying in his own bedroom upstairs, even as the Christmas bells on that cold, crisp morning sent cheering echoes through the stillness of the air.

We had, of course, left the house, as had all the other guests. Everyone felt the deepest possible sympathy for the beautiful young girl who had been so full of the joy of living but a few hours ago, and was now the pivot round which revolved the weird shadow of tragedy, of curious suspicions and of an ever-growing mystery. But at such times all strangers, acquaintances, and even friends in a house, are only an additional burden to an already overwhelming load of sorrow and of trouble.

We took up our quarters at the "Black Swan," in York. The local superintendent, hearing that Lady Molly had been actually a guest at Clevere on the night of the murder, had asked her to remain in the neighbourhood.

There was no doubt that she could easily obtain the chief's consent to assist the local police in the elucidation of this extraordinary crime. At this time both her reputation and her remarkable powers were at their zenith, and there was not a single member of the entire police force in the kingdom who would not have availed himself gladly of her help when confronted with a seemingly impenetrable mystery.

That the murder of Major Ceely threatened to become such no one could deny. In cases of this sort, when no robbery of any kind has accompanied the graver crime, it is the duty of the police and also of the coroner to try to find out, first and foremost, what possible motive there could be behind so cowardly an assault; and among motives, of course, deadly hatred, revenge, and animosity stand paramount.

But here the police were at once confronted with the terrible difficulty, not of discovering whether Major Ceely had an enemy at all, but rather which, of all those people who owed him a grudge, hated him sufficiently to risk hanging for the sake of getting him out of the way.

As a matter of fact, the unfortunate Major was one of those miserable people who seem to live in a state of perpetual enmity with everything and everybody. Morning, noon and night he grumbled, and when he did not grumble he quarrelled either with his own daughter or with the people of his household, or with his neighbours.

I had often heard about him and his eccentric, disagreeable ways from Lady Molly, who had known him for many years. She—like everybody in the county who otherwise would have shunned the old man—kept up a semblance of friendship with him for the sake of the daughter.

Margaret Ceely was a singularly beautiful girl, and as the Major was reputed to be very wealthy, these two facts perhaps combined to prevent the irascible gentleman from living in quite so complete an isolation as he would have wished.

Mammas of marriageable young men vied with one another in their welcome to Miss Ceely at garden parties, dances and bazaars. Indeed, Margaret had been surrounded with admirers ever since she had come out of the schoolroom. Needless to say, the cantankerous Major received these pretenders to his daughter's hand not only with insolent disdain, but at times even with violent opposition.

In spite of this the moths fluttered round the candle, and amongst this venturesome tribe none stood out more prominently than Mr. Laurence Smethick, son of the M.P. for the Pakethorpe division. Some folk there were who vowed that the young people were secretly engaged, in spite of the fact that Margaret was an outrageous flirt and openly encouraged more than one of her crowd of adorers.

Be that as it may, one thing was very certain—namely, that Major Ceely did not approve of Mr. Smethick any more than he did of the others, and there had been more than one quarrel between the young man and his prospective father-in-law.

On that memorable Christmas Eve at Clevere none of us could fail to notice his absence; whilst Margaret, on the other hand, had shown marked predilection for the society of Captain Glynne, who, since the sudden death of his cousin, Viscount Heslington, Lord Ullesthorpe's only son (who was killed in the hunting field last October, if you remember), had become heir to the earldom and its £40,000 a year.

Personally, I strongly disapproved of Margaret's behaviour the night of the dance; her attitude with regard to Mr. Smethick—whose constant attendance on her had justified the rumour that they were engaged—being more than callous.

On that morning of December 24th—Christmas Eve, in fact—the young man had called at Clevere. I remember seeing him just as he was being shown into the boudoir downstairs. A few moments later the sound of angry voices rose with appalling distinctness from that room. We all tried not to listen, yet could not fail to hear Major Ceely's overbearing words of rudeness to the visitor, who, it seems, had merely asked to see Miss Ceely, and had been most unexpectedly confronted by the irascible and extremely disagreeable Major. Of course, the young man speedily lost his temper, too, and the whole incident ended with a very unpleasant quarrel between the two men in the hall, and with the Major peremptorily forbidding Mr. Smethick ever to darken his doors again.

On that night Major Ceely was murdered.

II

Of course, at first, no one attached any importance to this weird coincidence. The very thought of connecting the idea of murder with that of the personality of a bright, good-looking young Yorkshireman like Mr. Smethick seemed, indeed, preposterous, and with one accord all of us who were practically witnesses to the quarrel between the two men, tacitly agreed to say nothing at all about it at the inquest, unless we were absolutely obliged to do so on oath.

In view of the Major's terrible temper, this quarrel, mind you, had not the importance which it otherwise would have had; and we all flattered ourselves that we had well succeeded in parrying the coroner's questions.

The verdict at the inquest was against some person or persons unknown; and I, for one, was very glad that young Smethick's name had not been mentioned in connection with this terrible crime.

Two days later the superintendent at Bishopthorpe sent an urgent telephonic message to Lady Molly, begging her to come to the police-station immediately. We had the use of a motor all the while that we stayed at the "Black Swan," and in less than ten minutes we were bowling along at express speed towards Bishopthorpe.

On arrival we were immediately shown into Superintendent Etty's private room behind the office. He was there talking with Danvers—who had recently come down from London. In a corner of the room, sitting very straight on a high-backed chair, was a youngish woman of the servant class, who, as we entered, cast a quick, and I thought suspicious, glance at us both.

She was dressed in a coat and skirt of shabby looking black, and although her face might have been called good-looking—for she had fine, dark eyes—her entire appearance was distinctly repellent. It suggested slatternliness in an unusual degree; there were holes in her shoes and in her stockings, the sleeve of her coat was half unsewn, and the braid on her skirt hung in loops all round the bottom. She had very red and coarse-looking hands, and undoubtedly there was a furtive expression in her eyes, which, when she began speaking, changed to one of defiance.

Etty came forward with great alacrity when my dear lady entered. He looked perturbed, and seemed greatly relieved at sight of her.

"She is the wife of one of the outdoor men at Clevere," he explained rapidly to Lady Molly, nodding in the direction of the young woman, "and she has come here with such a queer tale that I thought you would like to hear it."

"She knows something about the murder?" asked Lady Molly.

"Noa! I didn't say that!" here interposed the woman, roughly, "doan't you go and tell no lies, Master Inspector. I thought as how you might wish to know what my husband saw on the night when the Major was murdered, that's all; and I've come to tell you."

"Why didn't your husband come himself?" asked Lady Molly.

"Oh, Haggett ain't well enough—he—" she began explaining, with a careless shrug of the shoulders, "so to speak—"

"The fact of the matter is, my lady," interposed Etty, "this woman's husband is half-witted. I believe he is only kept on in the garden because he is very strong and can help with the digging. It is because his testimony is so little to be relied on that I wished to consult you as to how we should act in the matter."

"What is his testimony, then?"

"Tell this lady what you have just told us, Mrs. Haggett, will you?" said Etty, curtly.

Again that quick, suspicious glance shot into the woman's eyes. Lady Molly took the chair which Danvers had brought forward for her, and sat down opposite Mrs. Haggett, fixing her earnest, calm gaze upon her.

"There's not much to tell," said the woman, sullenly. "Haggett is certainly queer in his head sometimes—and when he is queer he goes wandering about the place of nights."

"Yes?" said my lady, for Mrs. Haggett had paused awhile and now seemed unwilling to proceed.

"Well!" she resumed with sudden determination, "he had got one of his queer fits on on Christmas Eve, and didn't come in till long after midnight. He told me as how he'd seen a young gentleman prowling about the garden on the terrace side. He heard the cry of 'Murder' and 'Help' soon after that, and ran in home because he was frightened."

"Home?" asked Lady Molly, quietly, "where is home?"

"The cottage where we live. Just back of the kitchen garden."

"Why didn't you tell all this to the superintendent before?"

"Because Haggett only told me last night, when he seemed less queerlike. He is mighty silent when the fits are on him."

"Did he know who the gentleman was whom he saw?"

"No, ma'am—I don't suppose he did—leastways he wouldn't say—but—"

"Yes? But?"

"He found this in the garden yesterday," said the woman, holding out a screw of paper which apparently she had held tightly clutched up to now, "and maybe that's what brought Christmas Eve and the murder back to his mind."

Lady Molly took the thing from her, and undid the soiled bit of paper with her dainty fingers. The next moment she held up for Etty's inspection a beautiful ring composed of an exquisitely carved moonstone surrounded with diamonds of unusual brilliance.

At the moment the setting and the stones themselves were marred by scraps of sticky mud which clung to them; the ring obviously having lain on the ground, and perhaps been trampled on for some days, and then been only very partially washed.

"At any rate you can find out the ownership of the ring," commented my dear lady after awhile, in answer to Etty's silent attitude of expectancy. "There would be no harm in that."

Then she turned once more to the woman.

"I'll walk with you to your cottage, if I may," she said decisively, "and have a chat with your husband. Is he at home?"

I thought Mrs. Haggett took this suggestion with marked reluctance. I could well imagine, from her own personal appearance, that her home was most unlikely to be in a fit state for a lady's visit. However, she could, of course, do nothing but obey, and, after a few muttered words of grudging acquiescence, she rose from her chair and stalked towards the door, leaving my lady to follow as she chose.

Before going, however, she turned and shot an angry glance at Etty.

"You'll give me back the ring, Master Inspector," she said with her usual tone of sullen defiance. "'Findings is keepings' you know."

"I am afraid not," replied Etty, curtly; "but there's always the reward offered by Miss Ceely for information which would lead to the apprehension of her father's murderer. You may get that, you know. It is a hundred pounds."

"Yes! I knew that," she remarked dryly, as, without further comment, she finally went out of the room.

III

My dear lady came back very disappointed from her interview with Haggett.

It seems that he was indeed half-witted—almost an imbecile, in fact, with but a few lucid intervals of which this present day was one. But, of course, his testimony was practically valueless.

He reiterated the story already told by his wife, adding no details. He had seen a young gentleman roaming on the terraced walk on the night of the murder. He did not know who the young gentleman was. He was going homewards when he heard the cry of "Murder," and ran to his cottage because he was frightened. He picked up the ring yesterday in the perennial border below the terrace and gave it to his wife.

Two of these brief statements made by the imbecile were easily proved to be true, and my dear lady had ascertained this before she returned it to me. One of the Clevere under-gardeners said he had seen Haggett running home in the small hours of that fateful Christmas morning. He himself had been on the watch for the cattle-maimers that night, and remembered the little circumstance quite plainly. He added that Haggett certainly looked to be in a panic.

Then Newby, another outdoor man at the Hall, saw Haggett pick up the ring in the perennial border and advised him to take it to the police.

Somehow, all of us who were so interested in that terrible Christmas tragedy felt strangely perturbed at all this. No names had been mentioned as yet, but whenever my dear lady and I looked at one another, or whenever we talked to Etty or Danvers, we all felt that a certain name, one particular personality, was lurking at the back of all our minds.

The two men, of course, had no sentimental scruples to worry them. Taking the Haggett story merely as a clue, they worked diligently on that, with the result that twenty-four hours later Etty appeared in our private room at the "Black Swan" and calmly informed us that he had just got a warrant out against Mr. Laurence Smethick on a charge of murder, and was on his way even now to effect the arrest.

"Mr. Smethick did *not* murder Major Ceely," was Lady Molly's firm and only comment when she heard the news.

"Well, my lady, that's as it may be!" rejoined Etty, speaking with that deference with which the entire force invariably addressed my dear lady; "but we have collected a sufficiency of evidence, at any rate, to justify arrest and, in my opinion, enough of it to hang any man. Mr. Smethick purchased the moonstone and diamond ring at Nicholson's in Coney Street about a week ago. He was seen abroad on Christmas Eve by several persons, loitering round the gates at Clevere Hall, somewhere about the time when the guests were leaving after the dance, and, again, some few moments after the first cry of 'Murder' had been heard. His own valet admits that his master did not get home that night until long after 2:00 a.m., whilst even Miss Granard here won't deny that there was a terrible quarrel between Mr. Smethick and Major Ceely less than twenty-four hours before the latter was murdered."

Lady Molly offered no remark to this array of facts which Etty thus pitilessly marshalled before us, but I could not refrain from exclaiming:

"Mr. Smethick is innocent, I am sure."

"I hope, for his sake, he may be," retorted Etty, gravely, "but somehow 'tis a pity that he don't seem able to give a good account of himself between midnight and two o'clock that Christmas morning."

"Oh!" I ejaculated, "what does he say about that?"

"Nothing," replied the man, dryly; "that's just the trouble."

Well, of course, as you who read the papers will doubtless remember, Mr. Laurence Smethick, son of Colonel Smethick, M.P., of Pakethorpe Hall, Yorks, was arrested on the charge of having murdered Major Ceely on the night of December 24th-25th, and, after the usual magisterial inquiry, was duly committed to stand his trial at the next York assizes.

I remember well that, throughout his preliminary ordeal, young Smethick bore himself like one who had given up all hope of refuting the terrible charges brought against him, and, I must say, the formidable number of witnesses which the police brought up against him more than explained that attitude.

Of course, Haggett was not called, but, as it happened, there were plenty of people to swear that Mr. Laurence Smethick was seen loitering round the gates of Clevere Hall after the guests had departed on Christmas Eve. The head gardener, who lives at the lodge, actually spoke to him, and Captain Glynne, leaning out of his brougham window, was heard to exclaim:

"Hello, Smethick, what are you doing here at this time of night?"

And there were others, too.

To Captain Glynne's credit, be it here recorded, he tried his best to deny having recognised his unfortunate friend in the dark. Pressed by the magistrate, he said obstinately:

"I thought at the time that it was Mr. Smethick standing by the lodge gates, but on thinking the matter over I feel sure that I was mistaken."

On the other hand, what stood dead against young Smethick was, firstly, the question of the ring, and then the fact that he was seen in the immediate neighbourhood of Clevere, both at midnight and again at about two, when some men, who had been on the watch for the cattle-maimers, saw him walking away rapidly in the direction of Pakethorpe.

What was, of course, unexplainable and very terrible to witness was Mr. Smethick's obstinate silence with regard to his own movements during those fatal hours on that night. He did not contradict those who said that they had seen him at about midnight near the gates of Clevere, nor his own valet's statements as to the hour when he returned home. All he said was that he could not account for what he did between the time when the guests left the Hall and he himself went back to Pakethorpe. He realised the danger in which he stood, and what caused him to be silent about a matter which might mean life or death to him could not easily be conjectured.

The ownership of the ring he could not and did not dispute. He had lost it in the grounds of Clevere, he said. But the jeweller in Coney Street swore that he had sold the ring to Mr. Smethick on the 18th of December, whilst it was a well-known and an admitted fact that the young man had not openly been inside the gates of Clevere for over a fortnight before that.

On this evidence Laurence Smethick was committed for trial. Though the actual weapon with which the unfortunate Major had been stabbed had not been found, nor its ownership traced, there was such a vast array of circumstantial evidence against the young man that bail was refused.

He had, on the advice of his solicitor, Mr. Grayson—one of the ablest lawyers in York—reserved his defence, and on that miserable afternoon at the close of the year, we all filed out of the crowded court feeling terribly depressed and anxious.

IV

My dear lady and I walked back to our hotel in silence. Our hearts seemed to weigh heavily within us. We felt mortally sorry for that good-looking young Yorkshireman, who, we were convinced, was innocent, yet at the same time seemed involved in a tangled web of deadly circumstances from which he seemed quite unable to extricate himself.

We did not feel like discussing the matter in the open streets, neither did we make any comment when presently, in a block in the traffic in Coney Street, we saw Margaret Ceely driving her smart dog-cart, whilst sitting beside her, and talking with great earnestness close to her ear, sat Captain Glynne.

She was in deep mourning, and had obviously been doing some shopping, for she was surrounded with parcels; so perhaps it was hypercritical to blame her. Yet somehow it struck me that just at the moment when there hung in the balance the life and honour of a man with whose name her own had oft been linked by popular rumour, it showed more than callous contempt for his welfare to be seen driving about with another man who, since his sudden access to fortune, had undoubtedly become a rival in her favours.

When we arrived at the "Black Swan," we were surprised to hear that Mr. Grayson had called to see my dear lady, and was upstairs waiting.

Lady Molly ran up to our sitting-room and greeted him with marked cordiality. Mr. Grayson is an elderly, dry-looking man, but he looked visibly affected, and it was some time before he seemed able to plunge into the subject which had brought him hither. He fidgeted in his chair, and started talking about the weather.

"I am not here in a strictly professional capacity, you know," said Lady Molly presently, with a kindly smile and with a view to helping him out of his embarrassment. "Our police, I fear me, have an exaggerated view of my capacities, and the men here asked me unofficially to remain in the neighbourhood and to give them my advice if they should require it. Our chief is very lenient to me, and has allowed me to stay. Therefore, if there is anything I can do—"

"Indeed, indeed there is!" ejaculated Mr. Grayson with sudden energy. "From all I hear, there is not another soul in the kingdom but you who can save this innocent man from the gallows."

My dear lady heaved a little sigh of satisfaction. She had all along wanted to have a more important finger in that Yorkshire pie.

"Mr. Smethick?" she said.

"Yes; my unfortunate young client," replied the lawyer. "I may as well tell you," he resumed after a slight pause, during which he seemed to pull himself together, "as briefly as possible what occurred on December 24th last and on the following Christmas morning. You will then understand the terrible plight in which my client finds himself, and how impossible it is for him to explain his actions on that eventful night. You will understand, also, why I have come to ask your help and your advice. Mr. Smethick considered himself engaged to Miss Ceely. The engagement had not been made public because of Major Ceely's anticipated opposition, but the young people had been very intimate, and many letters had passed between them. On the morning of the 24th Mr. Smethick called at the Hall, his intention then being merely to present his *fiancée* with the ring you know of. You remember the unfortunate *contretemps* that occurred: I mean the unprovoked quarrel sought by Major Ceely with my poor client, ending with the irascible old man forbidding Mr. Smethick the house.

"My client walked out of Clevere feeling, as you may well imagine, very wrathful; on the doorstep, just as he was leaving, he met Miss Margaret, and told her very briefly what had occurred. She took the matter very lightly at first, but finally became more serious, and ended the brief interview with the request that, since he could not come to the dance after what had occurred, he should come and see her afterwards, meeting her in the gardens soon after midnight. She would not take the ring from him then, but talked a good deal of sentiment about Christmas morning, asking him to bring the ring to her at night, and also the letters which she had written him. Well—you can guess the rest."

Lady Molly nodded thoughtfully.

"Miss Ceely was playing a double game," continued Mr. Grayson, earnestly. "She was determined to break off all relationship with Mr. Smethick, for she had transferred her volatile affections to Captain Glynne, who had lately become heir to an earldom and £40,000 a year. Under the guise of sentimental twaddle she got my unfortunate client to meet her at night in the grounds of Clevere and to give up to her the letters which might have compromised her in the eyes of her new lover. At two o'clock a.m. Major Ceely was murdered by one of his numerous enemies; as to which I do not know, nor does Mr. Smethick. He had just parted from Miss Ceely at the very moment when the first cry of 'Murder' roused Clevere from its slumbers. This she could confirm if she only would, for the two were still in sight of each other, she inside the gates, he just a little way down the road. Mr. Smethick saw Margaret Ceely run rapidly back towards the house. He waited about a little while, half hesitating what to do; then he reflected that his presence might be embarrassing, or even compromising to her whom, in spite of all, he still loved dearly; and knowing that there were plenty of men in and about the house to render what assistance was necessary, he finally turned his steps and went home a broken-hearted man, since she had given him the go-by, taken her letters away, and flung contemptuously into the mud the ring he had bought for her."

The lawyer paused, mopping his forehead and gazing with whole-souled earnestness at my lady's beautiful, thoughtful face.

"Has Mr. Smethick spoken to Miss Ceely since?" asked Lady Molly, after a while.

"No; but I did," replied the lawyer.

"What was her attitude?"

"One of bitter and callous contempt. She denies my unfortunate client's story from beginning to end; declared that she never saw him after she bade him 'good morning' on the doorstep of Clevere Hall, when she heard of his unfortunate quarrel with her father. Nay, more; she scornfully calls the whole tale a cowardly attempt to shield a dastardly crime behind a still more dastardly libel on a defenceless girl."

We were all silent now, buried in thought which none of us would have cared to translate into words. That the *impasse* seemed indeed hopeless no one could deny.

The tower of damning evidence against the unfortunate young man had indeed been built by remorseless circumstances with no faltering hand.

Margaret Ceely alone could have saved him, but with brutal indifference she preferred the sacrifice of an innocent man's life and honour to that of her own chances of a brilliant marriage. There are such women in the world; thank God I have never met any but that one!

Yet am I wrong when I say that she alone could save the

unfortunate young man, who throughout was behaving with such consummate gallantry, refusing to give his own explanation of the events that occurred on that Christmas morning, unless she chose first to tell the tale. There was one present now in the dingy little room at the "Black Swan" who could disentangle that weird skein of coincidences, if any human being not gifted with miraculous powers could indeed do it at this eleventh hour.

She now said, gently:

"What would you like me to do in this matter, Mr. Grayson? And why have you come to me rather than to the police?"

"How can I go with this tale to the police?" he ejaculated in obvious despair. "Would they not also look upon it as a dastardly libel on a woman's reputation? We have no proofs, remember, and Miss Ceely denies the whole story from first to last. No, no!" he exclaimed with wonderful fervour. "I came to you because I have heard of your marvellous gifts, your extraordinary intuition. Someone murdered Major Ceely! It was not my old friend Colonel Smethick's son. Find out who it was, then! I beg of you, find out who it was!"

He fell back in his chair, broken down with grief. With inexpressible gentleness Lady Molly went up to him and placed her beautiful white hand on his shoulder.

"I will do my best, Mr. Grayson," she said simply.

V

We remained alone and singularly quiet the whole of that evening. That my dear lady's active brain was hard at work I could guess by the brilliance of her eyes, and that sort of absolute stillness in her person through which one could almost feel the delicate nerves vibrating.

The story told her by the lawyer had moved her singularly. Mind you, she had always been morally convinced of young Smethick's innocence, but in her the professional woman always fought hard battles against the sentimentalist, and in this instance the overwhelming circumstantial evidence and the conviction of her superiors had forced her to accept the young man's guilt as something out of her ken.

By his silence, too, the young man had tacitly confessed; and if a man is perceived on the very scene of a crime, both before it has been committed and directly afterwards; if something admittedly belonging to him is found within three yards of where the murderer must have stood; if, added to this, he has had a bitter quarrel with the victim, and can give no account of his actions or whereabouts during the fatal time, it were vain to cling to optimistic beliefs in that same man's innocence.

But now matters had assumed an altogether different aspect. The story told by Mr. Smethick's lawyer had all the appearance of truth. Margaret Ceely's character, her callousness on the very day when her late *fiancé* stood in the dock, her quick transference of her affections to the richer man, all made the account of the events on Christmas night as told by Mr. Grayson extremely plausible.

No wonder my dear lady was buried in thought.

"I shall have to take the threads up from the beginning, Mary," she said to me the following morning, when after breakfast she appeared in her neat coat and skirt, with hat and gloves, ready to go out, "so, on the whole, I think I will begin with a visit to the Haggetts."

"I may come with you, I suppose?" I suggested meekly.

"Oh, yes!" she rejoined carelessly.

Somehow I had an inkling that the carelessness of her mood was only on the surface. It was not likely that she——my sweet, womanly, ultra-feminine, beautiful lady——should feel callously on this absorbing subject.

We motored down to Bishopthorpe. It was bitterly cold, raw, damp, and foggy. The chauffeur had some difficulty in finding the cottage, the "home" of the imbecile gardener and his wife.

There was certainly not much look of home about the place. When, after much knocking at the door, Mrs. Haggett finally opened it, we saw before us one of the most miserable, slatternly places I think I ever saw.

In reply to Lady Molly's somewhat curt inquiry, the woman said that Haggett was in bed, suffering from one of his "fits."

"That is a great pity," said my dear lady, rather unsympathetically, I thought, "for I must speak with him at once."

"What is it about?" asked the woman, sullenly. "I can take a message."

"I am afraid not," rejoined my lady. "I was asked to see Haggett personally."

"By whom, I'd like to know," she retorted, now almost insolently.

"I dare say you would. But you are wasting precious time. Hadn't you better help your husband on with his clothes? This lady and I will wait in the parlour."

After some hesitation the woman finally complied, looking very sulky the while.

We went into the miserable little room wherein not only grinding poverty but also untidiness and dirt were visible all round. We sat down on two of the cleanest-looking chairs, and waited whilst a colloquy in subdued voices went on in the room over our heads.

The colloquy, I may say, seemed to consist of agitated whispers on one part, and wailing complaints on the other. This was followed presently by some thuds and much shuffling, and presently Haggett, looking uncared-for, dirty, and unkempt, entered the parlour, followed by his wife.

He came forward, dragging his ill-shod feet and pulling nervously at his forelock.

"Ah!" said my lady, kindly; "I am glad to see you down, Haggett, though I am afraid I haven't very good news for you."

"Yes, miss!" murmured the man, obviously not quite comprehending what was said to him.

"I represent the workhouse authorities," continued Lady Molly, "and I thought we could arrange for you and your wife to come into the Union tonight, perhaps."

"The Union?" here interposed the woman, roughly. "What do you mean? We ain't going to the Union?"

"Well! but since you are not staying here," rejoined my lady, blandly, "you will find it impossible to get another situation for your husband in his present mental condition."

"Miss Ceely won't give us the go-by," she retorted defiantly.

"She might wish to carry out her late father's intentions," said Lady Molly with seeming carelessness.

"The Major was a cruel, cantankerous brute," shouted the woman with unpremeditated violence. "Haggett had served him faithfully for twelve years, and—"

She checked herself abruptly, and cast one of her quick, furtive glances at Lady Molly.

Her silence now had become as significant as her outburst of rage, and it was Lady Molly who concluded the phrase for her.

"And yet he dismissed him without warning," she said calmly.

"Who told you that?" retorted the woman.

"The same people, no doubt, who declare that you and Haggett had a grudge against the Major for this dismissal."

"That's a lie," asserted Mrs. Haggett, doggedly; "we gave information about Mr. Smethick having killed the Major because—"

"Ah," interrupted Lady Molly, quickly, "but then Mr. Smethick did not murder Major Ceely, and your information therefore was useless!"

"Then who killed the Major, I should like to know?"

Her manner was arrogant, coarse, and extremely unpleasant. I marvelled why my dear lady put up with it, and what was going on in that busy brain of hers. She looked quite urbane and smiling, whilst I wondered what in the world she meant by this story of the workhouse and the dismissal of Haggett.

"Ah, that's what none of us know!" she now said lightly; "some folks say it was your husband."

"They lie!" she retorted quickly, whilst the imbecile, evidently not understanding the drift of the conversation, was mechanically stroking his red mop of hair and looking helplessly all round him.

"He was home before the cries of 'Murder' were heard in the house," continued Mrs. Haggett.

"How do you know?" asked Lady Molly, quickly.

"How do I know?"

"Yes; you couldn't have heard the cries all the way to this cottage—why, it's over half a mile from the Hall!"

"He was home, I say," she repeated with dogged obstinacy.

"You sent him?"

"He didn't do it—"

"No one will believe you, especially when the knife is found."

"What knife?"

"His clasp knife, with which he killed Major Ceely," said Lady Molly, quietly; "see, he has it in his hand now."

And with a sudden, wholly unexpected gesture she pointed to the imbecile, who in an aimless way had prowled round the room whilst this rapid colloquy was going on.

The purport of it all must in some sort of way have found an echo in his enfeebled brain. He wandered up to the dresser whereon lay the remnants of that morning's breakfast, together with some crockery and utensils.

In that same half-witted and irresponsible way he had picked up one of the knives and now was holding it out towards his wife, whilst a look of fear spread over his countenance.

"I can't do it, Annie, I can't—you'd better do it," he said.

There was dead silence in the little room. The woman Haggett stood as if turned to stone. Ignorant and superstitious as she was, I suppose that the situation had laid hold of her nerves, and that she felt that the finger of a relentless Fate was even now being pointed at her.

The imbecile was shuffling forward, closer and closer to his wife, still holding out the knife towards her and murmuring brokenly:

"I can't do it. You'd better, Annie—you'd better—"

He was close to her now, and all at once her rigidity and nerve-strain gave way; she gave a hoarse cry, and snatching the knife from the poor wretch, she rushed at him ready to strike.

Lady Molly and I were both young, active and strong; and there was nothing of the squeamish *grande dame* about my dear lady when quick action was needed. But even then we had some difficulty in dragging Annie Hagget away from her miserable husband. Blinded with fury, she was ready to kill the man who had betrayed her. Finally, we succeeded in wresting the knife from her.

You may be sure that it required some pluck after that to sit down again quietly and to remain in the same room with this woman, who already had one crime upon her conscience, and with this weird, half-witted creature who kept on murmuring pitiably:

"You'd better do it, Annie—"

Well, you've read the account of the case, so you know what followed. Lady Molly did not move from that room until she had obtained the woman's full confession. All she did for her own protection was to order me to open the window and to blow the police whistle which she handed to me. The police-station fortunately was not very far, and sound carried in the frosty air.

She admitted to me afterwards that it had been foolish, perhaps, not to have brought Etty or Danvers with her, but she was supremely anxious not to put the woman on the alert from the very start, hence her circumlocutory speeches anent the workhouse, and Haggett's probable dismissal.

That the woman had had some connection with the crime, Lady Molly, with her keen intuition, had always felt; but as there was no witness to the murder itself, and all circumstantial evidence was dead against young Smethick, there was only one chance of successful discovery, and that was the murderer's own confession.

If you think over the interview between my dear lady and the Haggetts on that memorable morning, you will realise how admirably Lady Molly had led up to the weird finish. She would not speak to the woman unless Haggett was present, and she felt sure that as soon as the subject of the murder cropped up, the imbecile would either do or say something that would reveal the truth.

Mechanically, when Major Ceely's name was mentioned, he had taken up the knife. The whole scene recurred to his tottering mind. That the Major had summarily dismissed him recently was one of those bold guesses which Lady Molly was wont to make.

That Haggett had been merely egged on by his wife, and had been too terrified at the last to do the deed himself was no surprise to her, and hardly one to me, whilst the fact that the woman ultimately wreaked her own passionate revenge upon the unfortunate Major was hardly to be wondered at, in the face of her own coarse and elemental personality.

Cowed by the quickness of events, and by the appearance of Danvers and Etty on the scene, she finally made full confession.

She was maddened by the Major's brutality, when with rough, cruel words he suddenly turned her husband adrift, refusing to give him further employment. She herself had great ascendency over the imbecile, and had drilled him into a part of hate and of revenge. At first he had seemed ready and willing to obey. It was arranged that he was to watch on the terrace every night until such time as an alarm of the recurrence of the cattle-maiming outrages should lure the Major out alone.

This effectually occurred on Christmas morning, but not before Haggett, frightened and pusillanimous, was ready to flee rather than to accomplish the villainous deed. But Annie Haggett, guessing perhaps that he would shrink from the crime at the last, had also kept watch every night. Picture the prospective murderer watching and being watched!

When Haggett came across his wife he deputed her to do the deed herself.

I suppose that either terror of discovery or merely desire for the promised reward had caused the woman to fasten the crime on another.

The finding of the ring by Haggett was the beginning of that cruel thought which, but for my dear lady's marvellous powers, would indeed have sent a brave young man to the gallows.

Ah, you wish to know if Margaret Ceely is married? No! Captain Glynne cried off. What suspicions crossed his mind I cannot say; but he never proposed to Margaret, and now she is in Australia—staying with an aunt, I think—and she has sold Clevere Hall.

Gahan Wilson

The Inspector Ghote stories are a throwback to the Golden Age of Mystery. Bombay's intrepid CID representative dominates each moment in a way few detectives have since Charlie Chan and Philo Vance. And, in contrast to the more anonymous heroes who came to prominence in the hard-boiled era and beyond, Ganesh Ghote stays in the reader's mind as a presence long after the book has been closed.

Fortunately, unlike the great masters who created those heroes of the Golden Age, H.R.F. Keating is very much alive and working at the top of his form. His style, like his characters, is warm and ingratiating. He persuades his reader gently with the strength of his writing skills.

Keating is active in other areas of the mystery field, as an essayist, editor, and for a time, a distinguished mystery reviewer for the Times of London.

"Inspector Ghote and the Miracle Baby" first appeared in the Catholic Herald in England, and later in Ellery Queen's Mystery Magazine under the title "Inspector Ghote and the Miracle" in 1973. Unique among Christmas stories, it is highly satisfying with its understated humour. Detective fiction needs more heroes like Inspector Ghote, and more Ghote stories.

Inspector Ghote and the Miracle Baby

by H. R. F. Keating

W HAT HAS SANTA CLAUS got in store for me, Inspector Ghote said to himself, bleakly echoing the current cheerful Bombay newspaper advertisements, as he waited to enter the office of Assistant Commissioner Naik that morning of December 25th.

Whatever the A.C. had lined up for him, Ghote knew it was going to be nasty. Ever since he had recently declined to turn up for "voluntary" hockey, A.C. Naik had viewed him with sad-eyed disapproval. But what exact form would his displeasure take?

Almost certainly it would have something to do with the big Navy Week parade that afternoon, the chief preoccupation at the moment of most of the ever-excitable and drama-loving Bombayites. Probably he would be ordered out into the crowds watching the Fire Power demonstration in the bay, ordered to come back with a beltful of pickpocketing arrests.

"Come," the A.C.'s voice barked out.

Ghote went in and stood squaring his bony shoulders in front of the papers-strewn desk.

"Ah, Ghote, yes. Tulsi Pipe Road for you. Up at the north end. Going to be big trouble there. Rioting. Intercommunity outrages even."

Ghote's heart sank even deeper than he had expected. Tulsi Pipe Road was a two-kilometers-long thoroughfare that shot straight up from the Racecourse into the heart of a densely crowded mill district where badly paid Hindus, Muslims in hundreds and Goans by the thousand, all lived in prickling closeness, either in great areas of tumbledown hutments or in high tottering chawls, floor upon floor of massed humanity. Trouble between the religious communities there meant hell, no less.

"Yes, A.C.?" he said, striving not to sound appalled.

"We are having a virgin birth business, Inspector."

"Virgin birth, A.C. sahib?"

"Come, man, you must have come across such cases."

"I am sorry, A.C.," Ghote said, feeling obliged to be true to hard-won scientific principles. "I am unable to believe in virgin birth."

The A.C.'s round face suffused with instant wrath.

"Of course I am not asking you to believe in virgin birth, man! It is not you who are to believe: it is all those Christians in the Goan community who are believing it about a baby born two days ago. It is the time of year, of course. These affairs are always coming at Christmas. I have dealt with half a dozen in my day."

"Yes, A.C.," Ghote said, contriving to hit on the right note of awe.

"Yes. And there is only one way to deal with it. Get hold of the girl and find out the name of the man. Do that pretty damn quick and the whole affair drops away to nothing, like monsoon water down a drain."

"Yes, A.C."

"Well, what are you waiting for, man? Hop it!"

"Name and address of the girl in question, A.C. sahib."

The A.C.'s face darkened once more. He padded furiously over the jumble of papers on his desk top. And at last he found the chit he wanted.

"There you are, man. And also you will find there the name of the Head Constable who first reported the matter. See him straightaway. You have got a good man there, active, quick on his feet, sharp. If he could not make that girl talk, you will be having a first-class damn job, Inspector."

Ghote located Head Constable Mudholkar one hour later at the local chowkey where he was stationed. The Head Constable confirmed at once the blossoming dislike for a sharp bully that Ghote had been harboring ever since A.C. Naik had praised the fellow. And, what was worse, the chap turned out to be very like the A.C. in looks as well. He had the same round type of face, the same puffy-looking lips, even a similar soft blur of mustache. But the Head Constable's appearance was nevertheless a travesty of the A.C.'s. His face was simply, slewed.

To Ghote's prejudiced eyes, at the first moment of their encounter, the man's features seemed grotesquely distorted, as if in some distant time some god had taken one of the Head Constable's ancestors and had wrenched his whole head sideways between two omnipotent god-hands.

But, as the fellow supplied him with the details of the affair, Ghote forced himself to regard him with an open mind, and he then had to admit that the facial twist which had seemed so pronounced was in fact no more than a drooping corner of the mouth and of one ear being oddly longer than the other.

Ghote had to admit, too, that the chap was efficient. He had all the circumstances of the affair at his fingertips. The girl, named D'Mello, now in a hospital for her own safety, had been rigorously questioned both before and after the birth, but she had steadfastly denied that she had ever been with any man. She was indeed not the sort, the sole daughter of a Goan railway waiter on the Madras Express, a quiet girl, well brought up though her parents were poor enough; she attended Mass regularly with her mother, and the whole family kept themselves to themselves.

"But with those Christians you can never tell," Head Constable Mudholkar concluded.

Ghote felt inwardly inclined to agree. Fervid religion had always made him shrink inwardly, whether it was a Hindu holy man spending 20 years silent and standing upright or whether it was the Catholics, always caressing lifeless statues in their churches till glass protection had to be installed, and even then they still stroked the thick panes. Either manifestation rendered him uneasy.

That was the real reason, he now acknowledged to himself, why he did not want to go and see Miss D'Mello in the hospital where she would be surrounded by nuns amid all the trappings of an alien religion, surrounded with all the panoply of a newly found goddess.

Yet go and see the girl he must.

But first he permitted himself to do every other thing that might possibly be necessary to the case. He visited Mrs. D'Mello, and by dint of patient wheedling, and a little forced toughness, confirmed from her the names of the only two men that Head Constable Mudholkar—who certainly proved to know inside-out the particular chawl where the D'Mellos lived—had suggested as possible fathers. They were both young men—a Goan, Charlie Lobo, and a Sikh, Kuldip Singh.

The Lobo family lived one floor below the D'Mellos. But that one flight of dirt-spattered stairs, bringing them just that much nearer the courtyard tap that served the whole crazily leaning chawl, represented a whole layer higher in social status. And Mrs. Lobo, a huge, tightly fat woman in a brightly flowered Western-style dress, had decided views about the unexpected fame that had come to the people upstairs.

"Has my Charlie been going with that girl?" she repeated after Ghote had managed to put the question, suitably wrapped up, to the boy. "No, he has not. Charlie, tell the man you hate and despise trash like that."

"Oh, Mum," said Charlie, a teen-age wisp of a figure suffocating in a necktie beside his balloon-hard mother.

"Tell the man, Charlie."

And obediently Charlie muttered something that satisfied his passion-filled parent. Ghote put a few more questions for form's sake, but he realized that only by getting hold of the boy on his own was he going to get any worthwhile answers. Yet it turned out that he did not have to employ any cunning. Charlie proved to have a strain of sharp slyness of his own, and hardly had Ghote climbed the stairs to the floor above the D'Mellos where Kudlip Singh lived when he heard a whispered call from the shadow-filled darkness below.

"Mum's got her head over the stove," Charlie said. "She don't know I slipped out."

"There is something you have to tell me?" Ghote said, acting the indulgent uncle. "You are in trouble—that's it, isn't it?"

"My only trouble is Mum," the boy replied. "Listen, mister, I had to tell you. I love Miss D'Mello—yes, I love her. She's the most wonderful girl ever was."

"And you want to marry her, and because you went too far before—"

"No, no, no. She's far and away too good for me. Mister, I've never even said 'Good morning' to her in the two years we've lived here. But I love her, mister, and I'm not going to have Mum make me say different."

Watching him slip cunningly back home, Ghote made his mental notes and then turned to tackle Kuldip Singh, his last comparatively easy task before the looming interview at the nun-ridden hospital he knew he must have.

Kuldip Singh, as Ghote had heard from Head Constable Mudholkar, was different from his neighbors. He lived in this teeming area from choice not necessity. Officially a student, he spent all his time in a series of anti-social activities—protesting, writing manifestoes, drinking. He seemed an ideal candidate for the unknown and elusive father.

Ghote's suspicions were at once heightened when the young Sikh opened his door. The boy, though old enough to have a beard, lacked this status symbol. Equally he had discarded the obligatory turban of his religion. But all the Sikh bounce was there, as Ghote discovered when he identified himself.

"Policewallah, is it? Then I want nothing at all to do with you. Me and the police are enemies, bhai. Natural enemies."

"Irrespective of such considerations," Ghote said stiffly, "it is my duty to put to you certain questions concerning one Miss D'Mello."

The young Sikh burst into a roar of laughter.

"The miracle girl, is it?" he said. "Plenty of trouble for policemen there, I promise you. Top-level rioting coming from that business. The fellow who fathered that baby did us a lot of good."

Ghote plugged away a good while longer—the hospital nuns awaited—but for all his efforts he learned no more than he had in that first brief exchange. And in the end he still had to go and meet his doom.

Just what he had expected at the hospital he never quite formulated to himself. What he did find was certainly almost the exact opposite of his fears. A calm reigned. White-habited nuns, mostly Indian but with a few Europeans, flitted silently to and fro or talked quietly to the patients whom Ghote glimpsed lying on beds in long wards. Above them swung frail but bright paper chains in honor of the feast day, and these were all the excitement there was.

The small separate ward in which Miss D'Mello lay in a broad bed all alone was no different. Except that the girl was isolated, she seemed to be treated in just the same way as the other new mothers in the big maternity ward that Ghote had been led through on his way in. In the face of such matter-of-factness he felt hollowly cheated.

Suddenly, too, to his own utter surprise he found, looking down at the big calm-after-storm eyes of the Goan girl, that he wanted the story she was about to tell him to be true. Part of him knew that, if it were so, or if it was widely believed to be so, appalling disorders could result from the feverish religious excitement that was bound to mount day by day. But another part of him now simply wanted a miracle to have happened.

He began, quietly and almost diffidently, to put his questions. Miss D'Mello would hardly answer at all, but such syllables as she did whisper were of blank inability to name anyone as the father of her child. After a while Ghote brought himself, with a distinct effort of will, to change his tactics. He banged out the hard line. Miss D'Mello went quietly and totally mute.

Then Ghote slipped in, with adroit suddenness, the name of Charlie Lobo. He got only a small puzzled frown.

Then, in an effort to make sure that her silence was not a silence of fear, he presented, with equal suddenness, the name of Kuldip Singh. If the care-for-nothing young Sikh had forced this timid creature, this might be the way to get an admission. But instead there came something approaching a laugh.

"That Kuldip is a funny fellow," the girl said, with an out-of-place and unexpected offhandedness.

Ghote almost gave up. But at that moment a nun nurse appeared carrying in her arms a small, long, white-wrapped, minutely crying bundle—the baby.

While she handed the hungry scrap to its mother Ghote

stood and watched. Perhaps holding the child she would—?

He looked down at the scene on the broad bed, awaiting his moment again. The girl fiercely held the tiny agitated thing to her breast and in a moment or two quiet came, the tiny head applied to the life-giving nipple. How human the child looked already, Ghote thought. How much a man at two days old. The round skull, almost bald, as it might become again toward the end of its span. The frown on the forehead that would last a lifetime, the tiny, perfectly formed, plainly asymmetrical ears—

And then Ghote knew that there had not been any miracle. It was as he surmised, but with different circumstances. Miss D'Mello was indeed too frightened to talk. No wonder, when the local bully, Head Constable Mudholkar with his slewed head and its one ear so characteristically longer than the other, was the man who had forced himself on her.

A deep smothering of disappointment floated down on Ghote. So it had been nothing miraculous after all. Just a sad case, to be cleared up painfully. He stared down at the bed.

The tiny boy suckled energetically. And with a topsy-turvy welling up of rose-pink pleasure, Ghote saw that there had after all been a miracle. The daily, hourly, every-minute miracle of a new life, of a new flicker of hope in the tired world.

"Where did we go wrong, Mother? Where did we go wrong?"

If Poe is acknowledged to be the father of the mystery-detective story, Dickens's contribution places him chief among the midwives. His final book, the uncompleted Mystery of Edwin Drood, *is itself one of the great mysteries of literature. Dickens set up a fascinating story, then became physically incapacitated, leaving no clue to the solution. Subsequent Dickensians have tried their hands at it, but no version has been accepted as definitive.*

Dickens actually wrote several works about murder and investigation, including Barnaby Rudge, Hunted Down *and* Black House, *which features Inspector Bucket, the first important detective in English literature.*

Dickens also served as the editor of several periodicals in which his works were serialized. Dr. Marigold, *the work at hand, first appeared in one such publication,* All Year Round, *and is the story of a cheapjack (panhandler) and his daughter, little Sophy. Some of the chapters were written by Wilkie Collins, the author of* The Moonstone *and* The Woman in White. *The sixth chapter, "To Be Taken With A Grain of Salt," is a self-contained story entirely by Dickens's hand.*

By way of a prologue, bits from other chapters have been excerpted to give a picture of Dr. Marigold at Christmas. As he sits by the fire, a visitor appears with a story, a Christmas story, as Dickens himself called it, when he collected Dr. Marigold *into book form. Some liberties have been taken with the text, but the words that follow are all those of Charles Dickens. Only the omissions are mine.*

Dr. Marigold's Prescription

by Charles Dickens

I AM a Cheap Jack, and my own father's name was William Marigold. It was in his lifetime supposed by some that his name was William, but my own father always consistently said No, it was Willum. As to looking at the argument through the medium of the Register, William Marigold came into the world before Registers came up much—and went out of it too. They wouldn't have been greatly in his line neither, if they had chanced to come up before him!

I was born on the Queen's highway, but it was the King's at that time. A doctor was fetched to my mother by my own father, when it took place on a common; and in consequence of his being a very kind gentlemen, and accepting no fee but a tea-tray, I was named Doctor, out of gratitude and compliment to him. There you have me. Doctor Marigold.

The doctor having accepted a tea-tray, you'll guess that my father was a Cheap Jack before me. You are right, he was.

My father had been a lovely one in his time at the Cheap Jack work . . . But I top him. I don't say it because it's myself but because it has been universally acknowledged by all that has had the means of comparison.

I had had a first-rate autumn of it, and on the twenty-third of December, one thousand eight hundred and sixty-four, I found myself at Axbridge, Middlesex, clean sold out. So I jogged up to London with the old horse, light and easy, to have my Christmas Eve and Christmas Day alone by the fire . . . , and then to buy a regular new stock of goods all round, to sell 'em again and get the money.

I am a neat hand at cookery, and I'll tell you what I knocked up for my Christmas Eve dinner . . . I knocked up a beefsteak pudding for one, with two kidneys, a dozen oysters, and a couple of mushrooms thrown in. It's a pudding to put a man in a good humor with everything, except the two bottom buttons of his waistcoat. Having relished that pudding and cleared away, I turned the lamp low, and sat down by the light of the fire, watching it as it shone upon the backs of . . . books, . . . , before I dropped off dozing. . . .

I was on the road, off the road, in all sorts of places, north and south and west and east, winds liked best and winds liked least, here and there and gone astray, over the hills and far away . . . when I awoke with a start. . . .

I had started at a real sound . . . That tread . . . I believed I was a-going to see a . . . ghost.

The touch . . . was laid upon the outer handle of the door, the handle turned, and the door opened a little. . . .

Looking full at me . . . was a languid young man, which I attribute the distance between his extremities. He had a little head . . . weak eyes and weak knees, and altogether you couldn't look at him without feeling that there was greatly too much of him for his joints. . . .

"I am very glad to see you," says the Gentlemen. "Yet I have my doubts, Sir,", says I, "if you can be half as glad to see me as I am to see you."

The creature took off . . . a straw hat, and a quantity of dark curls fell about.

I might have been too high to fall into conversation with him, had it not been for my lonely feelings.

"Sir, . . . you are affected . . ."

This made our footing . . . easier.

"Come . . . Doctor Marigold must prescribe . . . the Best of Drinks."

He was amiable, though tired, . . . and such a languid young man, that I don't known how long it didn't take him to get this story out but it passed through his defective circulation to his top extremity in course of time.

TO BE TAKEN WITH A GRAIN OF SALT

I have always noticed a prevalent want of courage, even among persons of superior intelligence and culture, as to imparting their own psychological experiences when those have been of a strange sort. Almost all men are afraid that what they could relate in such wise would find no parallel or response in a listener's internal life, and might be suspected or laughed at. A truthful traveller, who should have seen some extraordinary creature in the likeness of a sea-serpent, would have no fear of mentioning it; but the same traveller, having had some singular presentiment, impulse, vagary of thought, vision (so called), dream, or other remarkable mental impression, would hesitate considerably before he would own to it. To this reticence I attribute much of the obscurity in which such subjects are involved. We do not habitually communicate our experiences of these subjective things as we do our experiences of objective creation. The consequence is, that the general stock of experience in this regard appears exceptional, and really is so, in respect of being miserably imperfect.

In what I am going to relate, I have no intention of setting up, opposing, or supporting, any theory whatever. I know the history of the Bookseller of Berlin, I have studied the case of the wife of a late Astronomer Royal as related by Sir David Brewster, and I have followed the minutest details of a much more remarkable case of Spectral Illusion occurring within my private circle of friends. It may be necessary to state as to this last, that the sufferer (a lady) was in no degree, however distant, related to me. A mistaken assumption on that head might suggest an explanation of a part of my own case,—but only a part,—which would be wholly without foundation. It cannot be referred to my inheritance of any developed peculiarity, nor had I never before any at all similar experience, nor have I ever had any at all similar experience since.

It does not signify how many years ago, or how few, a certain murder was committed in England, which attracted great attention. We hear more than enough of murderers as they rise in succession to their atrocious eminence, and I would bury the memory of this particular brute, if I could, as his body was buried, in Newgate Jail. I purposely abstain from giving any direct clew to the criminal's individuality.

When the murder was first discovered, no suspicion fell—or I ought rather to say, for I cannot be too precise in my facts, it was nowhere publicly hinted that any suspicion fell—on the man who was afterwards brought to trial. As no reference was at that time made to him in the newspapers, it is obviously impossible that any description of him can at that time have been given in the newspapers. It is essential that this fact be remembered.

Unfolding at breakfast my morning paper, containing the account of that first discovery, I found it to be deeply interesting, and I read it with close attention. I read it twice, if not three times. The discovery had been made in a bedroom, and, when I laid down the paper, I was aware of a flash—rush—flow—I do not know what to call it,—no word I can find is satisfactorily descriptive,—in which I seemed to see that bedroom passing through my room, like a picture impossibly painted on a running river. Though almost instantaneous in its passing, it was perfectly clear; so clear that I distinctly, and with a sense of relief, observed the absence of the dead body from the bed.

It was in no romantic place that I had this curious sensation, but in chambers in Piccadilly, very near to the corner of St. James's-street. It was entirely new to me. I was in my easy-chair at the moment, and the sensation was accompanied with a peculiar shiver which started the chair from its position. (But it is to be noted that the chair ran easily on castors.) I went to one of the windows (there are two in the room, and the room is on the second floor) to refresh my eyes with the moving objects down in Piccadilly. It was a bright autumn morning, and the street was sparkling and cheerful. The wind was high. As I looked out, it brought down from the Park a quantity of fallen leaves, which a gust took, and whirled into a spiral pillar. As the pillar fell and the leaves dispersed, I saw two men on the opposite side of the way, going from West to East. They were one behind the other. The foremost man often looked back over his shoulder. The second man followed him, at a distance of some thirty paces, with his right hand menacingly raised. First, the singularity and steadiness of this threatening gesture in so public a throughfare attracted my attention; and next, the more remarkable circumstance that nobody heeded it. Both men threaded their way among the other passengers with a smoothness hardly consistent even with the action of walking on a pavement; and no single creature, that I could see, gave them place, touched them, or looked after them. In passing before my windows, they both stared up at me. I saw their two faces very distinctly, and I knew that I could recognise them anywhere. Not that I had consciously noticed anything very remarkable in either face, except that the man who went first had an unusually lowering appearance, and that the face of the man who followed him was of the colour of impure wax.

I am a bachelor, and my valet and his wife constitute my whole establishment. My occupation is in a certain Branch Bank, and I wish that my duties as head of a Department were as light as they are popularly supposed to be. They kept me in town that autumn, when I stood in need of change. I was not ill, but I was not well. You may make the most that can be reasonably made of my feeling jaded, having a depressing sense upon me of a monotonous life, and being "slightly dyspeptic." I am assured by my renowned doctor that my real state of health at that time justifies no stronger description, and I quote his own from his written answer to my request for it.

As the circumstances of the murder, gradually unravelling, took stronger and stronger possession of the public mind, I kept them away from mine by knowing as little about them as was possible in the midst of the universal excitement. But I knew that a verdict of Wilful Murder had been found against the suspected murderer, and that he had been committed to Newgate for trial. I also knew that his trial had been postponed over one Sessions of the Central Criminal Court, on the ground of general prejudice and want of time for the preparation of the defence. I may further have known, but I believe I did not, when, or about when, the Sessions to which his trial stood postponed would come on.

My sitting-room, bedroom, and dressing-room, are all on one floor. With the last there is no communication but through the bedroom. True, there is a door in it, once communicating with the staircase; but a part of the fitting of my bath has been—and had then been for some years—fixed across it. At the same period, and as a part of the same arrangement, the door had been nailed up and canvased over.

I was standing in my bedroom late one night, giving some directions to my servant before he went to bed. My face was towards the only available door of communication with the dressing-room, and it was closed. My servant's back was towards that door. While I was speaking to him, I saw it open, and a man look in, who very earnestly and mysteriously beckoned to me. That man was the man who had gone second of the two along Piccadilly, and whose face was the colour of impure wax.

The figure, having beckoned, drew back, and closed the door. With no longer pause than was made by my crossing the bedroom, I opened the dressing-room door, and looked in. I had a lighted candle already in my hand. I felt no inward expectation of seeing the figure in the dressing-room, and I did not see it there.

Conscious that my servant stood amazed, I turned round to him, and said: "Derrick, could you believe that in my cool senses I fancied I saw a—" As I there laid my hand upon his breast, with a sudden start he trembled violently, and said, "O Lord, yes, Sir! A dead man beckoning!"

Now I do not believe that this John Derrick, my trusty and attached servant for more than twenty years, had any impression whatever of having seen any such figure, until I touched him. The change in him was so startling, when I touched him, that I fully believe he derived his impression in some occult manner from me at that instant.

I bade John Derrick bring some brandy, and I gave him a dram, and was glad to take one myself. Of what had preceded that night's phenomenon, I told him not a single word. Reflecting on it, I was absolutely certain that I had never seen that face before, except on the one occasion in Piccadilly. Comparing its expression when beckoning at the door with its expression when it had stared up at me as I stood at my window, I came to the conclusion that on the first occasion it had sought to fasten itself upon my memory, and that on the second occasion it had made sure of being immediately remembered.

I was not very comfortable that night, though I felt a certainty, difficult to explain, that the figure would not return. At daylight I fell into a heavy sleep, from which I was awakened by John Derrick's coming to my bedside with a paper in his hand.

This paper, it appeared, had been the subject of an altercation at the door between its bearer and my servant. It was a summons to me to serve upon a Jury at the forthcoming Sessions of the Central Criminal Court at the Old Bailey. I had never before been summoned on such a Jury, as John Derrick well knew. He believed—I am not certain at this hour whether with reason or otherwise—that that class of Jurors were customarily chosen on a lower qualification than mine, and he had at first refused to accept the summons. The man who served it had taken the matter very coolly. He had said that my attendance or non-attendance was nothing to him; there the summons was; and I should deal with it at my own peril, and not at his.

For a day or two I was undecided whether to respond to this call, or to take no notice of it. I was not conscious of the slightest mysterious bias, influence, or attraction, one way or other. Of that I am as strictly sure as of every other statement that I make here. Ultimately I decided, as a break in the monotony of my life, that I would go.

The appointed morning was a raw morning in the month of November. There was a dense brown fog in Piccadilly, and it became positively black and in the last degree oppressive East of Temple Bar. I found the passages and staircases of the Court-House flaringly lighted with gas, and the Court itself similarly illuminated. I *think* that, until I was so helped into the Old Court with considerable difficulty, I did not know into which of the two Courts sitting my summons would take me. But this must not be received as a positive assertion, for I am not completely satisfied in my mind on either point.

I took my seat in the place appropriated to Jurors in waiting, and I looked about the Court as well as I could through the cloud of fog and breath that was heavy in it. I noticed the

black vapour hanging like a murky curtain outside the great
windows, and I noticed the stifled sound of wheels on the
straw or tan that was littered in the street; also, the hum of the
people gathered there, which a shrill whistle, or a louder song
or hail than the rest, occasionally pierced. Soon afterwards,
the Judges, two in number, entered, and took their seats. The
buzz in the court was awfully hushed. The direction was given
to put the Murderer to the bar. He appeared there. And in that
same instant I recognized in him the first of the two men who
had gone down Piccadilly.

If my name had been called then, I doubt if I could have
answered to it audibly. But it was called about sixth or eighth
in the panel, and I was by that time able to say "Here!" Now,
observe. As I stepped into the box, the prisoner, who had
been looking on attentively, but with no sign of concern, became violently agitated, and beckoned to his attorney. The
prisoner's wish to challenge me was so manifest, that it occa-
sioned a pause, during which the attorney, with his hand upon
the dock, whispered with his client, and shook his head. I
afterwards had it from that gentleman, that the prisoner's first
affrighted words to him were, *"At all hazards, challenge that
man!"* But that, as he would give no reason for it, and admitted that he had not even known my name until he heard it
called and I appeared, it was not done.

Both on the ground already explained, that I wish to avoid
reviving the unwholesome memory of that Murderer, and also
because a detailed account of his long trial is by no means
indispensable to my narrative, I shall confine myself closely
to such incidents in the ten days and nights during which we,
the Jury, were kept together, as directly bear on my own curious personal experience. It is in that, and not in the Murderer, that I seek to interest my reader. It is to that, and not to
a page of the Newgate Calendar, that I beg attention.

I was chosen Foreman of the Jury. On the second morning
of the trial, after evidence had been taken for two hours (I
heard the church clocks strike), happening to cast my eyes
over my brother jurymen, I found an inexplicable difficulty in
counting them. I counted them several times, yet always with
the same difficulty. In short, I made them one too many.

I touched the brother juryman whose place was next me,

and I whispered to him, "Oblige me by counting us." He looked surprised by the request, but turned his head and counted. "Why," says he, suddenly, "we are Thirt—; but no, it's not possible. No. We are twelve."

According to my counting that day, we were always right in detail, but in the gross we were always one too many. There was no appearance—no figure—to account for it; but I had now an inward foreshadowing of the figure that was surely coming.

The Jury were housed at the London Tavern. We all slept in one large room on separate tables, and we were constantly in the charge and under the eye of the officer sworn to hold us in safe-keeping. I see no reason for suppressing the real name of that officer. He was intelligent, highly polite, and obliging, and (I was glad to hear) much respected in the City. He had an agreeable presence, good eyes, enviable black whiskers, and a fine sonorous voice. His name was Mr. Harker.

When we turned into our twelve beds at night, Mr. Harker's bed was drawn across the door. On the night of the second day, not being disposed to lie down, and seeing Mr. Harker sitting on his bed, I went and sat beside him, and offered him a pinch of snuff. As Mr. Harker's hand touched mine in taking it from my box, a peculiar shiver crossed him, and he said, "Who is this?"

Following Mr. Harker's eyes, and looking along the room, I saw again the figure I expected,—the second of the two men who had gone down Piccadilly. I rose, and advanced a few steps; then stopped, and looked round at Mr. Harker. He was quite unconcerned, laughed, and said in a pleasant way, "I thought for a moment we had a thirteenth juryman, without a bed. But I see it is the moonlight."

Making no revelation to Mr. Harker, but inviting him to take a walk with me to the end of the room, I watched what the figure did. It stood for a few moments by the bedside of each of my eleven brother jurymen, close to the pillow. It always went to the right-hand side of the bed, and always passed out crossing the foot of the next bed. It seemed, from the action of the head, merely to look down pensively at each recumbent figure. It took no notice of me, or of my bed, which was that nearest to Mr. Harker's. It seemed to go out where the moonlight came in, through a high window, as by an aërial flight of stairs.

Next morning at breakfast, it appeared that everybody present had dreamed of the murdered man last night, except myself, and Mr. Harker.

I now felt as convinced that the second man who had gone down Piccadilly was the murdered man (so to speak), as if it had been borne into my comprehension by his immediate testimony. But even this took place, and in a manner for which I was not at all prepared.

On the fifth day of the trial, when the case for the prosecution was drawing to a close, a miniature of the murdered man, missing from his bedroom upon the discovery of the deed, and afterwards found in a hiding-place where the Murderer had been seen digging, was put in evidence. Having been identified by the witness under examination, it was handed up to the Bench, and thence handed down to be inspected by the Jury. As an officer in a black gown was making his way with it across to me, the figure of the second man who had gone down Piccadilly impetuously started from the crowd, caught the miniature from the officer, and gave it to me with his own hands, at the same time saying, in a low and hollow tone,— before I saw the miniature, which was in a locket,—*"I was younger then, and my face was not then drained of blood."* It also came between me and the brother juryman to whom I would have given the miniature, and between him and the brother juryman to whom he would have given it, and so passed it on through the whole of our number, and back into my possession. Not one of them, however, detected this.

At table, and generally when we were shut up together in Mr. Harker's custody, we had from the first naturally discussed the day's proceedings a good deal. On that fifth day, the case for the prosecution being closed, and we having that side of the question in a completed shape before us, our discussion was more animated and serious. Among our number was a vestryman,—the densest idiot I have ever seen at large, —who met the plainest evidence with the most preposterous objections, and who was sided with by two flabby parochial parasites; all the three impanelled from a district so delivered over to Fever that they ought to have been upon their own trial for five hundred Murders. When these mischievous block-heads were at their loudest, which was towards midnight, while some of us were already preparing for bed, I again saw the murdered man. He stood grimly behind them, beckoning to me. On my going towards them and striking into the con-versation, he immediatley retired. This was the beginning of a separate series of appearances, confined to that long room in which *we* were confined. Whenever a knot of my brother jur-ymen laid their heads together, I saw the head of the murdered man among theirs. Whenever their comparison of notes was going against him, he would solemnly and irresistibly beckon to me.

It will be borne in mind that down to the production of the miniature, on the fifth day of the trial, I had never seen the Appearance in court. Three changes occurred now that we entered on the case for the defence. Two of them I will men-tion together, first. The figure was now in Court continually, and it never there addressed itself to me, but always to the person who was speaking at the time. For instance: the throat of the murdered man had been cut straight across. In the opening speech for the defence, it was suggested that the de-ceased might have cut his own throat. At that very moment, the figure, with its throat in the dreadful condition referred to (this it had concealed before), stood at the speaker's elbow, motioning across and across its windpipe, now with the right hand, now with the left, vigorously suggesting to the speaker himself the impossibility of such a wound having been self-inflicted by either hand. For another instance: a witness to character, a woman, deposed to the prisoner's being the most amiable of mankind. The figure at that instant stood on the floor before her, looking her full in the face, and pointing out the prisoner's evil countenance with an extended arm and an outstretched finger.

The third change now to be added impressed me strongly as the most marked and striking of all. I do not theorise upon it; I accurately state it, and there leave it. Although the Appear-ance was not itself perceived by those whom it addressed, its coming close to such persons was invariably attended by some trepidation or disturbance on their part. It seemed to me as if it were prevented, by laws to which I was not amenable, from fully revealing itself to others, and yet as if it could invisibly, dumbly, and darkly overshadow their minds. When the leading counsel for the defence suggested that hypothesis of suicide, and the figure stood at the learned gentleman's elbow, frightfully sawing at its severed throat, it is undeniable that the counsel faltered in his speech, lost for a few seconds the thread of his ingenious discourse, wiped his forehead with his handkerchief, and turned extremely pale. When the witness to character was confronted by the Appearance, her eyes most certainly did follow the direction of its pointed finger, and rest in great hesitation and trouble upon the prisoner's face. Two additional illustrations will suffice. On the eighth day of the trial, after the pause which was every day made early in the afternoon for a few minutes' rest and refreshment, I came back into court with the rest of the Jury some little time before the return of the Judges. Standing up in the box and looking about me, I thought the figure was not there, until, chancing to raise my eyes to the gallery, I saw it bending forward, and leaning over a very decent woman, as if to assure itself whether the Judges had resumed their seats or not. Immediatley afterwards that woman screamed, fainted, and was carried out. So with the venerable, sagacious, and patient Judge who conducted the trial. When the case was over, and he settled himself and his papers to sum up, the murdered man, entering by the Judges' door, advanced to his Lordship's desk, and looked eagerly over his shoulder at the pages of his notes which he was turning. A change came over his Lordship's face; his hand stopped; the peculiar shiver, that I knew so well, passed over him; he faltered, "Excuse me, gentlemen, for a few moments. I am somewhat oppressed by the vitiated air"; and did not recover until he had drunk a glass of water.

Through all the monotony of six of those interminable ten days,—the same Judges and others on the bench, the same Murderer in the dock, the same lawyers at the table, the same tones of question and answer rising to the roof of the Court, the same scratching of the Judge's pen, the same ushers going in and out, the same lights kindled at the same hour when there had been any natural light of day, the same foggy curtain outside the great windows when it was foggy, the same rain pattering and dripping when it was rainy, the same footmarks of turnkeys and prisoner day after day on the same sawdust, the same keys locking and unlocking the same heavy doors,—through all the wearisome monotony which made me feel as if I had been Foreman of the Jury for a vast period of time, and Piccadilly had flourished coevally with Babylon, the murdered man never lost one trace of his distinctness in my eyes, nor was he at any moment less distinct than anybody else. I must not omit, as a matter of fact, that I never once saw the Appearance which I call by the name of the murdered man look at the Murderer. Again and again I wondered, "Why does he not?" But he never did.

Nor did he look at me, after the production of the miniature, until the last closing minutes of the trial arrived. We retired to consider, at seven minutes before ten at night. The idiotic vestryman and his two parochial parasites gave us so much trouble that we twice returned into court to beg to have certain extracts from the Judges notes re-read. Nine of us had not the smallest doubt about those passages, neither, I believe, had any one in the Court; the dunderhead triumverate, however, having no idea but obstruction, disputed them for that very reason. At length we prevailed, and finally the Jury returned into Court at ten minutes past twelve.

The murdered man at that time stood directly opposite the Jury-box, on the other side of the Court. As I took my place, his eyes rested on me with great attention; he seemed satisfied, and slowly shook a great grey veil, which he carried on his arm for the first time, over his head and whole form. As I gave in our verdict, "Guilty," the veil collapsed, all was gone, and his place was empty.

The Murderer, being asked by the Judge, according to usage, whether he had anything to say before sentence of Death should be passed upon him, indistinctly muttered something which was described in the leading newspapers of the following day as "a few rambling, incoherent, and half-audible words, in which he was understood to complain that he had not had a fair trial, because the Foreman of the Jury was prepossessed against him." The remarkable declaration that he really made was this: *"My Lord, I knew I was a doomed man, when the Foreman of my Jury came into the box. My Lord, I knew he would never let me off, because before I was taken, he somehow got to my bedside in the night, woke me, and put a rope round my neck."*

Chief Inspector Doob of Scotland Yard arrived at Farnsworth Hall moments after the call had come in. It had been a drizzly Christmas Eve, and he had been nursing a head cold.

In the well-appointed sitting room of the home, he found Lord Carstairs, the wealthy industrialist, sprawled out across the floor, quite dead at the foot of an undecorated Christmas tree, blood still oozing from an ugly gash across the back of his bald head.

On a victorian settee nearby, Vivian Carstairs, his attractive widow sat sobbing into a lace handkerchief.

"I'm sorry to trouble you, Lady Carstairs," said Doob in his most solicitous voice, "but I'm afraid I'm going to need some kind of statement."

"Yes, Inspector," she said, composing herself. "I understand."

"As I told the constable, we were both upstairs in bed, when Arthur woke me, and said he thought he heard a burglar downstairs. The servants are all away, so he went downstairs to investigate."

"After a bit, when he didn't return, I decided to go downstairs myself. I took the poker from the bedroom fireplace just in case. It was dark downstairs. None of the lights seemed to be working.

"I thought I heard someone call to me from the sitting room. I went in to investigate, and something suddenly came toward me. I suppose I panicked and just swung at it. When I was able to get some light, I found poor Arthur, like that."

"I see," said Doob, considerately. "I wonder if it was possible that your husband had meant to do you some harm?"

"But, whatever for? I can think of no reason."

"My men say someone had tampered with the fuse box. And, what of your husband's recent attachment to a Miss Trixie Latouche?" continued Doob, removing a scented letter from the pocket of the dead man's dressing gown.

"The Duchess of Claymore? Tabloid stuff, I can assure you, Inspector. There was nothing to it," said the widow staunchly.

"Perhaps," conceded Doob, "but I think you had better come with us to police headquarters. The charge is premeditated murder."

WHAT MADE INSPECTOR DOOB SUSPICIOUS OF VIVIAN CARSTAIRS'S STORY?

Vivian Carstairs said she struck out with the poker as the person was coming towards her. Yet Lord Carstairs had been killed by a blow to the back of his head. She was subsequently convicted. Doob later married the Duchess of Claymore, after breaking her down during intensive interrogation.

The name Ellery Queen is synonymous with the American mystery story. As editor, author, collector, teacher, critic, lecturer, and anthologist, he has had a profound influence on the course of mystery writing.

Actually Queen is two people. Frederic Dannay and his cousin, the late Manfred B. Lee. (The fictional hero of most of their stories was also named Ellery Queen.) Queen the detective first appeared in The Roman Hat Mystery in 1929, and has since turned up in just about every form of mass communication ever devised, including television, radio and films.

The hallmark of an Ellery Queen story is its ingenuity. A classic Queen mystery takes a murder, proposes a number of different plausible solutions, then arrives at the correct one, usually the shrewdest of all.

In 1941, Lee and Dannay expanded their endeavors to a new monthly publication, Ellery Queen's Mystery Magazine, which became the keeper of the flame during the dark years when large publishing houses were turning away from mystery fiction in general and short stories in particular. It continues to dominate the field today.

With Lee's death, the Ellery Queen stories ceased, but Dannay continued his work to the end as editor-in-chief of the magazine, a latter-day Dr. Johnson in a field he had so tirelessly and effectively championed.

The Adventure of the Dauphin's Doll

by Ellery Queen

THERE IS A LAW among story-tellers, originally passed by Editors at the cries (they say) of their constituents, which states that stories about Christmas shall have children in them. This Christmas story is no exception; indeed, misopedists will complain that we have overdone it. And we confess in advance that this is also a story about Dolls, and that Santa Claus comes into it, and even a Thief; though as to this last, whoever he was—and that was one of the questions—he was certainly not Barabbas, even parabolically.

Another section of the statute governing Christmas stories provides that they shall incline towards Sweetness and Light. The first arises, of course, from the orphans and the never-souring savor of the annual Miracle; as for Light, it will be provided at the end, as usual, by that luminous prodigy, Ellery Queen. The reader of gloomier temper will also find a large measure of Darkness, in the person and works of one who, at least in Inspector Queen's harassed view, was surely the winged Prince of that region. His name, by the way, was not Satan, it was Comus; and this is paradox enow, since the original Comus, as everyone knows, was the god of festive joy and mirth, emotions not commonly associated with the Underworld. As Ellery struggled to embrace his phantom foe, he puzzled over this *non sequitur* in vain; in vain, that is, until Nikki Porter, no scorner of the obvious, suggested that he *might* seek the answer where any ordinary mortal would go at once. And there, to the great man's mortification, it was indeed to be found: On page 262b of Volume 6, *Coleb to Damasci*, of the 175th Anniversary edition of the *Encyclopaedia*

Britannica. A French conjuror of that name—Comus—performing in London in the year 1789 caused his wife to vanish from the top of a table—the very first time, it appeared, that this feat, uxorial or otherwise, had been accomplished without the aid of mirrors. To track his dark adversary's *nom de nuit* to its historic lair gave Ellery his only glint of satisfaction until that blessed moment when light burst all around him and exorcised the darkness, Prince and all.

But this is chaos.

Our story properly begins not with our invisible character but with our dead one.

Miss Ypson had not always been dead; *au contraire.* She had lived for seventy-eight years, for most of them breathing hard. As her father used to remark, "She was a very active little verb." Miss Ypson's father was a professor of Greek at a small Midwestern university. He had conjugated his daughter with the rather bewildered assistance of one of his brawnier students, an Iowa poultry heiress.

Professor Ypson was a man of distinction. Unlike most professors of Greek, he was a Greek professor of Greek, having been born Gerasymos Aghamos Ypsilonomon in Polykhnitos, on the island of Mytilini, "where," he was fond of recalling on certain occasions, "burning Sappho loved and sung"—a quotation he found unfailingly useful in his extracurricular activities; and, the Hellenic ideal notwithstanding, Professor Ypson believed wholeheartedly in immoderation in all things. This hereditary and cultural background explains the professor's interest in fatherhood—to his wife's chagrin, for Mrs. Ypson's own breeding prowess was confined to the barnyards on which her income was based—a fact of which her husband sympathetically reminded her whenever he happened to sire another wayward chick; he held their daughter to be nothing less than a biological miracle.

The professor's mental processes also tended to confuse Mrs. Ypson. She never ceased to wonder why instead of shortening his name to Ypson, her husband had not sensibly changed it to Jones. "My dear," the professor once replied, "you are an Iowa snob." "But nobody," Mrs. Ypson cried, "can spell it or pronounce it!" "This is a cross," murmured

Professor Ypson, "which we must bear with Ypsilanti." "Oh," said Mrs. Ypson.

There was invariably something Sibylline about his conversation. His favorite adjective for his wife was "ypsiliform," a term, he explained, which referred to the germinal spot at one of the fecundation stages in a ripening egg and which was, therefore, exquisitely *à propos*. Mrs. Ypson continued to look bewildered; she died at an early age.

And the professor ran off with a Kansas City variety girl of considerable talent, leaving his baptized chick to be reared by an eggish relative of her mother's, a Presbyterian named Jukes.

The only time Miss Ypson heard from her father—except when he wrote charming and erudite little notes requesting, as he termed it, *lucrum*—was in the fourth decade of his odyssey, when he sent her a handsome addition to her collection, a terra cotta play doll of Greek origin over three thousand years old which, unhappily, Miss Ypson felt duty-bound to return to the Brooklyn museum from which it had unaccountably vanished. The note accompanying her father's gift had said, whimsically: *"Timeo Danaos et dona ferentes."*

There was poetry behind Miss Ypson's dolls. At her birth the professor, ever harmonious, signalized his devotion to fecundity by naming her Cytherea. This proved the Olympian irony. For, it turned out, her father's philoprogenitiveness throbbed frustrate in her mother's stony womb; even though Miss Ypson interred five husbands of quite adequate vigor, she remained infertile to the end of her days. Hence it is classically tragic to find her, when all passion was spent, a sweet little old lady with a vague if eager smile who, under the name of her father, pattered about a vast and echoing New York apartment playing enthusiastically with dolls.

In the beginning they were dolls of common clay: a Billiken, a kewpie, a Kathe Kruse, a Patsy, a Foxy Grandpa, and so forth. But then, as her need increased, Miss Ypson began her fierce sack of the past.

Down into the land of Pharaoh she went for two pieces of thin desiccated board, carved and painted and with hair of strung beads, and legless—so that they might not run away

—which any connoisseur will tell you are the most superb specimens of ancient Egyptian paddle doll extant, far superior to those in the British Museum, although this fact will be denied in certain quarters.

Miss Ypson unearthed a foremother of "Letitia Penn," until her discovery held to be the oldest doll in America, having been brought to Philadelphia from England in 1699 by William Penn as a gift for a playmate of his small daughter's. Miss Ypson's find was a wooden-hearted "little lady" in brocade and velvet which had been sent by Sir Walter Raleigh to the first English child born in the New World. Since Virginia Dare had been born in 1587, not even the Smithsonian dared inpugn Miss Ypson's triumph.

On the old lady's racks, in her plate-glass cases, might be seen the wealth of a thousand childhoods, and some riches—for such is the genetics of dolls—possessed by children grown. Here could be found "fashion babies" from fourteenth century France, sacred dolls of the Orange Free State Fingo tribe, Satsuma paper dolls and court dolls from old Japan, beady-eyed "Kalifa" dolls of the Egyptian Sudan, Swedish birch-bark dolls, "Katcina" dolls of the Hopis, mammothtooth dolls of the Eskimos, feather dolls of the Chippewa, tumble dolls of the ancient Chinese, Coptic bone dolls, Roman dolls dedicated to Diana, *pantin* dolls which had been the street toys of Parisian exquisites before Madame Guillotine swept the boulevards, early Christian dolls in their *crèches* representing the Holy Family—to specify the merest handful of Miss Ypson's Briarean collection. She possessed dolls of pasteboard, dolls of animal skin, spool dolls, crabclaw dolls, eggshell dolls, cornhusk dolls, rag dolls, pinecone dolls with moss hair, stocking dolls, dolls of *bisque,* dolls of palm leaf, dolls of *papier-mâché,* even dolls made of seed pods. There were dolls forty inches tall, and there were dolls so little Miss Ypson could hide them in her gold thimble.

Cytherea Ypson's collection bestrode the centuries and took tribute of history. There was no greater—not the fabled playthings of Montezuma, or Victoria's, or Eugene Field's; not the collection at the Metropolitan, or the South Kensington, or the

royal palace in old Bucharest, or anywhere outside the en-
chantment of little girls' dreams.

It was made of Iowan eggs and the Attic shore, corn-fed
and myrtle-clothed; and it brings us at last to Attorney John
Somerset Bondling and his visit to the Queen residence one
December twenty-third not so very long ago.

December the twenty-third is ordinarily not a good time to
seek the Queens. Inspector Richard Queen likes his Christmas
old-fashioned; his turkey stuffing, for instance, calls for
twenty-two hours of over-all preparation and some of its ingredients are not readily found at the corner grocer's. And
Ellery is a frustrated gift-wrapper. For a month before
Christmas he turns his sleuthing genius to tracking down unusual wrapping papers, fine ribbons, and artistic stickers; and
he spends the last two days creating beauty.

So it was then when Attorney John S. Bondling called,
Inspector Queen was in his kitchen, swathed in a barbecue
apron, up to his elbows in *fines herbes*, while Ellery, behind
the locked door of his study, composed a secret symphony in
glittering fuchsia metallic paper, forest-green moiré ribbon,
and pine cones.

"It's almost useless," shrugged Nikki, studying Attorney
Bondling's card, which was as crackly-looking as Attorney Bondling. "You say you know the Inspector, Mr. Bondling?"

"Just tell him Bondling the estate lawyer," said Bondling
neurotically. "Park Row. He'll know."

"Don't blame me," said Nikki, "if you wind up in his stuffing. Goodness knows he's used everything else." And she
went for Inspector Queen.

While she was gone, the study door opened noiselessly for
one inch. A suspicious eye reconnoitered from the crack.

"Don't be alarmed," said the owner of the eye, slipping
through the crack and locking the door hastily behind him.
"Can't trust them, you know. Children, just children."

"Children!" Attorney Bondling snarled. "You're Ellery
Queen, aren't you?"

"Yes?"

"Interested in youth, are you? Christmas? Orphans, dolls,

that sort of thing?" Mr. Bondling went on in a remarkably nasty way.

"I suppose so."

"The more fool you. Ah, here's your father. Inspector Queen—!"

"Oh, that Bondling," said the old gentleman absently, shaking his visitor's hand. "My office called to say someone was coming up. Here, use my handkerchief; that's a bit of turkey liver. Know my son? His secretary, Miss Porter? What's on your mind, Mr. Bondling?"

"Inspector, I'm handling the Cytherea Ypson estate, and—"

"Nice meeting you, Mr. Bondling," said Ellery. "Nikki, the door is locked, so don't pretend you forgot the way to the bathroom . . ."

"Cytherea Ypson," frowned the Inspector. "Oh, yes. She died only recently."

"Leaving me with the headache," said Mr. Bondling bitterly, "of disposing of her Dollection."

"Her what?" asked Ellery, looking up from the key.

"Dolls—collection. Dollection. She coined the word."

Ellery put the key back in his pocket and stolled over to his armchair.

"Do I take this down?" sighed Nikki.

"Dollection," said Ellery.

"Spent about thirty years at it. Dolls!"

"Yes, Nikki, take it down."

"Well, well, Mr. Bondling," said Inspector Queen. "What's the problem? Christmas comes but once a year, you know."

"Will provides the Dollection be sold at auction," grated the attorney, "and the proceeds used to set up a fund for orphan children. I'm holding the public sale right after New Year's."

"Dolls and orphans, eh?" said the Inspector, thinking of Javanese black pepper and Country Gentleman Seasoning Salt.

"That's *nice*," beamed Nikki.

"Oh, is it?" said Mr. Bondling softly. "Apparently, young woman, you've never tried to satisfy a Surrogate. I've administered estates for nine years without a whisper against me, but let an estate involve the interests of just one little ba—little fatherless child, and you'd think from the Surrogate's attitude I was Bill Sykes himself!"

"My stuffing," began the Inspector.

"I've had those dolls catalogued. The result is frightening! Did you know there's no set market for the damnable things? And aside from a few personal possessions, the Dollection constitutes the old lady's entire estate. Sank every nickel she had in it."

"But it should be worth a fortune," protested Ellery.

"To whom, Mr. Queen? Museums always want such things as free and unencumbered gifts. I tell you, except for one item, those hypothetical orphans won't realize enough from that sale to keep them in—in bubble gum for two days!"

"Which item would that be, Mr. Bondling?"

"Number Eight-seventy-four," snapped the lawyer. "This one."

"Number Eight-seventy-four," read Inspector Queen from the fat catalogue Bondling had fished out of a large greatcoat pocket. "The Dauphin's Doll. Unique. Ivory figure of a boy Prince eight inches tall, clad in court dress, genuine ermine, brocade, velvet. Court sword in gold strapped to waist. Gold circlet crown surmounted by single blue brilliant diamond of finest water, weight approximately 49 carats—"

"How many carats?" exclaimed Nikki.

"Larger than the *Hope* and the *Star of South Africa,*" said Ellery, with a certain excitement.

"—appraised," continued his father, "at one hundred and ten thousand dollars."

"Expensive dollie."

"Indecent!" said Nikki.

"This indecent—I mean exquisite royal doll," the Inspector read on, "was a birthday gift from King Louis XVI of France to Louis Charles, his second son, who became dauphin at the death of his elder brother in 1789. The little dauphin was proclaimed Louis XVII by the royalists during the French Revolution while in custody of the *sans-culottes*. His fate is shrouded in mystery. Romantic, historic item."

"*Le prince perdu*. I'll say," muttered Ellery. "Mr. Bondling, is this on the level?"

"I'm an attorney, not an antiquarian," snapped their visitor. "There are documents attached, one of them a sworn statement—holograph—by Lady Charlotte Atkyns, the English actress-friend of the Capet family—she was in France during the Revolution—or purporting to be in Lady Charlotte's hand. It doesn't matter, Mr. Queen. Even if the history is bad, the diamond's good!"

"I take it this hundred-and-ten-thousand dollar dollie constitutes the bone, as it were, or that therein lies the rub?"

"You said it!" cried Mr. Bondling, cracking his knuckles in a sort of agony. "For my money the Dauphin's Doll is the only negotiable asset of that collection. And what's the old lady do? She provides by will that on the day preceding Christmas the Cytherea Ypson Dollection is to be publicly displayed . . . on the main floor of Nash's Department Store! *The day before Christmas, gentlemen!* Think of it!"

"But why?" asked Nikki, puzzled.

"Why? Who knows why? For the entertainment of New York's army of little beggars, I suppose! Have you any notion how many peasants pass through Nash's on the day before Christmas? My cook tells me—she's a very religious woman—it's like Armageddon."

"Day before Christmas," frowned Ellery. "That's tomorrow."

"It does sound chancy," says Nikki anxiously. Then she brightened. "Oh, well, maybe Nash's won't co-operate, Mr. Bondling."

"Oh, won't they!" howled Mr. Bondling. "Why, old lady Ypson had this stunt cooked up with that gang of peasant-purveyors for years! They've been snapping at my heels ever since the day she was put away!"

"It'll draw every crook in New York," said the Inspector, his gaze on the kitchen door.

"Orphans," said Nikki. "The orphans' interests *must* be protected." She looked at her employer accusingly.

"Special measures, Dad," said Ellery.

"Sure, sure," said the Inspector, rising. "Don't you worry

about this, Mr. Bondling. Now if you'll be kind enough to excu——"

"Inspector Queen," hissed Mr. Bondling, leaning forward tensely, "that is not all."

"Ah." Ellery briskly lit a cigaret. "There's a specific villain in this piece, Mr. Bondling, and you know who he is."

"I do," said the lawyer hollowly, "and then again I don't. I mean, it's Comus."

"Comus!" the Inspector screamed.

"Comus?" said Ellery slowly.

"Comus?" said Nikki. "Who dat?"

"Comus," nodded Mr. Bondling. "First thing this morning. Marched right into my office, bold as day—must have followed me; I hadn't got my coat off, my secretary wasn't even in. Marched in and tossed this card on my desk."

Ellery seized it. "The usual, Dad."

"His trademark," growled the Inspector, his lips working.

"But the card just says 'Comus,' " complained Nikki. "Who—?"

"Go on, Mr. Bondling!" thundered the Inspector.

"And he calmly announced to me," said Bondling, blotting his cheeks with an exhausted handkerchief, "that he's going to steal the Dauphin's Doll tomorrow, in Nash's."

"Oh, a maniac," said Nikki.

"Mr. Bondling," said the old gentleman in a terrible voice, "just what did this fellow look like?"

"Foreigner—black beard—spoke with a thick accent of some sort. To tell you the truth, I was so thunderstruck I didn't notice details. Didn't even chase him till it was to late."

The Queens shrugged at each other, Gallically.

"The old story," said the Inspector; the corners of his nostrils were greenish. "The brass of the colonel's monkey and when he does show himself nobody remembers anything but beards and foreign accents. Well, Mr. Bondling, with Comus in the game it's serious business. Where's the collection right now?"

"In the vaults of the Life Bank & Trust, Forty-third Street branch."

"What time are you to move it over to Nash's?"

"They wanted it this evening. I said nothing doing. I've made special arrangements with the bank, and the collection's to be moved at seven-thirty tomorrow morning."

"Won't be much time to set up," said Ellery thoughtfully, "before the store opens its doors." He glanced at his father.

"You leave Operation Dollie to us, Mr. Bondling," said the Inspector grimly. "Better give me a buzz this afternoon."

"I can't tell you, Inspector, how relieved I am—"

"Are you?" said the old gentleman sourly. "What makes you think he won't get it?"

When Attorney Bondling had left, the Queens put their heads together, Ellery doing most of the talking, as usual. Finally, the Inspector went into the bedroom for a session with his direct line to Headquarters.

"Anybody would think," sniffed Nikki, "you two were planning the defense of the Bastille. Who is this Comus, anyway?"

"We don't know, Nikki," said Ellery slowly. "Might be anybody. Began his criminal career about five years ago. He's in the grand tradition of Lupin—a saucy, highly intelligent rascal who's made stealing an art. He seems to take a special delight in stealing valuable things under virtually impossible conditions. Master of make-up—he's appeared in a dozen different disguises. And he's an uncanny mimic. Never been caught, photographed, or fingerprinted. Imaginative, daring —I'd say he's the most dangerous thief operating in the United States."

"If he's never been caught," said Nikki skeptically, "how do you know he commits these crimes?"

"You mean and not someone else?" Ellery smiled pallidly. "The techniques mark the thefts as his work. And then, like Arsène, he leaves a card—with the name 'Comus' on it—on the scene of each visit."

"Does he usually announce in advance that he's going to swipe the crown jewels?"

"No." Ellery frowned. "To my knowledge, this is the first such instance. Since he's never done anything without a reason, that visit to Bondling's office this morning must be part of his greater plan. I wonder if—"

The telephone in the living room rang clear and loud.

Nikki looked at Ellery. Ellery looked at the telephone.

"Do you suppose—?" began Nikki. But then she said, "Oh, it's too absurd!"

"Where Comus is involved," said Ellery wildly, "nothing is too absurd!" and he leaped for the phone. "Hello!"

"A call from an old friend," announced a deep and hollowish male voice. "Comus."

"Well," said Ellery. "Hello again."

"Did Mr. Bondling," asked the voice jovially, "persuade you to 'prevent' me from stealing the Dauphin's Doll in Nash's tomorrow?"

"So you know Bondling's been here."

"No miracle involved, Queen. I followed him. Are you taking the case?"

"See here, Comus," said Ellery. "Under ordinary circumstances I'd welcome the sporting chance to put you where you belong. But these circumstances are not ordinary. That doll represents the major asset of a future fund for orphaned children. I'd rather we didn't play catch with it. Comus, what do you say we call this one off?"

"Shall we say," asked the voice gently, "Nash's Department store—tomorrow?"

*   *   *

Thus the early morning of December twenty-fourth finds Messrs. Queen and Bondling, and Nikki Porter, huddled on the iron sidewalk of Forty-third Street before the holly-decked windows of the Life Bank & Trust Company, just outside a double line of armed guards. The guards form a channel between the bank entrance and an armored truck, down which Cytherea Ypson's Dollection flows swiftly. And all about gapes New York, stamping callously on the aged, icy face of the street against the uncharitable Christmas wind.

Now is the winter of his discontent, and Mr. Queen curses.

"I don't know what you're beefing about," moans Miss Porter.

"You and Mr. Bondling are bundled up like Yukon prospectors. Look at *me*."

"It's that rat-hearted public relations tripe from Nash's,"

says Mr. Queen murderously. "They all swore themselves to secrecy, Brother Rat included. Honor! Spirit of Christmas!"

"It was all over the radio last night," whimpers Mr. Bondling. "And in this morning's papers."

"I'll cut his creep's heart out. Here! Velie, keep those people away!"

Sergeant Velie says good-naturedly from the doorway of the bank, "You jerks stand back." Little does the Sergeant know the fate in store for him.

"Armored trucks," says Miss Porter bluishly. "Shotguns."

"Nikki, Comus made a point of informing us in advance that he meant to steal the Dauphin's Doll in Nash's Department Store. It would be just like him to have said that in order to make it easier to steal the doll en route."

"Why don't they hurry?" shivers Mr. Bondling. "Ah!"

Inspector Queen appears suddenly in the doorway. His hands clasp treasure.

"Oh!" cries Nikki.

New York whistles.

It is magnificence, an affront to democracy. But street mobs, like children, are royalists at heart.

New York whistles, and Sergeant Thomas Velie steps menacingly before Inspector Queen, Police Positive drawn, and Inspector Queen dashes across the sidewalk between the bristling lines of guards with the Dauphin's Doll in his embrace.

Queen the Younger vanishes, to materialize an instant later at the door of the armored truck.

"It's just immorally, hideously beautiful, Mr. Bondling," breathes Miss Porter, sparkly-eyed.

Mr. Bondling cranes, thinly.

ENTER *Santa Claus, with bell*.

*   *   *

Santa. Oyez, oyez. Peace, good will. Is that the dollie the radio's been yappin' about, folks?

Mr. B. Scram.

Miss P. Why, Mr. Bondling.

Mr. B. Well, he's got no business here. Stand back, er, Santa. Back!

Santa. What eateth you, my lean and angry friend? Have you no compassion at this season of the year?

Mr. B. Oh . . . Here! (*Clink.*) Now will you *kindly* . . . ?

Santa. Mighty pretty dollie. Where they takin' it, girlie?

Miss P. Over to Nash's, Santa.

Mr. B. You asked for it. Officer!!!

Santa (hurriedly). Little present for you girlie. Compliments of Santy. Merry, merry.

Miss P. For *me*? (EXIT *Santa, rapidly, with bell.*) Really, Mr. Bondling, was it necessary to . . . ?

Mr. B. Opium for the masses! What did that flatulent faker hand you, Miss Porter? What's in that unmentionable envelope?

Miss P. I'm sure I don't know, but isn't it the most touching idea? Why it's addressed to *Ellery*. Oh! Elleryyyyyy!

Mr. B (EXIT *excitedly*). Where is he? You—! Officer! Where did that baby-deceiver disappear to? A Santa Claus . . . !

Mr. Q (*entering on the run*). Yes? Nikki, what is it? What's happened?

Miss P. A man dressed as Santa Claus just handed me this envelope. It's addressed to you.

Mr. Q. Note? (*He snatches it, withdraws a miserable slice of paper from it on which is block-lettered in pencil a message which he reads aloud with considerable expression.*) "Dear Ellery, Don't you trust me? I said I'd steal the Dauphin in Nash's emporium today and that's exactly where I'm going to do it. Yours—" Signed . . .

Miss P (*craning*). "Comus." That Santa?

Mr. Q. (Sets his manly lips. An icy wind blows.)

*   *   *

Even the master had to acknowledge that their defenses against Comus were ingenious.

From the Display Department of Nash's they had requisitioned four miter-jointed counters of uniform length. These they had fitted together, and in the center of the hollow square thus formed they had erected a platform six feet high. On the counters, in plastic tiers, stretched the long lines of Miss Ypson's babies. Atop the platform, dominant, stood a great chair of handcarved oak, filched from the Swedish Modern section of the Fine Furniture Department; and on this Valhalla-like throne, a huge and rosy rotundity, sat Sergeant Thomas Velie of Police Headquarters, morosely grateful for the anonymity endowed by the scarlet suit and the jolly mask and whiskers of his appointed role.

Nor was this all. At a distance of six feet outside the counters shimmered a surrounding rampart of plate glass, borrowed in its various elements from *The Glass Home of the Future* display on the sixth floor rear, and assembled to shape an eight foot wall quoined with chrome, its glistening surfaces flawless except at one point, where a thick glass door had been installed. But the edges fitted intimately and there was a formidable lock in the door, the key to which lay buried in Mr. Queen's right trouser pocket.

It was 8:54 A.M. The Queens, Nikki Porter, and Attorney Bondling stood among store officials and an army of plainclothesmen on Nash's main floor surveying the product of their labors.

"I think that about does it," muttered Inspector Queen at last. "Men! Positions around the glass partition."

Twenty-four assorted gendarmes in mufti jostled one another. They took marked places about the wall, facing it and grinning up at Sergeant Velie. Sergeant Velie, from his throne, glared back.

"Hagstrom and Piggott—the door."

Two detectives detached themselves from a group of reserves. As they marched to the glass door, Mr. Bondling plucked at the Inspector's overcoat sleeve. "Can all these men be trusted, Inspector Queen?" he whispered. "I mean, this fellow Comus—"

"Mr. Bondling," replied the old gentleman coldly, "you do your job and let me do mine."

"But—"

"Picked men, Mr. Bondling! I picked 'em myself."

"Yes, yes, Inspector. I merely thought I'd—"

"Lieutenant Farber."

A little man with watery eyes stepped forward.

"Mr. Bondling, this is Lieutenant Geronimo Farber, Headquarters jewelry expert. Ellery?"

Ellery took the Dauphin's Doll from his greatcoat pocket, but he said, "If you don't mind, Dad, I'll keep holding on to it."

Somebody said, "Wow," and then there was silence.

"Lieutenant, this doll in my son's hand is the famous Dauphin's Doll with the diamond crown that—"

"Don't touch it, Lieutenant, please," said Ellery. "I'd rather nobody touched it."

"The doll," continued the Inspector, "has just been brought here from a bank vault which it ought never to have left, and Mr. Bondling, who's handling the Ypson estate, claims it's the genuine article. Lieutenant, examine the diamond and give us your opinion."

Lieutenant Farber produced a *loupe*. Ellery held the dauphin securely, and Farber did not touch it.

Finally, the expert said: "I can't pass an opinion about the doll itself, of course, but the diamond's a beauty. Easily worth a hundred thousand dollars at the present state of the market —maybe more. Looks like a very strong setting, by the way."

"Thanks Lieutenant. Okay, son," said the Inspector. "Go into your waltz."

Clutching the dauphin, Ellery strode over to the glass gate and unlocked it.

"This fellow Farber," whispered Attorney Bondling in the Inspector's hairy ear. "Inspector, are you absolutely sure he's—?"

"He's really Lieutenant Farber?" The Inspector controlled himself. "Mr. Bondling, I've known Gerry Farber for eighteen years. Calm yourself."

Ellery was crawling perilously over the nearest counter. Then, bearing the dauphin aloft, he hurried across the floor of the enclosure to the platform.

Sergeant Velie whined, "Maestro, how in hell am I going to sit here all day without washin' my hands?"

But Mr. Queen merely stooped and lifted from the floor a heavy little structure faced with black velvet consisting of a floor and a backdrop, with a two-armed chromium support. This object he placed on the platform directly between Sergeant Velie's massive legs.

Carefully, he stood the Dauphin's Doll in the velvet niche. Then he clambered back across the counter, went through the glass door, locked it with the key, and turned to examine his handiwork.

Proudly the prince's plaything stood, the jewel in his little golden crown darting "on pale electric streams" under the concentrated tide of a dozen of the most powerful floodlights in the possession of the great store.

"Velie," said Inspector Queen, "you're not to touch that doll. Don't lay a finger on it."

The Sergeant said, "Gaaaaa."

"You men on duty. Don't worry about the crowds. Your job is to keep watching that doll. You're not to take your eyes off it all day. Mr. Bondling, are you satisfied?" Mr. Bondling seemed about to say something, but then he hastily nodded. "Ellery?"

The great man smiled. "The only way he can get that bawbie," he said, "is by well-directed mortar fire or spells and incantations. Raise the portcullis!"

*   *   *

Then began the interminable day, *dies irae*, the last shopping day before Christmas. This is traditionally the day of the inert, the procrastinating, the undecided, and the forgetful, sucked at last into the mercantile machine by the perpetual pump of Time. If there is peace upon earth, it descends only afterward; and at no time, on the part of anyone embroiled, is there good will toward men. As Miss Porter expresses it, a cat fight in a bird cage would be more Christian.

But on this December twenty-fourth, in Nash's, the normal bedlam was augmented by the vast shrilling of thousands of children. It may be, as the Psalmist insists, that happy is the man that hath his quiver full of them; but no bowmen surrounded Miss Ypson's darlings this day, only detectives carrying revolvers, not a few of whom forbore to use same only by the most heroic self-discipline. In the black floods of humanity overflowing the main floor little folks darted about like electrically charged minnows, pursued by exasperated maternal shrieks and the imprecations of those whose shins and rumps and toes were at the mercy of hot, happy little limbs; indeed, nothing was sacred, and Attorney Bondling was seen to quail and wrap his greatcoat defensively about him against the savage innocence of childhood. But the guardians of the law, having been ordered to simulate store employees, possessed no such armor; and many a man earned his citation that day for unique cause. They stood in the millrace of the tide; it churned about them, shouting, "Dollies! *Dollies!*" until the very word lost its familiar meaning and became the insensate scream of a thousand Loreleis beckoning strong men to destruction below the eye-level of their diamond Light.

But they stood fast.

And Comus was thwarted. Oh, he tried. At 11:18 A.M. a tottering old man holding to the hand of a small boy tried to wheedle Detective Hagstrom into unlocking the glass door "so my grandson here—he's terrible nearsighted—can get a closer look at the pretty dollies." Detective Hagstrom roared, "Rube!" and the old gentleman dropped the little boy's hand violently and with remarkable agility lost himself in the crowd. A spot investigation revealed that, coming upon the boy, who had been crying for his mommy, the old gentleman had promised to find her. The little boy, whose name—he said—was Lance Morganstern, was removed to the Lost and Found Department; and everyone was satisfied that the great thief had finally launched his attack. Everyone, that is, but Ellery Queen. He seemed puzzled. When Nikki asked him why, he merely said: "Stupidity, Nikki. It's not in character."

At 1:46 P.M., Sergeant Velie sent up a distress signal. He had, it seemed, to wash his hands. Inspector Velie scrambled off his perch, clawed his way over the counter, and pounded urgently on the inner side of the glass door. Ellery let him out, relocking the door immediately, and the Sergeant's red-clad figure disappeared on the double in the general direction of the main-floor gentlemen's relief station, leaving the dauphin in solitary possession of the dais.

During the Sergeant's recess, Inspector Queen circulated among his men repeating the order of the day.

The episode of Velie's response to the summons of Nature caused a temporary crisis. For at the end of the specified fifteen minutes he had not returned. Nor was there a sign of him at the end of a half hour. An aide dispatched to the relief station reported back that the sergeant was not there. Fears of foul play were voiced at an emergency staff conference held then and there and counter-measures were being planned even as, at 2:35 P.M., the familiar Santa-clad bulk of the Sergeant was observed battling through the lines, pawing at his mask.

"Velie," snarled Inspector Queen, "where have you been?"

"Eating my lunch," growled the Sergeant's voice, defensively. "I been taking my punishment like a good soldier all this damn day, Inspector, but I draw the line at starvin' to death in the line of duty."

"Velie—!" choked the Inspector; but then he waved his hand feebly and said, "Ellery, let him back in there."

And that was very nearly all. The only other incident of note occurred at 4:22 P.M. A well-upholstered woman with a red face yelled, "Stop! Thief! He grabbed my pocketbook! Police!" about fifty feet from the Ypson exhibit. Ellery instantly shouted, *"It's a trick! Men, don't take your eyes off that doll!"* "It's Comus disguised as a woman," exclaimed Attorney Bondling, as Inspector Queen and Detective Hesse wrestled the female figure through the mob. She was now a wonderful shade of magenta. "What are you *doing?*" she screamed. "Don't arrest *me!*—catch that crook who stole my pocketbook!" "No dice, Comus," said the Inspector. "Wipe off that make-up." "McComas?" said the woman loudly. "My name is Rafferty, and all these folks saw it. He was a fat man with a mustache." "Inspector," said Nikki Porter, making a surreptitious scientific test. "This is a female. Believe me." And so, indeed it proved. All agreed that the mustachioed fat man had been Comus, creating a diversion in the desperate hope that the resulting confusion would give him an opportunity to steal the little dauphin.

"Stupid, stupid," muttered Ellery, gnawing his fingernails.

"Sure," grinned the Inspector. "We've got him nibbling his tail, Ellery. This was his do-or-die pitch. He's through."

"Frankly," sniffed Nikki, "I'm a little disappointed."

"Worried," said Ellery, "would be the word for me."

*   *   *

Inspector Queen was too case-hardened a sinner's nemesis to lower his guard at his most vulnerable moment. When the 5:30 bells bonged and the crowds began struggling toward the exits, he barked: "Men, stay at your posts. Keep watching that doll!" So all hands were on the *qui vive* even as the store emptied. The reserves kept hustling people out. Ellery, standing on an Information booth, spotted bottlenecks and waved his arms.

At 5:50 P.M. the main floor was declared out of the battle zone. All stragglers had been herded out. The only persons visible were the refugees trapped by the closing bell on the upper floors, and these were pouring out of elevators and funneled by a solid line of detectives and accredited store personnel to the doors. By 6:05 they were a trickle; by 6:10 even the trickle had dried up. And the personnel itself began to disperse.

"No, men!" called Ellery sharply from his observation post. "Stay where you are till all the store employees are out!" The counter clerks had long since disappeared.

Sergeant Velie's plaintive voice called from the other side of the glass door. "I got to get home and decorate my tree. Maestro, make with the key."

Ellery jumped down and hurried over to release him. Detective Piggott jeered, "Going to play Santa to your kids tomorrow morning, Velie?" at which the Sergeant managed even through his mask to project a four-letter word distinctly, forgetful of Miss Porter's presence, and stamped off toward the gentlemen's relief station.

"Where you going, Velie?" asked the Inspector, smiling.

"I got to get out of these x-and-dash Santy clothes somewheres, don't I?" came back the Sergeant's mask-muffled tones, and he vanished in a thunderclap of his fellow-officers' laughter.

"Still worried, Mr. Queen?" chuckled the Inspector.

"I don't understand it." Ellery shook his head. "Well, Mr. Bondling, there's your dauphin, untouched by human hands."

"Yes. Well!" Attorney Bondling wiped his forehead happily. "I don't profess to understand it, either, Mr. Queen. Unless it's simply another case of an inflated reputation . . ." He clutched the Inspector suddenly. "Those men!" he whispered. *"Who are they?"*

"Relax, Mr. Bondling," said the Inspector good-naturedly. "It's just the men to move the dolls back to the bank. Wait a minute, you men! Perhaps, Mr. Bondling, we'd better see the dauphin back to the vaults ourselves."

"Keep those fellows back," said Ellery to the Headquarters men, quietly, and he followed the Inspector and Mr. Bondling into the enclosure. They pulled two of the counters apart at one corner and strolled over to the platform. The dauphin was winking at them in a friendly way. They stood looking at him.

"Cute little devil," said the Inspector.

"Seems silly now," beamed Attorney Bondling. "Being so worried all day."

"Comus must have had *some* plan," mumbled Ellery.

"Sure," said the Inspector. "That old man disguise. And that purse-snatching act."

"No, no, Dad. Something clever. He's always pulled something clever."

"Well, there's the diamond," said the lawyer comfortably. "He didn't."

"Disguise . . ." muttered Ellery. "It's always been a disguise. Santa Claus costume—he used that once—this morning in front of the bank . . . Did we see a Santa Claus around here today?"

"Just Velie," said the Inspector, grinning. "And I hardly think—"

"Wait a moment, please," said Attorney Bondling in a very odd voice.

He was staring at the Dauphin's Doll.

"Wait for what, Mr. Bondling?"

"What's the matter?" said Ellery, also in a very odd voice.

"But . . . not possible . . ." stammered Bondling. He snatched the doll from its black velvet repository. *"No!"* he howled. *"This isn't the dauphin! It's a fake—a copy!"*

Something happened in Mr. Queen's head— a little *click!* like the turn of a switch. And there was light.

"Some of you men!" he roared. *"After Santa Claus!"*

"Who, Mr. Queen?"

"What's he talkin' about?"

"After who, Ellery?" gasped Inspector Queen.

"What's the matter?"

"I dunno!"

"Don't stand here! *Get him!*" screamed Ellery, dancing up and down. "The man I just let out of here! The Santa who made for the men's room!"

Detectives started running, wildly.

"But Ellery," said a small voice, and Nikki found that it was her own, "that was Sergeant Velie."

"It was *not* Velie, Nikki! When Velie ducked out just before two o'clock to relieve himself, *Comus waylaid him!* It was Comus who came back in Velie's Santa Claus rig, wearing Velie's whiskers and mask! *Comus has been on this platform all afternoon!*" He tore the dauphin from Attorney Bondling's grasp. "Copy . . . ! Somehow he did it, he did it."

"But Mr. Queen," whispered Attorney Bondling, "his voice. He spoke to us . . . in Sergeant Velie's voice."

"Yes, Ellery," Nikki heard herself saying.

"I told you yesterday Comus is a great mimic, Nikki. Lieutenant Farber! Is Farber still here?"

The jewelry expert, who had been gaping from a distance, shook his head as if to clear it and shuffled into the enclosure.

"Lieutenant," said Ellery in a strangled voice. "Examine this diamond . . . I mean, *is* it a diamond?"

Inspector Queen removed his hands from his face and said froggily, "Well, Gerry?"

Lieutenant Farber squinted once through his *loupe*. "The hell you say. It's strass—"

"It's what?" said the Inspector piteously.

"Strass, Dick—lead glass—paste. Beautiful job of imitation—as nice as I've ever seen."

"Lead me to that Santa Claus," whispered Inspector Queen.

But Santa Claus was being led to him. Struggling in the grip of a dozen detectives, his red coat ripped off, his red pants around his ankles, but his whiskery mask still on his face, came a large shouting man.

"But I tell you," he was roaring, "I'm Sergeant Tom Velie! Just take the mask off—that's all!"

"It's a pleasure," growled Detective Hagstrom, trying to

break their prisoner's arm, "we're reservin' for the Inspector."

"Hold him, boys," whispered the Inspector. He struck like a cobra. His hand came away with Santa's face.

And there, indeed, was Sergeant Velie.

"Why it's Velie," said the Inspector wonderingly.

"I only told you that a thousand times," said the Sergeant, folding his great hairy arms across his great hairy chest. "Now who's the so-and-so who tried to bust my arm?" Then he said, "My pants!" and, as Miss Porter turned delicately away, Detective Hagstrom humbly stooped and raised Sergeant Velie's pants.

"Never mind that," said a cold, remote voice.

It was the master, himself.

"Yeah?" said Sergeant Velie, hostilely.

"Velie, weren't you attacked when you went to the men's room just before two?"

"Do I look like the attackable type?"

"You did go to lunch?—in person?"

"And a lousy lunch it was."

"It was *you* up here among the dolls all afternoon?"

"Nobody else, Maestro. Now, my friends, I want action. Fast patter. What's this all about? Before," said Sergeant Velie softly, "I lose my temper."

While divers Headquarters orators delivered impromptu periods before the silent Sergeant, Inspector Richard Queen spoke.

"Ellery. Son. How in the name of the second sin did he do it?"

"Pa," replied the master, "you got me."

*   *   *

Deck the hall with boughs of holly, but not if your name is Queen on the evening of a certain December twenty-fourth. If your name is Queen on that lamentable evening you are seated in the living room of a New York apartment uttering no falalas but staring miserably into a somber fire. And you have company. The guest list is short, but select. It numbers two, a Miss Porter and a Sergeant Velie, and they are no comfort.

No, no ancient Yuletide carol is being trolled; only the silence sings.

Wail in your crypt, Cytherea Ypson; all was for nought; your little dauphin's treasure lies not in the empty coffers of the orphans but in the hot clutch of one who took his evil inspiration from a long-crumbled specialist in vanishments.

Speech was spent. Should a wise man utter vain knowledge and fill his belly with the east wind? He who talks too much commits a sin, says the Talmud. He also wastes his breath; and they had now reached the point of conservation, having exhausted the available supply.

Item: Lieutenant Geronimo Farber of Police Headquarters had examined the diamond in the genuine dauphin's crown a matter of seconds before it was conveyed to its sanctuary in the enclosure. Lieutenant Farber had pronounced the diamond a diamond, and not merely a diamond, but a diamond worth in his opinion over one hundred thousand dollars.

Question: Had Lieutenant Farber lied?

Answer: Lieutenant Farber was (a) a man of probity, tested in a thousand fires, and (b) he was incorruptible. To (a) and (b) Inspector Richard Queen attested violently, swearing by the beard of his personal Prophet.

Question: Had Lieutenant Farber been mistaken?

Answer: Lieutenant Farber was a nationally famous police expert in the field of precious stones. It must be presumed that he knew a real diamond from a piece of lapidified glass.

Question: Had it *been* Lieutenant Farber?

Answer: By the same beard of the identical prophet, it had been Lieutenant Farber and no facsimile.

Conclusion: The diamond Lieutenant Farber had examined immediatley preceding the opening of Nash's doors that morning had been the veritable diamond of the dauphin, the doll had been the veritable Dauphin's Doll, and it was this genuine article which Ellery with his own hands had carried into the glass-enclosed fortress and deposited between the authenticated Sergeant Velie's verified feet.

Item: All day—specifically, between the moment the dauphin had been deposited in his niche until the moment he was discovered to be a fraud; that is, during the total period in which a theft-and-substitution was even theoretically possible —no person whatsoever, male or female, adult or child, had set foot within the enclosure except Sergeant Thomas Velie, alias Santa Claus.

> *Question:* Had Sergeant Velie switched dolls, carrying the genuine dauphin concealed in his Santa Claus suit, to be cached for future retrieval or turned over to Comus or a confederate of Comus's, during one of his two departures from the enclosure?
>
> *Answer (by Sergeant Velie):**
>
> *Confirmation:* Some dozens of persons with police training and specific instructions, not to mention the Queens themselves, Miss Porter, and Attorney Bondling, testified unqualifiedly that Sergeant Velie had not touched the doll, at any time, all day.
>
> *Conclusion:* Sergeant Velie could not have stolen, and therefore he did not steal, the Dauphin's Doll.

Item: All those deputized to watch the doll swore that they had done so without lapse or hindrance the everlasting day; moreover, that at no time had anything touched the doll— human or mechanical—either from inside or outside the enclosure.

> *Question:* The human vessel being frail, could those so swearing have been in error? Could their attention have wandered through weariness, boredom, *et cetera?*
>
> *Answer:* Yes, but not all at the same time, by the laws of probability. And during the only two diversions of the danger period, Ellery himself testified that he had kept his eyes on the dauphin and that nothing whatsoever had approached or threatened it.

Item: Despite all of the foregoing, at the end of the day they had found the real dauphin gone and a worthless copy in its place.

"It's brilliantly, unthinkably clever," said Ellery at last. "A master illusion. For, of course, it *was* an illusion . . ."

"Witchcraft," groaned the Inspector.

*Deleted.—*Editor.*

"Mass mesmerism," suggested Nikki Porter.

"Mass bird gravel," growled the Sergeant.

Two hours later Ellery spoke again.

"So Comus had a worthless copy of the dauphin all ready for the switch," he muttered. "It's a world-famous dollie, been illustrated countless times, minutely described, photographed . . . All ready for the switch, but how did he make it? How? How?"

"You said that," said the Sergeant, "once or forty-two times."

"The bells are tolling," sighed Nikki, "but for whom? Not for us." And indeed, while they slumped there, Time, which Seneca named father of truth, had crossed the threshold of Christmas; and Nikki looked alarmed, for as that glorious song of old came upon the midnight clear, a great light spread from Ellery's eyes and beatified the whole contorted countenance, so that peace sat there, the peace that approximateth understanding; and he threw back that noble head and laughed with the merriment of an innocent child.

"Hey," said Sergeant Velie, staring.

"Son," began Inspector Queen, half-rising from his armchair; when the telephone rang.

"Beautiful!" roared Ellery. "Oh, exquisite! How did Comus make the switch, eh? Nikki—"

"From somewhere," said Nikki, handing him the telephone receiver, "a voice is calling, and if you ask me it's saying 'Comus.' Why not ask him?"

"Comus," whispered the Inspector, shrinking.

"Comus," echoed the Sergeant, baffled.

"Comus?" said Ellery heartily. "How nice. Hello there! Congratulations."

"Why, thank you," said the familiar deep and hollow voice. "I called to express my appreciation for a wonderful day's sport and to wish you the merriest kind of Yuletide."

"You anticipate a rather merry Christmas yourself, I take it."

"Laeti triumphantes," said Comus jovially.

"And the orphans?"

"They have my best wishes. But I won't detain you, Ellery.

If you'll look at the doormat outside your apartment door, you'll find on it—in the spirit of the season—a little gift, with the compliments of Comus. Will you remember me to Inspector Queen and Attorney Bondling?"

Ellery hung up, smiling.

On the doormat he found the true Dauphin's Doll, intact except for a contemptible detail. The jewel in the little golden crown was missing.

*   *   *

"It was," said Ellery later, over pastrami sandwiches, "a fundamentally simple problem. All great illusions are. A valuable object is placed in full view in the heart of an impenetrable enclosure, it is watched hawkishly by dozens of thoroughly screened and reliable trained persons, it is never out of their view, it is not once touched by human hand or any other agency, and yet, at the expiration of the danger period, it is gone—exchanged for a worthless copy. Wonderful. Amazing. It defies the imagination. Actually, it's susceptible—like all magical hocus-pocus—to immediate solution if only one is able—as I was not—to ignore the wonder and stick to the fact. But then, the wonder is there for precisely that purpose: to stand in the way of the fact.

"What is the fact?" continued Ellery, helping himself to a dill pickle. "The fact is that between the time the doll was placed on the exhibit platform and the time the theft was discovered no one and no thing touched it. Therefore between the time the doll was placed on the platform and the time the theft was discovered *the dauphin could not have been stolen*. It follows, simply and inevitably, that the dauphin must have been stolen *outside that period*.

"Before the period began? No. I placed the authentic dauphin inside the enclosure with my own hands; at or about the beginning of the period, then, no hand but mine had touched the doll—not even, you'll recall, Lieutenant Farber's.

"Then the dauphin must have been stolen after the period closed."

Ellery brandished half the pickle. "And who," he demanded solemnly, "is the only one besides myself who handled that doll after the period closed and before Lieutenant Farber pronounced the diamond to be paste? The only one?"

The Inspector and the Sergeant exchanged puzzled glances, and Nikki looked blank.

"Why, Mr. Bondling," said Nikki, "and he doesn't count."

"He counts very much, Nikki," said Ellery, reaching for the mustard, "because the facts say Bondling stole the dauphin at that time."

"Bondling!" The Inspector paled.

"I don't get it," complained Sergeant Velie.

"Ellery, you must be wrong," said Nikki. "At the time Mr. Bondling grabbed the doll off the platform, the theft had already taken place. It was the worthless copy he picked up."

"That," said Ellery, reaching for another sandwich, "was the focal point of his illusion. How do we know it was the worthless copy he picked up? Why, he said so. Simple, eh? He said so, and like the dumb bunnies we were, we took his unsupported word as gospel."

"That's right!" mumbled his father. "We didn't actually examine the doll till quite a few seconds later."

"Exactly," said Ellery in a munchy voice. "There was a short period of beautiful confusion, as Bondling knew there would be. I yelled to the boys to follow and grab Santa Claus —I mean, the Sergeant here. The detectives were momentarily demoralized. You, Dad, were stunned. Nikki looked as if the roof had fallen in. I essayed an excited explanation. Some detectives ran; others milled around. And while all this was happening—during those few moments when nobody was watching the genuine doll in Bondling's hand because everyone thought it was a fake—Bondling calmly slipped it into one of his greatcoat pockets and from the other produced the worthless copy which he'd been carrying there all day. When I did turn back to him, it was the copy I grabbed from his hand. And his illusion was complete.

"I know," said Ellery dryly. "It's rather on the let-down side. That's why illusionists guard their professional secrets so closely; knowledge is disenchantment. No doubt the incredulous amazement aroused in his periwigged London audience by Comus the French conjuror's dematerialization of his wife from the top of a table would have suffered the same fate if he'd revealed the trap door through which she had dropped. A good trick, like a good woman, is best in the dark. Sergeant, have another pastrami."

"Seems like funny chow to be eating early Christmas morning," said the Sergeant, reaching. Then he stopped. Then he said, "Bondling," and shook his head.

"Now that we know it was Bondling," said the Inspector, who had recovered a little, "it's a cinch to get that diamond back. He hasn't had time to dispose of it yet. I'll just give downtown a buzz—"

"Wait, Dad," said Ellery.

"Wait for what?"

"Whom are you going to sic the dogs on?"

"What?"

"You're going to call Headquarters, get a warrant, and so on. Who's your man?"

The Inspector felt his head. "Why . . . Bondling, didn't you say?"

"It might be wise," said Ellery, thoughtfully searching with his tongue for a pickle seed, "to specify his alias."

"Alias?" said Nikki. "Does he have one?"

"What alias, Son?"

"Comus."

"*Comus!*"

"*Comus?*"

"Comus."

"Oh, come off it," said Nikki, pouring herself a shot of coffee, straight, for she was in training for the Inspector's Christmas dinner. "How could Bondling be Comus when Bondling was with us all day?—and Comus kept making disguised appearances all over the place . . . that Santa who gave me the note in front of the bank—the old man who kidnapped Lance Morganstern—the fat man with the mustache who snatched Mrs. Rafferty's purse."

"Yeah," said the Sergeant. "How?"

"These illusions die hard," said Ellery. "Wasn't it Comus who phoned a few minutes ago to rag me about the theft? Wasn't it Comus who said he'd left the stolen dauphin— minus the diamond—on our doormat? Therefore Comus is Bondling.

"I told you Comus never does anything without a good reason," said Ellery. "Why did 'Comus' announce to 'Bondling' that he was *going* to steal the Dauphin's Doll? Bondling told us that—putting the finger on his *alter ego*—because he wanted us to believe he and Comus were separate individuals. He wanted us to watch for *Comus* and take *Bondling* for granted. In tactical execution of this strategy, Bondling provided us with three 'Comus'-appearances during the day—obviously, confederates.

"Yes," said Ellery, "I think, Dad, you'll find on backtracking that the great thief you've been trying to catch for five years has been a respectable estate attorney on Park Row all the time, shedding his quiddities and his quillets at night in favor of the soft shoe and the dark lantern. And now he'll have to exchange them all for a number and a grilled door. Well, well, it couldn't have happened at a more appropriate season; there's an old English proverb that says the Devil makes his Christmas pie of lawyers' tongues. Nikki, pass the pastrami."

Highlights of last year's
Wassail Bowl Game

"That's enough—you don't have to carry the ball any further!"

The name Thomas Hardy has meant sure-fire gloom and doom for a century. To students of his craft, a Hardy work, set amid the wild midlands of Wessex, promises fatalism and man struggling unsuccessfully against nature. To the dedicated undergraduate embarking on a course in English literature, a comprehensive assignment on Hardy becomes like an extended holiday with a religious martyr. First depression sets in. Later only electro-shock therapy can restore the will to live. No one has ever gone to Thomas Hardy for light reading.

Some of this grimness surely reflects Hardy's own frustrations with life. He had always hoped to become a writer and poet but a strong-willed father dictated a career in architecture. Only after his literary success was assured did he devote himself entirely to the work he loved.

What a surprise then, to discover this almost frivolous adventure of a juvenile detective among so much adversity and pessimism. "The Thieves Who Couldn't Help Sneezing" is startling proof that man cannot live on misery alone. Not even Thomas Hardy.

The Thieves Who Couldn't Help Sneezing

by Thomas Hardy

MANY YEARS AGO, when oak-trees now past their prime were about as large as elderly gentlemen's walking-sticks, there lived in Wessex a yeoman's son, whose name was Hubert. He was about fourteen years of age, and was as remarkable for his candor and lightness of heart as for his physical courage, of which, indeed, he was a little vain.

One cold Christmas Eve his father, having no other help at hand, sent him on an important errand to a small town several miles from home. He travelled on horseback, and was detained by the business till a late hour the evening. At last, however, it was completed; he returned to the inn, the horse was saddled, and he started on his way. His journey homeward lay through the Vale of Blackmore, a fertile but somewhat lonely district, with heavy clay roads and crooked lanes. In those days, too, a great part of it was thickly wooded.

It must have been about nine o'clock when, riding along amid the overhanging trees upon his stout-legged cob, Jerry, and singing a Christmas carol, to be in harmony with the season, Hubert fancied that he heard a noise among the boughs. This recalled to his mind that the spot he was traversing bore an evil name. Men had been waylaid there. He looked at Jerry, and wished he had been of any other color than light gray; for on this account the docile animal's form was visible even here in the dense shade. "What do I care?" he said aloud, after a few minutes of reflection. "Jerry's legs are too nimble to allow any highwayman to come near me."

"Ha! ha! indeed," was said in a deep voice; and the next moment a man darted from the thicket on his right hand, another man from the thicket on his left hand, and another from a tree-trunk a few yards away. Hubert's bridle was seized, he was pulled from his horse, and although he struck out with all his might, as a brave boy would naturally do, he was over-powered. His arms were tied behind him, his legs bound tightly together, and he was thrown into the ditch. The robbers, whose faces he could now dimly perceive to be artificially blackened, at once departed, leading off the horse.

As soon as Hubert had a little recovered himself, he found that by great exertion he was able to extricate his legs from the cord; but, in spite of every endeavor, his arms remained bound as fast as before. All, therefore, that he could do was to rise to his feet and proceed on his way with his arms behind him, and trust to chance for getting them unfastened. He knew that it would be impossible to reach home on foot that night, and in such a condition; but he walked on. Owing to the confusion which this attack caused in his brain, he lost his way, and would have been inclined to lie down and rest till morning among the dead leaves had he not known the danger of sleeping without wrappers in a frost so severe. So he wandered further onwards, his arms wrung and numbed by the cord which pinioned him, and his heart aching for the loss of poor Jerry, who never had been known to kick, or bite, or show a single vicious habit. He was not a little glad when he discerned through the trees a distant light. Towards this he made his way, and presently found himself in front of a large mansion with flanking wings, gables, and towers, the battlements and chimneys showing their shapes against the stars.

All was silent; but the door stood wide open, it being from this door that the light shone which had attracted him. On entering he found himself in a vast apartment arranged as a dining-hall, and brilliantly illuminated. The walls were covered with a great deal of dark wainscoting, formed into moulded panels, carvings, closet-doors, and the usual fittings of a house of that kind. But what drew his attention most was the large table in the midst of the hall, upon which was spread a sumptuous supper, as yet untouched. Chairs were placed around, and it appeared as if something had occurred to interrupt the meal just at the time when all were ready to begin.

Even had Hubert been so inclined, he could not have eaten

in his helpless state, unless by dipping his mouth into the
dishes, like a pig or cow. He wished first to obtain assistance;
and was about to penetrate further into the house for that purpose when he heard hasty footsteps in the porch and the
words, "Be quick!" uttered in the deep voice which had
reached him when he was dragged from the horse. There was
only just time for him to dart under the table before three men
entered the dining-hall. Peeping from beneath the hanging
edges of the tablecloth, he perceived that their faces, too,
were blackened, which at once removed any remaining doubts
he may have felt that these were the same thieves.

"Now, then," said the first—the man with the deep voice
—"let us hide ourselves. They will all be back again in a
minute. That was a good trick to get out of the house—eh?"

"Yes. You well imitated the cries of a man in distress," said
the second.

"Excellently," said the third.

"But they will soon find out that it was a false alarm.
Come, where shall we hide? It must be some place we can
stay in for two or three hours, till all are in bed and asleep.
Ah! I have it. Come this way! I have learnt that the further
closet is not opened once in a twelve-month; it will serve our
purpose exactly."

The speaker advanced into a corridor which led from the
hall. Creeping a little farther forward, Hubert could discern
that the closet stood at the end, facing the dining-hall. The
thieves entered it, and closed the door. Hardly breathing, Hubert glided forward, to learn a little more of their intention, if
possible; and, coming close, he could hear the robbers whispering about the different rooms where the jewels, plate, and
other valuables of the house were kept, which they plainly
meant to steal.

They had not been long in hiding when a gay chattering of
ladies and gentlemen was audible on the terrace without. Hubert felt that it would not do to be caught prowling about the
house, unless he wished to be taken for a robber himself; and
he slipped softly back to the hall, out the door, and stood in a
dark corner of the porch, where he could see everything without being himself seen. In a moment or two a whole troop of
personages came gliding past him into the house. There were

an elderly gentleman and lady, eight or nine young ladies, as many young men, besides half-a-dozen menservants and maids. The mansion had apparently been quite emptied of its occupants.

"Now, children and young people, we will resume our meal," said the old gentleman. "What the noise could have been I cannot understand. I never felt so certain in my life that there was a person being murdered outside my door."

Then the ladies began saying how frightened they had been, and how they had expected an adventure, and how it had ended in nothing at all.

"Wait a while," said Hubert to himself. "You'll have adventure enough by-and-by, ladies."

It appeared that the young men and women were married sons and daughters of the old couple, who had come that day to spend Christmas with their parents.

The door was then closed, Hubert being left outside in the porch. He thought this a proper moment for asking their assistance; and, since he was unable to knock with his hands, began boldly to kick the door.

"Hullo! What disturbance are you making here?" said a footman who opened it; and, seizing Hubert by the shoulder, he pulled him into the dining-hall. "Here's a strange boy I have found making a noise in the porch, Sir Simon."

Everybody turned.

"Bring him forward," said Sir Simon, the old gentleman before mentioned. "What were you doing there, my boy?"

"Why, his arms are tied!" said one of the ladies.

"Poor fellow!" said another.

Hubert at once began to explain that he had been waylaid on his journey home, robbed of his horse, and mercilessly left in this condition by the thieves.

"Only to think of it!" exclaimed Sir Simon.

"That's a likely story," said one of the gentlemen-guests, incredulously.

"Doubtful, hey?" asked Sir Simon.

"Perhaps he's a robber himself," suggested a lady.

"There is a curiously wild, wicked look about him, certainly, now that I examine him closely," said the old mother.

Hubert blushed with shame; and, instead of continuing his

story, and relating that robbers were concealed in the house, he doggedly held his tongue, and half resolved to let them find out their danger for themselves.

"Well, untie him," said Sir. Simon. "Come, since it is Christmas Eve, we'll treat him well. Here, my lad; sit down in that empty seat at the bottom of the table, and make as good a meal as you can. When you have had your fill we will listen to more particulars of your story."

The feast then proceeded; and Hubert, now at liberty, was not at all sorry to join in. The more they ate and drank the merrier did the company become; the wine flowed freely, the logs flared up the chimney, the ladies laughed at the gentlemen's stories; in short, all went as noisily and as happily as a Christmas gathering in old times possibly could do.

Hubert, in spite of his hurt feelings at their doubts of his honesty, could not help being warmed both in mind and in body by the good cheer, the scene, and the example of hilarity set by his neighbors. At last he laughed as heartily at their stories and repartees as the old Baronet, Sir Simon, himself. When the meal was almost over one of the sons, who had drunk a little too much wine, after the manner of men in that century, said to Hubert, "Well, my boy, how are you? Can you take a pinch of snuff?" He held out one of the snuff-boxes which were then becoming common among young and old throughout the country.

"Thank you," said Hubert, accepting a pinch.

"Tell the ladies who you are, what you are made of, and what you can do," the young man continued, slapping Hubert upon the shoulder.

"Certainly," said our hero, drawing himself up, and thinking it best to put a bold face on the matter. "I am a traveling magician."

"Indeed!"

"What shall we hear next?"

"Can you call up spirits from the vasty deep, young wizard?"

"I can conjure up a tempest in a cupboard," Hubert replied.

"Ha-ha!" said the old Baronet, pleasantly rubbing his hands. "We must see this performance. Girls, don't go away: here's something to be seen."

"Not dangerous, I hope?" said the old lady.

Hubert rose from the table. "Hand me your snuff-box, please," he said to the young man who had made free with him. "And now," he continued, "without the least noise, follow me. If any of you speak it will break the spell."

They promised obedience. He entered the corridor, and, taking off his shoes, went on tiptoe to the closet door, the guests advancing in a silent group at a little distance behind him. Hubert next placed a stool in front of the door, and, by standing upon it, was tall enough to reach to the top. He then, just as noiselessly, poured all the snuff from the box along the upper edge of the door, and, with a few short puffs of breath, blew the snuff through the chink into the interior of the closet. He held up his finger to the assembly, that they might be silent.

"Dear me, what's that?" said the old lady, after a minute or two had elapsed.

A suppressed sneeze had come from inside the closet.

Hubert held up his finger again.

"How very singular," whispered Sir Simon. "This is most interesting."

Hubert took advantage of the moment to gently slide the bolt of the closet door into its place. "More snuff," he said, calmly.

"More snuff," said Sir Simon. Two or three gentlemen passed their boxes, and the contents were blown in at the top of the closet. Another sneeze, not quite so well suppressed as the first, was heard: then another, which seemed to say that it would not be suppressed under any circumstances whatever. At length there arose a perfect storm of sneezes.

"Excellent, excellent for one so young!" said Sir Simon. "I am much interested in this trick of throwing the voice—called, I believe, ventriloquism."

"More snuff," said Hubert.

"More snuff," said Sir Simon. Sir Simon's man brought a large jar of the best scented Scotch.

Hubert once more charged the upper chink of the closet, and blew the snuff into the interior, as before. Again he charged, and again, emptying the whole contents of the jar. The tumult of sneezes became really extraordinary to listen to—there was no cessation. It was like wind, rain, and sea battling in a hurricane.

"I believe there are men inside, and that it is no trick at all!" exclaimed Sir Simon, the truth flashing on him.

"There are," said Hubert. "They are come to rob the house, and they are the same who stole my horse."

The sneezes changed to spasmodic groans. One of the thieves, hearing Hubert's voice, cried, "Oh! mercy! mercy! Let us out of this!"

"Where's my horse?" said Hubert.

"Tied to the tree in the hollow behind Short's Gibbet. Mercy! mercy! let us out, or we shall die of suffocation!"

All the Christmas guests now perceived that this was no longer sport, but serious earnest. Guns and cudgels were procured; all the men-servants were called in, and arranged in position outside the closet. At a signal Hubert withdrew the bolt, and stood on the defensive. But the three robbers, far from attacking them, were found crouching in the corner, gasping for breath. They made no resistance; and, being pinioned, were placed in an outhouse till the morning.

Hubert now gave the remainder of his story to the assembled company, and was profusely thanked for the services he had rendered. Sir Simon pressed him to stay over the night, and accept the use of the best bedroom the house afforded, which had been occupied by Queen Elizabeth and King Charles successively when on their visits to this part of the country. But Hubert declined, being anxious to find his horse Jerry, and to test the truth of the robbers' statements concerning him.

Several of the guests accompanied Hubert to the spot behind the gibbet, alluded to by the thieves as where Jerry was hidden. When they reached the knoll and looked over, behold! there the horse stood, uninjured, and quite unconcerned. At sight of Hubert he neighed joyfully; and nothing could exceed Hubert's gladness at finding him. He mounted, wished his friends "Good-night!" and cantered off in the direction they pointed out, reaching home safely about four o'clock in the morning.

Gahan Wilson

It is unusual to see the name Stanley Ellin without a word like *brilliant* or *great* preceding it. He has been synonymous with quality in the mystery field for some 34 years. In 1981 the Mystery Writers of America honored him as one of their Grand Masters.

A story such as "Death on Christmas Eve" is an instructive joy to any student interested in the art of writing. The pacing, the characterization, the description and plot development all mesh like the parts of a Swiss watch to produce a work of art that really "ticks."

He started his career with a bang back in 1948 with the much-admired story "The Specialty of the House," and continued delivering new small masterpieces at the rate of one a year to a grateful readership until his death in 1986.

Perhaps this deliberation explains his success, for an Ellin story is never out of print for long. Anthologists would be hard pressed to put together a first-rate collection without him. Fortunately, they seldom try.

In 1979, his first 35 stories were assembled into a collection called The Specialty of the House and Other Stories. *Like Chopin's nocturnes, Escoffier's recipes, and Hitchcock's suspense films, it is an assemblage of work so distinguished as to redefine the word greatness in that art.*

Death on Christmas Eve

by Stanley Ellin

As a child I had been vastly impressed by the Boerum house. It was fairly new then, and glossy; a gigantic pile of Victorian rickrack, fret-work, and stained glass, flung together in such chaotic profusion that it was hard to encompass in one glance. Standing before it this early Christmas Eve, however, I could find no echo of that youthful impression. The gloss was long since gone; woodwork, glass, metal, all were merged to a dreary gray, and the shades behind the windows were drawn completely so that the house seemed to present a dozen blindly staring eyes to the passerby.

When I rapped my stick sharply on the door, Celia opened it.

"There is a doorbell right at hand," she said. She was still wearing the long outmoded and badly wrinkled black dress she must have dragged from her mother's trunk, and she looked, more than ever, the image of old Katrin in her later years: the scrawny body, the tightly compressed lips, the colorless hair drawn back hard enough to pull every wrinkle out of her forehead. She reminded me of a steel trap ready to snap down on anyone who touched her incautiously.

I said, "I am aware that the doorbell has been disconnected, Celia," and walked past her into the hallway. Without turning my head, I knew that she was glaring at me; then she sniffed once, hard and dry, and flung the door shut. Instantly we were in a murky dimness that made the smell of dry rot about me stick in my throat. I fumbled for the wall switch, but Celia said sharply, "No! This is not the time for lights."

I turned to the white blur of her face, which was all I could see of her. "Celia," I said, "spare me the dramatics."

"There has been a death in this house. You know that."

"I have good reason to," I said, "but your performance now does not impress me."

"She was my own brother's wife. She was very dear to me."

I took a step toward her in the murk and rested my stick on her shoulder. "Celia," I said, "as your family's lawyer, let me give you a word of advice. The inquest is over and done with, and you've been cleared. But nobody believed a word of your precious sentiments then, and nobody ever will. Keep that in mind, Celia."

She jerked away so sharply that the stick almost fell from my hand. "Is that what you have come to tell me?" she said.

I said, "I came because I knew your brother would want to see me today. And if you don't mind my saying so, I suggest that you keep to yourself while I talk to him. I don't want any scenes."

"Then keep away from him yourself!" she cried. "He was at the inquest. He saw them clear my name. In a little while he will forget the evil he thinks of me. Keep away from him so that he can forget."

She was at her infuriating worst, and to break the spell I started up the dark stairway, one hand warily on the balustrade. But I heard her follow eagerly behind, and in some eerie way it seemed as if she were not addressing me, but answering the groaning of the stairs under our feet.

"When he comes to me," she said, "I will forgive him. At first I was not sure, but now I know. I prayed for guidance, and I was told that life is too short for hatred. So when he comes to me I will forgive him."

I reached the head of the stairway and almost went sprawling. I swore in annoyance as I righted myself. "If you're not going to use lights, Celia, you should, at least, keep the way clear. Why don't you get that stuff out of here?"

"Ah," she said, "those are all poor Jessie's belongings. It hurts Charlie to see anything of hers, I knew this would be the best thing to do—to throw all her things out."

Then a note of alarm entered her voice. "But you won't tell Charlie, will you? You won't tell him?" she said, and kept repeating it on a higher and higher note as I moved away from her, so that when I entered Charlie's room and closed the door behind me it almost sounded as if I had left a bat chittering behind me.

As in the rest of the house, the shades in Charlie's room were drawn to their full length. But a single bulb in the chandelier overhead dazzled me momentarily, and I had to look twice before I saw Charlie sprawled out on his bed with an arm flung over his eyes. Then he slowly came to his feet and peered at me.

"Well," he said at last, nodding toward the door, "she didn't give you any light to come up, did she?"

"No," I said, "but I know the way."

"She's like a mole," he said. "Gets around better in the dark than I do in the light. She'd rather have it that way too. Otherwise she might look into a mirror and be scared of what she sees there."

"Yes," I said, "she seems to be taking it very hard."

He laughed short and sharp as a sea-lion barking. "That's because she's still got the fear in her. All you get out of her now is how she loved Jessie, and how sorry she is. Maybe she figures if she says it enough, people might get to believe it. But give her a little time and she'll be the same old Celia again."

I dropped my hat and stick on the bed and laid my overcoat beside them. Then I drew out a cigar and waited until he fumbled for a match and helped me to a light. His hand shook so violently that he had hard going for a moment and muttered angrily at himself. Then I slowly exhaled a cloud of smoke toward the ceiling, and waited.

Charlie was Celia's junior by five years, but seeing him then it struck me that he looked a dozen years older. His hair was the same pale blond, almost colorless so that it was hard to tell if it was graying or not. But his cheeks wore a fine, silvery stubble, and there were huge blue-black pouches under his eyes. And where Celia was braced against a rigid and uncompromising backbone, Charlie sagged, standing or sitting, as if he were on the verge of falling forward. He stared at me and tugged uncertainly at the limp mustache that dropped past the corners of his mouth.

"You know what I wanted to see you about, don't you?" he said.

"I can't imagine," I said, "but I'd rather have you tell me."

"I'll put it to you straight," he said. "It's Celia. I want to see her get what's coming to her. Not jail. I want the law to take her and kill her, and I want to be there to watch it."

A large ash dropped to the floor, and I ground it carefully into the rug with my foot. I said, "You were at the inquest, Charlie; you saw what happened. Celia's cleared, and unless additional evidence can be produced, she stays cleared."

"Evidence! My God, what more evidence does anyone need! They were arguing hammer and tongs at the top of the stairs. Celia just grabbed Jessie and threw her down to the bottom and killed her. That's murder, isn't it? Just the same as if she used a gun or poison or whatever she would have used if the stairs weren't handy?"

I sat down wearily in the old leather-bound armchair there and studied the new ash that was forming on my cigar. "Let me show it to you from the legal angle," I said, and the monotone of my voice must have made it sound like a well-memorized formula. "First, there were no witnesses."

"I heard Jessie scream and I heard her fall," he said doggedly, "and when I ran out and found her there, I heard Celia slam her door shut right then. She pushed Jessie and then scuttered like a rat to be out of the way."

"But you didn't *see* anything. And since Celia claims that she wasn't on the scene, there were no witnesses. In other words, Celia's story cancels out your story, and since you weren't an eyewitness you can't very well make a murder out of what might have been an accident."

He slowly shook his head.

"You don't believe that," he said. "You don't really believe that. Because if you do, you can get out now and never come near me again."

"It doesn't matter what I believe; I'm showing you the legal aspects of the case. What about motivation? What did Celia have to gain from Jessie's death? Certainly there's no money or property involved; she's as financially independent as you are."

Charlie sat down on the edge of his bed and leaned toward me with his hands resting on his knees. "No," he whispered, "there's no money or property in it."

I spread my arms helplessly. "You see?"

"But you know what it is," he said. "It's me. First, it was the old lady with her heart trouble any time I tried to call my soul my own. Then when she died and I thought I was free, it was Celia. From the time I got up in the morning until I went to bed at night, it was Celia every step of the way. She never had a husband or a baby—but she had me!"

I said quietly, "She's your sister, Charlie. She loves you," and he laughed that same unpleasant, short laugh.

"She loves me like ivy loves a tree. When I think back now, I still can't see how she did it, but she would just look at me a certain way and all the strength would go out of me. And it was like that until I met Jessie... I remember the day I brought Jessie home, and told Celia we were married. She swallowed it, but that look was in her eyes the same as it must have been when she pushed Jessie down those stairs."

I said, "But you admitted at the inquest that you never saw her threaten Jessie or do anything to hurt her."

"Of course I never *saw!* But when Jessie would go around sick to her heart every day and not say a word, or cry in bed every night and not tell me why, I knew damn well what was going on. You know what Jessie was like. She wasn't so smart or pretty, but she was good-hearted as the day was long, and she was crazy about me. And when she started losing all that sparkle in her after only a month, I knew why. I talked to her and I talked to Celia, and both of them just shook their heads. All I could do was go around in circles, but when it happened, when I saw Jessie lying there, it didn't surprise me. Maybe that sounds queer, but it didn't surprise me at all."

"I don't think it surprised anyone who knows Celia," I said, "but you can't make a case out of that."

He beat his fist against his knee and rocked from side to side. "What can I do?" he said. "That's what I need you for —to tell me what to do. All my life I never got around to doing anything because of her. That's what she's banking on now—that I won't do anything, and that she'll get away with it. Then after a while, things'll settle down, and we'll be right back where we started from."

I said, "Charlie, you're getting yourself all worked up to no end."

He stood up and stared at the door, and then at me. "But I can do something," he whispered. "Do you know what?"

He waited with bright expectancy of one who has asked a clever riddle that he knows will stump the listener. I stood up facing him, and shook my head slowly. "No," I said. "Whatever you're thinking, put it out of your mind."

"Don't mix me up," he said. "You know you can get away with murder if you're as smart as Celia. Don't you think I'm as smart as Celia?"

I caught his shoulders tightly. "For God's sake, Charlie," I said, "don't start talking like that."

He pulled out of my hands and went staggering back against the wall. His eyes were bright, and his teeth showed behind his drawn lips. "What should I do?" he cried. "Forget everything now that Jessie is dead and buried? Sit here until Celia gets tired of being afraid of me and kills me too?"

My years and girth had betrayed me in that little tussle with him, and I found myself short of dignity and breath. "I'll tell you one thing," I said. "You haven't been out of this house since the inquest. It's about time you got out, if only to walk the streets and look around you."

"And have everybody laugh at me as I go!"

"Try it," I said, "and see. Al Sharp said that some of your friends would be at his bar and grill tonight, and he'd like to see you there. That's my advice—for whatever it's worth."

"It's not worth anything," said Celia. The door had been opened, and she stood there rigid, her eyes narrowed against the light in the room. Charlie turned toward her, the muscles of his jaw knotting and unknotting.

"Celia," he said, "I told you never to come into this room!"

Her face remained impassive. "I'm not *in* it. I came to tell you that your dinner is ready."

He took a menacing step toward her. "Did you have your ear at the door long enough to hear everything I said? Or should I repeat it for you?"

"I heard an ungodly and filthy thing," she said quietly, "an invitation to drink and roister while this house is in mourning. I think I have every right to object to that."

He looked at her incredulously and had to struggle for words. "Celia," he said, "tell me you don't mean that! Only the blackest hypocrite alive or someone insane could say what you've just said, and mean it."

That struck a spark in her. "Insane!" she cried. "*You* dare use that word? Locked in your room, talking to yourself, thinking heaven knows what!" She turned to me suddenly. "You've talked to him. You ought to know. Is it possible that—"

"He is as sane as you, Celia," I said heavily.

"Then he should know that one doesn't drink in saloons at a time like this. How could you ask him to do it?"

She flung the question at me with such an air of malicious triumph that I completely forgot myself. "If you weren't preparing to throw out Jessie's belongings, Celia, I would take that question seriously!"

It was a reckless thing to say, and I had instant cause to regret it. Before I could move, Charlie was past me and had Celia's arms pinned in a paralyzing grip.

"Did you dare go into her room?" he raged, shaking her savagely. "Tell me!" And then, getting an immediate answer from the panic in her face, he dropped her arms as if they were red hot, and stood there sagging with his head bowed.

Celia reached out a placating hand toward him. "Charlie," she whimpered, "don't you see? Having her things around bothers you. I only wanted to help you."

"Where are her things?"

"By the stairs, Charlie. Everything is there."

He started down the hallway, and with the sound of his uncertain footsteps moving away I could feel my heartbeat slowing down to its normal tempo. Celia turned to look at me, and there was such a raging hatred in her face that I knew only a desperate need to get out of that house at once. I took my things from the bed and started past her, but she barred the door.

"Do you see what you've done?" she whispered hoarsely. "Now I will have to pack them all over again. It tires me, but

I will have to pack them all over again—just because of you."

"That is entirely up to you, Celia," I said coldly.

"You," she said. "You old fool. It should have been you along with her when I—"

I dropped my stick sharply on her shoulder and could feel her wince under it. "As your lawyer, Celia," I said, "I advise you to exercise your tongue only during your sleep, when you can't be held accountable for what you say."

She said no more, but I made sure she stayed safely in front of me until I was out in the street again.

From the Boerum house to Al Sharp's Bar and Grill was only a few minutes walk, and I made it in good time, grateful for the sting of the clear winter air in my face. Al was alone behind the bar, busily polishing glasses, and when he saw me enter he greeted me cheerfully. "Merry Christmas, counsellor," he said.

"Same to you," I said, and watched him place a comfortable-looking bottle and a pair of glasses on the bar.

"You're regular as the seasons, counsellor," said Al, pouring out two stiff ones. "I was expecting you along right about now."

We drank to each other and Al leaned confidingly on the bar. "Just come from there?"

"Yes," I said.

"See Charlie?"

"And Celia," I said.

"Well," said Al, "that's nothing exceptional. I've seen her too when she comes by to do some shopping. Runs along with her head down and that black shawl over it like she was being chased by something. I guess she is at that."

"I guess she is," I said.

"But Charlie, he's the one. Never see him around at all. Did you tell him I'd like to see him some time?"

"Yes," I said. "I told him."

"What did he say?"

"Nothing. Celia said it was wrong for him to come here while he was in mourning."

Al whistled softly and expressively, and twirled a forefinger at his forehead. "Tell me," he said, "do you think it's safe for them to be alone together like they are? I mean, the way things stand, and the way Charlie feels, there could be another case of trouble there."

"It looked like it for a while tonight," I said. "But it blew over."

"Until next time," said Al.

"I'll be there," I said.

Al looked at me and shook his head. "Nothing changes in that house," he said. "Nothing at all. That's why you can figure out all the answers in advance. That's how I knew you'd be standing here right about now talking to me about it."

I still could smell the dry rot of the house in my nostrils, and I knew it would take days before I could get it out of my clothes.

"This is one day I'd like to cut out of the calendar permanently," I said.

"And leave them alone to their troubles. It would serve them right."

"They're not alone," I said. "Jessie is with them. Jessie will always be with them until that house and everything in it is gone."

Al frowned. "It's the queerest thing that ever happened in this town, all right. The house all black, her running through the streets like something hunted, him lying there in that room with only the walls to look at, for—when was it Jessie took that fall, counsellor?"

By shifting my eyes a little I could see in the mirror behind Al the reflection of my own face: ruddy, deep jowled, a little incredulous.

"Twenty years ago," I heard myself saying. "Just twenty years ago tonight."

"It's here, again, Henri!"

If anyone ever challenged the throne of Agatha Christie, it was Margery Allingham. It was not unreasonable to suppose that Allingham was the author Christie chose when she wanted to curl up with a good mystery. Both women were masters of the genteel English setting. Both were tremendously prolific in their prime.

But, after World War II, Allingham seemed to grow tired of her series character Albert Campion. He had bowed to much acclaim in the 1929 book The Crime at Black Dudley, *but had become peripheral to the action of her post-war stories. When he returned to center stage it was in the role of government agent. At the height of her popularity, she was mentioned with Christie and Dorothy Sayers, but she is less well-remembered today. Her last book,* Cargo of Eagles, *was completed after her death by her husband Philip Youngman Carter, who added to the Campion series with two entries of his own.*

Margery Allingham was particularly inspired by the combination of crime and Christmas for she left four remarkable stories, all with Albert Campion: "On Christmas Day in the Morning," "Murder Under the Mistletoe," "The Man With the Sack," and the following tale, which has been out of print in this country for over thirty years. Among its delights are some moments aboard a train speeding away from wartime London. It is Allingham at her best—and that you shall find is very good indeed.

243

The Case is Altered

by Margery Allingham

M<small>R. ALBERT CAMPION</small>, sitting in a first-class smoking
compartment, was just reflecting sadly that an atmosphere of stultifying decency could make even Christmas
something of a stuffed-owl occasion, when a new hogskin
suitcase of distinctive design hit him on the knees. At that
same moment a golf bag bruised the shins of the shy young
man opposite, an armful of assorted magazines burst over the
pretty girl in the far corner, and a blast of icy air swept round
the carriage. There was the familiar rattle and lurch which
indicates that the train has started at last, a squawk from a
receding porter, and Lance Feering arrived before him apparently by rocket.

"Caught it," said the newcomer with the air of one confi-
dently expecting congratulations, but as the train bumped
jerkily he teetered back on his heels and collapsed between the
two young people on the opposite seat.

"My dear chap, so we noticed," murmured Campion, and
he smiled apologetically at the girl, now disentangling herself
from the shellburst of newsprint. It was his own disarming
my-poor-friend-is-afflicted variety of smile that he privately
considered infallible, but on this occasion it let him down.

The girl, who was in the early twenties and was slim and
fair, with eyes like licked brandy-balls, as Lance Feering ine-
legantly put it afterwards, regarded him with grave interest.
She stacked the magazines into a neat bundle and placed them
on the seat opposite before returning to her own book. Even
Mr. Feering, who was in one of his more exuberant moods,
was aware of that chilly protest. He began to apologize.

Campion had known Feering in his student days, long before he had become one of the foremost designers of stage décors in Europe, and was used to him, but now even he was impressed. Lance's apologies were easy but also abject. He collected his bag, stowed it on a clear space on the rack above the shy young man's head, thrust his golf things under the seat, positively blushed when he claimed his magazines, and regarded the girl with pathetic humility. She glanced at him when he spoke, nodded coolly with just enough graciousness not to be gauche, and turned over a page.

Campion was secretly amused. At the top of his form Lance was reputed to be irresistible. His dark face with the long mournful nose and bright eyes were unhandsome enough to be interesting and the quick gestures of his short painter's hands made his conversation picturesque. His singular lack of success on this occasion clearly astonished him and he sat back in his corner eyeing the young woman with covert mistrust.

Campion resettled himself to the two hours' rigid silence which etiquette demands from first-class travelers who, although they are more than probably going to be asked to dance a reel together if not to share a bathroom only a few hours hence, have not yet been introduced.

There was no way of telling if the shy young man and the girl with the brandy-ball eyes knew each other, and whether they too were en route for Underhill, Sir Philip Cookham's Norfolk place. Campion was inclined to regard the coming festivities with a certain amount of lugubrious curiosity. Cookham himself was a magnificent old boy, of course, "one of the more valuable pieces in the Cabinet," as someone had once said of him, but Florence was a different kettle of fish. Born to wealth and breeding, she had grown blasé towards both of them and now took her delight in notabilities, a dangerous affectation in Campion's experience. She was some sort of remote aunt of his.

He glanced again at the young people, caught the boy unaware, and was immediately interested.

The illustrated magazine had dropped from the young man's hand and he was looking out of the window, his mouth drawn down at the corners and a narrow frown between his thick eyebrows. It was not an unattractive face, too young for strong character but decent and open enough in the ordinary way. At that particular moment, however, it wore a revealing expression. There was recklessness in the twist of the mouth and sullenness in the eyes, while the hand which lay upon the inside arm-rest was clenched.

Campion was curious. Young people do not usually go away for Christmas in this top-step-at-the-dentist's frame of mind. The girl looked up from her book.

"How far is Underhill from the station?" she inquired.

"Five miles. They'll meet us." The shy young man turned to her so easily and with such obvious affection that any romantic theory Campion might have formed was knocked on the head instantly. The youngster's troubles evidently had nothing to do with love.

Lance had raised his head with bright-eyed interest at the gratuitous information and now a faintly sardonic expression appeared upon his lips. Campion sighed for him. For a man who fell in and out of love with the abandonment of a seal round a pool, Lance Feering was an impossible optimist. Already he was regarding the girl with that shy despair which so many ladies had found too piteous to be allowed to persist. Campion washed his hands of him and turned away just in time to notice a stranger glancing in at them from the corridor. It was a dark and arrogant young face and he recognized it instantly, feeling at the same time a deep wave of sympathy for old Cookham. Florence, he gathered, had done it again.

Young Victor Preen, son of old Preen of the Preen Aero Company, was certainly notable, not to say notorious. He had obtained much publicity in his short life for his sensational flights, but a great deal more for adventures less creditable; and when angry old gentlemen in the armchairs of exclusive clubs let themselves go about the blackguardliness of the younger generation, it was very often of Victor Preen that they were thinking.

He stood now a little to the left of the compartment window, leaning idly against the wall, his chin up and his heavy lids drooping. At first sight he did not appear to be taking any interest in the occupants of the compartment, but when the shy young man looked up, Campion happened to see the swift glance of recognition, and of something else, which passed between them. Presently, still with the same elaborate casualness, the man in the corridor wandered away, leaving the other staring in front of him, the same sullen expression still in his eyes.

The incident passed so quickly that it was impossible to define the exact nature of that second glance, but Campion was never a man to go imagining things, which was why he was surprised when they arrived at Minstree station to hear Henry Boule, Florience's private secretary, introducing the two and to notice that they met as strangers.

It was pouring with rain as they came out of the station, and Boule, who, like all Florence's secretaries, appeared to be suffering from an advanced case of nerves, bundled them all into two big Daimlers, a smaller car, and a shooting-brake. Campion looked round him at Florence's Christmas bag with some dismay. She had surpassed herself. Besides Lance there were at least half a dozen celebrities: a brace of political highlights, an angry looking lady novelist, Nadja from the ballet, a startled R.A., and Victor Preen, as well as some twelve or thirteen unfamiliar faces who looked as if they might belong to Art, Money, or even mere Relations.

Campion became separated from Lance and was looking for him anxiously when he saw him at last in one of the cars, with the novelist on one side and the girl with brandy-ball eyes on the other, Victor Preen making up the ill-assorted four.

Since Campion was an unassuming sort of person he was relegated to the brake with Boule himself, the shy young man and the whole of the luggage. Boule introduced them awkwardly and collapsed into a seat, wiping the beads from off his forehead with a relief which was a little too blatant to be tactful.

Campion, who had learned that the shy young man's name was Peter Groome, made a tentative inquiry of him as they sat jolting shoulder to shoulder in the back of the car. He nodded.

"Yes, it's the same family," he said. "Cookham's sister married a brother of my father's. I'm some sort of relation, I suppose."

The prospect did not seem to fill him with any great enthusiasm and once again Campion's curiosity was piqued. Young Mr. Groome was certainly not in a seasonable mood.

In the ordinary way Campion would have dismissed the matter from his mind, but there was something about the youngster which attracted him, something indefinable and of a despairing quality, and moreover there had been that curious intercepted glance in the train.

They talked in a desultory fashion throughout the uncomfortable journey. Campion learned that young Groome was in his father's firm of solicitors, that he was engaged to be married to the girl with the brandy-ball eyes, who was a Miss Patricia Bullard of an old north country family, and that he thought Christmas was a waste of time.

"I hate it," he said with a sudden passionate intensity which startled even his mild inquisitor. "All this sentimental good-will-to-all-men-business is false and sickening. There's no such thing as good-will. The world's rotten."

He blushed as soon as he had spoken and turned away.

"I'm sorry," he murmured, "but all this bogus Dickensian stuff makes me writhe."

Campion made no direct comment. Instead he asked with affable inconsequence, "Was that young Victor Preen I saw in the other car?"

Peter Groome turned his head and regarded him with the steady stare of the wilfully obtuse.

"I was introduced to someone with a name like that, I think," he said carefully. "He was a little baldish man, wasn't he?"

"No, that's Sir George." The secretary leaned over the luggage to give the information. "Preen is the tall young man, rather handsome, with the very curling hair. He's *the* Preen, you know." He sighed. "It seems very young to be a millionaire, doesn't it?"

"Obscenely so," said Mr. Peter Groome abruptly, and returned to his despairing contemplation of the landscape.

Underhill was *en fête* to receive them. As soon as Campion observed the preparations, his sympathy for young Mr. Groome increased, for to a jaundiced eye Lady Florence's display might well have proved as dispiriting as Preen's bank balance. Florence had "gone all Dickens," as she said herself at the top of her voice, linking her arm through Campion's, clutching the R.A. with her free hand, and capturing Lance with a bright birdlike eye.

The great Jacobean house was festooned with holly. An eighteen foot tree stood in the great hall. Yule logs blazed on iron dogs in the wide hearths and already the atmosphere was thick with that curious Christmas smell which is part cigar smoke and part roasting food.

Sir Philip Cookham stood receiving his guests with pathetic bewilderment. Every now and again his features broke into a smile of genuine welcome as he saw a face he knew. He was a distinguished-looking old man with a fine head and eyes permanently worried by his country's troubles.

"My dear boy, delighted to see you. Delighted," he said, grasping Campion's hand. "I'm afraid you've been put over in the Dower House. Did Florence tell you? She said you wouldn't mind, but I insisted that Feering went over there with you and also young Peter." He sighed and brushed away the visitor's hasty reassurances. "I don't know why the dear girl never feels she has a party unless the house is so over-crowded that our best friends have to sleep in the annex," he said sadly.

The "dear girl," looking not more than fifty-five or her sixty years, was clinging to the arm of the lady novelist at that particular moment and the two women were emitting mirthless parrot cries at each other. Cookham smiled.

"She's happy, you know," he said indulgently. "She enjoys this sort of thing. Unfortunately I have a certain amount of urgent work to do this weekend, but we'll get in a chat, Campion, some time over the holiday. I want to hear your news. You're a lucky fellow. You can tell your adventures."

The lean man grimaced. "More secret sessions, sir?" he inquired.

The Cabinet Minister threw up his hands in a comic but expressive little gesture before he turned to greet the next guest.

As he dressed for dinner in his comfortable room in the small Georgian dower house across the park, Campion was inclined to congratulate himself on his quarters. Underhill itself was a little too much of the ancient monument for strict comfort.

He had reached the tie stage when Lance appeared. He came in very elegant indeed and highly pleased with himself. Campion diagnosed the symptoms immediately and remained irritatingly incurious.

Lance sat down before the open fire and stretched his sleek legs.

"It's not even as if I were a good looking blighter, you know," he observed invitingly when the silence had become irksome to him. "In fact, Campion, when I consider myself I simply can't understand it. Did I so much as speak to the girl?"

"I don't know," said Campion, concentrating on his dressing. "Did you?"

"No." Lance was passionate in his denial. "Not a word. The hard-faced female with the inky fingers and the walrus mustache was telling me her life story all the way home in the car. This dear little poppet with the eyes was nothing more than a warm bundle at my side. I give you my dying oath on that, And yet—well, it's extraordinary, isn't it?"

Campion did not turn round. He could see the artist quite well through the mirror in front of him. Lance had a sheet of note-paper in his hand and was regarding it with that mixture of feigned amusement and secret delight which was typical of his eternally youthful spirit.

"Extraordinary," he repeated, glancing at Campion's unresponsive back. "She had nice eyes. Like licked brandy-balls."

"Exactly," agreed the lean man by the dressing table. "I thought she seemed very taken up with her fiancé, young Master Groome, though," he added tactlessly.

"Well, I noticed that, you know," Lance admitted, forgetting his professions of disinterest. "She hardly recognized my existence in the train. Still, there's absolutely no accounting for women. I've studied 'em all my life and never understood 'em yet. I mean to say, take this case in point. That kid ignored me, avoided me, looked through me. And yet look at this. I found it in my room when I came up to change just now."

Campion took the note with a certain amount of distaste. Lovely women were invariably stooping to folly, it seemed, but even so he could not accustom himself to the spectacle. The message was very brief. He read it at a glance and for the first time that day he was conscious of that old familiar flicker down the spine as his experienced nose smelled trouble. He re-read the five lines.

> "There is a sundial on a stone pavement just off the drive. We saw it from the car. I'll wait ten minutes there for you half an hour after the party breaks up tonight."

There was neither signature nor initial, and the summons broke off as baldly as it had begun.

"Amazing, isn't it?" Lance had the grace to look shame-faced.

"Astounding." Campion's tone was flat. "Staggering, old boy. Er—fishy."

"Fishy?"

"Yes, don't you think so?" Campion was turning over the single sheet thoughtfully and there was no amusement in the pale eyes behind his horn-rimmed spectacles. "How did it arrive?"

"In an unaddressed envelope. I don't suppose she caught my name. After all, there must be some people who don't know it yet." Lance was grinning impudently. "She's batty, of course. Not safe out and all the rest of it. But I liked her eyes and she's very young."

Campion perched himself on the edge of the table. He was still very serious.

"It's disturbing, isn't it?" he said, "Not nice. Makes one wonder."

"Oh, I don't know." Lance retrieved his property and tucked it into his pocket. "She's young and foolish, and it's Christmas."

Campion did not appear to have heard him. "I wonder," he said. "I should keep the appointment, I think. It may be unwise to interfere, but yes, I rather think I should."

"You're telling me." Lance was laughing. "I may be wrong, of course," he added defensively, "but I think that's a cry for help. The poor girl evidently saw that I looked a dependable sort of chap and—er—having her back against the wall for some reason or other she turned instinctively to the stranger with the kind face. Isn't that how you read it?"

"Since you press me, no. Not exactly," said Campion, and as they walked over to the house together he remained thoughtful and irritatingly uncommunicative.

Florence Cookham excelled herself that evening. Her guests were exhorted "to be young again," with the inevitable result that Underhill contained a company of irritated and exhausted people long before midnight.

One of her ladyship's more erroneous beliefs was that she was a born organizer, and that the real secret of entertaining people lay in giving everyone something to do. Thus Lance and the R.A.—now even more startled-looking than ever—found themselves superintending the decoration of the great tree, while the girl with the brandy-ball eyes conducted a small informal dance in the drawing room, the lady novelist scowled over the bridge table, and the ballet star refused flatly to arrange amateur theatricals.

Only two people remained exempt from this tyranny. One was Sir Philip himself, who looked in every now and again, ready to plead urgent work awaiting him in his study whenever his wife pounced upon him, and the other was Mr. Campion, who had work to do on his own account and had long mastered the difficult art of self-effacement. Experience had taught him that half the secret of this maneuver was to keep discreetly on the move and he strolled from one party to another, always ready to look as if he belonged to any one of them should his hostess's eye ever come to rest upon him inquiringly.

For once his task was comparatively simple. Florence was in her element as she rushed about surrounded by breathless assistants, and at one period the very air in her vicinity seemed to have become thick with colored paper-wrappings, yards of red ribbons and a colored snowstorm of little address tickets as she directed the packing of the presents for the Tenants' Tree, a second monster which stood in the ornamental barn beyond the kitchens.

Campion left Lance to his fate, which promised to be six or seven hours' hard labor at the most moderate estimate, and continued his purposeful meandering. His lean figure drifted among the company with an apparent aimlessness which was deceptive. There was hidden urgency in his lazy movements and his pale eyes behind his spectacles were inquiring and unhappy.

He found Patricia Bullard dancing with young Preen, and paused to watch them as they swung gracefully by him. The man was in a somewhat flamboyant mood, flashing his smile and his noisy witticisms about him after the fashion of his kind, but the girl was not so content. As Campion caught sight of her pale face over her partner's sleek shoulder his eyebrows rose. For an instant he almost believed in Lance's unlikely suggestion. The girl actually did look as though she had her back to the wall. She was watching the doorway nervously and her shiny eyes were afraid.

Campion looked about him for the other young man who should have been present, but Peter Groome was not in the ballroom, nor in the great hall, nor yet among the bridge tables in the drawing-room, and half an hour later he had still not put in an appearance.

Campion was in the hall himself when he saw Patricia slip into the anteroom which led to Sir Philip's private study, that holy of holies which even Florence treated with a wholesome awe. Campion had paused for a moment to enjoy the spectacle of Lance, wild eyed and tight lipped, wrestling with the last of the blue glass balls and tinsel streamers on the Guests' Tree, when he caught sight of the flare of her silver skirt disappearing round a familiar doorway under one branch of the huge double staircase.

It was what he had been waiting for, and yet when it came his disappointment was unexpectedly acute, for he too had liked her smile and her brandy-ball eyes. The door was ajar when he reached it, and he pushed it open an inch or so farther, pausing on the threshold to consider the scene within. Patricia was on her knees before the paneled door which led into the inner room and was trying somewhat ineffectually to peer through the keyhole.

Campion stood looking at her regretfully, and when she straightened herself and paused to listen, with every line of her young body taut with the effort of concentration, he did not move.

Sir Philip's voice amid the noisy chatter behind him startled him, however, and he swung round to see the old man talking to a group on the other side of the room. A moment later the girl brushed past him and hurried away.

Campion went quietly into the anteroom. The study door was still closed and he moved over to the enormous period fireplace which stood beside it. This particular fireplace, with its carved and painted front, its wrought iron dogs and deeply recessed inglenooks, was one of the showpieces of Underhill.

At the moment the fire had died down and the interior of the cavern was dark, warm, and inviting. Campion stepped inside and sat down on the oak settle, where the shadows swallowed him. He had no intention of being unduly officious, but his quick ears had caught a faint sound in the inner room and Sir Philip's private sanctum was no place for furtive movements when its master was out of the way. He had not long to wait.

A few moments later the study door opened very quietly and someone came out. The newcomer moved across the room with a nervous, unsteady tread, and paused abruptly, his back to the quiet figure in the inglenook.

Campion recognized Peter Groome and his thin mouth narrowed. He was sorry. He had liked the boy.

The youngster stood irresolute. He had his hands behind him, holding in one of them a flamboyant parcel wrapped in the colored paper and scarlet ribbon which littered the house. A sound from the hall seemed to fluster him, for he spun round, thrust the parcel into the inglenook which was the first hiding place to present itself, and returned to face the new arrival. It was the girl again. She came slowly across the room, her hands outstretched and her face raised to Peter's.

In view of everything, Campion thought it best to stay

where he was, nor had he time to do anything else. She was speaking urgently, passionate sincerity in her low voice.

"Peter, I've been looking for you. Darling, there's something I've got to say and if I'm making an idiotic mistake then you've got to forgive me. Look here, you wouldn't go and do anything silly, would you? Would you, Peter? Look at me."

"My dear girl." He was laughing unsteadily and not very convincingly with his arms around her. "What on earth are you talking about?"

She drew back from him and peered earnestly into his face.

"You wouldn't, would you? Not even if it meant an awful lot. Not even if for some reason or other you felt you *had* to. Would you?"

He turned from her helplessly, a great weariness in the lines of his sturdy back, but she drew him round, forcing him to face her.

"Would he what, my dear?"

Florence's arch inquiry from the doorway separated them so hurriedly that she laughed delightedly and came briskly into the room, her gray curls a trifle disheveled and her draperies flowing.

"Too divinely young, I love it!" she said devastatingly. "I must kiss you both. Christmas is the time for love and youth and all the other dear charming things, isn't it? That's why I adore it. But, my dears, not here. Not in this silly poky little room. Come along and help me, both of you, and then you can slip away and dance together later on. But don't come in this room. This is Philip's dull part of the house. Come along this minute. Have you seen my precious tree? Too incredibly distinguished, my darlings, with two great artists at work on it. You shall both tie on a candle. Come along."

She swept them away like an avalanche. No protest was possible. Peter shot a single horrified glance towards the fireplace, but Florence was gripping his arm; he was thrust out into the hall and the door closed firmly behind him.

Campion was left in his corner with the parcel less than a dozen feet away from him on the opposite bench. He moved over and picked it up. It was a long flat package wrapped in holly-printed tissue. Moreover, it was unexpectedly heavy and the ends were unbound.

He turned it over once or twice, wrestling with a strong disinclination to interfere, but a vivid recollection of the girl with the brandy-ball eyes, in her silver dress, her small pale face alive with anxiety, made up his mind for him and, sighing, he pulled the ribbon.

The typewritten folder which fell on to his knees surprised him at first, for it was not at all what he had expected, nor was its title, "Report on Messrs. Anderson and Coleridge, Messrs. Saunders, Duval and Berry, and Messrs. Birmingham and Rose," immediately enlightening, and when he opened it at random a column of incomprehensible figures confronted him. It was a scribbled pencil note in a precise hand at the foot of one of the pages which gave him his first clue.

"These figures are estimated by us to be a reliable forecast of this firm's full working capacity,"

Two hours later it was bitterly cold in the garden and a thin white mist hung over the dark shrubbery which lined the drive when Mr. Campion, picking his way cautiously along the clipped grass verge, came quietly down to the sundial walk. Behind him the gabled roofs of Underhill were shadowy against a frosty sky. There were still a few lights in the upper windows, but below stairs the entire place was in darkness.

Campion hunched his greatcoat about him and plodded on, unwonted severity in the lines of his thin face.

He came upon the sundial walk at last and paused, straining his eyes to see through the mist. He made out the figure standing by the stone column, and heaved a sigh of relief as he recognized the jaunty shoulders of the Christmas tree decorator. Lance's incurable romanticism was going to be useful at last, he reflected with wry amusement.

He did not join his friend but withdrew into the shadows of a great clump of rhododendrons and composed himself to wait. He intensely disliked the situation in which he found himself. Apart from the extreme physical discomfort involved, he had a natural aversion towards the project on hand, but little fair-haired girls with shiny eyes can be very appealing.

It was a freezing vigil. He could hear Lance stamping about

in the mist, swearing softly to himself, and even that supremely comic phenomenon had its unsatisfactory side.

They were both shivering and the mist's damp fingers seemed to have stroked their very bones when at last Campion stiffened. He had heard a rustle behind him and presently there was a movement in the wet leaves, followed by the sharp ring of feet on the stones. Lance swung round immediately, only to drop back in astonishment as a tall figure bore down.

"Where is it?"

Neither the words nor the voice came as a complete surprise to Campion, but the unfortunate Lance was taken entirely off his guard.

"Why, hello, Preen," he said involuntarily. "What the devil are you doing here?"

The newcomer had stopped in his tracks, his face a white blur in the uncertain light. For a moment he stood perfectly still and then, turning on his heel, he made off without a word.

"Ah, but I'm afraid it's not quite so simple as that, my dear chap."

Campion stepped out of his friendly shadows and as the younger man passed, slipped an arm through his and swung him round to face the startled Lance, who was coming up at the double.

"You can't clear off like this," he went on, still in the same affable, conversational tone. "You have something to give Peter Groome, haven't you? Something he rather wants?"

"Who the hell are you?" Preen jerked up his arm as he spoke and might have wrenched himself free had it not been for Lance, who had recognized Campion's voice and, although completely in the dark, was yet quick enough to grasp certain essentials.

"That's right, Preen," he said, seizing the man's other arm in a bear's hug. "Hand it over. Don't be a fool. Hand it over."

This line of attack appeared to be inspirational, since they felt the powerful youngster stiffen between them.

"Look here, how many people know about this?"

"The world—" Lance was beginning cheerfully when Campion forstalled him.

"We three and Peter Groome," he said quietly. "At the moment Sir Philip has no idea that Messrs. Preen's curiosity concerning the probable placing of Government orders for aircraft parts has overstepped the bounds of common sense. You're acting alone, I suppose?"

"Oh, lord, yes, of course." Preen was cracking dangerously, "If my old man gets to hear of this I—oh, well, I might as well go and crash."

"I thought so." Campion sounded content. "Your father has a reputation to consider. So has our young friend Groome. You'd better hand it over."

"What?"

"Since you force me to be vulgar, whatever it was you were attempting to use as blackmail, my precious young friend," he said. "Whatever it may be, in fact, that you hold over young Groome and were trying to use in your attempt to force him to let you have a look at a confidential Government report concerning the orders which certain aircraft firms were likely to receive in the next six months. In your position you could have made prettty good use of them, couldn't you? Frankly, I haven't the faintest idea what this incriminating document may be. When I was young, objectionably wealthy youths accepted I.O.U.s from their poorer companions, but now that's gone out of fashion. What's the modern equivalent? An R.D. check, I suppose?"

Preen said nothing. He put his hand in an inner pocket and drew out an envelope which he handed over without a word. Campion examined the slip of pink paper within by the light of a pencil torch.

"You kept it for quite a time before trying to cash it, didn't you?" he said. "Dear me, that's rather an old trick and it was never admired. Young men who are careless with their accounts have been caught out like that before. It simply wouldn't have looked good to his legal-minded old man, I take it? You two seem to be hampered by your respective papas' integrity. Yes, well, you can go now."

Preen hesitated, opened his mouth to protest, but thought better of it. Lance looked after his retreating figure for some little time before he returned to his friend.

"Who wrote that blinking note?" he demanded.

"He did, of course," said Campion brutally. "He wanted to see the report but was making absolutely sure that young Groome took all the risks of being found with it."

"Preen wrote the note," Lance repeated blankly.

"Well, naturally," said Campion absently. "That was obvious as soon as the report appeared in the picture. He was the only man in the place with the necessary special information to make use of it."

Lance made no comment. He pulled his coat collar more closely about his throat and stuffed his hands into his pockets.

All the same the artist was not quite satisfied, for, later still, when Campion was sitting in his dressing-gown writing a note at one of the little escritories which Florence so thoughtfully provided in her guest bedrooms, he came padding in again and stood warming himself before the fire.

"Why?" he demanded suddenly. "Why did I get the invitation?"

"Oh, that was a question of luggage." Campion spoke over his shoulder. "That bothered me at first, but as soon as we fixed it onto Preen that little mystery became blindingly clear. Do you remember falling into the carriage this afternoon? Where did you put your elegant piece of gent's natty suitcasing? Over young Groome's head. Preen saw it from the corridor and assumed that the chap was sitting *under his own bag!* He sent his own man over here with the note, told him not to ask for Peter by name but to follow the nice new pigskin suitcase upstairs."

Lance nodded regretfully. "Very likely," he said sadly. "Funny thing. I was sure it was the girl."

After a while he came over to the desk. Campion put down his pen and indicated the written sheet.

> "Dear Groome," it ran, "I enclose a little matter that I should burn forthwith. The package you left in the inglenook is still there, right at the back on the left-hand side, cunningly concealed under a pile of logs. It has not been seen by anyone who could possibly understand it. If you nipped over

very early this morning you could return it to its appointed place without any trouble. If I may venture a word of advice, it is never worth it."

The author grimaced. "It's a bit avuncular," he admitted awkwardly, "but what else can I do? His light is still on, poor chap. I thought I'd stick it under his door."

Lance was grinning wickedly.

"That's fine," he murmured. "The old man does his stuff for reckless youth. There's just the signature now and that ought to be as obvious as everything else has been to you. I'll write it for you. 'Mery Christmas. Love from Santa Claus.'"

"You win," said Mr. Campion.

The Murder for Christmas
Guide to Gift Giving

Obviously there should be a standard value for a certain type of Christmas present. One may give what one will to one's own family or particular friends; that is all right. But in a Christmas house-party there is a pleasant interchange of parcels, of which the string and the brown paper and the kindly thought are the really important ingredients, and the gift inside is nothing more than an excuse for these things. It is embarrassing for you if Jones has apologised for his brown paper with a hundred cigars and you have only excused yourself with twenty-five cigarettes; perhaps still more embarrassing if it is you who have lost so heavily on the exchange. An understanding that the contents were to be worth five shillings exactly would avoid this embarrassment.

And now ... I am reminded of the ingenuity of a friend of mine, William by name, who arrived at a large country house for

Christmas without any present in his bag. He had expected neither to give nor to receive anything, but to his horror he discovered on the 24th that everybody was preparing a Christmas present for him, and that it was taken for granted that he would require a little privacy and brown paper on Christmas Eve for the purpose of addressing his own offerings to others. He had wild thoughts of telegraphing to London for something to be sent down, and spoke to other members of the house-party in order to discover what sorts of presents would be suitable.

"What are you giving our host?" he asked one of them.

"Mary and I are giving him a book," said John, referring to his wife.

William then approached the youngest son of the house, and discovered that he and his next brother Dick were sharing in this, that, and the other. When he had heard this, William retired to his room and thought profoundly.

He was the first down to breakfast on Christmas morning. All the places at the table were piled high with presents. He looked at John's place. The top parcel said, "To John and Mary from Charles." William took out his fountain-pen and added a couple of words to the inscription. It then read, "To John and Mary from Charles and William," and in William's opinion looked just as effective as before. He moved on to the next place. "To Angela from Father," said the top parcel. "And William," wrote William. At his hostess' place he hesitated for a moment. The first present there was for "Darling Mother, from her loving children." It did not seem that an "and William" was quite suitable. But his hostess was not to be deprived of William's kindly thought; twenty seconds later the handkerchiefs "from John and Mary and William" expressed all the nice things which he was feeling for her. He passed on to the next place....

It is of course impossible to thank every donor of a joint gift; one simply thanks the first person whose eye one happens to catch. Sometimes William's eye was caught, sometimes not. But he was spared fall embarrassment; and I can recommend his solution of the problem with perfect confidence to those who may be in a similar predicament next Christmas.

A.A. Milne

If we are to have more stories of the calibre of those that appeared previously in this collection, we must look to the slush piles of our magazines to provide them. Slush piles are those towering stacks of unsolicited manuscripts that come through the mail in search of publication. Cursed by writers, disparaged by editors, they are nevertheless a necessary, even vital, in this time of dwindling short story markets.

As few writers are born with agents in attendance, or publishers standing by, waiting to record each precious word, most are forced to find their readership through painful trial and error. They will read junk and feel they can do better. They will want to attract the attention of a successful agent, but will be unable because they are unknown. They will hope, then, that some astute editor will discover them in a slush pile. But how? And when?

"Mother's Milk" is a story from a slush pile. It was once headed for the pages of Mystery Magazine but has been re-routed here. That it finds publication is no doubt a matter of some luck. Or is there more to the story than that?

Is Mines to become another Hoch or Keating? Or will he join the legion of "also-published" authors who have their day and are gone? Only time and the reader can tell.

Mother's Milk

by James Mines

IT HAD SNOWED in the night, and more was predicted by evening. The cold that had accompanied it penetrated closed windows and doors, trying to get at the sickly heat inside.

I had come upstairs about ten to collect her breakfast tray and listen to the usual recitation of mid-morning maladies. After twenty years of a ritual like this, the ear develops a selective deafness. It hears without listening.

It was remarkable, then, that I caught it. Just a trivial little observation. A single chord in a symphony of blabber like:

"And another thing. That new nurse Mrs. Fletcher is not suitable. Not suitable at all. My evening milk was cold again last night. And," she continued, drawing the bedding around her, "she spent the entire night in the sitting room around the corner. What does she have in there? A sailor?"

"I wouldn't know, Mother," I answered, watching her parched, puckered lips open and close.

She tossed her white head contemptuously and buried it in the morning paper.

"She's no better than the others. What's wrong with people nowadays? Pride in working doesn't interest them any more."

Mother could give any banality the force of a Supreme Court judgment.

"I suppose I will have to let her go after the holidays," she concluded.

I was shifting uncomfortably in my place at the end of the bed.

"Now, here's something. Vitamins that kill people. Some sort of plant food. Carried off one unfortunate already."

There was a certain glee in her thin, screechy voice. Mother got a big kick out of stories about other people's misfortunes. The Jonestown disaster had her walking on air for weeks.

She looked back at me and shook her head dramatically. "It's getting so a person can't take a glass of water without worrying about what's in it."

She laid the paper aside for a quiet moment of cosmic contemplation, as she stared meaningfully off into space. This familiar gesture of social concern had, by now, reached such a level of unsurpassed fraudulency that it deserved to be preserved in the Smithsonian.

"As if I didn't have enough to worry about, what with this terrible dizziness and weakness I suffer from. And my arthritis—and bad circulation," the thought made her stir in the mound of pillows. "You know, it hasn't been easy for me."

I wanted to tell her she could probably still take on an entire football team single-handed, but I suppressed the thought.

"The worst of all has been my allergies."

I knew we'd get around to them. We always did.

"There are so many things I don't tolerate. Why if it wasn't for all my allergies, I'd have been up and around years ago. I must be·so very careful. I don't react to things like normal people."

She sighed with heartfelt self-pity.

"I shall never forget that awful attack I had after Dr. Snavely gave me the penicillin injection."

I was sure she was going to recite the Great Event all over again, highlighting every gasp and welt and bead of sweat, but luckily I was spared.

Her recall of this fabled episode was confined to making her watery blue eyes project more than their usual amount of bogus suffering.

The tray was beginning to feel like lead. My arms ached to get out of there.

"I guess there's no use trying to hide it. I *am* feeling poorly today. I've asked for Miss Livesey to send for Dr. Snavely."

She never let up. Not once in eighty years.

"She told me," I said, reassuringly. "He'll be by about 3."

"I don't know where I'd be if it weren't for him. He is the only doctor in town decent enough to make house calls."

I wanted to add that he was the only doctor in town with time to make house calls. Bernard M. Snavely, M.D. was a rare medical specimen—a doctor who outlives his practice. Five years ago he'd closed his office on Beecher Street and returned to the comforts of the Chesterton Club where he passed his final hours playing poker, smoking cigars and downing healthy shots of Corby's whiskey. Concerns of public health no longer troubled him.

It is true, that between hands, he did administer to the needs of a few contemporaries like Mother. But as these last patients passed on, he took grateful solace in the uninterrupted company of Kings and Queens, panatellas, and those comforting shots of Corby's restorative.

I have heard from those in a position to know that Dr. Snavely's retirement had a salutory effect on the health of the community. At the end, his trade had become all tricks. Whatever he had once known of the substance of medicine was long since forgotten.

But Mother, of course, would have none other.

"I'm very reluctant to complain," I realized she was saying, "but the Cream of Wheat had lumps in it. I've told Miss Livesey what havoc they wreak with my dentures."

As she closed her eyes to savor this havoc more fully, I whisked the paper off the bed and stepped quickly out into the hall.

I avoided looking in the hall mirror as I passed. The things I had seen there recently had upset me. Scared me, if you want to know the truth.

Thin wisps of colorless hair over long expanses of pale scalp, puffy creases of skin beneath my eyes, spidery little blood vessels around my nose—I realized that time was eating away at me.

I'd planned so carefully for some good years—a studio apartment in New York, a box at the Met, stimulating friends whose interests extended beyond the livestock report. And I'd assumed that, by now, I'd be enjoying them.

When I came home from college after father died, it was

just to be for a few months, until Mother had a chance to get back on her feet. But somehow it went on and on.

At first, I didn't notice that time was passing. Then suddenly it was almost all gone. What had made it really painful was the realization that time was making me look like *her*.

I was terrified. Panicked. I had to do something. All that money Dad had left would be squandered on nurses and medical care. I was having nightmares about being left here, poor, alone and dying in a town I'd always hated.

I was desperate for a way out.

"How is she?" Molly Livesey's brogue purred as she took the tray I'd brought into the kitchen.

"She said there were lumps in the Cream of Wheat. They irritate her dentures."

Molly's eyes flared for a moment. "That woman hasn't got a grateful bone in her body. If she were my mother, I'd have done something to irritate her dentures long ago, and in no uncertain terms."

She threw her head back in defiance.

"She's just sick and afraid," I said in a deliberately bland voice. "We have to try and understand."

She let out a laugh that sounded like a snort and carried the tray over to the sink.

I took the paper and a fresh cup of coffee and retired to the dining room and the inner satisfaction that acknowledged martyrdom brings.

The article about the plant food vitamins was the sort of bilge newspapers pass off as "human interest" and bury among the clothing ads on page eighteen.

The problem had come to light following the sudden death of a child in Georgia. Apparently the mother had discovered her sleeping through her favorite television show and immediately suspected something was wrong. Paramedics were dispatched, but, by the time the child reached the hospital, she was dead.

An autopsy disclosed nothing. Then a playmate recalled seeing the child eating a pellet from a planter in the hall. The pellet was checked and found to be Mullen's African Violet Vitamins, a commonly used product that has been on the market for years. Investigators discovered the pellet contained succinyl-choline-alginate, a substance similar to one used in anesthesia.

Once ingested, this unpronounceable drug set off a series of chemical reactions that slowly paralyzed the diaphragm. The victim becomes drowsy, falls asleep and suddenly ceases breathing. Death follows in two to three hours.

Investigators said that since the pellet had no taste, it gave no warning of its lethal properties. As it was later metabolized into a number of harmless by-products, even after death, it was virtually untraceable, unless one knew what to look for.

Naturally, consumer advocates were outraged, and the FDA was ordering Mullen's African Violet Vitamins off the market. An agency spokesman refused to speculate about other deaths, saying only that he found it hard to believe any responsible adult would take plant vitamins.

I put the paper down and took a long sip of coffee. After ten years of disappointing books and toiletry items, Mother was finally going to get the kind of Christmas present she'd always dreamed of—the biggest funeral this town had ever seen.

About two, I made my run to the flower shop across town. The entrance to the shopping mall was backed up for two blocks, and hordes of last minute shoppers were everywhere. Everywhere, that is, but Eldon Stillwell's forgotten white frame shop across the street.

There everything was predictably quiet. Only a splattering of red poinsettias awaiting purchase gave any sense of time.

I looked around casually and finally selected an unexceptional specimen from the shelf of African violets.

"How's the old lady?" Eldon wanted to know as I set the plant on the chipped linoleum counter.

"Good as can be expected," I answered safely.

The long, porous face nodded as the purchase was rung up.

"You know," I began innocently, "we've had such rotten luck lately with African violets. I wonder if there isn't some sort of plant food or fertilizer you might recommend."

"Look over there," he said, indicating a dusty shelf in the back of the room.

I went over and picked up the yellowed carton of Mullen's Vitamins I had spotted earlier.

And that was that.

It had hardly been much of a calculated risk. Eldon Stillwell, of uncertain health and less certain store hours, lived in the backwater of human events. It was common knowledge that he had not so much as glanced at a paper since that unfortunate Mr. Nixon was hounded out of office by lackeys of the Left Wing Press.

The chances of his seeing the article were non-existent. And who would tell him? I'll bet I was the only other person in the store all day.

The next challenge was getting the stuff into Mother's evening milk. I'd have to distract Mrs. Fletcher, who always prepared it. Maybe I could get her out of the room by pretending to hear Mother call. Maybe somebody at the door.

Then a stroke of genius. I'd tell her I'd read there was a Lawrence Welk special on the TV. She wouldn't be able to get at the set fast enough. And I'd have the milk all to myself.

The African violet, box, receipt and bag went into the trash barrel in the garage, stuffed down on the bottom beneath the garbage. The tube of pellets went into my pocket.

So far, so good.

"Oh, am I glad to see you," Molly began, as I came in the back door to the kitchen. "Dr. Snavely called. He won't be able to come over until early evening. Morris Murchison's had another heart attack. He's gone over to the hospital with him."

"That's too bad," I answered vaguely.

"You better believe it," she huffed, waving a spatula in the air. "Your mother had a fit when I told her. One thing she's never been able to understand is other people getting sick when she's not feeling well."

She was waving the spatula all over the place. "Why, when she found out Morris Murchison was taking Dr. Snavely away from her, I thought she'd go over there and finish him off herself."

"Now, Mother's not like that," I said in my best Jimmy Stewart voice.

"You go up and talk to her. I got better things to do than go up and down stairs all day. Why, if I had any sense left in me, I'd leave right now!"

The spatula came down with a wallop against the wooden table.

Ten years ago Mary Margaret Livesey made the mistake of taking herself seriously. She quit and went to work for a relentlessly bland couple named Cerillo who'd come to town to manage the local RCA plant. That lasted two months. When she discovered this distressingly sensible couple would give her nothing to complain about, she came back claiming "mother needed her."

Mother never needed anyone. Except, perhaps, for an occasional odd job.

Morris Murchison's heart provided a minor delay, but it just meant more time for careful planning. Another hour or two wouldn't matter.

By six o'clock, the minor delay had become a major inconvenience. I was nervous, excited and impatient to act. Anticipation had overwhelmed me.

I tried several things to distract my thinking. None of them worked.

The wait was driving me crazy. Dr. Snavely should have come and gone long ago.

By seven o'clock my nerves were shot. I needed a couple of drinks to settle myself. Still no doctor.

I thought of trying to get him on the phone. But, no, that was not good. No need to seem impatient or overwrought on the phone. Someone might notice, and wonder later on.

"I'm going now," Molly announced, appearing in the doorway dressed like Sir Edmund Hilary. The metal clips on her boots had rattled noisily as she clomped across the floor. "Hope he gets here soon. That Fletcher woman's been here an hour and your mother's already made a meal out of her."

She finished tying her scarf and stomped to the front door.

"Well, good night. See you, Monday," she called.

I watched her go down the front walk to her car. Powdery flakes were falling into gusts of wind that danced them across the frozen ground and slammed them into trees and houses. Another cold night. I wouldn't miss it in New York.

I looked at the clock again and then at my hands. Nothing much I could do but fix myself another drink.

After three and a half hours of television I couldn't begin to remember as I was seeing it, I got up from the chair and looked out the window again. Snow was coming down in truckloads.

The old buzzard was not coming. His devotion to my mother's frequent calls was one of the beautiful things in life. But beauty must fade, and this was the night to do it.

Finally, I could not wait any longer. I put my hand in my pocket, gripped the bottle and headed for the stairs.

Mrs. Fletcher met me at the top, flitting round like a bird whose worm has been stolen.

"Oh, she's terrible, just terrible tonight."

I pushed past her and went into the room.

"Where's Dr. Snavely," Mother wanted to know, as though I had somehow hidden him.

"Still at the hospital with Morris Murcheson."

"Oh, come now, no one really expects me to believe that. That old faker doesn't have a heart to attack. They're probably both over at the Chesterton Club playing cards right now."

"Would you like to call over there and find out?" I asked boldly, fingering the bottle in my pocket.

"Absolutely not! I will not give him the satisfaction of thinking I'm calling all over the county for him."

She looked at me indignantly, and pouted, "Doesn't he realize how serious my condition could be?"

"Mother, for God's sakes. I'm sure he'll be here first thing in the morning."

She impaled me with a glance.

"I could be dead by morning. I could be dead now for all he knows. Or cares."

I could see this was getting nowhere.

I signaled to Mrs. Fletcher that it was time for Mother's milk. I was unremarkably calm and controlled. And Mother sensed it.

Tears appeared in her eyes. Her body relaxed. There was no fight now.

"It's so terrible to get old," she whined pathetically. "So

terrible. And you've been such a comfort to me. So unselfish."

She reached out and took me in her arms, kissing and caressing my face, holding me close to her body. I felt sorry for her. Genuinely sorry. But it was only the knowledge that she would never inflict this on me again that made it bearable.

"Here we are," chirped Mrs. Fletcher brightly, coming into the room. I thought she was referring to the glass of milk in her hand, until I saw the desiccated Ghost of Medicine Past file in behind her.

"About time," Mother snapped at him. "Hope we didn't interrupt a winning streak."

Snavely smiled cheerily and set his bag on a chair.

I grabbed the milk and nudged Mrs. Fletcher from the room.

Dr. Snavely's arrival had caught me off guard. I realized how reckless I had been. In the end, it would probably work to my advantage. He could say at the funeral he had thought it was another minor illness. Another false alarm. Maybe he hadn't taken her complaints seriously enough.

I took the milk back to the kitchen on the pretext of keeping it hot. Mrs. Fletcher returned to the safety of the sitting room and her copy of *Locked Doors*.

I watched carefully as I dropped each pellet into the glass. If one had killed a child, all twelve should do nicely for Mother.

I watched as they sank slowly below the white surface, dissolving slowly until the spoon detected nothing at the bottom.

I checked again. No telltale sediment. Nothing on the sides. No taste. No smell. And soon, no Mother.

A door banged loudly upstairs. Mother had made short work of Dr. Snavely.

"Well," he said, arching his scrawny white eyebrows as I met him on the stairs, "she's just having a few extra beats. Nothing serious, mind you. Probably just excitement, but I'll leave instructions with Mrs. Fletcher just in case."

"Thanks, that will make me feel a lot better. She just didn't seem like herself today."

He looked back at me in momentary disbelief, and then

scrambled down the wooden stairs with the nurse in full retreat.

I looked at the glass again. It looked perfectly harmless. There was a stillness in the house, now, broken only by the whispered voices in the foyer.

Mother was still fuming in her bed. "In the morning, I want you to call over to the hospital and see if Dr. Snavely was there or not. I will not be made a fool of."

"Yes, mother," I murmured, setting the glass beside the bed.

I started straightening out the blankets and fluffing up the pillows. Out of the corner of my eye, I saw her take the glass in hand and bring it closer.

"I might have died," she said, resting it in her hands for a moment.

I was trying not to look directly at the glass.

"I might have died waiting for that man," she repeated incredulously. The glass inched closer to her mouth.

"Now don't think about it. Just try and get a good night's sleep," I said, nervously trying to soothe her.

She put the glass down without drinking. "How can I get a good night's sleep knowing that a man I have trusted for years could care so little for my well-being."

I thought I was going to start screaming at her. She couldn't do this to me now.

She brought the glass back up to her lips and stopped short, looking into it.

My heart stopped beating.

"It's not warm enough. Cold milk promotes indigestion."

But she put the glass to her lips and drained the contents. As the white liquid disappeared I felt only relief. Total relief.

I took the empty glass and watched her lie back and close her eyes. This is how I would find her in the morning. Sleeping peacefully. Forever.

I reached over and turned out the light beside the bed.

"Oh!"

It was Mother's voice. I snapped the light back on. She was sitting upright in bed. Gasping. Wheezing.

Something was wrong. Her face was red and swollen. She was grunting and flailing her arms toward me.

I looked at the glass. What had happened?

She was trying to scream but all that came out was breathy gurgling. She grabbed my arm.

The veins around her eyes protruded out. The eyes themselves were bulging and bloodshot. Copious yellow mucus spilled from her mouth. The matted white curls on her head seemed alive and writhing.

Her grip tightened. The other arm shot out suddenly, catching the lamp beside the bed, sending it crashing to the floor.

The door flew open. Dr. Snavely was inside.

"Get some adrenalin from my bag," he yelled.

I tried to speak but my tongue would not work.

The nurse hurried into the room with a hypodermic. The old man grabbed it and jabbed it into Mother's hip.

Her other hand was at the front of my shirt.

"It's all right. It's all right," he was shouting at both of us. "I'm going to send her into the hospital tonight. Don't worry. She's going to be all right."

Somehow I knew she would.

"What did you give her?" he asked, looking curiously at the glass in my hand. The glass I had planned to put in the garbage disposal.

I heard myself give an answer, but it was like hearing someone else's voice. I could feel the glass leave my hand. I could feel her grip easing. Something was said around me.

Then I knew. It was just like "the penicillin shot."

But it couldn't be.

It was impossible.

Who ever heard of anyone being allergic to poison?

"Good heavens—this must mean we've practically finished him off."

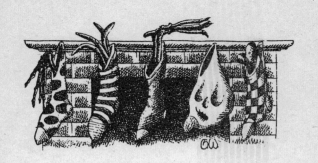

G. K. Chesterton would be surprised if he were to return and discover that his reputation rested primarily on his Father Brown stories. He was, after all, a celebrated critic, social historian, poet and biographer. He was one of the leading lights of Fabian Socialism, and an important member of England's intellectual elite. In 1922 he converted to Roman Catholicism and began a new career as religious proselytizer and Anglo-Catholic pundit.

His Father Brown stories, begun in 1911, chronicle his fascination with an institution he sought to portray in moral and ethical terms. Some critics complained that Chesterton gave his readers too much of a Sunday School lesson with his stories, but all agreed that Father Brown was and is one of the most important detectives of all time.

"The Flying Stars" is one of the earliest of the stories and features Flambeau, the master crook, who functions primarily as Father Brown's Moriarty (and then as his reformed aide) in the series of 51 adventures.

Admittedly some of the Father Brown stories seem a little fustian and talky today, but the great ones, such as "The Flying Stars," have a humanity and genuine social concern that transcends all else. Likewise, it ensures that Chesterton's tales of the little cleric are still read and appreciated, and will continue to be, as long as crime continues to fascinate and challenge readers.

The Flying Stars

by G. K. Chesterton

"THE MOST BEAUTIFUL CRIME I ever committed," Flambeau would say in his highly moral old age, "was also, by a singular coincidence, my last. It was committed at Christmas. As an artist I had always attempted to provide crimes suitable to the special season or landscapes in which I found myself, choosing this or that terrace or garden for a catastrophe, as if for a statuary group. Thus squires should be swindled in long rooms panelled with oak; while Jews, on the other hand, should rather find themselves unexpectedly penniless among the lights and screens of the Café Riche. Thus, in England, if I wished to relieve a dean of his riches (which is not so easy as you might suppose), I wished to frame him, if I make myself clear, in the green lawns and grey towers of some cathedral town. Similarly, in France, when I had got money out of a rich and wicked peasant (which is almost impossible), it gratified me to get his indignant head relieved against a grey line of clipped poplars, and those solemn plains of Gaul over which broods the mighty spirit of Millet.

"Well, my last crime was a Christmas crime, a cheery, cosy, English middle-class crime; a crime of Charles Dickens. I did it in a good old middle-class house near Putney, a house with a crescent of carriage drive, a house with a stable by the side of it, a house with the name on the two outer gates, a house with a monkey tree. Enough, you know the species. I really think my imitation of Dickens's style was dexterous and literary. It seems almost a pity I repented the same evening."

Flambeau would then proceed to tell the story from the inside; and even from the inside it was odd. Seen from the outside it was perfectly incomprehensible, and it is from the outside that the stranger must study it. From this standpoint the drama may be said to have begun when the front doors of the house with the stable opened on the garden with the monkey tree, and a young girl came out with bread to feed the birds on the afternoon of Boxing Day. She had a pretty face, with brave brown eyes; but her figure was beyond conjecture, for she was so wrapped up in brown furs that it was hard to say which was hair and which was fur. But for the attractive face she might have been a small toddling bear.

The winter afternoon was reddening towards evening, and already a ruby light was rolled over the bloomless beds, filling them, as it were, with the ghosts of the dead roses. On one side of the house stood the stable, on the other an alley or cloister of laurels led to the larger garden behind. The young lady, having scattered bread for the birds (for the fourth or fifth time that day, because the dog ate it), passed unobtrusively down the lane of laurels and into a glimmering plantation of evergreens behind. Here she gave an exclamation of wonder, real or ritual, and looking up at the high garden wall above her, beheld it fantastically bestridden by a somewhat fantastic figure.

"Oh, don't jump, Mr. Crook," she called out in some alarm; "it's much too high."

The individual riding the party wall like an aerial horse was a tall, angular young man, with dark hair sticking up like a hair brush, intelligent and even distinguished lineaments, but a sallow and almost alien complexion. This showed the more plainly because he wore an aggressive red tie, the only part of his costume of which he seemed to take any care. Perhaps it was a symbol. He took no notice of the girl's alarmed adjuration, but leapt like a grasshopper to the ground beside her, where he might very well have broken his legs.

"I think I was meant to be a burglar," he said placidly, "and I have no doubt I should have been if I hadn't happened to be born in that nice house next door. I can't see any harm in it, anyhow."

"How can you say such things?" she remonstrated.

"Well," said the young man, "if you're born on the wrong side of the wall, I can't see that it's wrong to climb over it."

"I never know what you will say or do next," she said.

"I don't often know myself," replied Mr. Crook; "but then I am on the right side of the wall now."

"And which is the right side of the wall?" asked the young lady, smiling.

"Whichever side you are on," said the young man named Crook.

As they went together through the laurels towards the front garden a motor horn sounded thrice, coming nearer and nearer, and a car of splendid speed, great elegance, and a pale green colour swept up to the front doors like a bird and stood throbbing.

"Hullo, hullo!" said the young man with the red tie, "here's somebody born on the right side, anyhow. I didn't know, Miss Adams, that your Santa Claus was so modern as this."

"Oh, that's my godfather, Sir Leopold Fischer. He always comes on Boxing Day."

Then, after an innocent pause, which unconsciously betrayed some lack of enthusiasm, Ruby Adams added:

"He is very kind."

John Crook, journalist, had heard of that eminent City magnate; and it was not his fault if the City magnate had not heard of him; for in certain articles in *The Clarion* or *The New Age* Sir Leopold had been dealt with austerely. But he said nothing and grimly watched the unloading of the motor-car, which was rather a long process. A large, neat chauffeur in green got out from the front, and a small, neat manservant in grey got out from the back, and between them they deposited Sir Leopold on the doorstep and began to unpack him, like some very carefully protected parcel. Rugs enough to stock a bazaar, furs of all the beasts of the forest, and scarves of all the colours of the rainbow were unwrapped one by one, till they revealed something resembling the human form; the form of a friendly, but foreign-looking old gentleman, with a grey goat-like beard and a beaming smile, who rubbed his big fur gloves together.

Long before this revelation was complete the two big doors of the porch had opened in the middle, and Colonel Adams (father of the furry young lady) had come out himself to invite his eminent guest inside. He was a tall, sunburnt, and very silent man, who wore a red smoking-cap like a fez, making him look like one of the English Sirdars or Pashas in Egypt. With him was his brother-in-law, lately come from Canada, a big and rather boisterous young gentleman-farmer, with a yellow beard, by name James Blount. With him also was the more insignificant figure of the priest from the neighbouring Roman Church; for the colonel's late wife had been a Catholic, and the children, as is common in such cases, had been trained to follow her. Everything seemed undistinguished about the priest, even down to his name, which was Brown; yet the colonel had always found something companionable about him, and frequently asked him to such family gatherings.

In the large entrance hall of the house there was ample room even for Sir Leopold and the removal of his wraps. Porch and vestibule, indeed, were unduly large in proportion to the house, and formed, as it were, a big room with the front door at one end, and the bottom of the staircase at the other. In front of the large hall fire, over which hung the colonel's sword, the process was completed and the company, including the saturnine Crook, presented to Sir Leopold Fischer. That venerable financier, however, still seemed struggling with portions of his well-lined attire, and at length produced from a very interior tail-coat pocket, a black oval case which he radiantly explained to be his Christmas present for his god-daughter. With an unaffected vain-glory that had something disarming about it he held out the case before them all; it flew open at a touch and half-blinded them. It was just as if a crystal fountain had spurted in their eyes. In a nest of orange velvet lay like three eggs, three white and vivid diamonds that seemed to set the very air on fire all round them. Fischer stood beaming benevolently and drinking deep of the astonishment and ecstasy of the girl, the grim admiration and gruff thanks of the colonel, the wonder of the whole group.

"I'll put 'em back now, my dear," said Fischer, returning the case to the tails of his coat. "I had to be careful of 'em coming down. They're the three great African diamonds called 'The Flying Stars,' because they've been stolen so often. All the big criminals are on the track; but even the rough men about in the streets and hotels could hardly have kept their hands off them. I might have lost them on the road here. It was quite possible."

"Quite natural, I should say," growled the man in the red tie. "I shouldn't blame 'em if they had taken 'em. When they ask for bread, and you don't even give them a stone, I think they might take the stone for themselves."

"I won't have you talking like that," cried the girl, who was in a curious glow. "You've only talked like that since you became a horrid what's-his-name. You know what I mean. What do you call a man who wants to embrace the chimney-sweep?"

"A saint," said Father Brown.

"I think," said Sir Leopold, with a supercilious smile, "that Ruby means a Socialist."

"A radical does not mean a man who lives on radishes," remarked Crook, with some impatience; "and a Conservative does not mean a man who preserves jam. Neither, I assure you, does a Socialist mean a man who desires a social evening with the chimney-sweep. A Socialist means a man who wants all the chimneys swept and all the chimney-sweeps paid for it."

"But who won't allow you," put in the priest in a low voice, "to own your own soot."

Crook looked at him with an eye of interest and even respect. "Does one want to own soot?" he asked.

"One might," answered Brown, with speculation in his eye. "I've heard that gardeners use it. And I once made six children happy at Christmas when the conjuror didn't come, entirely with soot—applied externally."

"Oh, splendid," cried Ruby. "Oh, I wish you'd do it to this company."

The boisterous Canadian, Mr. Blount, was lifting his loud voice in applause, and the astonished financier his (in some considerable deprecation), when a knock sounded at the double front doors. The priest opened them, and they showed again the front garden of evergreens, monkey-tree and all, now gathering gloom against a gorgeous violet sunset. The scene thus framed was so coloured and quaint, like a back scene in a play, that they forgot a moment the insignificant figure standing in the door. He was dusty-looking and in a frayed coat, evidently a common messenger. "Any of you gentlemen Mr. Blount?" he asked, and held forward a letter doubtfully. Mr. Blount started, and stopped in his shout of assent. Ripping up the envelope with evident astonishment he read it; his face clouded a little, and then cleared, and he turned to his brother-in-law and host.

"I'm sick at being such a nuisance, colonel," he said, with the cheery colonial conventions; "but would it upset you if an old acquaintance called on me here tonight on business? In point of face it's Florian, that famous French acrobat and comic actor; I knew him years ago out West (he was a French-Canadian by birth), and he seems to have business for me, though I hardly guess what."

"Of course, of course," replied the colonel carelessly. "My dear chap, any friend of yours. No doubt he will prove an acquisition."

"He'll black his face, if that's what you mean," cried Blount, laughing. "I don't doubt he'd black everyone else's eyes. I don't care; I'm not refined. I like the jolly old pantomime where a man sits on his top hat."

"Not on mine, please," said Sir Leopold Fischer, with dignity.

"Well, well," observed Crook, airily, "don't let's quarrel. There are lower jokes than sitting on a top hat."

Dislike of the red-tied youth, born of his predatory opinions and evident intimacy with the pretty godchild, led Fischer to say, in his most sarcastic, magisterial manner: "No doubt you have found something much lower than sitting on a top hat. What is it, pray?"

"Letting a top hat sit on you, for instance," said the Socialist.

"Now, now, now," cried the Canadian farmer with his barbarian benevolence, "don't let's spoil a jolly evening. What I say is let's do something for the company tonight. Not blacking faces or sitting on hats, if you don't like those—but something of the sort. Why couldn't we have a proper old English pantomime—clown, columbine, and so on. I saw one when I left England at twelve years old, and it's blazed in my brain like a bonfire ever since. I came back to the old country only last year, and I find the thing's extinct. Nothing but a lot of snivelling fairy plays. I want a hot poker and a policeman made into sausages, and they give me princesses moralising by moonlight, Blue Birds, or something. Blue Beard's more in my line, and him I liked best when he turned into the pantaloon."

"I'm all for making a policeman into sausages," said John Crook. "It's a better definition of Socialism than some recently given. But surely the get-up would be too big a business."

"Not a scrap," cried Blount, quite carried away. "A harlequinade's the quickest thing we can do, for two reasons. First, one can gag to any degree; and, second, all the objects are household things—tables and trowel-horses and washing baskets, and things like that."

"That's true," admitted Crook, nodding eagerly and walking about. "But I'm afraid I can't have my policeman's uniform? Haven't killed a policeman lately."

Blount frowned thoughtfully a space, and then smote his thigh. "Yes, we can!" he cried. "I've got Florian's address here, and he knows every *costumier* in London. I'll 'phone him to bring a police dress when he comes." And he went bounding away to the telephone.

"Oh, it's glorious, godfather," cried Ruby, almost dancing. "I'll be columbine and you shall be pantaloon."

The millionaire held himself stiff with a sort of heathen solemnity. "I think, my dear," he said, "you must get someone else for pantaloon."

"I will be pantaloon, if you like," said Colonel Adams, taking his cigar out of his mouth, and speaking for the first and last time.

"You ought to have a statue," cried the Canadian, as he came back, radiant, from the telephone. "There, we are all fitted. Mr. Crook shall be clown; he's a journalist and knows all the oldest jokes. I can be harlequin, that only wants long legs and jumping about. My friend Florian 'phones he's bringing the police costume; he's changing on the way. We can act it in this very hall, the audience sitting on those broad stairs opposite, one row above another. These front doors can be the back scene, either open or shut. Shut, you see an English interior. Open, a moonlit garden. It all goes by magic."

And snatching a chance piece of billiard chalk from his pocket, he ran it across the hall floor, half-way between the front door and the staircase, to mark the line of the footlights.

How even such a banquet of bosh was got ready in time remained a riddle. But they went at it with that mixture of recklessness and industry that lives when youth is in a house; and youth was in that house that night, though not all may have isolated the two faces and hearts from which it flamed. As always happens, the invention grew wilder and wilder through the very tameness of the *bourgeois* conventions from which it had to create. The columbine looked charming in an outstanding skirt that strangely resembled the large lamp-shade in the drawing-room. The clown and pantaloon made themselves white with flour from the cook, and red with rouge from some other domestic, who remained (like all true Christian benefactors) anonymous. The harlequin, already clad in silver paper out of cigar boxes, was, with difficulty, prevented from smashing the old Victorian lustre chandeliers, that he might cover himself with resplendent crystals. In fact he would certainly have done so, had not Ruby unearthed some old pantomime paste jewels she had worn at a fancy dress party as the Queen of Diamonds. Indeed, her uncle, James Blount, was getting almost out of hand in his excitement; he was like a schoolboy. He put a paper donkey's head unexpectedly on Father Brown, who bore it patiently, and even found some private manner of moving his ears. He even essayed to put the paper donkey's tail to the coat-tails of Sir Leopold Fischer. This, however, was frowned down. "Uncle is too absurd," cried Ruby to Crook, round whose shoulders she had seriously placed a string of sausages. "Why is he so wild?"

"He is harlequin to your columbine," said Crook. "I am only the clown who makes the old jokes."

"I wish you were the harlequin," she said, and left the string of sausages swinging.

Father Brown, though he knew every detail done behind the scenes, and had even evoked applause by his transformation of a pillow into a pantomime baby, went round to the front and sat among the audience with all the solemn expectation of a child at his first matinée. The spectators were few, relations, one or two local friends, and the servants; Sir Leopold sat in the front seat, his full and still fur-collared figure largely obscuring the view of the little cleric behind him; but it has never been settled by artistic authorities whether the cleric lost much. The pantomime was utterly chaotic, yet not contemptible; there ran through it a rage of improvisation which came chiefly from Crook the clown. Commonly he was a clever man, and he was inspired tonight with a wild omniscience, a folly wiser than the world, that which comes to a young man who has seen for an instant a particular expression on a particular face. He was supposed to be the clown, but he was really almost everything else, the author (so far as there was an author), the prompter, the scene-painter, the scene-shifter, and, above all, the orchestra. At abrupt intervals in the outrageous performance he would hurl himself in full costume at the piano and bang out some popular music equally absurd and appropriate.

The climax of this, as of all else, was the moment when the two front doors at the back of the scene flew open, showing the lovely moonlit garden, but showing more prominently the famous professional guest; the great Florian, dressed up as a policeman. The clown at the piano played the constabulary chorus in the "Pirates of Penzance," but it was drowned in the deafening applause, for every gesture of the great comic actor was an admirable though restrained version of the carriage and manner of the police. The harlequin leapt upon him and hit him over the helmet; the pianist playing "Where did you get that hat?" he faced about in admirably simulated astonishment, and then the leaping harlequin hit him again (the pianist suggesting a few bars of "Then we had another one"). Then the harlequin rushed right into the arms of the policeman and fell on top of him, amid a roar of applause. Then it was that the strange actor gave that celebrated imitation of a dead man, of which the fame still lingers round Putney. It was almost impossible to believe that a living person could appear so limp.

The athletic harlequin swung him about like a sack or twisted or tossed him like an Indian club; all the time to the most maddeningly ludicrous tunes from the piano. When the harlequin heaved the comic constable heavily off the floor the clown played "I arise from dreams of thee." When he shuffled him across his back, "With my bundle on my shoulder," and when the harlequin finally let fall the policeman with a most convincing thud, the lunatic at the instrument struck into a jingling measure with some words which are still believed to have been, "I sent a letter to my love and on the way I dropped it."

At about this limit of mental anarchy Father Brown's view was obscured altogether; for the City magnate in front of him rose to his full height and thrust his hands savagely into all his pockets. Then he sat down nervously, still fumbling, and then stood up again. For an instant it seemed seriously likely that he would stride across the footlights; then he turned a glare at the clown playing the piano; and then he burst in silence out of the room.

The priest had only watched for a few more minutes the absurd but not inelegant dance of the amateur harlequin over his splendidly unconscious foe. With real though rude art, the harlequin danced slowly backwards out of the door into the garden, which was full of moonlight and stillness. The vamped dress of silver paper and paste, which had been too glaring in the footlights, looked more and more magical and silvery as it danced away under a brilliant moon. The audience was closing in with a cataract of applause, when Brown felt his arm abruptly touched, and he was asked in a whisper to come into the colonel's study.

He followed his summoner with increasing doubt, which was not dispelled by a solemn comicality in the scene of the study. There sat Colonel Adams, still unaffectedly dressed as a pantaloon, with the knobbed whalebone nodding above his brow, but with his poor old eyes sad enough to have sobered a Saturnalia. Sir Leopold Fischer was leaning against the mantelpiece and heaving with all the importance of panic.

"This is a very painful matter, Father Brown," said Adams. "The truth is, those diamonds we all saw this afternoon seem to have vanished from my friend's tail-coat pocket. And as you—"

"As I," supplemented Father Brown, with a broad grin, "was sitting just behind him—"

"Nothing of the sort shall be suggested," said Colonel Adams, with a firm look at Fischer, which rather implied that some such thing *had* been suggested. "I only ask you to give me the assistance that any gentleman might give."

"Which is turning out his pockets," said Father Brown, and proceeded to do so, displaying seven and sixpence, a return ticket, a small silver crucifix, a small breviary, and a stick of chocolate.

The colonel looked at him long, and then said, "Do you know, I should like to see the inside of your head more than the inside of your pockets. My daughter is one of your people, I know; well, she has lately—" and he stopped.

"She has lately," cried out old Fischer, "opened her father's house to a cut-throat Socialist, who says openly he would steal anything from a richer man. This is the end of it. Here is the richer man—and none the richer."

"If you want the inside of my head you can have it," said Brown rather wearily. "What it's worth you can say afterwards. But the first thing I find in that disused pocket is this: that men who mean to steal diamonds don't talk Socialism. They are more likely," he added demurely, "to denounce it."

Both the others shifted sharply and the priest went on:

"You see, we know these people, more or less. That Socialist would no more steal a diamond than a Pyramid. We ought to look at once to the one man we don't know. The fellow acting the policeman—Florian. Where is he exactly at this minute, I wonder."

The pantaloon sprang erect and strode out of the room. An interlude ensued, during which the millionaire stared at the priest, and the priest at his breviary; then the pantaloon returned and said, with *staccato* gravity, "The policeman is still lying on the stage. The curtain has gone up and down six times; he is still lying there."

Father Brown dropped his book and stood staring with a look of blank mental ruin. Very slowly a light began to creep in his grey eyes, and then he made the scarcely obvious answer.

"Please forgive me, colonel, but when did your wife die?"

"Wife!" replied the staring soldier, "she died this year two months. Her brother James arrived just a week too late to see her."

The little priest bounded like a rabbit shot. "Come on!" he cried in quite unusual excitement. "Come on! We've got to go and look at that policeman!"

They rushed on to the now curtained stage, breaking rudely past the columbine and clown (who seemed whispering quite contentedly), and Father Brown bent over the prostrate comic policeman.

"Chloroform," he said as he rose; "I only guessed it just now."

There was a startled stillness, and then the colonel said slowly, "Please say seriously what all this means."

Father Brown suddenly shouted with laughter, then stopped, and only struggled with it for instants during the rest of his speech. "Gentlemen," he gasped, "there's not much time to talk. I must run after the criminal. But this great French actor who played the policeman—this clever corpse the harlequin waltzed with and dandled and threw about—he was—" His voice again failed him, and he turned his back to run.

"He was?" called Fischer inquiringly.

"A real policeman," said Father Brown, and ran away into the dark.

There were hollows and bowers at the extreme end of that leafy garden, in which the laurels and other immortal shrubs showed against sapphire sky and silver moon, even in that mid-winter, warm colours as of the south. The green gaiety of the waving laurels, the rich purple indigo of the night, the moon like a monstrous crystal, make an almost irresponsible romantic picture; and among the top branches of the garden trees a strange figure is climbing, who looks not so much romantic as impossible. He sparkles from head to heel, as if clad in ten million moons; the real moon catches him at every movement and sets a new inch of him on fire. But he swings, flashing and successful, from the short tree in this garden to the tall, rambling tree in the other, and only stops there because a shade has slid under the smaller tree and has unmistakably called up to him.

"Well, Flambeau," says the voice, "you really look like a Flying Star; but that always means a Falling Star at last."

The silver, sparkling figure above seems to lean forward in the laurels and, confident of escape, listens to the little figure below.

"You never did anything better, Flambeau. It was clever to come from Canada (with a Paris ticket, I suppose) just a week after Mrs. Adams died, when no one was in a mood to ask questions. It was cleverer to have marked down the Flying Stars and the very day of Fischer's coming. But there's no cleverness, but mere genius, in what followed. Stealing the stones, I suppose, was nothing to you. You could have done it by sleight of hand in a hundred other ways besides that pretence of putting a paper donkey's tail to Fischer's coat. But in the rest you eclipsed yourself."

The silvery figure among the green leaves seems to linger as if hypnotised, though his escape is easy behind him; he is staring at the man below.

"Oh, yes," says the man below, "I know all about it. I know you not only forced the pantomime, but put it to a double use. You were going to steal the stones quietly; news came by an accomplice that you were already suspected, and a capable police officer was coming to rout you up that very night. A common thief would have been thankful for the warning and fled; but you are a poet. You already had the clever notion of hiding the jewels in a blaze of false stage jewellery. Now, you saw that if the dress were a harlequin's the appearance of a policeman would be quite in keeping. The worthy officer started from Putney police station to find you, and walked into the queerest trap ever set in this world. When the front door opened he walked straight on to the stage of a Christmas pantomime, where he could be kicked, clubbed, stunned and drugged by the dancing harlequin, amid roars of laughter from all the most respectable people in Putney. Oh, you will never do anything better. And now, by the way, you might give me back those diamonds."

The green branch on which the glittering figure swung, rustled as if in astonishment; but the voice went on:

"I want you to give them back, Flambeau, and I want you to give up this life. There is still youth and honour and humour in you; don't fancy they will last in that trade. Men may keep a sort of level of good, but no man has ever been able to

keep on one level of evil. That road goes down and down.
The kind man drinks and turns cruel; the frank man kills and
lies about it. Many a man I've known started like you to be an
honest outlaw, a merry robber of the rich, and ended stamped
into slime. Maurice Blum started out as an anarchist of princi-
ple, a father of the poor; he ended a greasy spy and tale-bearer
that both sides used and despised. Harry Burke started his free
money movement sincerely enough; now he's sponging on a
half-starved sister for endless brandies and sodas. Lord Amber
went into wild society in a sort of chivalry; now he's paying
blackmail to the lowest vultures in London. Captain Barillon
was the great gentleman-apache before your time; he died in a
madhouse, screaming with fear of the 'narks' and receivers
that had betrayed him and hunted him down. I know the
woods look very free behind you, Flambeau; I know that in a
flash you could melt into them like a monkey. But some day
you will be an old grey monkey, Flambeau. You will sit up in
your free forest cold at heart and close to death, and the tree-
tops will be very bare."

Everything continued still, as if the small man below held
the other in the tree in some long invisible leash; and he went
on:

"Your downward steps have begun. You used to boast of
doing nothing mean, but you are doing something mean tonight. You are leaving suspicion on an honest boy with a good
deal against him already; you are separating him from the
woman he loves and who loves him. But you will do meaner
things than that before you die."

Three flashing diamonds fell from the tree to the turf. The
small man stooped to pick them up, and when he looked up
again the green cage of the tree was emptied of its silver bird.

The restoration of the gems (accidentally picked up by Father Brown, of all people) ended the evening in uproarious
triumph; and Sir Leopold, in his height of good humour, even
told the priest that though he himself had broader views, he
could respect those whose creed required them to be cloistered
and ignorant of this world.

"Oh, yeah, and forget that idea I had about hiring girl elves."